Dedication

for Randy Matthews

Acknowledgements

Without the assistance of several people, this book would not be. These people are, first, my brother, Randy Matthews, and then Sally Sutherland, Patricia Gilmore, Robert Arthur, and Pat Meiwes. Each contributed far in excess of what could be expected or hoped for based on family, friendship, or love of reading. I also thank my publisher, Evan Swensen, who had the courage to take on this project.

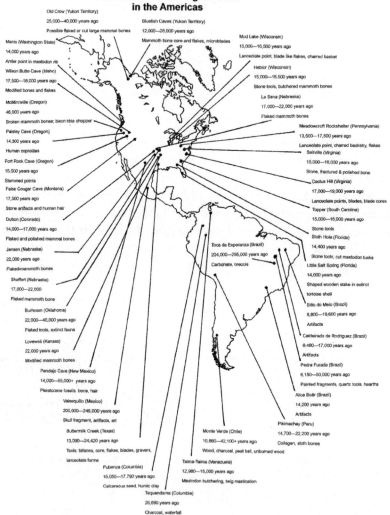

Pre-Clovis Archaeological Sites in the Americas

Old Crow (Yukon Territory)
25,000—40,000 years ago
Possible flaked or cut large mammal bones

Bluefish Caves (Yukon Territory)
12,000—28,000 years ago
Mammoth bone core and flakes, microblades

Manis (Washington State)
14,000 years ago
Antler point in mastodon rib

Wilson Butte Cave (Idaho)
17,500—18,000 years ago
Modified bones and flakes

McMinnville (Oregon)
46,000 years ago
Broken mammoth bones; bison tibia chopper

Paisley Cave (Oregon)
14,300 years ago
Human coprolites

Fort Rock Cave (Oregon)
15,500 years ago
Stemmed points

False Cougar Cave (Montana)
17,500 years ago
Stone artifacts and human hair

Dutton (Colorado)
14,000—17,000 years ago
Flaked and polished mammal bones

Jensen (Nebraska)
22,000 years ago
Flaked mammoth bones

Shaffert (Nebraska)
17,000—22,000
Flaked mammoth bone

Burnham (Oklahoma)
22,000—40,000 years ago
Flaked tools, extinct fauna

Lovewell (Kansas)
22,000 years ago
Modified mammoth bones

Pendejo Cave (New Mexico)
14,000—55,000+ years ago
Pleistocene fossils, bone, hair

Valsequillo (Mexico)
200,000—245,000 years ago
Skull fragment, artifacts, art

Buttermilk Creek (Texas)
13,090—24,420 years ago
Tools: bifaces, core, flakes, blades, gravers, lanceolate forms

Pubenza (Columbia)
15,050—17,790 years ago
Calcareous seed, humic clay

Tequendama (Columbia)
26,890 years ago
Charcoal, waterfall

Mud Lake (Wisconsin)
15,000—16,500 years ago
Lanceolate point, blade like flakes, charred basket

Hebior (Wisconsin)
15,000—16,500 years ago
Stone tools, butchered mammoth bones

La Sena (Nebraska)
17,000—22,000 years ago
Flaked mammoth bones

Meadowcroft Rockshelter (Pennsylvania)
13,500—17,500 years ago
Lanceolate point, charred basketry, flakes

Saltville (Virginia)
15,000—16,000 years ago
Stone, fractured & polished bone

Cactus Hill (Virginia)
17,000—19,000 years ago
Lanceolate points, blades, blade cores

Topper (South Carolina)
15,000—16,000 years ago
Stone tools

Sloth Hole (Florida)
14,400 years ago
Stone tools, cut mastodon tusks

Little Salt Spring (Florida)
14,000 years ago
Shaped wooden stake in extinct tortoise shell

Sitio do Meio (Brazil)
8,800—18,600 years ago
Artifacts

Caldeirado de Rodriguez (Brazil)
9,480—17,000 years ago
Artifacts

Pedra Furada (Brazil)
6,150—50,000 years ago
Painted fragments, quartz tools, hearths

Alice Boër (Brazil)
14,200 years ago
Artifacts

Pikimachay (Peru)
14,700—22,200 years ago
Collagen, sloth bones

Toca da Esperanza (Brazil)
204,000—295,000 years ago
Carbonate, breccia

Monte Verde (Chile)
10,860—42,100+ years ago
Wood, charcoal, peat ball, unburned wood

Taima-Taima (Venezuela)
12,980—15,000 years ago
Mastodon butchering, twig mastication

8

Introduction

Zamimolo's Story, 50,000 BC is the third novel in the Winds of Change series that focuses on the peopling of the Americas. In this novel, a small group of the People migrates by boat to Central America from China/Mongolia. They have to adjust to environmental extremes, not only from temperature change, lack of seasonal variation to annual summer, but also to the entirely different set of living creatures in the environment. These include Volkswagen-sized armadillos and twenty-foot tall sloths.

I have also included the terror birds which were supposed to have gone extinct prior to 50,000 BC, but some remained into the 17,000 years ago range according to an article by Herculano Alvarenga and others in 2010. South America had been an island and wildlife was unique to that land in the way that the fauna of Australia or Madagascar differs from anything else on earth today. A few million years ago, the Americas connected via Central America. Despite the connection, South America remained a strange land. Animals did begin to migrate north from South America to North America and the other way around once the lands connected. The chart below provides an example of the size comparison of four species of terror birds and a human of today.

Other animals the People would have encountered were: the camel (macrauchenias) and horse (Hippidion),

the rhino-like toxodon that the Nola Nola call glar and stegomastodon,

the elephant (cuvieronius) and the smilodon.

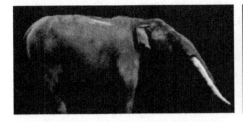 

Finally, the People had to adjust with no less impact to people from significantly different cultures whose mores did not necessarily match their own. The novel series deals with two issues:

Clovis-First vs. Pre-Clovis Views

Clovis-First View: Clovis-First is an opinion that no humans were in the Americas until the Holocene (11,700 years ago to present). Proponents of that view are C. Vance Haynes, Aleš Hrdlička, Paul Martin, and Tim Flannery. The Clovis-First View recognizes no Pre-Clovis sites in the Americas. Along with the Clovis-First View is the idea that intelligence along with body shape evolved.

Pre-Clovis View: Pre-Clovis is an opinion that humans were in the Americas in the Pleistocene (2.6 million to 11,700 years ago), and may have been present here as far back as hundreds of thousands of years ago. Pre-Clovis proponents are: Thomas Dillehay, James Adovasio, Christopher Hardaker, and Michael Cremo. They point to some 400 Pre-Clovis sites in the Americas, a few of which are shown on the chart on page 8. This view conceives that humans have always had the same level of intelligence; they just applied it to different sets of circumstances and built on different bases.

The Intellectual Level and Life Styles of Neanderthals

Neanderthals have been viewed as hunched over, dark-skinned brutes without the function of spoken language. We know today that Neanderthals had fair skin, and some had red hair and blue eyes; could speak as well as we can; were intellectually bright (catching dolphins, something which can't be done from shore); killed mega fauna with spears; and survived temperatures that would challenge our best outdoors men and women today; buried their dead with red ochre and flowers; and cared for their disabled. It might be noted that many people today carry residual Neanderthal DNA.

The series explores the Pre-Clovis View and speculates on the mores and lifestyles of a People who could endure for hundreds of thousands of years without killing off others or their own kind. The series demonstrates how the various humans might have merged Neanderthals, *Homo erectus,* Cro-magnons, and Denisovans—raising the question whether these groups are the same species, since they can reproduce viable young (at this point the *Homo erectus* connection is unproven lacking DNA from *Homo erectus*).

Zamimolo's Story, 50,000 BC begins with an abduction, because the People don't know the signs of the animal life, having just arrived in Central America. The People fail to realize silence in the bugs and frogs reflects an observed change in the environment. The abduction has a profound effect on Zamimolo, one of the leaders of his People. Can the ways of other groups of people affect the mores and actions of the People? Read to discover.

Caution: The books in this series contain numbers of people. Some readers lose the story trying to grasp every name. As a writer, I could not chop the characters out, because they have function and/or they are part of a family, but some are just not vital. After studying this issue, I have taken the chart showing the families and people of groups, and I marked the names of those whose roles are the most relevant in bold type. Some characters may not even be listed on the chart. I'd urge readers just to keep reading when the names become a little difficult. There's no need to fix every name. Check with the chart, if you have questions.

Zamimolo's Story, 50,000 BC contains a bibliography.
For more information see: http://booksbybonnye.com
For a compilation of articles regarding early man, see my Author Facebook page at:
Facebook: https://www.facebook.com/pages/Bonnye-Matthews/484231424 985849?ref=hl#

THE PEOPLE

Deity: Wisdom

Wise One: **Pikotal, Pikotek**

Tukyatuk + Meninkua	Golmid + Colitoba	Rustumarin + Uilo	Tokatumeta + Foliflio
Kih	Jup	**Linpint**	Dimutenka
Zamimolo	**Olomaru-mia**	**Grakumashi**	Obi
Numing	Milukima	Latumala	Mimiputash
Kada	Ramuduku	Gifi	Remu
Hutapska	Allumelk	Ekemento	Urkumit
Inrusk	Colkibut	Yakak	Wislopie
Tas	Flanilk	Oaq	Nob
Molar	**Picota**		**Jalutui**

NOLA NOLA

Deity: Creator of All

Chief Uvela	**Ahma**
Mechalu	Albigrimpa
Oscola	**Pipto**
Bul	**Token**
Tuna	**Coshiga**
Kiahmuha	Rur
Dooderido	Flukua
Sima	Mohu

SOUTHERN KAPOTONOK

Deity: Maker

Chief Hirmit
Tomarghi
Yok (Wise One)
Lomah
Kumoha
Dop

NORTHERN KAPOTONOK

Deity: Maker

Chief Paaku
Ba
Kolpatin
Met, Vil, Gu, For,
Poo, Soklinatu,
Opt (Wise One)

ALITUKIT

Deity: ------

Students: Hoft, Kit

Masters: Gu, Lipin, Theu
Bognuru, Alikuat

NOTE: Names in bold are the primary characters. Not all characters are listed.

Chapter 1

There was a hush among the People. The only sounds were from the waves crashing on the shore below them, the light wind, a few frogs just beginning to break the peace in the distance, night bugs, and the crackling fire. The hunters sat cross-legged on flat stones that gathered into a semi-circle reflecting their former cave arrangement for council meetings. The women sat on skins laid on the sand just beyond the men. Children sat or reclined on skins with their mothers. It was as yet a moonless night but the profusion of stars provided light from the cloud-free sky. It was their first night in their new land. Glad to be off the boat and on land again, there was not a single complaint heard all day—even when the boat left.

The Wise One, who sat at the forefront near the fire, his bundle from the ancients beside him, remained silent for a long time as he pieced together memories of the rugged long boat trip to this new land. Something troubled his spirit, but he couldn't identify the cause. He put his hand on the leather bundle. Only rarely did he unwind it. The bundle contained a piece of a meteorite, a yellow rock owl that seemed to glow, a gold nugget, a piece of jade, a purple sea shell with holes along one side, a piece of a grouping of white crystals, and many other small special things. There was a tiny piece of animal gut folded to hold some black dust that was supposed to be a feather. It was reputed to hold much power. Some legends said it was from a raven from the time when animals and humans talked to each other. The Wise One had no idea of the meaning of all the items in the bundle, only that he was charged with keeping them because they had been with the People since the beginning of time.

Despite the still and quiet, the Wise One's mind web raced backwards through time as far as he could go in his life and then almost regrettably turned and came forward to this place by the sea. His pathetically thin frame showed his bones in sharp contrast to the normally well-fleshed People. Across the sea to the west from where they'd come, he'd been covered with skins to keep the cold away. Here he shed the skins that covered him in favor of a leather loincloth only because of the oppressive heat. The People were silently shocked at how emaciated he'd become. They had seen his sunken cheeks, but his chest showed every rib and his bones protruded just below his waist. His beard was scant. He had little hair atop his head. The tops of his ears stuck out as they always had. Some of his teeth were missing. Yet the man at age seventy still retained a mind web sharper than anyone else. The People saw him as something more than a man, though they'd never have said that aloud. To them he'd always been there and would always be there. He had to be. There was no one to replace him. He was their rock on land, anchor on the sea.

The starry sky reminded the old man of the glowing light in the water he'd sometimes seen, as their boat progressed to this new land. Sparks from the flames seemed to aim for the sky to join the twinkling lights there. A sense of auspicious delight infused the tired People. To find a new home with warmth after the cold temperatures they'd survived for so long was a relief.

"Has he nodded off?" Oaq asked quietly with an elbow poke to his brother, Ekemento.

"I don't think so," Ekemento whispered back.

Uilo, their mother, used a hand sign to quiet them.

Zamimolo smiled at Olomaru-mia from across the other side of the semi-circle. Zamimolo had dark brown hair, almost black. His gently sloping forehead and brow ridges showed his ancestry lay with the old People. His father was fully old People from the extreme far west. He looked just like his father except for eye color. His eyes were brown; his father's, dark blue. Olomaru-mia was also part old People and Minguat. Her light red hair mixed with gold was her crowning beauty. Her eyes were green. They remembered the characteristics of People, though they'd been told that all were People and differences were not important from the beginning of time. Each had a sense of ancestry simply from the traits they bore. Olomaru-mia's hair was long and hung in tight spirals to her waist. It was soft and she kept it clean and shining, fully combed. Zamimolo sat on the far other side of the semi-circle from her with nothing blocking their view of each other. They would join in a few days when the People settled into their new location. They had waited for a long time and now that the sea trip was behind them, they would spend the rest of their lives joined. Olomaru-mia smiled back at Zamimolo and tilted her head in the way that melted his belly. Her smile told him how she loved him. His smile returned the message. She sat on the far outside edge of the group watching her little sisters, Flanilk and Picota. She decided to make a quick trip to the privy before the meeting began, so she asked Milukima, her fourteen-year-old sister, to watch Flanilk and Picota while she relieved herself.

Linpint touched Zamimolo's shoulder and asked, "Would you like to accompany me on a quick safety check of this country tomorrow to see if others are nearby? We also need to know what animals live here and what our dangers are. We've already seen some differences."

"Of course," Zamimolo replied, relishing a trip through the new country.

"Based on what Rustumarin and Golmid have seen, there appear to be no hearth fires in this area now, but others could have come here from time to time. We'd find traces. See that set of hills over there. I thought we might climb to the top to see what we can from the highest point."

"First light?" Zamimolo asked.

"No reason to make it any later," Linpint agreed.

The Wise One raised both arms to the sky. He cleared his throat. A few hunters noticed that even the bugs and frogs quieted for the old man. Silence was profound. The Wise One began, the silence broken by his voice.

"First let us thank Wisdom for our safe travel from our cold, old land to this warm, new land. We ask that Wisdom will keep us here as safely as in our old land and that our days will be long on the earth." He paused. "And may I never have to travel the sea on a boat again!" He spat towards the fire. Laughter moved through the group. Almost everyone concurred.

A dark man moved silently up from an arroyo, crouching beside a wind shaped tree at a crest in the sand near the People. He didn't move. He'd seen the girl leave the group, positioned himself, and waited, hardly breathing. Olomaru-mia heard the Wise One and rose to hurry back to the group. She passed a stunted tree growing in sea grass and fell to her knees, wondering at the sand on her lips as she fell into a deep sleep. The man had struck a blow as fast as a serpent strike to her left temple. He wrapped her hands in skins and tied them tightly at the wrists with several knots, each one tight. He placed a piece of leather into her mouth and secured it with a strap around her mouth, tying it at the back of her head, careful not to cut off her ability to breathe. He lifted her over his shoulders to hang like a speared deer around his neck and headed quickly towards the river's edge always keeping to where he'd seen many people walk. He glanced furtively toward the light of the fire. There was no moon so the next few moments should tell whether he retained his prize or was discovered. His skin was far darker than that of these people and would not reflect much of the little light available. Hers would. He walked into the water not quite waist deep and began to move as quickly as possible upriver in that direction in the dark. He knew in a brief time he would be far beyond sight and there would be no tracks to follow. He wanted as much distance as he could gain before light. He counted on luck to get him as far south as the path that would lead to the mountain pass. He wanted to reach it before light. If he succeeded he could cross the mountain and the valley below before hunters could find his tracks—if his luck held. He was certain that once over the taller mountain, they'd never find him, but he had to do that undetected.

Back at the fire the story began. Zamimolo stared at the Wise One. He would listen carefully to every word, though he had heard the stories over and over. Each time to him it was as if they were new. He let go of the plans for the next day and gave all his thought to the Wise One.

The Wise One sat erect; he looked slightly up at the sky breathing deeply as he began, "This is a very, very old story. It is the story of Kukuk-na and Timkut-na. Timkut-na and Kukuk-na were hunters. They had trekked far looking for meat to feed the People. It was a time of drought and meat was not easy to find."

"The men went to places where they had known deer to gather. There were none. They went to places where trees grew in groves providing shade from the sun for animals. There were no animals there. They went to the highlands where they'd found grazers. There were none. They went to the lowlands and found nothing. Hunger was everywhere, but they were determined that they would not let their People starve, if they could help it."

"Kukuk-na and Timkut-na were exhausted. They looked for a place to sleep. Wisdom was sucking color from the land fast. Below them was a grove of trees and they stumbled towards it. Timkut-na was the first to arrive. He noticed a spring that had not dried up. He kneeled and began to drink, for his thirst was great. Suddenly he felt a hit on his hand. A serpent had been harboring in the grass beside him, and it bit his hand. He noticed it was a cobra. He cursed himself for being so careless. Kukuk-na arrived. He saw what had happened, and Timkut-na showed him the direction the cobra had gone. Kukuk-na found the snake and killed it. He looked for others and found none. There was no cure for the bite. Either Timkut-na would live or die."

"Kukuk-na tried to make a lean-to from what was available. He helped Timkut-na put out his sleeping skins and lie down. He made a fire. He handed Timkut-na a piece of jerky, but the hunter declined. He wasn't hungry. Kukuk-na ate it. Timkut-na's hand was beginning to hurt severely. He became nauseated and vomited, but there was nothing in his stomach to get rid of but a little water. His eyelids were drooping and his hand and arm were swelling. He was in obvious pain. Kukuk-na was agonizing over his friend. He kept the fire going and watched over Timkut-na carefully. Timkut-na slept fitfully. When Wisdom restored color to the land, Kukuk-na saw that Timkut-na was struggling to breathe. He saw him breathe his last."

"Kukuk-na took the digging tool Timkut-na carried in his backpack and dug the best he could to bury Timkut-na. When he had him in the hole and covered by dirt, he still needed to find more dirt to cover his friend. He did not want any animals to dig the man up. Slowly he brought more dirt and covered the body. Then he found rocks and covered the mound. In the distance he heard what sounded like voices. He thought it was just his being alone that he was hearing things that weren't there."

"Kukuk-na sat by the lean-to and wept. He wept because his People hungered. He wept because there were no animals to feed his People. He wept because he and Timkut-na were starving. He wept because Timkut-na died. He wept because he was alone."

"The voices came closer. Kukuk-na didn't notice. It was two hunters from his People. They had found meat. They came to call the hunters home."

"This story is the reason we always check thoroughly for snakes and spiders when we look at a place to camp or live. Even if you are terribly tired, you must look to be certain that the place you are planning to stay is free of harmful living things. Timkut-na died because his thirst was more important than his safety."

The Wise One let the words move over the People. The story was as ancient as the stars. He wondered whether the People would get the significances. "Why did I choose this story, this night?" he asked, his voice cracking like the wood in the fire pit.

Tokatumeta held his arms outstretched, palms up. The Wise One nodded towards him.

Tokatumeta said, "We have faced drought and fewer animals. We who are here chose to leave the others and have traveled in search of a better life, where it is not so cold. We need to take care for our own safety in this land. We need to use much caution until we know this new place. The few animals we've observed on shore don't look much like those we are accustomed to seeing. There are probably many differences."

The People made quiet noises indicating agreement. The volume of the frogs' nightly song was increasing substantially.

The Wise One was pleased. He continued. "What is our plan for the next few days?"

Linpint held his arms outstretched, palms up. The Wise One nodded to him and Linpint said, "At first light Zamimolo and I will travel the area to make sure we are alone. We will look for a suitable place to make our home." He nodded back towards the Wise One.

Rustumarin held his arms outstretched, palms up. The Wise One nodded and Rustumarin said, "Golmid and I will hunt the hills that lie to the east." He nodded back towards the Wise One.

Tokatumeta held his arms outstretched, palms up. At the nod from the Wise One, he said, "I will accompany several of the women to the place where the rocks come to the shore just north of here. We should be able to find some sea life there. I will assure the safety of the women gatherers." He nodded back to the Wise One.

The Wise One searched the People. No other arms were held outstretched. "The council ends," he said. There was some talking among the People, and then they headed toward the places they had set up for sleeping.

Milukima asked Colitoba, her mother, "Where's Olomaru-mia?"

"I don't know. When did you last see her?"

"Just before the Wise One began, she left to relieve herself. I haven't seen her since. She asked me to watch Flanilk and Picota."

Colitoba was jolted. Olomaru-mia had been gone too long. She was not one to wander off. She was not one to miss a council meeting. Zamimolo had attended the council, so she wasn't with him. Colitoba found Golmid and asked him to find Olomaru-mia, explaining what had happened.

Golmid whistled a loud sharp whistle. All the hunters gathered to hear his words.

Golmid explained what he'd learned. Zamimolo felt as if a war club had hit his belly. Something must be wrong. Olomaru-mia would never just wander off. She'd scream if there were strangers among them—if she saw them. The men constructed torches of the wood they could find. Most wood had been used for the fire. The hunters searched the area of the place they stayed, calling her name repeatedly. She did not respond to calls. They could find nothing unusual at all. It was as if she'd vanished.

"We cannot track in the dark," Grakumashi shouted.

"We have to try!" Golmid said defiantly. His daughter was missing. She must be found.

Feeling very uncomfortable and disoriented, Olomaru-mia returned slowly to consciousness. She opened her eyes to find herself being carried, draped across someone's shoulders. It made no sense. There was something horrible in her mouth and a hand grasped her left arm. She wiggled struggling to free herself, thinking she must be having a bad dream. The grasp on her arm tightened and a grasp tightening on her leg assured her this was no dream and that she was in danger. She panicked. She was forcibly held on the shoulders of someone she didn't know. His smell was not familiar at all. He was walking in water. She was horrified to realize that her hands were covered so her fingers were of no value. She continued to fight to get down. She knew to find his eyes so she could try to gouge them out. She couldn't reach them. Kicking was a waste of effort.

Mechalu, her captor, slid her to her feet. He said to her, "No fighting."

Olomaru-mia was shocked that she could understand the man. She stood there gaping at him. Then her anger rose and she kicked his shin and began to run away, having no idea where to run. She could not see the campfire anywhere.

Mechalu grabbed her by the hair. He didn't have time for this. He slapped her face hard.

Olomaru-mia raised her hand to her face. She was hurt and angry. She could make no intelligible sound, just gurgling deep in her throat, but tears fell plentifully.

"No fighting! No running!" Mechalu repeated the words. Olomaru-mia began to pummel his chest with her fists in the covers he'd put on them. She reached up to pull over her head the strip holding the leather in her mouth.

Mechalu hit her head again. She slumped and he caught her and placed her back where he'd had her before she awakened. Why did she fight when she knew she couldn't win? he wondered. Maybe she thinks she can find a way, he considered, and resolved to watch with special care.

Zamimolo's belly was ripped. He knew that nothing should have kept Olomaru-mia from him. He suspected darkly that a person had taken her, but there was no evidence anywhere that was the case. If he knew which way to turn, he'd do whatever was required, but he was mystified. Even he admitted it was futile to search in the dark.

"Zami," Linpint said quietly, "Tomorrow we will cover this entire area. We'll know which way to go. I will help you. We'll get her back."

"You think it's theft, too?" Zamimolo asked.

Linpint held his teeth together tightly for a moment. "I can think of no other reason for her to be missing. Someone could have observed us on our arrival and waited for the right moment. We thought we were safe when we weren't. It's frightening."

"Instead of fear I feel enraged," Zamimolo said. "Olomaru-mia must be terrified."

The Wise One walked over to the two men. He had pulled a skin across his shoulders. He looked at Zamimolo. "It's clearly abduction. I'm so sorry. Wait until first light. Then, try your hardest to find the trail. I think it will take much time, but I *know* that one day *you will find her again*." The Wise One walked back to the fire saddened by the event.

Zamimolo sank to his knees. He knew the Wise One would not have said those words if they hadn't been prophetic. It would take much time. Olomaru-mia would be terrified. He had to find her, but he couldn't help her this night. He thought of her sweetness and kindness and feared the worst for her. Tears fell from his eyes. He lay on his side on the sand. He couldn't sleep. He vowed to kill anyone who harmed her.

Rays of light were hinting the sun's appearance to the east. Mechalu was tired, but he'd made it to the pathway to the mountain pass. The pathway was stony, so it would cover tracks well. The girl had regained consciousness, but she had not continued to make a nuisance of herself. She was still. Once he reached the mountains and gained some elevation, he would feel safe. It was still fairly dark in the forest. He released Olomaru-mia to her feet. He tied a rope to her ankle and tied the other end of the rope to a large rock. He removed the gag but kept her hands covered. He took a piece of jerky and handed her one.

"Let me starve," she replied, refusing it, breaking the forest silence. "I'd rather die than be here." She turned from him.

In the trees howler monkeys set off a noise that scared her terribly. She looked but saw nothing. She didn't know what was making the noise.

"Stop fighting. Eat," Mechalu shouted, pulling her back around.

Olomaru-mia glared at him.

"Eat, or I hit you," he said trying to communicate slowly and clearly, showing her with his hands what he meant. He knew she was frightened, but he had a long way to go and she would need to walk. He couldn't carry her all the way back to his land in the east. It wasn't much food, but she had to eat. He also had to make sure she feared him enough to obey him.

Olomaru-mia didn't get all his words, but she understood enough to hear the threat. She took the jerky and ate a piece listening to the monkeys.

"You have husband?" he asked.

She pretended not to understand though the words were close enough that she knew exactly what he was asking. He pushed her down and answered his own question. She was outraged, but she could not fight back. She berated herself for not answering the simple question. In the struggle the strap to the bag that Zamimolo had made for her broke. The strap slid from around her neck and the bag came to rest just inside the skin of her tunic.

"You have no husband," he said flatly. "Soon you will." He couldn't believe the woman he'd chosen for his own was a virgin. He was so lucky. No one had ever had her. He'd be first. He'd seen her hair from a distance. It drew him. She was the one he wanted, but he'd been willing to take what he could get stealthily in the dark of night. When she left the group and he could steal her so easily, he realized his luck was stronger than he thought. And, then, to have her as a virgin made him know his luck was potent. She also appeared to understand him fairly well. He wondered what else luck would bring him on this trial of his manhood. To become fully men, his people required a young man to make a trip to the western sea from where they'd come many generations ago. They had to go alone with only hand knives, no spears. They had to return with some evidence of their valor, something they'd keep the rest of their lives, a treasure—something no one else could touch ever. He'd done very well. Somehow he sensed he'd found a good woman. She would be his wife.

Again, Olomaru-mia understood. Join her captor! Had he no mind web? she wondered. She was promised to Zamimolo. She adored Zamimolo. Where was he? Would she ever see him again? Her belly ripped apart. How could Wisdom have let this happen? Where was Wisdom? Didn't Wisdom care? She'd listened to the stories carefully at night. She'd carefully followed Wisdom's teaching. Why was this happening to her? To Zamimolo? Hatred for her captor washed over her repeatedly. The screeching continued, joined by very loud birds, one of which she could see. It was huge with red, yellow, green, and blue feathers and an enormous beak. She'd never seen anything like it. Her head hurt.

"You're filth, evil, mean, vile!" she shouted at Mechalu, tossing her jerky to the woods.

He understood. "It is the way of the world, Little One. Just the way of the world. The lucky and strong get what they want. Others suffer for lack of it." He retrieved the jerky and handed it to her. "Eat!" he said forcefully.

"No!" she said with equal force.

He shoved her to the ground. He bit off a piece of the jerky, chewed it, pinched her nose until she had to open her mouth to breathe and then he spit the jerky into her mouth and held her mouth closed. She could not fight. "Swallow!" he demanded.

Olomaru-mia held out as long as she could and finally swallowed. He was sitting atop her and she was miserable. He was a tall man. If he held out his arm, she could walk under it. She shed more tears silently.

"Now, will you eat it, or must I feed you?"

Crestfallen, she nodded affirmatively, tears falling. She ate it, swallowing much of it whole. He drank from his water bag and offered it to her. She drank.

"We walk." Mechalu pulled her up, untied the rope from the rock and her ankle, and tied it around her neck. He tied the other end to his leather loincloth belt. He reapplied the gag. He tied her hands together behind her so she could not remove the gag. He followed the path leading upward into the mountain. Left behind in grass beside the path was the little bag Zamimolo had made her. She didn't feel it slide from her tunic when she got up. She walked behind Mechalu. Her belly ripped with each step farther from Zamimolo and her People. Tears fell unchecked. They'd never find her. For comfort, she tried to feel the little bag Zamimolo had made her. It hung around her neck. He had attached a seashell to the flap. She treasured it. It wasn't there! It was a tie to her beloved. She was sure it had been there earlier, but it was no longer there. More tears fell as she stumbled along behind Mechalu. She loved the little bag and the promise that it contained. It was a symbol of their love forever. It was gone. Was the promise gone? Cold fear enveloped her. The noise of the monkeys was diminishing with distance. Birds and insect noise replaced it.

Light had just returned, and the People were busy getting ready to search widely for their missing member. Zamimolo and Linpint were ready to depart. They made a wide sweep beginning at the water's edge, arcing out into the land, and going to the edge of the water north of them. Then they returned to the start point and made another wide sweep from the water's edge arcing onto the land and back to the water's edge south of where they began. They could find tracks nowhere. They had been certain they would find something. They did another arc from the midpoint of the first arc north to the midpoint of the arc at the water's edge south. Nothing. It struck them that the abductor must have walked away in the water or had a boat. There were no tracks on land from man or beast. The abductor must have approached them from the water, unless it was a bird, but they dismissed that idea as absurd.

Zamimolo sought out the Wise One. "Wise One, may I talk with you?"

"Of course," he said.

"Will you give me guidance as to where I should look first?"

The old man slowly sat on the sandy ground. He appeared to have entered into the world of spirits. Zamimolo also sat. He waited patiently. The sun continued to rise higher and higher in the sky.

Finally, the Wise One looked up directly into the eyes of Zamimolo. "He is taking her to the other salt sea to the east. He will treat her well. He will go southeast from here along the river and then east. There is a path through the mountains, but it connects with many other paths, and I can give you no better direction. Where he goes is far from here by more than a moon's reckoning. He speaks our language from long ago. Zamimolo, if you pursue her, it will take the better part of your life. Do you understand me? As painful as it may feel to you, you can let her go and know she will not be treated badly."

Zamimolo stared at the old man. "How can I not try to find her? She has been my life!"

"She will not be abused. She will always be treated well. At least know that. It will take a long time to find her, and by then she won't be the same person you know now. When you see her, you will both have white hair."

"How can she be different? We love each other. She was *stolen*."

"I simply know what I'm given. I don't get all the details."

"I should go southeast? I should look for a path through the mountains?" Zamimolo asked.

The old man nodded. Zamimolo got up and gave the old man a hand to help him up. The old man put his hand on Zamimolo's shoulder and shook his head. He turned and walked away.

Zamimolo found Linpint and told him what the Wise One had said. "It's probably better that I go alone, my friend. According to the Wise One, I'll be white-haired old before I find her." A gull soared overhead. Zamimolo wished he could fly to find Olomaru-mia with greater speed and sight.

Linpint looked sadly at his friend. "I'll give four seasons to help you. The loss of my wife keeps me disinterested in women right now, so an adventure might just be a good thing. Come, Zamimolo, let's head southeast."

As they began to depart friends and family came to wish the two young men well. They had backpacks filled to the brim with jerky and bed rolls atop their backpacks. Each carried two spears and extra points. They carried several water bags apiece. They walked down the riverbank following the direction Olomaru-mia had already been taken according to the Wise One. So much time had passed.

The small mountains were some distance from them. Grasshoppers moved through the grass at their approach as they walked the riverbank. To find a path through the mountains would require a lot of guessing. As they walked, Linpint wondered how many paths there could be that went through the mountains, paths that could be accessed from the shoreline. The mountains extended as far as he could see. He guessed there could be endless paths.

Back at the site where the People camped, there was great concern. That someone had stealthily taken one of the People while all hunters were awake remained in the forefront of the mind webs of all. They'd been invaded. They felt a need to find a place to live that provided a sense of security, safety from others who might want to steal from them. Their first thought was to the hills. The mountains to the north were appealing for they seemed to be elevated well enough and did not form a long range, so they would be able to keep watch over approaches to their place with the few People they had. Access to their new place would have to be more observable at heights rather than down on the flat land near the river, where washes cut out depths in the land enabling a stranger to hide from view. This had not been a problem in their old land where People were rare. The hazards were different in this place.

Tukyatuk and Grakumashi gathered their weapons and told the Wise One they were off to the mountains of the north to determine whether that would make a good place to live. The mountains were not far. They were certain they could get there and back before night. They moved swiftly. As they left some of the women began to move outward from the camp to look for greens to accompany their night meal. Children were admonished to remain at camp. They complied easily fearing that one step outside the bounds of the camp would result in immediate abduction.

Having pushed hard to climb the animal path through dense vegetation, Mechalu and Olomaru-mia began to descend until they reached a flat place overlooking a broad valley. Olomaru-mia was astonished at the wildlife. There was a herd of animals that had elephant-like short trunks but looked like camels. There were several elephants: one with long straight tusks and another with up-curving tusks. There were several really odd animals that had a hump on their backs and long tails with a ball at the end. They were so numerous. Olomaru-mia had never seen so many animals together in one place at one time. A large iridescent blue and black butterfly flew right by her, causing her to jump. She was astonished at its beauty and followed it with her eyes until it was out of sight. Mechalu took off the gag and band. He untied her hands from behind her. Mechalu reasoned that noise could not travel to pursuers from their location—yet.

Momentarily forgetting her situation, Olomaru-mia asked with interest pointing to the animals below, "What are they?"

Mechalu used his hands to show a partial trunk and a slight hump on the back and said, "trunked camel." He explained they lived in herds. Then he pointed to the elephant, moved his hands from his jaw straight down, and said, "long-tooth elephant." He pointed to the other elephant taking his hand and moving it down from his jaw and then upward and said, "curved-tooth elephant." Finally, he pointed to the huge animal with a great hump and balled tail and said, "spiked-tail armadillo."

She pointed to the animals in the same sequence and said, "trunked camel, long-tooth elephant, curved-tooth elephant, spiked-tail armadillo."

"Very good," Mechalu said with a genuine smile, astonished at her speed in learning the names of animals. He pointed for her to sit. She complied. He handed her more of the dried meat. She ate some. It wasn't worth fighting over every little thing, she'd learned. She took the offered water bag. Then, her feeling shifted. This man had stolen her. Why was she talking to him? She hated him! Where was Zamimolo?

Something squealed and crashed through the brush. Olomaru-mia tried to curl up in a tight ball crossing her arms over her ankles and ducking her head. The posture made Mechalu smile. It was only a tapir, probably startled by them. He guessed correctly that if she was so frightened, neither she nor any pursuers knew how to judge from animal noises what was occurring in the forest. He had the advantage.

Mechalu left the area for cover behind vegetation to make water. She had the same need, so she pointed to the same direction. He held the rope and motioned for her to go. She had hoped to be free and possibly make a run, but realized that he was in good shape and she was not after the long boat travel. She also had a great fear of the forest through which they traveled. It was far different from the forests at home. She returned and sat watching the beasts below. They were all animals that ate plants. They were food. There were so many!

Mechalu indicated that they needed to move along down the mountain. When he began to stuff the gag into Olomaru-mia's mouth, he hesitated. She shook her head with a negative.

"You will remain silent?" he asked. Based on distant animal noises he had heard as they climbed and crested the mountain, he knew no humans had entered the forest. He reasoned that they'd make the camp location long before pursuers could reach the top of the mountain. He could dispense with the gag temporarily.

She nodded affirmatively. He put the gag in his bag. He led down the path to the lowland where they would camp for the night. He knew the path even in the dark though the paths forked frequently. That evening she tried to imagine how to break free and follow the trail back to her People. She feared the constant noises and strange animals whose habits she didn't know. It was too overpowering. Even without the fears, it seemed that her hope of escape was vain. There had been so many forks in the path that she didn't remember the way back. She couldn't follow the path of the sun in the forest. She reasoned she might find her way back by crossing the mountain and finding the water, but then she didn't know whether he'd walked a river or the sea. She despaired. It was getting dark fast on this east side of the mountain. Mechalu wanted to get across the valley as soon as they could see when the sun's rays first appeared, and he wanted to do it without leaving a trail. If others were close to the top of the mountain, he did not wish to be seen crossing below. It would make their trek much harder to follow if they weren't tracked across the valley.

Zamimolo and Linpint had followed the river's edge until they noticed a pile of rocks. The rock pile was in disarray but it seemed unlikely to them that those rocks would be in that location along a sandy beach unless placed there by people because they were different rocks from what lay about. Both wondered whether they marked a path in the mountains. As quickly as possible, they used the rock pile as an indicator and walked straight for the mountain. After some inspection, they found a path. They followed it, occasionally recognizing that the path had been used recently, but they could not tell whether it was by people or animals.

It was becoming dark when Linpint noticed something out of place in the grass at the edge of the path ahead. He bent over and picked up the little bag Zamimolo had made for Olomaru-mia. He handed it silently to his friend.

"The strap broke. Do you think she intentionally left us a marker?" Zamimolo asked the rhetorical question. He yearned for her. He hoped it would be as easy to continue to follow her. He hoped she'd leave more signs, but she was not a hunter. She wasn't trained. "Do you want to stop here?" he asked. It was getting very dark. He could stay in a place where he knew she'd been.

"Yes. We could push on to the top of the mountain but we'd be doing it in the dark and there could be bears or something we've never seen in this forest. We are in a land of unknown hazards." Linpint was ready to rest.

Back at camp the women had returned with limpets, mussels, and clams. The women who remained at camp had a pouch filled with water ready for the seafood to which they'd add hot rocks from the fire pit to heat the water as soon as the seafood was added. To the boil just before taking up the soup, women added greens they'd found nearby. Each person got a bowl and was served. The People were hungry. Finally, Tukyatuk and Grakumashi emerged from the dark. They found their bowls and ate the seafood soup.

The People cleaned up from the evening meal and prepared for the council meeting.

In the mountains Mechalu and Olomaru-mia had reached the valley. He had led her in the dark to the east a good way into the valley. Frogs were calling; birds made their night songs; monkeys shouted before settling down. She wondered about his eyes, for her vision was not good enough for her to have moved so quickly in the dark. He had carefully edged around trees to disguise their tracks. He had taken her arm to lead her in the dark. They reached the rock shelter he had been seeking and put their few burdens down. He took the rope away from Olomaru-mia's neck and tied her ankles together. With another shorter rope he tied her wrists together behind her. He tied a rope from her feet to one of his feet with a knot that would pull free with a single tug. Mechalu was very tired. He'd had little sleep in the last couple of days, and he didn't want to lose his prize by sleeping. The thought that she might chew a rope or signal their location with a scream bothered him, so he put the gag back on with the leather strip to hold it. He tied it tightly.

Then, he gently put his hand on her head where he'd hit her to make her sleep. It had bruised. He wondered whether it hurt. This was a tough way of getting a wife, he mused, but he had chosen a great one. He held her to him for a moment, stroking her arm, thinking of the tenderness that would exist from now into the future. She stiffened and began to panic, wondering what was in his mind. He kissed her forehead. He circled her in his arms with her head on his chest. She could hear his heartbeat. She could hear familiar sounds of crickets and other strange bug noises including katydids and cicadas, making her wonder whether it was all one bug or several. The thought of creepy things was unsettling.

Mechalu held her there seemingly lost in thought for a while. Mechalu could envision the ceremony at home when he would join with this girl. He would have her as wife because she was his prize of valor. No one could touch her—not even the elders. He would be kind to her, and she would be a good wife to him. She would birth him many children. He smiled.

Olomaru-mia was despairing. He pulled her to him and lay on his side behind her, his arms still about her. Her arms ached, but she could not tell him. He began to slide his hand down her side curving in at her waist and raising up at her hip. She froze. It seemed, however, that he was just interested in stroking her, nothing more. She had heard stories about people who were stolen. They were treated badly and women were more often than not raped. Yet, he had not harmed her, except to render her unconscious. She thought she should consider herself fortunate for his treatment of her, but she reminded herself that she could allow herself to hold only hatred for him. He was a thief. Despite her discomfort, fear of the forest noise, and agony at separation from her People, she slept.

The council meeting of the People that night was a time of discomfort. All the people except Olomaru-mia, Zamimolo, and Linpint were attending. Night noise from the frogs and the wind was loud. Fear was present as if serpents had invaded their midst. Never had the People in their lifetimes experienced abduction from their number. It was terrifying that one person could be snatched so silently from among them without a trail to follow. A few murmured that spirits had done it.

Numing held out his arms, palms up. The Wise One nodded to him.

"Tonight, Obi and I will guard so that all may sleep," he offered. The Wise One nodded acceptance.

Tukyatuk and Grakumashi were eager to share their day's trip. The Wise One nodded to Tukyatuk whose arms were held out, palms up.

Tukyatuk said, "We went to the mountains to the north. They are not very tall but are of sufficient height to make it possible for us to assign only two people to stand watch atop the highest peak, where they'd have a full view of any attempt to gain access to the upper levels from the flat land below. In addition, there is a small cave near the summit and a lake. We should be safe until we choose a better place. We think that after the morning meal, we should pack up to leave for the mountain."

Rustumarin held his arms out, palms up. The Wise One nodded.

Rustumarin asked, "With a cave and water available, was there no sign of human life, if only a temporary hearth?"

Grakumashi held his arms out, palms up. The Wise One nodded.

Grakumashi began, "There is no sign of human presence anywhere. Not even ancient small hearths. We examined the area carefully. The only paths are made by animals. It seems to be a safe place at least until we become more familiar with our surroundings. We also looked from up there to see whether fires were visible anywhere in our area. We could find none."

Suddenly hunters first and then others among the People began to strike their left palm with their right fist. It was a sign that all agreed with the proposal. As quickly as the sound began, it ceased. The council adjourned. In the daylight they'd move to the mountains. Maybe on the mountain they could lay down the fear that gripped them.

The first rays of sun were not yet lightening the sky when a wiggling and muffled sound from Olomaru-mia awakened Mechalu. Slowly he looked to see what the cause of the sound was and noticed a snake about as long as he was tall was making its way toward the place where they lay together. He released the tie on his leg, reached for his knife, and moved to the side of the snake's path. In an instant he grabbed the snake by the head and severed its head from its body. Olomaru-mia lay there terrified. Trussed as she was, she had been incapable of getting away from the venomous snake. Howler monkeys shouted to each other, also aware of the snake, and Olomaru-mia felt she couldn't cope any longer. Mechalu threw the snake and the head a far distance from where they would be walking. Olomaru-mia trembled. Mechalu moved beside her and held her in his arms, something which brought her instant comfort to be followed quickly afterward with a strong attempt to shake him off. She was determined not to forget he was her captor and never to be trusted. She had mixed feelings: she didn't know the forest and feared it, needing protection Mechalu would provide. Yet, he was a man who had stolen her from her People. She depended on a man whom she could not forgive. It was confusing.

Mechalu understood she had mixed feelings about him. He knew time would change that. He was a patient man. He untied her ankles and retied the rope around her neck. He wanted to crest the mountain ahead of them as quickly as possible. He left Olomaru-mia's gag in place for fear that a sound from her could alert any followers as to their location. Followers could be near the crest of the mountain they'd just left. He left her hands tied behind her. He was eager to get on the way. He moved into the tall grass to relieve himself, realizing he'd made it hard for her to do the same. He led her to a place where she was off the path, so she could make water. She emerged from the grasses dispirited. It appeared that another day of trekking would be taking place with the gag in and her hands tied behind her. Mechalu headed towards the mountain. Clouds were gathering overhead and it appeared that rain would come. He jerked the rope to encourage her to move faster on the trail that led up the mountain. It was not comfortable to have the rope jerking her neck, but she did respond with a quicker step. At first they traveled an animal trail. That gave way to a path that looked as if humans had used it. It was broader and the vegetation overhead and to the sides had been broken away. They followed that path until the clouds parted and the sun was overhead. They shifted off to an animal trail.

Nearing the sun's zenith, voices rang out in the valley far to the north calling her. Olomaru-mia tried with everything in her body to reply but came out with only a small gagged sound that wouldn't travel. She knew the voices. They were far away, but she knew them. That's why she'd been gagged. Now, she understood. She fell to her knees, ignoring the jerk on the rope on her neck. She wept and wept. Mechalu felt compassion, but realized that they had made it safely without giving evidence of their route through the forest. He realized that the men had followed the obvious paths through the forest heading north, not the subtle ones they'd used to head south. Clouds were gathering again, darker ones, making it clear that a rainstorm was on the way.

Any pathway evidence that existed would be obliterated soon. Despite the fact that Mechalu believed they were safe from detection, he was concerned enough that he went to her and hit her head, causing Olomaru-mia to sleep again. He carried her, wanting to crest the mountain before she could do anything to alert the callers to her position. He knew the men had called from the north end of the top of the first, smaller mountain. He was well ahead of them and far south. With her on his shoulders again, he rushed up the mountain, feeling fed by extraordinary determination to keep his prize of valor. Nearing the mountaintop, Olomaru-mia waked up, but did not fight being carried like a speared animal. Zami would not find her. She wondered whether she should give up. In despair she decided to will herself to die.

With the sun descending Mechalu crested the mountain, which was quite a bit taller than the one they crossed the previous day. Once on the other side and partway down the mountain, he put Olomaru-mia down and had her walk. He followed an animal trail to a broad open land about a third of the way down the mountain. Mechalu stopped, removing Olomaru-mia's gag and untying her hands from behind her, so they could eat some jerky and drink water. Olomaru-mia put the jerky in her mouth and then spit it into her mittens and buried it in the vegetation out of sight of Mechalu. Both were becoming dehydrated. Olomaru-mia began to weep. She knew that Zamimolo was an expert tracker, but she didn't believe that he could possibly find her now, and rain was starting to fall, becoming heavier over time. Mechalu was moving so fast she had trouble keeping up. Sometimes she fell. He would help her up and then he'd straighten out the vegetation where she'd fallen. He seemed angry with her as if he believed she did it intentionally. She did not realize he thought she was leaving signs for the trackers. Her head hurt badly. She knew he must stop hitting her head or he'd damage or disorder her mind web, if he hadn't already.

At another stop Mechalu sat beside her noticing her weeping. He felt sorry that she had to hurt, but he knew he'd be a good husband to her. She had no worries. He put his hands on her head and caused her to look at him. "What is your name?" he asked.

She looked at him in disbelief that he'd ask such a question then. She was soaking wet and pain ripped her belly to be separated from Zamimolo and her People. And he wanted to know her name?

"What is your name?" he asked again.

"Olomaru-mia," she said in an angry voice. Thunder boomed nearby.

"Say it slowly," he said.

Olomaru-mia had no desire to talk to her abductor. She stared off into the distance.

Mechalu grabbed her hair and pulled her head about roughly, so she looked at him again with an edge of fear. "Say your name slowly," he demanded.

Olomaru-mia complied, hoping that lightning would strike her. The night bug chorus was gaining volume.

Mechalu repeated her name. He asked if he'd said it correctly.

She nodded.

He repeated it several more times. Then he added, "I am Mechalu."

Olomaru-mia just looked at him.

"Say my name," he demanded.

She glared at him.

Mechalu was losing patience. He'd been kind to her. Once again, he said gentler, "Say my name."

She looked away, and fast as a snake he struck her cheek hard.

"Say my name," he growled.

She did.

"Say it again!" he insisted, poised to strike again.

She complied in tears.

He stood and pulled her by the hand to stand. He retied her hands behind her, but he put the gag in his bag. He pulled on the rope and the two continued down the mountain. By nightfall they'd reach a rock shelter with a cairn he'd built. It was located around the toe of another mountain. They would finally have a comfortable night.

Light came to the west side of the first mountain where Zamimolo and Linpint spent the night. As soon as they could see clearly, they gathered their backpacks and began to hike the rest of the way up the mountain. They quickly lost the track of the two they followed, but they reasoned that if they crested the hill they might see Olomaru-mia and her captor or captors. He hoped she'd make noise somehow to alert them, but she had never been taught what to do in such a case. No story told what the captive should do. They traveled upwards as quickly as they could. Part way up the hill, Linpint fell into a cave under tree roots. It had been obscured by the leafy vine ground cover in the forest. Linpint was in it to his arms. Zamimolo helped him out, and they continued.

In an area where no trees grew just a little higher on the hill, they stopped on the grass to have something to eat and some water. Linpint lay on his back looking at the heavy sky, noticing the smell of rain. Soon they'd be drenched. Zamimolo was grateful to be outside the heavy forest for a while. He didn't care for the darkness and sense of foreboding he felt in a dense forest. A crashing noise brought both of the men to their feet. At the edge of the clearing, a huge ground sloth was pulling at a tree and it had fallen to lean on another tree. The tree hold wasn't good, and soon the tree would crash to the ground. The tree didn't bother them at all. The shaggy coated ground sloth was a great concern. The boatmen had warned them about these animals. The beasts could move at a rate almost as fast as a man could. They stood four times the height of a fully-grown man. Their nails were something to avoid. They could strike out with their arms at an alarming speed. Normally they ate plants, but some people said they also ate meat, taking over the kills of the long-tooth cat. Zamimolo and Linpint had no desire to verify that comment. Apparently, the sloth hadn't detected their presence. They put on their backpacks just as the rain began to fall in huge drops.

They went back into the forest quietly and continued up the mountain. Rain abated briefly as they crested. The men called to Olomaru-mia. They called to each direction, first east, then south, then west, then north. They repeated the process several times. Each time they listened with great care. There was no return call, no rock fall such as a gagged hunter might create with an intentional kick. Nothing. All seemed to be a forest without people. There was no indication anywhere that would lead them to Olomaru-mia. They decided that when they returned to the People they'd insist that all People learn the things hunters do if they were lost, so if they were stolen they'd know how to alert followers with signs or sounds. The men were dismayed in the present. Mountains continued seemingly forever. Olomaru-mia seemed to have vanished.

Zamimolo stood looking eastward. The Wise One had said to go east. He looked at Linpint, "How can I hope to find her in this forested mountainous land? I feel dispirited. I sense defeat. And the forest noise here is deafening!"

"We have hardly tried yet, my friend. Let's continue over the side of this mountain to see if we can find a place to spend the night. There are ways to find her. Perhaps we'll find other people living here who can help us. Don't give up so easily."

Mechalu led Olomaru-mia around the toe of the final mountain of the day. It was dusk. It would be fully dark by the time they reached their destination. He was eager to reach his rock shelter and cache. It was the place he had spent much of his time since he'd been on his test of manhood valor. He'd been gone for a long time. In this specific place, however, he had come to feel at home, though it was a long way from his real home. Olomaru-mia was extremely tired. Her foot had been seriously injured on a sharp stick, and it continued to bleed. She walked on it almost relishing the pain, hoping to hasten her death by blood loss. Mechalu had been striving to reach his place and did not stop often. When they did stop, she had eaten nothing, burying the food she'd been given in the vegetation where they'd stop, when Mechalu was looking elsewhere. She carefully concealed the foot injury, hoping Mechalu would not smell the blood.

At dark, when Olomaru-mia could not see well, Mechalu pointed to the rock shelter. He'd made places inside the protective cover of rock to sit and even to sleep. Skins were laid over branches that were designed to keep the sleeper off the ground. He led her to a place to sit while he began to spin wood between his hands to create a spark for a fire, anticipating a warming fire in the firepit. Firewood had been placed in stacks around the rock shelter. Mechalu was so intent on what he did that he neglected to untie her hands or remove the gag. Olomaru-mia no longer wept. She wanted to die and would do whatever she could to hasten the process. And when she reached Wisdom, she wanted to ask why this had been permitted to happen. She felt empty. Few thoughts crossed her mind web. The sound of the fire starter barely reached her. The constant forest noises no longer caused her great alarm. She faded.

Mechalu got the ember and blew it into flames. He set what he carried in his hands carefully under the logs he had stacked, ready for his return. The fire in the pit he'd dug and surrounded with rocks came to life from a tiny ember. In a short time a real fire was burning and he could see. Mechalu turned to Olomaru-mia and realized she looked terrible. No longer was there anger, but in its place was an emptiness that disturbed him. Something wasn't right. He realized she was still gagged and her hands were tied. He went to her and remedied the things he had neglected. She was lifeless. Her cheeks were bright red.

"What's the matter?" he asked.

37

She was silent. This was different, he noticed. It wasn't like her intentionally ignoring him earlier in the day, flaring at him from anger. She was just not there. It sent an alert resounding through Mechalu that he could not ignore. First, he smelled and then he saw the blood and realized her foot was badly injured. He wondered how much blood she'd lost. Mechalu got a wooden bowl he'd made and ran to the pond. He filled the bowl and put it near Olomaru-mia. He took a small pouch from his backpack. He put her foot in the bowl and washed it thoroughly, noticing that she hardly flinched when he pressed on the wound to clean it out. He knew it should hurt severely. He also noticed that her skin was very hot as from a fever, not exertion. He guessed that she'd had the foot injury for quite some time, but she hadn't let him know. He took some skins and dried her foot. He reached into his bag and pulled out a tiny leather folded pouch. Inside were two bone needles. He took some hair that he'd removed from a horse neck a while ago. He threaded the needle and holding her foot so she couldn't move it, he sewed the wound together. She barely showed that she felt it. Mechalu took a pinch of herbs from his pouch. He opened the folded neck of another pouch and extracted some honey directly onto the wound. He sprinkled the herbs on the honey. Then he brought the leather up to her foot and pressed the herbs and honey against the wound. He wrapped the soft leather around her foot and tied the wrap with narrow strips of leather. He wrapped the whole foot and tied it securely.

Mechalu went to his bed and checked the bedding to be sure that no snakes or spiders were lurking among the branches or skins. He laid Olomaru-mia on the bed. He got a bag, went back to the pond, and filled the bag. He returned and hung the bag on a piece of rock that stuck out from the wall. Olomaru-mia seemed to be sleeping. He removed the tunic that Olomaru-mia was wearing and took a piece of soft leather from his cache and wet it in the bag. He laid the wet leather on her chest, hoping to reduce her fever. She lay there as if in another world. Mechalu was worried that his valor prize might not survive. He got another piece of leather, wet it, and put it on her body from the ribs to her knees. Mechalu took the remains of the water and tried to dribble some into her mouth. That was very slow but successful. He had forgotten his hunger. All he sought was to heal her.

He lifted the leather piece off her chest and fanned her with it. He noticed that her nipples were pink, not the dark brown with which he was familiar. It made him smile. He re-wet the cloth, put it back in place, and then did the same with the other piece of leather. He stared at her in the firelight while he fanned her. Her pubic hair was the light reddish golden color of the hair on her head! He had never seen such a thing. He was shocked that he hadn't noticed earlier. It was uncharacteristic for him to miss something like that. He lifted her arm. Her underarm hair was also light. He could even see bluish blood vessels through her skin. He wanted to touch her, but he restrained himself. He intended to join with her. For no reason that he could explain, he blushed. He could feel it coming, and it was a significant blush. He was grateful that nobody had observed him. He lifted her hands and noticed that one of the knuckles on her left hand was stiff. He couldn't bend the finger at the place of stiffness without breaking it. He wondered at it as a curiosity. He covered her back with the wet skin and sought something to eat. Jerky would suffice, he decided. After he ate, he dribbled more water into her mouth. He wanted to be sure that she had plenty of water, even if it took all night.

Olomaru-mia stirred. She saw him through slitted eyes fanning her with a wet piece of leather, which dripped water onto her skin. She was shivering. Her mind web could not piece together what was happening, and she drifted back to sleep. Over the days that followed, she regained consciousness briefly and saw Mechalu taking care of her. She still had difficulty understanding where she was, why she was there, and where the People were. Before she could do much reasoning, she would fall back into fitful, feverish sleep, amidst the noise of monkeys, birds, and bugs. So much noise.

Meanwhile, the People had packed up and moved for safety to the mountain site discovered earlier by Tukyatuk and Grakumashi. The cave was adequate for the present, but if the group grew, they would have to look elsewhere. Water from the pond was good, but they soon expanded water-catching small channels in the rock of the cave exterior to channel rain into containers made from carefully sewed leather skins. For drinking they pre-ferred the rainwater. Wildlife abounded on the flat land below them and from their vantage point, they could easily see where the hunters should go for meat. The camel was the most abundant grazer below. They were not hard to harvest, not like the elephants or giant armadillos. The armadillos had either spiked tails or smooth, fat tails. They had managed to kill a few, but the meat of the camel had far greater appeal and was much easier to spear. They also really liked the taste of the animal that resembled the rhino, but it was a snarly beast and not at all easy to spear.

Colitoba sat on the stone by the hearth. Her gaze was unfocused. She toyed with a piece of split leather at the bottom edge of her tunic.

Meninkua squatted beside her. "You still hurt?" Meninkua's long dark graying hair shone in the light, her dark brown eyes filled with sympathy. The People had all loved Olomaru-mia.

"Of course. The Wise One said she would not be found until she has white hair and by then she will no longer be the same person we know. How could I lose my precious daughter so fast? I fear what is happening to her."

"No one could have known this would happen. There were no signs of human life around the area where we chose to camp. Hunters checked it long before dark. It had to have been done stealthily. But the Wise One said she'll be treated well." Meninkua brushed off some small biting insects.

"Sometimes I wonder if he really knows."

"Don't search for trouble, my friend. The Wise One wouldn't say that unless the Spirit of Wisdom told him."

Colitoba looked up. "I know. It's just hard not to worry. She has been such a good child and you and I know what mostly happens to girls who are stolen."

"Maybe the Wise One knows that this is somehow different."

"I sincerely hope so."

"Come, my friend, we can find some greens for tonight."

"Let me get the leather sling for carrying Picota," she replied getting up. "I'll be ready then." She knew she had to do her part for the People.

The two women and their daughters, Molar and Flanilk, followed the women down the hill in search of supplementary greens for the night meal. They waved at Folifilo, the youngest of the four eldest wives. She had speared some fish and was bringing them up to the cave as they descended. The fish were threaded through the mouth and gill on a thin rope. Meninkua estimated that there were at least ten fish.

Down on the flat land the women observed the young children practicing with slingshots at leather targets. Kih, Meninkua's eldest son, was overseeing the slingshot practice. Obi was watching the spear practice of the older children. Across the flat land to the north, they could see that someone had speared a camel and was far along in the butchering process. This place seemed good.

By a small creek Jup, Colitoba's eldest son, and his wife, Gifi, sat with their feet in the water. Gifi's face was drawn.

"I'm still frightened," she said with her shoulders held up high.

"Now that we have our home, there is no need, sweet Gifi. The lookouts will assure that nobody creeps up on us now."

"But with Olomaru-mia it was so fast. She would have fought. It seems she had no way to know anyone was there or to resist."

"My dear, you make the choice. Either you live your life in fear or you don't. Fear is no longer reasonable. You can choose to turn loose of the fear."

"How?"

"Just trust."

"Trust?" Gifi was dumbfounded.

"Trust the lookouts, the hunters, the fact that no tracks have been found so there are not many of these people. Keep your nose, eyes, and ears aware of your surroundings as you do anyway for snakes and wild animals. Then, there is no need to fear. We hunters think it was a single person who happened to see us land, who waited until dark, took Olomaru-mia, and then left to return to his people, wherever they live—which isn't near here, or we'd see traces of their hearth fires. You are as safe as you can be. Nobody is ever completely safe. Just go ahead and live your life fearlessly, for you can now." He put his arm around her.

"You aren't afraid?"

"Not as soon as we moved here. I've seen the lookout places. You can see all directions. We put the people who see the best there. We are as safe as we were back home." He hugged her to him.

"I'll try."

"My wife, I ask you to live fearlessly—not try. When you say, 'I'll try,' you give yourself the ability to continue in fear. Declare to yourself that you'll live fearlessly. Then do it. It's something you must control."

She reached for his hands and held them. She searched his face, coming to rest on his dark blue eyes. "I will live fearlessly." She filled herself with determination.

The two embraced and then returned to the chores they'd been doing.

In the mountains, Zamimolo and Linpint had awakened and begun to continue to the east following a path that seemed recently used. At their movement, howler monkeys set off amazing, seemingly endless cacophony of ear splitting sounds. The men looked at each other and shrugged. The path led to another path that was clearly one used by people, and they were encouraged. Human evidence was not recent, but they hoped it would lead to people who could give them directions where to look. It led northeast to a river showing traces of human presence. The men followed the river to a valley, which in six days brought them to the sea. The sandy beach was lovely. If they stood facing the water, to their right a good distance away was a hill rising from the sand. The same was true of the view to the left. They realized that the shore consisted of both sandy beaches and hillsides at the water's edge. They knew this sea was a different sea from the one they crossed to the new land. As hunters, they knew the direction they had traveled. They realized the land they had chosen for this migration was a narrow land.

They agreed to travel on, keeping the sea to their right. Keeping the sea to their right was more to the east than heading in the other direction, which seemed to head toward the south, and their choice seemed tied to human use. They hoped to find some people who could give them guidance on where to look for Olomaru-mia.

Back at the rock shelter Mechalu was still greatly concerned. He had left Olomaru-mia briefly to hunt and had returned with a camel. He had butchered it and had the meat cooking. He cleaned up at the lake and returned to find Olomaru-mia sitting up looking confused.

"How are you feeling?" he asked.

"I have seen you taking care of me. Who are you?"

"I am Mechalu. We have traveled a long distance together. You injured your foot. You seem better now."

Olomaru-mia looked at her foot and realized she was undressed.

"Where is my tunic?" she asked horrified.

"Here," Mechalu handed it to her.

"Why did you take my tunic?" she asked.

"Because you had a high fever and I had to soak you with wet cloths." Mechalu assessed the situation. She looked terribly weak and he wasn't at all sure that she was well yet. He squatted beside her and put his head against hers. "Your fever has gone," he said.

She realized she had leather circles threaded with leather through slits tied to her hands.

"What is this?" she asked indignantly. "Get this off me!"

"Shhhhhh," he took her by the shoulders and laid her back down gently.

She resisted with every bit of energy she had, which was very little.

He held her down. "Stop struggling. You've been very sick. You need rest."

"Where is Zamimolo?" she asked near panic.

"Who is Zamimolo?"

"He is the man I will join. Where is he?"

Mechalu thought carefully. Should he bring it all up? Would it help her get better to face reality so soon again?

"I don't know where he is," he answered truthfully. "You have been very sick. When you are better, I'll take you to my people."

"I don't want to be separated from my People," she sobbed, reaching for the little bag at her neck. It wasn't there.

"What did you do with my little bag?"

"What bag?"

"The one that hangs on a leather strip around my neck. It's missing."

"You must have lost it in the forest. I haven't seen it."

Olomaru-mia felt something like a memory rising and it fell flat, irretrievable. She was so tired. Mechalu brought some branches over to her and laid a soft piece of leather over them so she could rise up a little. She watched him with the animal he was cooking and fell back to sleep. A while later she reawakened.

In a growl she demanded, "Get these things off my hands!"

He came over and realized she'd lost the fear he'd carefully instilled in her. He kneeled at her side. "No," he said forcefully, staring hard directly into her eyes threateningly.

"Why?" she demanded not cowed.

"I put them there for a reason. They will stay there until that reason no longer exists."

"At least have the courage to tell me why you did such a thing."

"No!" he said emphatically. He went to her and took the small rope and with purpose and staring into her face, he tied her feet together. "It isn't a matter of courage," he muttered.

A shock went through Olomaru-mia, a memory tried to surface, but she could not quite grasp it. With her hands wrapped, there was no way she could untie the rope that tied her feet together.

"Am I a captive?" she asked, her voice tinged with horror.

"You could say so," Mechalu replied.

Olomaru-mia tried hard to capture the memory, but it remained outside her grasp. She was silent. She knew she was a captive. She would think on that. It was, however, hard to think. She was so tired.

Finally, she rose up on an elbow and asked, "If I'm a captive, why did you take care of me when I was sick. Why didn't you leave me to die and go your way?"

"You are not well yet. I didn't leave you because I will take you to my people. There you will join with me."

"I will not. I am promised to Zamimolo."

"Zamimolo is lost. You are coming with me. I cannot leave you in the forest alone. An animal would kill you to eat you."

"That would be fine with me."

"Not with me."

"Who are you?"

"My name is Mechalu, Olomaru-mia."

Again, the memory came so close only to fade away.

"I really want to go home," she whimpered.

"Olomaru-mia, your people have moved, and I have no idea where they are now. Hear me. You are going to come with me to my people. You will be my wife. I will take good care of you. You will not be harmed. You will be loved. Stop whining over what was lost and get used to what will be."

Olomaru-mia stared at him. She understood what he was saying. She just couldn't put the pieces of the recent past together. This stranger planned to be her husband and told her Zamimolo and her people were nowhere to be found. She wondered whether they'd taken a boat back to the home they'd left for this new land. She was so very confused and the bug noise was not helping her to feel better or think straight.

Mechalu took some of the meat that had cooked thoroughly on the outside and sliced it, laying the pieces on a slab of wood. He walked over to the bed where Olomaru-mia lay and sat beside her. He handed her a piece of the meat.

Olomaru-mia took it and ate. It was wonderful, she thought. She became full very fast but enjoyed the meat. She thanked Mechalu and dozed. As night came on, Mechalu got a large skin and stretched out beside Olomaru-mia. She awakened and asked him what he was doing.

"I am sleeping here on my bed beside you as I have for the last six nights. Lie back, be still, and sleep."

Olomaru-mia was shocked to think that she'd been sleeping beside this stranger. She wanted to remain awake all night, but she could not manage to stay awake for any length of time at all. Soon she slept.

In the morning she awakened beside Mechalu. The memory came again and Olomaru-mia remembered that Mechalu had stolen her. She remembered Zamimolo calling to her from the mountaintop. Mechalu had made her unconscious, even though she couldn't reply with a gag on. She remembered wanting to die. Mechalu had taken good care of her she admitted to herself. Off and on while sick, she saw that. Even with her death wish, he wouldn't let her die. Her emotions ripped apart. She didn't know what to think or feel anymore. She didn't move for fear of awakening Mechalu. She reasoned that what Mechalu said was true: her People had probably moved from fear that another would be stolen, and Zamimolo was probably lost in the forest with another hunter, probably Linpint. They would surely find their way back to the People since hunters were trained to do that.

When Mechalu awakened, he realized Olomaru-mia was awake. He untied her feet so she was free to leave the area to make water. She probably wouldn't run, he thought, because she clearly had no idea where she was and the forest sounds frightened her. In time she'd learn to interpret those noises, but he was glad that time was not yet. He reheated the meat and sliced it. He brought her some.

"Mechalu," she said, "I really wish you'd let me die. I really wanted to die. If I cannot have Zamimolo and be with my People, I would rather die."

He laid down the wooden slab where he'd put the meat for their morning meal. He held her shoulders very tightly and looked into her green eyes. "That is a very ungracious thing to say. The Creator made you to live. He has made it so that what you thought your life would be has changed. The expectation is that you will make the best of what is, not wish to die. For you to wish to die is ungracious to the Creator and to me. I will take care of you. You will have my children. They cannot be born without you. I do not wish to hear any more of your complaints. What is—is!"

Olomaru-mia was shocked. His people had a Creator. That Creator must be very like Wisdom. Was she being ungracious to Wisdom? Wisdom had, after all, allowed this to happen. At that moment Olomaru-mia lost her fight. She attributed her state to the winds of change, the exhalation of Wisdom that turned lives of the People upside down and caused much consternation. Zamimolo and her People were gone to her. She realized she depended on Mechalu to keep her safe and feed her, neither of which could she do. It was clear that he'd do all he could to keep her from death. She didn't want to recognize that dependency, but it was real. She knew that she was going to have to change herself into someone new. Mechalu handed her some meat. She took it and thanked him. She ate.

Olomaru-mia looked up. "Mechalu, you have hit my head and made me sleep too much. If you continue to do that you will disorder my mind web, and I'll be no use to me, you, or anyone else. Have you not seen people who have head injuries?"

"I think it's safe to assure you now that no longer will I make you sleep. At the same time, you are to stop fighting, and you must obey me. You will not try to escape or remain silent about injury. In addition, this you must swear—if you hear your name called by those who search for you, you will not respond. If you do reply to a call, my hunters and I will track down the callers. You will watch us skin them slowly for three days while they are tied to the ground, kill them, and know you are responsible. These are our forests. We can find them, while they cannot find us. Do you swear?"

Olomaru-mia was horrified. They'd skin living People! Who could think of such an awful thing to do? It was outrageous. It spoke of a sick mind web. What manner of people were they? she wondered. Nausea tinged the edges of her belly. "In the face of Wisdom, I will swear," she said in a very subdued voice.

After some time Mechalu asked, "Is there anything I can get for you?"

"A comb," she replied having earlier noticed that there were many tangles in her hair.

"What's that?" he asked not familiar with the word.

Olomaru-mia explained the word and the use for it. She drew a picture in the dirt. Mechalu understood but told her they didn't have combs but that he would try to make one for her. He told her they cut their hair, but he didn't want hers cut. He thought her hair was beautiful just like it was.

Mechalu pushed her down and told her to sleep. Soon, he knew, they needed to continue their trek home. She needed to regain strength to make that trek. He got a piece of hard wood and brought it to sit near her. He began to carve a comb. It would have more spaces than the one she had used, but it would work.

Suddenly the forest became uncharacteristically quiet. Olomaru-mia sat upright. A rumbling noise was followed by great waves in the earth, as if they were on the ocean. It continued for some time. Trees swayed back and forth and a rock fell from the overhead shelter. Then there was silence. All became still.

Olomaru-mia was surprised but not frightened. She'd experienced earth-quakes in her life, not this large, perhaps, but some did quite a lot of damage. She waited to discover whether others would follow. Mechalu pushed her back down and told her again to sleep. He explained that earthquakes were very common in this land. Sometimes they'd cause a dwelling to fall, but normally they did no damage at all.

Olomaru-mia knew from Ki'ti's Understanding, a story told at campfires about the reason for the winds of change when Mt. Baambas erupted. It told that the winds of change were always for good purpose, even when the People could not detect the reason. She tried to find a good purpose for her capture, but she could find no reason for what happened to her. She thought on Mechalu's words, "What is—is." It did not take long before she closed her eyes and drifted off to sleep, Olomaru-mia wondered as she did just who she was. She was no longer certain she knew her own identity.

Chapter 2

Linpint stood on the white beach sand and inhaled deeply the salt air. It was another gray day. He wondered when the sun and blue sky would return. He loved the appearance of the blue green water. This new sea on the other side of the narrow land where they had decided to make their new home came as a real surprise. He walked to the water's edge. After the storm they'd witnessed the night before, he wondered whether there would be objects washed up near the shore. He was not disappointed. His brief walk at the edges of the water showed several shells shaped like snail shells but huge and obviously from animals that lived under the water. He picked up two of them and realized the animals were still inside the shells but had pulled a piece of hard substance across the entryway to protect themselves. With his fingernail he tapped on the protective shield of the animal. The tap on the protective shield, unlike skin of the animal, made noise. He carried them back to the place where the two men spent the night.

"What have you brought?" Zamimolo asked.

"It looks like two sea snails," Linpint replied holding up his treasures that were twice as long as his hand. "We eat fresh food from the sea this day."

Zamimolo went to the sea and partly filled a large leather bag with seawater. He picked up some green seaweed, swished it in the sea, and dumped it into the bag. He hung the bag on a nearby broken tree limb and, using tongs made from bent wood, he added several fist-sized stones from the edge of the fire to the bag. Soon they'd eat. Already he was salivating.

Linpint took the time to run a comb through his hair. He pulled it back and fastened his hair at the top back of his head with a collar held together with a wooden pin that went through the three holes of the leather. It worked well to keep his hair from his eyes. Zamimolo had chosen the same means of controlling his hair. Some men wore theirs loose or cut. There was no one way to fix hair, though not too long ago all grown men would have had long loose hair unless they hunted and then they'd use a single braid down the back. The young men would have had hair cut shoulder length, held in place with a band around the forehead to the back of the head, until they made their first large kill.

"As big as those things are, I think we should add some more hot rocks," Zamimolo said.

"Good idea," Linpint replied. He got up, removed the rocks from the bag, and added several others that were white hot. The water immediately boiled.

Zamimolo had pulled two pieces of woody material from a palm tree and put it beside the bag to receive the shells.

"It has to be ready," Linpint said as the savor of the meat wafted on the salt air. He put a shell on each of the servers Zamimolo had found. The animals inside the shells had erupted from them. To the servers Linpint added equal parts of the seaweed. "Hot food and a lovely place to eat it. This is tasty!" he exclaimed with sincerity.

"I wouldn't mind eating jerky and being back at the place with **all** People present," Zamimolo said acerbically.

Linpint couldn't help but notice how bitter Zamimolo was becoming from the abduction of Olomaru-mia. He knew bitterness would do his friend no good, but didn't know how to help. Zamimolo rebuffed his suggestions each time Linpint offered, so Linpint kept silent. In his own case, he knew the outcome of the loss of a wife. Her body lay in the sea. She fell overboard on the trip to the new land. He had no hope. Zamimolo did, but the Wise One had effectively quashed it. He tried to remain sympathetic without encouraging the bitterness.

Zamimolo poured the remains of the cooking bag water on the fire, tied the bag to his backpack, covered the fire pit with sand, and gathered his few things together. He stood looking out at the sea wondering again where Olomaru-mia was. He was eager to follow the path that led along the edge of the water. Linpint shrugged on his backpack and was ready.

The two men left their temporary residence and headed along the path with the sea on their right side. They searched each time they reached a high point for traces of hearth fires, but saw none. For days they traveled, always with the sea on their right. Occasionally they'd see very small islands off to the right. Infrequently they'd see a small fire pit that had been used moons ago.

Linpint marveled at the parrots, for he'd never seen birds like these. A pair took wing as they approached, showing their brilliant red underwings and underbellies. Both men were becoming accustomed to the raucous noise of the birds and monkeys, but they still lacked understanding of the signals their sounds provided.

Zamimolo's belly continued to be ripped apart with the loss of Olomaru-mia. "If I ever find the man who took her," he said with half chewed peccary in his mouth one evening, "I've resolved to kill him. I dream of killing him."

Linpint was alarmed. To hunt to find Olomaru-mia was one thing; to hunt to kill a man, quite another. The latter was vengeance. The stories made it clear that vengeance was a killer of those who used it. It was not in keeping with the order of the winds of change, something to which Wisdom expected the People to adjust.

"Zami, you are ignoring the story of Gambul and Mangot. I fear for the health of your mind web, if you continue these thoughts." Linpint was horrified. He didn't like what was happening to his friend at all, but he had no sense of how to reach him. From Zamimolo's scowl it was clear that his words had a very different effect from what he had intended.

"Nobody who listens to those stories has any idea how I feel!" Zamimolo spat out the words, his hands clenched tightly and his jaw muscles bulged.

"So you think you're the only person who has lost the love of his life?"

"I'm sorry," Zamimolo looked at Linpint with softer eyes. "I know you still grieve. What I just said is self-centered and unkind. I am just so undone." His hands relaxed but the muscles in his jaw did not.

"Zami, if you continue on with the desire for vengeance, I will leave you to return to the People. You are my friend, but I will not watch you destroy yourself. It's not as if you don't know better. You would be searching for the wrong thing for all the wrong reasons. I will not choose to help with that."

Zamimolo listened to Linpint. His friend had been saying these words in different ways for many days. He knew the truth of the words. He heard them with his ears but they never got deep enough to affect his belly, the source of his fire of vengeance. He knew Linpint was his friend—all a friend could be. Linpint's words would throw water on the fire that was building in his belly, Zamimolo admitted, but the water was not enough to extinguish the fire.

51

Zamimolo resolved at least to keep the fire banked. By hiding the embers, he hoped to have his friend beside him for the seasons promised. He didn't wish to be alone. Maybe, he thought, he could get past these vengeful feelings.

"You're right. Thank you, Linpint. I have hated the man instead of what he did. I have seen the man for what he did rather than who he is. There is, perhaps, a difference. I will correct my mind web as we walk today," he said, wondering whether he might actually be able to do what his words said. Both men climbed into trees near the water to prepare for sleep.

The next day the two were nearing the summit of a great bald hill, when Linpint exclaimed, "There in the far distance is a fire!"

Zamimolo rushed over to see where Linpint pointed. Sure enough, smoke was rising.

The two men moved as rapidly as they could to reach the fire. When they reached a small hill, they looked down on a fire. Near the fire, someone appeared to sleep. They walked down the hill quietly. A young man rose up and turned to face them.

"Who are you?" he asked them, in words close enough to theirs for them to understand.

"I am Linpint. This is Zamimolo."

"I am Tomarghi of the Kapotonok. I ran from a big-tooth cat in the forest. I have injured my leg. The big-tooth cat left when I made it into the sea. I came for the turtle eggs. The turtles should arrive any night now."

The men were unsure what a big-tooth cat was but were more concerned with Tomarghi's injury. Zamimolo bent down beside the young man, his concern obvious. "Let me look at that," he said. "Tomarghi, your leg is broken. Between the two of us, we can get it put in place to restrict movement so it can heal, but it will be very painful. You have displaced the bones. Once we get it put in place and held there, we can help you return home."

"I would be grateful for help," he said wincing. "I feared that the cat would return tonight and I'd have to remain in the water in the dark wondering whether the cat would overcome its fear of water or go away. I do not fear pain to fix my leg. I need my leg and am useless like this. I know how it is. I broke this same one when I was younger. I feared staying in water to avoid the cat today, because sometimes the pain causes me to sleep the sleep that is undesired."

Zamimolo knew well how to set a leg. He had done it numbers of times. He spoke little and went straight to work. Linpint had not been involved in bone setting so he simply followed the instructions of Zamimolo. He went to find straight sticks. The young man seemed to have many leather strips. Fortunately the bone had not broken through the skin. When they finished, they talked about how best to get him home. Linpint favored a leather strip fixed to two poles that would make a stretcher. Zamimolo finally agreed.

"There is another way," Tomarghi said quietly.

"What's that?" Zamimolo asked.

"Find two straight sticks in there," he said pointing to the trees. "Look for ones that have outstretched arms at the end of the stick. They should be as long as from my armpit to my ankle."

"Are you in your proper mind web?" Zamimolo asked.

Tomarghi laughed. "Yes. We call these sticks crutches. With them we are slow but can walk without assistance when a leg breaks."

Zamimolo and Linpint looked at each other. They were interested, so they hurried to get a sense of the length of pole needed and went quickly to the forest. Zamimolo found one first. Then Linpint found one with a slightly longer arm on one side. They hurried back to the young man.

Linpint said, "We can just break off this long arm from the crutch."

"It would be good to leave it. It might be useful to carry something," the young man replied. "Do you have any furred skin?"

"I have some," Linpint offered, holding up a piece.

"My father will replace it. Will you cut it in half?"

Linpint cut the furred piece in half and handed it to the young man. He carefully lined the arms of the crutch and tied leather around the fur to keep it in place. With help he stood up and showed the men how to use the crutches. Zamimolo and Linpint were amazed. They had never thought of something like that. It made such good sense.

"You will come to my home?" he asked.

"Of course! After all this work, you don't think we'd leave you to the big-tooth cat, do you?" Zamimolo teased.

"Thank you," he replied already with his backpack shrugged on and heading for home.

They discovered that Tomarghi was a long way from home. As they walked, Linpint said that he thought they should stop for something to eat and drink. Tomarghi had no food with him. He had made a long run and intended to eat turtle eggs and then return with eggs for the people.

At their rest stop Linpint said, "Hold your crutches just like you use them," while he made marks on the wood. "There, that's good." He opened his backpack and took some leather strips. He wound the leather strips tightly around the pole just below where Tomarghi held onto it. What he tried to do was to give the young man's hands a grip on the peeled wood to prevent his hands from slipping down, something he'd observed as they walked. The bottom part of the leather extended farther out from the pole to stop the hand from slipping down. Tomarghi tried the handgrips and was delighted. They sat and ate jerky and Zamimolo passed around the water skin.

While they ate, they discussed the big-tooth cat. Linpint described their cave lion from where they had lived. From the descriptions, they realized both talked about very big cats, but the cats were not the same. Zamimolo was amazed that just because water separated these two lands, the animals were so very, very different. He and Linpint made the crossing and there were people here, recognizable people. Why, he wondered, were the animals so different?

They continued up the beach and by evening were within sight of Tomarghi's home on a hillside above the water. Birds were singing their evening songs and the night bugs were beginning to make their noises. In the distance a shriek resounded, then disappeared in the noise of insects and frogs.

Armed village hunters hurried to greet the men, since there was no expectation that three men might approach. They recognized Tomarghi quickly and realized that the two men had helped him. That brought great pleasure and welcome from the hunters, one of whom relieved Tomarghi of his backpack. They would celebrate with dancing and a feast for the travelers. The people had already eaten.

The hunters led them to the fire circle. They leaned their weapons against the Chief's hut, and told the strangers to do the same. Weapons were placed on one side of the entry to the hut. The men showed the strangers where to rest their backpacks against the other side of the entry to the hut.

Zamimolo and Linpint studied the dwellings used by these people. Instead of all living together, there were numbers of small huts formed from tree trunks leaned into one another. Huts were built on a mound of earth packed tightly. Linpint correctly assumed the raised level was to prevent rain from entering the hut's living area. Leafed limbs covered the tree trunks and gray moss, which hung from some trees, was stuffed into the matrix of the leafy limbs. Large, stiff leaves radiating in a part circle from a single stem covered the structure for waterproofing against the rains. They overlapped each other at the sides and the one above hung over the ones below. Smoke from a tiny hearth could exit through a hole in the top of the structure where the trunks came together. Linpint and Zamimolo found them interesting, but too dark and confining.

Two hunters showed Zamimolo and Linpint to a place at the fire circle the most distant from the Chief's house, where they sat beside each other with a hunter to either side of them. People began to gather at the circle taking places that seemed assigned, while talking occurred but was subdued as the people observed the strangers. As with the fire seating of the People, the men sat forming the innermost circle and the women and children gathered outside the inner circle, usually behind husbands or fathers.

When all were seated quiet among the people came quickly. Tomarghi's father came from his hut and took his seat. He had a hat on his head that was band-shaped, not covering the top of his head. Somehow, the headband of the hat supported feathers of incredible colors. The feathers stuck straight up from the headband. Some were long and thin, others long and wide and some at the edge of the headband were soft and fluffy. Zamimolo and Linpint were fascinated almost to forgetting to listen. They had never seen anything like it. Around the Chief's neck was a short cape also made of feathers. The color of it all was vibrant and eye-catching. The Chief squatted at his place and sat down cross-legged.

He looked at the strangers. "We welcome you to our humble village," he said in a hoarse voice. "You have helped Tomarghi and we are obligated to you."

Zamimolo started to speak, to say there was no obligation but Linpint's silent hunter pressure against him communicated to him not to move or reply.

"We are Kapotonok, the turtle people. My name is Hirmit. I am Chief. The old man to my right is our spiritual leader, Yok. Tomarghi is my son. These are our people." The Chief began to name each person around the circle. At the sound of their name, each person nodded to the strangers.

"You are?" Chief Hirmit asked.

Linpint said, "I am Linpint of the People from beyond the western sea. This is Zamimolo. We just traveled here from our cold land across the sea to find a warmer place to live. We found a place here up a wide inlet where we set up our temporary camp. One of our women was stolen. Zamimolo and I search for her."

"She is not here or Tomarghi would have told you. We do not steal women, but we do like to meet other people to secure women for our young men and men for our young women. In our tradition, young women go to live where the man lives. We have several young women here who need husbands."

Linpint pressed Zamimolo hard to hold his silence.

"Your People and the Kapotonok are one people from the beginning, people from the western sea. The mariners who travel the western sea are the reason we can understand each other. They are like the land travelers of old, who shared the differences from place to place, so all understood the world a little better. That has been their job since life began. They kept our original language alive. There are some people living here who came from the eastern sea who are very difficult to understand when they speak. We can understand them but it's difficult until you get used to the way they use their words. We have been separated from them by great distance since just after the Maker formed people. It is as though they are different people, but that is not true. We all have our differences, but we are all people. You'll discover this for yourself."

The Chief rose while all the others remained seated. "You must be tired from your search. We will feed you. We will have music while you eat. Stay where you are and enjoy your time with us."

The Chief entered his hut and returned shortly afterward without the hat and cape. A few women rose and brought turtle shells filled with sea-food, seaweed, and fruits. The color was somewhat like the Chief's feathers. A huge shell was placed before Zamimolo and Linpint and a smaller one before Tomarghi.

The sea turtle was the symbol of Tomarghi's people. They centered their lives around it. Shells were useful for making many things including combs, digging tools, bowls, containers. Many of the young women wore necklaces of turtle nails or seashells, while men wore cat or condor nails or camel teeth. One man with scars on his left side wore a huge tooth on a strip of leather around his neck. Tomarghi told Linpint it was the tooth of a big-tooth cat that the man had killed when it attacked him. The big-tooth cat had two of these teeth among its upper teeth and it used them to stab. Most people didn't survive attacks by the big-tooth cat. Linpint couldn't imagine a cat with a tooth that large. He wondered how it closed its mouth.

"You must stay for the turtle feast," Chief Hirmit told the men. "We only take five turtles a year from a beach, because we want them to return. We only take them after they have laid their eggs. We take eggs from that many nests. Many beaches are sacred to the turtles. They visit them each year to lay their eggs. It is something to see! Go with our hunters tomorrow to the beach where you found Tomarghi and bring back turtles and eggs. We will have a great feast from the sea when you return. You will see what has happened on that beach since the beginning of time."

They sat watching the dancing and listened to the music. The music, it struck Zamimolo, sounded much in rhythm with waves, rising and falling.

If he shut his eyes, he could see himself back on the boat. It almost seemed that the insects were in harmony with the music of the drum and shell instruments. Zamimolo felt that was just his mind web playing tricks. In the distance he heard monkeys sounding aggravated over something, but the sound quieted as quickly as it began.

Across the circle Linpint noticed an old man looking at Tomarghi's leg. He felt the leg carefully nodding from time to time. He examined the wrapping and the way Zamimolo had tied the splints. He looked at the handgrips on the crutches. He rose from where he sat and found his way to Zamimolo, while Linpint watched one of the young girls dance to the drum. She was smiling at him, leaning back seemingly with invitation. Linpint found her extremely attractive.

"Tomarghi tells me you are responsible for preparing his leg to heal."

Zamimolo nodded.

"You have done good work. Very good work. I like the handgrips on the crutch."

"Thank you," Zamimolo said. "Linpint is responsible for the handgrips."

"You do good work, too." The old man looked at Linpint and put his hand on his shoulder. His hand felt like a weak bird's foot, but it was surprisingly warm.

"Both of you have suffered loss," the old man muttered.

Zamimolo was alert. Where'd he get that information? he wondered. He assumed the man was like their Wise One.

"Do you want to choose a woman from among ours? We have some who need husbands." The old man searched their faces.

"I am looking for the woman who was promised to me. We came by boat recently and she was abducted. I want to find **her**," Zamimolo responded rudely.

The old man turned from Linpint and put his warm weak hand on Zamimolo's shoulder. "You will not find her until you are both too old. You will both be very different people then. Best you find another young woman. The Maker makes it clear. You need to turn loose of her. You grasp at air, not your former love." The old man had a fleeting vision of a very dark-skinned man with a pale-skinned girl with golden red hair. He knew the approximate place where the man lived.

"How do you know this?" Zamimolo asked.

"It's written in the wind. Can you not hear the wind? It tells all to those who learn to listen."

"I cannot hear it, but the Wise One of our People can hear it. He said the same thing you said."

"And you will ruin the life you were given by refusing to heed our words. You have no wisdom! You'll find her when she has white hair, if you keep searching. If you continue to search and find her, you'll be the undoing of her good life. Sight of you will kill her. You need to go home. To continue your search will avail you nothing. She will join and love another. Return to your people. Live and have a good life. This land provides very well for those who live. Both of you are like dead men."

"If you were me, would you give up?"

"Yes, because I hear and heed the winds. I have the wisdom of the wind. You are going against the winds and that is a task with no reward, like fishing all day and catching nothing or going to pick fruit only to find the monkeys have taken all that's fit to eat. Were you not taught to respect your elders and to listen carefully to your Wise One?"

"Of course, I was taught that. I yearn for Olomaru-mia. We have loved since early childhood. She is my all."

"No more. She is now someone else's all. She will join soon and will love the man with the dark skin, darker than mine. He already loves her. They will have many children and their life will be very good."

"Where do the people with the dark skin live?"

"Because you will not hear the words of the wind, I will not give you that information precisely. All I will tell you is to go north. Follow the edge of the sea, if you must continue this wrongdoing. You will need to follow the edge of the sea for four seasons." The old man knew he must get the word to his people to tell the men the same thing if asked. Only he and the Chief would know they were sending the men in the wrong direction. The Kapotonok knew of the dark people to the north who came from the rising sun. Only he and the Chief were old enough to remember the dark men of the south who came from the setting sun. He would send two runners to the nearest villages related to his, villages to the north. He would tell those to the north of this quest and what to tell the young men. The young men didn't seem to understand that their continued search could set off a war. If they went north and reached the Alitukit, those warriors would scare them off, if not kill them outright. Better to sacrifice these two than start a war, he thought.

Linpint had wandered down to the water's edge. He heard the music and realized there was dancing at the fire. Suddenly he felt a hand on his shoulder. The smiling girl had arrived so silently he hadn't heard her. Linpint turned and put his hands on her shoulders. She smiled at him looking directly into his eyes.

She beckoned to him, saying nothing. She did not need to say anything. She had already shown where her interest lay. He followed her into some tall grasses by the water and there they spent much time in pleasure. Had he been asked, Linpint would have sworn he wasn't ready for this, but his body said otherwise. They enjoyed each other until they both were satiated, and they returned to the fire and their huts.

The next day, Zamimolo was eager to head north, so he and Linpint told the Chief that they appreciated the offer to remain for the turtle feast, but that they needed to be on their way. The Chief gave them food that would last for a long time to carry with them. He gave them his best wishes for a good trip telling them that they'd have to cross rivers, but bridges frequently crossed those rivers. The widest, hardest to cross rivers had bridges. They'd have to walk upriver quite a distance to find the bridge.

The next morning the sun rose in a cloudless sky. The men ate with the people and then left heading north, never giving thought that they might have been tricked. Tricks were not part of the way they ordered their mind webs. Zamimolo pondered the words of the old man about the wind's telling him things and wondered whether that was the same as the winds of change he knew. It disturbed him a lot that the Wise One and the old man both told him the same thing. Zamimolo did not understand how seeing him could kill Olomaru-mia. The Wise One of the People had not told him that.

"Linpint, what did the old man mean when he said sight of me would kill Olomaru-mia. Did he mean literally that she would die?"

"I don't know what he meant, but it disturbs me that two people who understand Wisdom have told you not to do what you're doing, because it will not serve to meet your goals. Now, we hear it could result in Olomaru-mia's death. I think you should reconsider."

"It just doesn't make sense. How could seeing me kill Olomaru-mia?"

"I only know that what sounds reasonable to our mind webs is not all there is to life, Zami. It certainly isn't all there is to Wisdom."

Mechalu uncovered the wrapping on Olomaru-mia's foot. The foot had healed well and the redness had gone. It still caused her some pain, and he was convinced that she should not walk on her foot unprotected. He replaced the covering.

"You know how to cut leather strips, do you not?" he asked.

"Yes. Of course. What do you want?"

"I want some thin but strong strips. I have leather in that pile that you can use. We need to head for home, and I want something to protect your feet. Your feet are soft. I will make foot coverings for both your feet. Is there much pain from your foot now?"

"No more than I can tolerate. I can walk on it." The thought of trekking was intimidating, but she would not hold him back.

Mechalu looked at her standing with the sun behind her. Her energy had increased since he'd taken care to heal her foot and provide good food. She kept her hair properly combed and pulled back. The sun made it glow all about her. The sight of her overwhelmed him. He strode purposely to her and circled her in his arms, pressing her as if he might crush her. The action took her by complete surprise and her body, instead of rejecting him, responded. He kissed her passionately and then held her away from him, leaving her mind web spinning.

"Ah, your beauty and strength took me by surprise, Olomaru-mia. I forgot myself for a moment. Because we will join, I cannot have you until we complete the ceremony at home. It gives me great joy, though, that you responded. We will have such a great life filled with passion and children. I must be much more careful."

Olomaru-mia was dumbfounded. She did not reply to Mechalu, turning inward to her own thoughts. What was she doing responding to this man, her abductor, the thief! She rebuked herself. She was promised to Zamimolo. Then she reminded herself of the winds of change. Is this what Wisdom had planned for her all along. Was her response to Mechalu pleasing to Wisdom? It was all too confusing. She turned away from giving time to those thoughts and went to the leather. Her hands were free now and she was able to use the flint knife to cut the leather. What differences a few days made.

Olomaru-mia took the hard stiff leather piece and used it to back up the softer leather she'd cut for the strips. She cut carefully trying to make the strips he'd requested as parallel and straight as possible. She was grateful that Mechalu thought to make foot coverings for her. He had some good qualities. She also knew he was strong and experienced passion.

By evening Mechalu had finished the foot coverings. Fur lined the bottom of the foot coverings. By taking flexible leather he had covered her foot and brought all the corners up to her ankle where he had threaded the leather strips through slits and tied the whole together. He had then wrapped strips around the foot covering to smooth it to fit her foot. The foot coverings would definitely protect her feet.

"We leave in the morning," he told her.

Olomaru-mia was not pleased. She realized that the closer she approached his home, the closer she came to a fixed change in her life. Once she joined Mechalu, she would find herself in an irrevocable bond. She understood that Zamimolo would not find her to prevent this joining. She tried to resign herself to it, but that thread of hope would not break. She walked to the tall grass to relieve herself.

"Stop!" Mechalu shouted. "Don't move," he said evenly as he ran to where she stood.

Olomaru-mia did not move, wondering what threat existed.

Mechalu hacked at a branch above her with an elongated blade on a wooden handle, and a snake in brilliant yellow fell to the ground in two pieces.

"What is that?" she asked breathless.

"It's a poisonous snake," he replied. "Look," he held the two pieces up for her to examine. The snake was the length of his arm.

"It's beautiful," she admitted.

"It's poisonous," he said flatly. Mechalu could not find beauty in anything poisonous. "You must avoid them. Snakes can be colorful like this or match the plants on which they rest. Look to branches above you not only at the ground. Look for color and shape." Mechalu felt an urgency to get her home to his people. Harmful snakes or other animals rarely entered the village.

"I will do that," she replied.

When the first rays of light hit their sleeping place, Mechalu got up and checked his backpack. He had made a smaller one for Olomaru-mia. He checked hers also. Both contained all that they planned to take with them on this final trek.

Olomaru-mia started to put on the foot coverings Mechalu had made, but he hurried over to put them on her. First, however, he wanted to check the site of the foot injury. He decided to wash it again and reapply the honey and herbs. Satisfied that the wound was healing well, he wrapped the foot. He placed the fur insert against the sole of her foot. Then he added the foot covering. He tied the strips around the foot covering well, but not too tightly. He went to his cache of leather and put a few extra pieces in his backpack.

Olomaru-mia had put fruit on the servers. To the fruit Mechalu had added some roasted peccary meat. Olomaru-mia had seen the animal when Mechalu brought it to camp. It reminded her of the boars she'd occasionally eaten before they traveled to this new land. She could not detect a difference in the taste of boar and peccary. The two ate without talking.

Olomaru-mia broke the silence. "Are you going to tie my hands and put that rope around my neck?"

"Do you plan to obey me?" Mechalu asked instead of answering.

"Yes," she admitted convincingly.

"Then, no, I will not tie you up."

Olomaru-mia was grateful for the choice. She hated being tied. It was uncomfortable, but worse—it was demeaning. She realized it depended on her. Either she was a captive in which case she would be tied, or she was Mechalu's future wife in which case she was free. For her to try to escape was futile. She'd only die in the forests. She'd choose freedom from the ropes.

They shrugged on their backpacks and headed out. Olomaru-mia was surprised that they began to climb another mountain. She was also beginning to understand that Mechalu understood the forest and its pathways very well. She followed dutifully carefully staying right behind him.

As they gained elevation, the clouds settled on the mountain gently, as if they were birds lowering themselves on egg-filled nests. Olomaru-mia realized they were walking inside clouds. The blurriness that the clouds created added a different note of scenic beauty to the eyes of Olomaru-mia. It drew from her a sense of respect, a quiet of step that otherwise might not be there.

Later in the day they reached the seashore. Mechalu had a temporary camp in the trees not far from the beach. They went to the shore and laid down their burdens. Each began to do the work that would be required for them to eat. Mechalu had gone down the beach while Olomaru-mia gathered wood for a fire and laid out implements that might be useful if they intended to cook anything. Mechalu did not think to share his plans, but rather he would wander off and return with food of some type.

Olomaru-mia walked down to the water's edge. She stood looking back at the mountain they'd crossed. It wasn't the tallest they'd been across, but it was a mountain. She looked at the clouds that drifted almost imperceptibly from north to south across the neck of the mountain as if it wore a fluffy white rabbit skin about its neck and shoulders for warmth in the evening. Above the mountain moving not fast but quicker than the lower clouds, there were darker clouds moving from south to north. She wondered at the wind blowing in opposite directions at different speeds and, shading her eyes, she looked at the sky, thinking of Wisdom and the winds of change. Between the clouds she could see the setting sun's rays. The beauty of the place did not escape her. The turquoise water, the very light colored sand contrasting with the palm trees at the shore and forest with every green color and shape possible beyond, trimmed by white clouds and darker ones, and the sun's rays as it began to descend was breathtaking to her. She fought the sense of assurance that all would be well with a sense of duty to what had been. She knew she had to let go of the past, but she continued to carry it as a burden.

Mechalu arrived with a number of crabs without pinchers. He had removed them. He pulled out the cooking bag and Olomaru-mia immediately fashioned the place where the bag would hang near the stones they would drop in the bag for boiling.

"What are those things?" she asked.

"Crabs," he replied. "See here. These are the claws. I remove them so nobody gets hurt. Have you ever eaten crab?"

"No." She looked at him and the crabs. The crabs looked hard. She touched one and it was very hard.

"How do you eat it?" she asked.

"First, you need to know how to cook it. See this red color?" He showed her a leaf. You cook the crab until it turns red like this. I'll crack them for you, show you what to eat, and how to remove the meat. It is a wonderful food. Go to the sea, find the light green sea plant at the edge of the water, and bring some up to go with the crabs. It is not like leaves on a tree but rather like this." Using a crab claw, he drew a clumpy looking blob with curly outer edges in the sand. "We'll add it to the bag just before we eat."

Olomaru-mia had no trouble finding the seaweed Mechalu described. She brought it back and by then it was time to add it to the bag. The crabs were almost red. Mechalu reached both the top and bottom shells from the back, using pressure to pull the top of the shell from the bottom with his fingers. He showed her the yellow material in the center, which she could eat if she liked it, and the gray fingers atop the crab's body to avoid. He used his knife to split the hard structures on either side of the crab to get at the crab's meat. Mechalu cracked open the claw, pressing his knife against the shell on one side, just splitting the shell, not going all the way through, and then on the other so that the meat came out whole. He placed some claw meat on one leaf and some on another, handing one to Olomaru-mia. She delighted in the taste of the crab and the seaweed. She learned fast to open the crabs and to get at the meat. Having no knife of her own to open the claws, she had to share Mechalu's. Both ate their fill using a twig to pull out the few hard-to-reach pieces of crabmeat. Mechalu had no need to ask what she thought of it. She had meticulously picked every piece of meat from the shells. The sky was filling with stars and the fire was pleasantly warm. Olomaru-mia remembered the cold of their former home. She considered this a much more convenient way to live.

"How is your foot?" Mechalu asked, stretched out on a piece of leather, his head propped on his hand from a bent arm.

"It is almost well. The foot coverings were a very good help. My foot hurt only a little. Thank you."

Mechalu nodded. "That's good." Mechalu was pleased with himself. "Tomorrow we walk along the shore. You won't need foot coverings there. We will look for boats. If we see boats, we will step into the trees and hide until I can determine who sails. You must be quiet. Understand?"

"Yes, I understand."

"You will remain silent?"

"I will."

"Good. I will not need to stuff your mouth with leather. Some people from the far south try to capture others. They travel by boat. They make captives do their work. We must take care not to cross their paths."

Olomaru-mia mused at the incongruity of his concern about capture while she sat there captured. She certainly didn't wish to be captured to be used as a slave. She knew about slaves. When one of her People was too difficult to live with, either they would be traded as slaves to boatmen or be killed. Most preferred death. It did not sound as if Mechalu intended to use her as a slave but rather have her as a wife. Still, she reasoned, he had captured her. At least she knew him. He treated her well. She didn't want to be captured by anyone else.

The sky which had been gray for days was clear. Mechalu had made a quick sleeping place for the night in the limbs of a tree by lacing broken dead branches among the living tree branches. He circled the trunk of the tree, careful to cover the bark with his urine. He laid a skin over the branches. They climbed up the trunk and lay there in the branches with leaves and stars above them. Olomaru-mia had never thought to sleep in a tree. The gentle movement from the wind rocked her and calmed her weary soul. To suspend thought and worry for a time to gaze upon something as beautiful as the night sky gave her peace, something she had not felt for quite a while.

Mechalu gently pulled her to him and hugged her dispassionately. He felt her body melt against his. They had come a long way together; they had a long way to go. She had ceased to fight him. He believed that he was finally winning her. They drifted off to sleep.

Dawn brought crashing noises through the forest. It seemed that an elephant was chasing something at the edge of the forest. It bellowed and birds and monkeys screamed. Only the bugs seemed to quiet themselves. The elephant was moving to the north, so the two of them climbed from the tree, took their things, and made their way to the beach. They headed south as quickly as possible. They could see broken trees to their right in a swath created by the elephant. They had no desire to be near that big animal while it was being so fearsome.

As they walked, Mechalu took Olomaru-mia's hand and she did not withdraw it. He looked to the water and no boats were visible. His ears, always attuned to the sounds of the forest, told him that after the incident with the elephant, at least no people were in the forest. All had returned to normal. Normal included the ground sloth that was at the edge of the forest, eating leaves from the top of a tree. Mechalu pointed it out to Olomaru-mia who wanted to flee to the water.

"Calm yourself," Mechalu said quietly, holding her hands tightly, "As long as you don't aggravate the giant, it won't bother you. It's just eating the leaves it likes above all others." The sloth stood on its feet and used its tail for support. It was easily four times the height of Mechalu.

They passed the ground sloth, and it paid no attention to them. Olomaru-mia was dumbfounded. She kept looking back to see whether it followed. It didn't.

Mechalu went from walking with her hand-in-hand to walking with his arm around her, above her short backpack, and his hand on her shoulder. Again, she did not pull away. He pointed out various trees, telling her which ones bore edible fruit, which were good for wood fires, which bore nuts. She tried to learn all the new information. Sometimes it felt overwhelming. He showed her parrots, snakes, and monkeys that she had not seen. He showed her how to see the forest and understand what it had to tell as well as show. He told her to listen. The forest was relatively quiet. He told her it was a time of resting. No snakes were threatening monkeys or birds; big animals were not prowling nearby. They did not trouble the forest animals, because they walked along the shore, far enough from the forest to be viewed as safe. No people were in the forest. Somewhere in the walk, Olomaru-mia gently put her hand on Mechalu's back at the side of his backpack. He avoided showing any reaction at all, but his joy was great.

"We will eat crab again?" Olomaru-mia asked him.

"You liked it enough to choose it two nights in a row?"

"I didn't get my fill yet," she replied smiling a genuine smile.

"This evening, I'll show you how to find and catch them. We'll hunt together for crabs and end this day with a feast."

Olomaru-mia looked up at him and smiled again.

Deep from the forest the sound of a cat's growl and shriek rolled outward to their ears.

Olomaru-mia stopped dead in her tracks. "What was that?" she asked, frightened.

"Big-tooth cat," Mechalu replied. It has probably threatened another animal to stay away from its kill.

"You can understand that from its sound?"

"This is thick forest. You have to learn what the sounds mean to live here. It's not a mystery. You just have to learn to hear."

"You've made me see that my eyes don't know how to see this place, and my ears don't know how to hear it. What else is there I must learn to survive here?"

"Olomaru-mia, do what I tell you. Obey me. I love you. So, look first to me. Then, when I tell you about the way to understand the sounds you just heard, store that information carefully, so the next time you'll understand. As you learn to use your eyes and ears, you'll find it easier to know what you see and hear. Did you live in open spaces in your old land?"

"No, we lived in forests, but the animals were not as plentiful and they mostly stayed in the valleys. We never saw the animals I've seen here."

It was Mechalu's turn to be surprised. "You never saw a sloth until today?"

"No."

"What about elephants?"

"We had elephants, but they didn't look like these. Do bears live here?"

"We have only one bear. It's black. Its head when on all legs is higher than our tallest man's head. Fortunately, bears don't live near where we live. They live much farther south. I have seen some when I was younger."

"The animals here don't seem to frighten you, but to me it's a place where you can become overpowered by beasts at every turn. This land seems so unsafe."

They stood at the water's edge. They faced each other and Mechalu put his arms gently around her. "That's why you need a husband, Olomaru-mia. I know this place and how to protect us and the children we'll have. I know how to use the amazing numbers and variety of food in this place to see that we never hunger. This is a great land. Do not fear it—just depend on me and my people to assure your safety. Learn what's safe and what isn't. It won't take you long. Then, do what's expected of you to keep the balance of work even.

"I am not lazy, Mechalu."

"I am certain your words are true. You are wonderful, Olomaru-mia."

While they hugged, Olomaru-mia felt a stabbing pain in her belly. To be listening to those words, to feel comfortable in the presence of her abductor still caused her pangs of guilt. She also reckoned that if Wisdom would cause the winds of change to bring her life to this, she should continue to yield to it. Her conflict hadn't resolved, but it had become easier to face when it arose. She tried to tell the guilt it was time for it to leave, but that didn't really work.

"Do you see the second hill on the shoreline? It appears gray in color from here."

"Yes."

"That's where we stop for the night. Let's move."

The two picked up the things they were carrying and moved down the beach. Olomaru-mia discovered that her skin was a little sore and red. She said nothing, but it hurt.

When they finally made camp on the bluff overlooking the water, Mechalu commented on the redness of her skin. By then it was much redder.

"It hurts," she admitted.

Mechalu felt the heat of it. He put a skin in the shade of several trees and pointed for her to sit there. "I'll be back," he said vanishing into the forest. Shortly afterwards, he returned with a succulent plant. He squeezed the leaves to drain the liquid on his fingertips. He put the liquid on her shoulders, forearms, nose, forehead, the places where she had the most discomfort. Her feet were red and swollen. He covered them with the liquid from the plant.

"Your skin does not seem well suited to this land," Mechalu said while gently putting the liquid they used for burns on her flaming face. "Your skin rejects the intensity of light we accept as normal. You were fine in the forest. Out on the beach you seem to cook. We will have to keep you shaded."

"Do your people live in the forest or in the sun?"

"We live at the edge, but there is much sun. You remain here while I go for crabs." Mechalu stood before her, looking carefully at all her exposed skin to see whether he'd missed anything.

The two feasted on crabs again. Olomaru-mia loved the taste of the animals, and she found it delightful that it carried its own bowl, for she tended to place the meat in the upper shell before eating it. That evening, Mechalu also brought two soft-shelled crabs. Olomaru-mia didn't care for them at all. Mechalu had roasted them over the fire instead of boiling them. She was convinced that boiling them would not have made an improvement.

Before they slept, Mechalu made a very thin skin cover to go around Olomaru-mia's neck to protect her shoulders. He also designed a cover for each foot that circled the ankle and had a hole cut for the big toe to stick through to hold the cover over the top of the foot. Mechalu had never had to solve skin problems from the sun. He learned as Olomaru-mia had problems from it. He had brought her some plants she requested. Some of the boatmen had hats made from woven plant leaves. She would try to make a head covering to protect the skin on her face. She reasoned that would also reduce sun in her eyes. The two worked together quietly, listening to the waves breaking and the forest bugs and animals preparing for night. For the next day's trek, she would be protected.

They slept that night listening to sounds of a storm at such a distance that they could not see the clouds. Mechalu told her the storm would not bother them, and it didn't. The next morning they continued their walk along the beach. After several days, Olomaru-mia realized they were going in a different direction. Instead of heading to the south, they were moving more eastwardly. They continued day after day coming closer and closer to his home.

Zamimolo and Linpint hadn't gone many days before Linpint began to shiver. The sun on their skin from days of trekking had burned both of them, but Linpint seemed to have the worst of it. Zamimolo had provided a quiet space at the edge of the forest in good shade. He laid skins under and over Linpint and went to find a water source to replenish their water bags. Zamimolo's shoulders, nose, and forehead seemed the most tender places on his skin. Both men had the tops of their feet burnt. Zamimolo gathered some long leaves and noticed a small fall of water from the edge of the hillside. He tasted it and the water was good. He filled both bags and tied them off. He gathered the bags and the leaves and headed back to Linpint, feeling the edges of nausea himself.

Back at the camp, they both were cautious about drinking too fast. They did spend much time in drinking a small amount and waiting and then repeating the process. Zamimolo felt better, but Linpint still seemed very sick. Zamimolo felt him. His skin was hot. Zamimolo took the leaves and quickly weaved a temporary hat for Linpint. Then he helped him to undress, and both headed to the water. After a short while in the water, Linpint began to feel a little better. He did not feel good, but the chills and high fever had gone. They returned to the edge of the forest and Zamimolo fixed Linpint a resting place in the trees where he would be surrounded by breezes for cooling.

Later when Linpint was feeling better and it was almost dark, Zamimolo asked, "Why did we have no problems on the boat but now on land the sun burns us?"

Linpint looked at him as if the question were too simple. "Zami, all of the traveling People were on the lower, shaded deck. We didn't get the hottest part of the sun. We only went to the upper deck when there were big storms, and then they put us in huts."

"How did I forget that?" he wondered.

"We have to make some protection from the sun for our heads, shoulders, and feet," Linpint said, speaking, he felt, as if from a fog.

"I think we should stay here for a few days," Zamimolo added, "until we get the protection made and have a chance to feel better. There is fruit around us and I can find some meat to spear when the sun returns. I may be able to find some sea snails like the ones we ate after the storm. They were so good."

"They were good," Linpint said, actually feeling hunger for the first time all day. "Is there any jerky left?"

Zamimolo looked in his backpack and found two good-sized sticks. He handed one to Linpint and rested against the tree trunk to eat his.

As darkness grew, Linpint said, "Zami, are you awake?"

"Yes. I was just about to get up to gather wood for a fire."

"I don't think that's a good idea. There is a boat on the water far away. I don't think it wise to signal where we are to boatmen we don't know."

"Where?" Zamimolo was shocked. He'd been scanning the sea for boats.

"See that tiny island off to the southeast? It's just south of that. See it now?"

"My friend, your eyes see very well! I had missed it altogether, and I've been searching the water for boats. You're right about no fire.

"Do you think we're safe from discovery here?" Linpint asked.

"Just to be safe, I will move us back tonight and tomorrow when it's better light, I'll find a place that will be safe for a few days."

"Once you find a place, Zami, I can help move us. I am feeling a lot better now that it's not so hot."

Zamimolo headed to the woods. Near the place where he found the water, there was good space for them to camp. The trees more than adequately hid their place from view from the water. He hurried back to Linpint and the two of them moved the camp. Zamimolo went to the sand and in the moonlight, he took a leafed branch and smoothed out their footprints in the sand from earlier going into the water to cool off Linpint. Fortunately, they had walked in the water as they traveled, and those footprints would have washed out.

The next morning they realized the boat was just off shore from them. Both were very uneasy and maintained strict silence and no movement. They saw people with dark skin. They could not understand the words of the people at all. They appeared to be looking for something, but the men could not imagine what they sought. They dug in the sand and put something in bags. Occasionally they'd laugh. At length, the men who had come to shore got back in the small boat and rowed out to the larger one just off shore. They tied the small boat to the larger one and lifted a small square sail and left, heading north.

When the men were completely out of sight, Zamimolo went to the shore to see if he could understand why the men had gone there. Then he saw what looked like what the Kapotonok people had wanted them to see, turtles laying eggs in the sand—but the turtles were gone. Their slider tracks remained. Zamimolo released a sigh, realizing that he had removed their tracks just hours earlier. It appeared that these boatmen had the same view of caring for the turtles. They did not disturb all the nests, just some. Zamimolo headed back and started a fire. He took a cooking bag, filled it with water, and hung it on a rock protrusion. He took a grass bag and returned to the shore while Linpint watched from his perch where he was making grass hats.

Zamimolo returned with his bag filled. "We have turtle eggs for our morning meal!" he said triumphantly. "They were collecting turtle eggs, and just like the Kapotonok people, they didn't take all of them—just enough for their own needs."

"How good it was that you wiped out our tracks! They'd have found us otherwise."

"It's always good to be careful. We already know there are some who live nearby who steal people."

"Zami," Linpint whispered, "What in the name of provident Wisdom is that?"

Zamimolo looked in the direction that Linpint was looking. Above them on the hill was a brownish-looking animal that resembled a turtle but was twice in length the height of a man. It had a boxy shaped head and a fat tail. It was grazing. The animal's heavily-shelled body made him think that hunters would find it difficult to spear one. Maybe they'd have to flip it to see a soft spot a spear could pierce.

Zamimolo let out a short snort. "At least they won't eat us!"

Linpint laughed aloud. In light of the frustration, sunburn pain, and nausea of the last few days, it seemed fitting to laugh at the utterly strange creature grazing on the hillside. It was a creature they had no need to fear as a predator.

Zamimolo dropped hot rocks in the cooking bag. He carefully washed off each egg and dropped them one by one gently into the bag. The eggs were soft and his fingers made depressions in the shell surface. There were nearly a hundred eggs. He decided to cook only a portion of them and save the others for later. When the water cooled slightly, the men decided the eggs had probably cooked adequately. They began to eat. The meal definitely was larger than most of their meals, except at feasting times. They peeled the eggs and made a pile of the soft shells. No sooner had the shell pile begun to form than ants appeared and headed straight for them. The men quickly scooped up the shells on the ground and threw them towards a dead tree as far as they could, having no interest in a large number of ants as neighbors.

"These eggs have a strange, unpleasant aftertaste. I like bird eggs better."

"I agree," Linpint said. "And these shells are strangely soft. But, it's food."

"Do you think those people are the ones who took Olomaru-mia? Their boat could explain why we haven't found traces of them."

"Zami, I think she could be anywhere. We're in a strange land among strange creatures and plants. It's hot and we sweat. The sun burns our skin. Animals, birds, and bugs are rudely loud. Day is about the same length as night. I am overwhelmed with just the day-to-day effort of getting to know this place. It's too soon to be able to make the assumptions we could have made if this occurred back where we used to live. Who would have thought to eat peeled turtle eggs, but here we are doing it."

"You think this is futile?"

"I do for the present, my friend. We just do not know this land well enough. We are strangers here."

"Do you wish to return to our People now?"

"Well, of course. Nevertheless, I promised you four seasons. You know that I keep my promises. The better question would be, whether you want to return to our People now?"

"I waver on my answer. I want to believe that just beyond the next hill or turn, we'll find her. I don't have anything in my mind web that would support that belief. In fact, I have clear evidence that isn't the case. I feel driven by the pain of the loss of Olomaru-mia. Sometimes I'm blinded by that pain." Tears welled up in Zamimolo's eyes and he unashamedly wept.

Zamimolo continued, "This morning when the boat was here and people collected turtle eggs, I hardly breathed fearing they'd see us. Then I realized they didn't know about Olomaru-mia and the People, because they were too casual about what they were doing. They didn't look into the trees, because they didn't expect to find anyone here. It made me feel safe, and it tore my belly."

"I understand," Linpint said as he tossed the last of his turtle shells toward the dead tree.

A human shout rang out behind them on the hill. The two men looked at each other with concern. It sounded like someone was hurt. They heard an elephant belligerently sounding its warning, and then the ground noise from its run reached them audibly, and they felt it through the ground. Monkeys and birds were contributing chatter and shrieks, their contribution to the confusing noise. They stood and picked up their spears.

"Wait," Linpint cautioned. "Let's put on our sun protection first. We've taken about all we can take. Look at my skin. It's peeling off!" He pulled a piece of dry skin from his shoulder about the size of the palm of his hand.

The men put on their conical hats made of long leaves, their shoulder protectors that wrapped and tied around their necks, and the foot coverings that surrounded their ankles with a skirt-like circle. They gathered their weapons and began to climb the hill to reach the level from where they'd heard the shout. The enormous animal had moved away.

When they first reached the hilltop, they saw nothing. No large animals were anywhere and they didn't see people. Something moved in the grass and they noticed it was the arm of a man. They ran to him. The man must have been hunting and had a bad time of it, they thought, until they noticed the puncture marks.

"Did he try to fight with a wolf by himself?" Zamimolo asked.

"He's been bit badly in the side. Where are his people? He's not as dark skinned as the people we saw this morning. He looks more like the Kapotonok."

From the edge of the forest, Linpint heard a moan. He ran to the place, leaving Zamimolo with the bitten man.

"There's another here," he called to Zamimolo. "This one is bruised badly. There's a dead wolf here beside a camel carcass. There's a dead man here also."

Zamimolo and Linpint lifted the semi-conscious men to their burnt shoulders and carried them to their place at the bottom of the hill. They treated the open wounds with honey and wrapped them. Zamimolo realized they were running very short on skins and honey. The man with the wolf bite was running a fever. Linpint took leather skins and wet them, laying them across the chest of the man.

Linpint took a couple of spears and went back up the hill to pick up the camel carcass for the evening meal. He opened and gutted it quickly, leaving the entrails for carrion eaters. He dragged the dead man a distance from the entrails. He returned to their camp and began to skin the animal. They would prepare it for roasting so that by evening they would have food.

By high sun, the first man awakened. He said words that sounded like those of the Kapotonok. The men showed him his living friend who'd been bitten. The man wanted to know where the third man was. They explained his body was up on the hill. He had died.

The man wept at first loudly and then more subdued. The dead man was his father.

When he regained some composure, Linpint asked him, "Where are your people?"

"We live on a hill above the sea to the north. It is not far from here. It just requires following the water's edge." He marked in the sand sunrise, high sun, sunset, dark. He showed half of the distance from high sun to sunset. Linpint realized that the distance was not long. Zamimolo looked at it.

"I'll go to get help," he offered. "After yesterday, I'm in better shape than you," he looked at Linpint. "You can take care of these people, while I go for help."

"Good. Be safe, Zami." Linpint was glad he didn't have to walk any distance in the sun. Even with the sun protection, his skin was still very sore.

"I will," he said with assurance. Wearing his green hat and sun protection, Zamimolo walked as quickly as he could north on the beach.

Shortly after Zamimolo left, the man who'd been bitten waked.

"Met? Met? Where are you?"

"I am here, Foo. A wolf bit you. People are caring for us. One has gone for help."

"Where's Soklinatu?" Foo asked still very foggy of mind web.

Tears filled Met's eyes. "My father's gone, Foo. He's with the Maker."

Foo wept. "He was the best, Met. The best." The exertion was extreme and Foo slipped back into sleep.

The camel roast was beginning to smell, but it was not ready at all. Linpint filled the cooking bag and hung it. He put several good-sized hot rocks into the bag and carefully added some turtle eggs. When the water had cooled, he took the eggs and placed them carefully on a green leaf. He handed it to Met.

"See that dead tree over there?" Linpint asked.

"Yes."

"That's where we've been throwing the shells," Linpint said.

Met looked at him quizzically, but when he peeled the shell from the egg, he tossed the shells to the place Linpint had shown him. At his home, he would have dropped the shells at his feet and the women would have swept them away.

"Why remove the shells so far?" Met finally chose to satisfy his curiosity.

"Because as soon as we dropped them nearby, they attracted ants. We prefer not to have ants around us.

"The ants you find here are not the bad ants," Met said, tossing some shells in the direction of the dead tree.

"I don't know what you mean by bad ants."

"I mean the ones that sting people."

"I thought all ants bit people." Linpint was confused. Was there a special ant that wanted to bite people? He'd believe anything about bugs in this new land.

"I mean the ones that bite people with their mouths while stinging them with their tails. They leave nasty sores."

Zamimolo wasn't eager to see those ants. Met's face was showing pain. He asked, "Met, do you hurt?"

"Yes, there is a lot of pressure on my air bladders. When the elephant ran by and hit my chest with its big tooth, it must have done some damage. I'll probably be fine in a few days. It seemed anxious when it saw the fresh killed wolf or maybe it was something else. I don't think my ribs are broken, but I'm not sure." Met closed his eyes. It hurt to breathe.

"Did you and Foo kill the wolf?" Linpint asked.

"Oh, no. It was my father and me. We had killed a small camel and the wolf wanted it. Foo was bit and stumbled off. Between my father and me, we killed it."

"I am cooking the camel."

"I thought you were cooking it. When my people arrive, they will bring home my father's body to bury. I hope nothing bothers it."

"This morning, Met, there were some people who came in a boat and gathered turtle eggs from the sand. They didn't see us here. Their skins were darker than yours."

"You saw the Alitukit. They live far north of us. They are a peaceful people as long as you don't disturb them."

"What do you mean, 'disturb them.'"

"They don't want others to live on their land."

"Would they steal people?" Linpint asked watching Met's face carefully.

"I really don't know. I want to say they wouldn't, but I don't know them that well. Some of our elder hunters could probably answer your question. Why are you asking?"

"My friend, Zamimolo, seeks the girl who was to become his wife. We arrived by boat from the sea to the west. The night of the day we arrived, she was stolen. We have been trying to find her. She seems to have vanished. He is breaking inside from the loss."

"Because of your kindness, I wish I could help. It just doesn't sound like something the Alitukit would do. I don't know any people who steal other people. It makes no sense."

"Is there any way I can make you more comfortable?" Linpint asked.

"I would like to lie flat on the earth for a while to sleep, if possible."

"Here, let me help." Linpint smoothed out the ground and laid a skin under Met. The man looked very tired. "While you rest, I will bring the body of your father down here so we can protect it."

Met smiled weakly and shut his eyes.

Linpint put on his sun protection again and climbed up the slope to the hilltop. He picked up the dead man, carried him down the hill, and placed the body in the shade downwind of their camp.

As the sun began to go down behind the hills, Linpint saw Zamimolo and the men walking along the shoreline. The camel was well done and ready for hungry people. Met and Foo both still slept. Linpint went to meet the men. Zamimolo made introductions and the men headed toward the camp. When they arrived, Met awakened.

Lumikna, their healer, went straight to Met. He felt his skin and discovered that he was not feverish. He checked the hunter over and found severely tender places in multiple locations, and assessed damage as painful but not life threatening.

"Gu, wrap his chest carefully. Some ribs are questionable," Lumikna said quietly.

He went to Foo. That was different. The bite was serious and showed inflammation around the puncture marks. Foo was feverish, and Lumikna could not rouse him.

While Lumikna checked Foo, two of the men, Ta and For, asked where to find the body of Soklinatu. Linpint walked them to the place.

Ta looked at Linpint. "Would you share some camel with us before we take the body home? I am hungry."

"Of course," Linpint replied. "The camel was hunted and killed by your people. I'll set up your food right away. Come back to camp."

To make servers, Linpint pulled some fibrous material from the coconut tree nearest the campsite and cut off a steaming hunk of camel roast for the men. He sliced the meat hunks on the coconut fiber servers and handed one each to Ta and For. He had placed some fruit and a few boiled eggs on each server. The men ate ravenously. Linpint served the others and finally himself.

Night noise of the forest had begun. The sky was clear and there was a fragrance from some flowering plants on the outgoing breeze. Zamimolo noticed Lumikna looking at Gu. Ever so slightly, he shook his head negatively. Zamimolo correctly deduced that Lumikna did not expect Foo to survive.

Lumikna looked up at Zamimolo. "I know we planned to stay here overnight, but I have changed my mind. We'll use the two stretchers to carry Foo and the body of Soklinatu home as soon as we finish eating. Would you accompany Met home tomorrow? He is able to walk but may need to stop to rest frequently."

"It would be our pleasure to help in any way we can," Zamimolo replied.

The men set up the stretchers. Ta and For carried the body; Vil and Gu transported Foo. Much light remained when they left. Zamimolo marveled at the speed of their arrival, assessment, and departure. They wasted no time. Lumikna thanked Zamimolo and Linpint and the men left.

Met lay on the skin. He was full from the camel and felt very tired. He was grateful that he wouldn't have to make the long walk until the next day.

Normally, he'd have thought of the walk as very short. It grew longer the worse he felt. He slept.

The next day the men got up, ate some of the remaining camel, packed their things, and headed to Met's home to the north.

When they arrived just before high sun, there was a meeting identical to the one where Chief Hirmit presided. Chief Paaku presided at the meeting. He explained that they and the people of Chief Hirmit were both Kapotonok. Their village had become too large, so their group had migrated north. He explained that his people live almost all year much farther north, but they come to the edge of the sea for the turtle time and the chance to see relatives. It made better use of the land and kept from overhunting the animals. He said the Kapotonok had once come from the western sea. They had lived in this land longer than their stories could remember. Their people stretched along the edge of the sea to the north and the south but more to the south. They knew peoples from the north to the south of this huge land. Some of those people regularly traveled the western seas to this day both to the north and to the south, such as the boatmen who brought them to this land. He told of people from the eastern sea who traveled from a land far away, the Alitukit. He said they rarely met with them because the Alitukit were distrustful of strangers. There was a language difference. They could make themselves understood, but it was tedious and frustrating.

Zamimolo introduced Linpint to the men. He told the men of his People who lived in the forests of the north across the sea, of the deep snows, and the cold. He told of their knowledge of a warm land where it didn't snow, where there was room for many People. He said that they split much as had the Kapotonok, primarily because some yearned for warmth. It would also make animals more available to those who remained behind. He told of their arrival at a large inlet where they turned in to set up temporary camp and of the abduction of Olomaru-mia. They explained they were in this part of the land searching for her.

Chief Paaku looked at an older man, Opt. "Do you know anything?"

Opt looked into Zamimolo's eyes with eyes black as coal—eyes that bored into Zamimolo's belly. "You are dishonoring the Maker, young man. Men who know the Maker have told you this. The girl you seek belongs to another now. You will not find her until you both have white hair. If you find her, she will die because you dishonor the Maker. Why put her life at risk? You will not get what you want—her for your wife. She is now another's. Go home, straighten your life, find a wife, and live right. Find a way to atone for your dishonoring the Maker." Opt looked at Linpint. "You encourage your friend to dishonor the Maker by staying with him. You need to leave here for your home. Already your seed grows in the belly of a woman. Find her. Make her your wife. You will find none better. Care well for those children. Teach them to honor the Maker. One will become a Chief of renown. Another will make a discovery that will help people. You are both wasting your lives now. Respect what is, for what is—is. You are powerless to change it. I repeat, both of you are wasting your lives."

Both Zamimolo and Linpint were amazed at the words of the old man. Linpint had heard this three times now. He felt uneasy, but inwardly he resolved not to continue north with Zamimolo but rather to return home after a stop at the other Kapotonok village. He wondered what Zamimolo would do. Zamimolo was also uneasy. He felt responsible for causing future harm to Linpint if he continued this quest. He did not want to fight Wisdom, and he was certain the word Maker meant Wisdom. It became clear to him that his pursuit was likely futile and that he needed to straighten his life without Olomaru-mia.

Chief Paaku interrupted their thoughts. "We have need of a man and a woman exchange to keep lines from becoming too close. We would like to travel to your home to see whether a trade is possible."

Linpint looked up. "I have tried to fulfill my promise to my friend, but after the words of Opt, I have reconsidered. I will return home. Opt is right. It is possible that my seed grows in the belly of a woman of the Kapotonok. I will ask that she come home with me."

"Good!" Opt interrupted.

Linpint continued, "If your people wish to come with me to explore a swap, I'll be glad for the company."

"I will accompany you with my daughter, Ba, and nephew Kolpatin," the Chief replied. "There may be others. Now, let us have music and dance. It is early but the time to celebrate is here." The circle disbanded, musical instruments appeared, and women began to start roasting for the evening meal. Zamimolo was in a whirlwind. He couldn't believe that Linpint had agreed to leave the pursuit in front of strangers, before telling him. Yet, he could understand that after three wise men had said the same thing, it was time to change. Even he would return home, wherever that was now.

Ba, a lovely, very young woman went to Zamimolo. Her very long dark hair braided down her back, caught with a small leather tie. Tendrils framed her face and neck. She was beautiful, but seemed unaware. "Zamimolo," she said quietly, "You look so sad. I am very sorry to hear that your first experience in this great land was sadness."

"I am trying hard to get past it, but it's still like a new wound." He wanted her to leave him but did not want to appear rude.

"You appear to be distraught. I am going to work on the muscles in your shoulders and neck. It will help them to relax. You only need to sit there. You can enjoy the music while I work. I need to get some things from my hut and will be right back."

Zamimolo was undone. He didn't want a strange girl working on his muscles, but he didn't know how to get out of the situation, so he just accepted it as something he had to do. Linpint heard the exchange and was amused. He pretended not to have heard.

The music began. There were two drums beating slightly differently, one slower and deeply resounding, the other faster with more beats in the same time. A flute played a high pitch. Gourds filled with something made rattling sounds. There was a piece of wood with a deep groove. A man used two sticks to tap out sounds from the grooved piece of wood. Sometimes instead of tapping the grooved piece, the two sticks would tap together. A few people made whistling music; some hummed.

When Ba returned, Zamimolo noticed she hummed. Not loud, but he could hear her. Ba wore a soft leather short skirt, as did all the Kapotonok women. Women only wore the short skirts. Women of the People covered their breasts with their tunics. These women were uncovered. She did not seem to have skin burned from the sun. He wondered why. As she hummed, she took some succulent plants and placed them on a piece of hard leather. She cut the tip of the leaf and dripped liquid onto her hand. She used what seemed to Zamimolo to be a large quantity. She rubbed her palms together and went to kneel behind him. She began to smooth the liquid into his skin on the tops of his shoulders. It was very soothing. It took some of the sting from the burn. She smoothed the liquid all over his shoulders and down his arms, and then began to massage those muscles with strength for which he was not prepared. He did not expect that anyone so tiny could possibly cause him pain, but this was serious work on muscles. He had no idea his muscles were so tight. She could just look at him and know? He did not understand. He had been sitting curved over, resting his arms and forehead on his knees. Her breasts were brushing against his back, and he found himself becoming aroused. Quickly, he sat up straight.

"It would be a lot easier if you lie down on your belly," she said quietly.

Zamimolo didn't know what to do, so he did what she suggested. She placed the leather with the plants next to his arm and straddled his back. He lay there like a trodden toad. Unseen, Linpint was stifling laughter. He'd been through something similar in the other village. Somehow, Linpint didn't expect this event to plant a seed in her belly, however.

Ba worked for a long time on Zamimolo's shoulders and neck muscles. When she finished, Zamimolo thanked her profusely. He felt a sense of freedom, of release from too much tightness. Zamimolo found Linpint.

"You really surprised me. Couldn't you have told me, before you told strangers?"

"I know I should have warned you, but the words were out of my mouth almost before I thought them. It is time to return home, Zami."

"I just wanted to let you know that I can see the reason to return home. These wise men are seeing something I cannot see, but they are bringing words from Wisdom to me. I do not want to be at odds with Wisdom."

"Nor I."

Zamimolo walked over to Chief Paaku. "We have listened to Opt and with what we have been told, we are ready to return home tomorrow. Do you have any honey to spare and some strips of leather. We run low on both."

"Linpint desires to find the girl from the other village. Her name is Lomah. Linger here a few days and we will accompany you to meet your people. We will not leave tomorrow but will send a message to bring Lomah here, if she is willing, along with any others. We will cross directly to the western sea and one of my friends will take us by boat to your inlet. Having her come here will be faster than for us to go there and return. And, yes, Zamimolo, we can replace your honey and leather." The Chief smiled, knowing Zamimolo had no idea how they'd get the message out.

"How will you tell them what the plan is?" Zamimolo asked, curiosity burning his mind web.

"Drums."

"What?" Zamimolo said, incredulous.

"You will see and hear tonight. Meanwhile I will show you with these pebbles." He laid five pebbles on the ground. He drew the eastern line of the edge of the sea in the sand. "These are the rivers you crossed to get here," he said. "The pebbles are example drum sites. We send a message to this drum. They pass it along to the next drum and we hear it to know they have passed on what we said accurately. The third drum site passes it on until it gets to the farthest point, the other village. There are more than five sites. These sites remain even when we are not here. A long line of these sites exists all along the west from north to south. We remain in communication."

Zamimolo was dumbfounded. A communication system that covered so much territory was more than he could take in so quickly. He marveled at the idea.

"Go, enjoy the music, we are about to eat. Then, later there will be dancing. You have some time to relax. Make the most of it," he said with a smile.

Zamimolo found Linpint and told him about the drums. Linpint was equally astonished. They were eager to hear the drums and observe them at work. The two men went to the fire circle and stood against trees. They watched the young people dancing in between their jobs of readying for the evening meal. These were the happiest people Zamimolo and Linpint had seen for a long time. There was a fallen log with a flat top at the edge of their temporary village. The Kapotonok used it for the placement of food in large turtle shell bowls or smaller servers. People would take their food or be served from there. Zamimolo watched Ba dance in with bowls and servers and dance back to return with more. Her movement fascinated him. He could not take his eyes from her. Suddenly pain gripped his belly. What, he wondered, was he doing permitting himself to become captivated by a woman, a very young one at that, when Olomaru-mia remained abducted? Then he realized that, according to the wise man from this group of people, Olomaru-mia had already joined with someone else. Somehow, he believed that the old man knew truth, even if he could not begin to understand how. Even if it hurt him from his head to his toes. For the first time in his life Zamimolo questioned everything he'd ever been taught. Then he rebounded to his first belief, Wisdom was good; Wisdom held all things together; Wisdom shared important information with a person obligated to share it with others. Wisdom produced the winds of change and expected people not only to adjust to it but also to find the blessing in it. Zamimolo realized that he had not had a single thought of this event as a blessing at all. It was important to do that. He would think on that. Ba danced past the edge of the fire pit. Fleetingly Zamimolo thought that if they joined she'd be in a longer length tunic instantly, a tunic with a top. He immediately wondered at his own thoughts. She dressed properly for the group in which she lived. The Kapotonok thought nothing of women's bared breasts. Who was he to have thoughts as an outsider? He found Linpint and shared his thoughts.

"I've had the same thoughts. I will gladly join Lomah, but she will wear a longer tunic and stop running about in short skirts with exposed breasts."

"But, Linpint, I had this thought about someone with whom I'd not thought to join."

"You heard the wise old man. Olomaru-mia has already joined another. You need look elsewhere, my friend. Olomaru-mia is not available, even if you found her. Maybe part of your mind web is already acting on that information. Ba would make a great wife for you, and she certainly finds you attractive. You know you'll never get through tomorrow without another massage." Linpint grinned lasciviously.

Zamimolo pushed him. The two laughed. Gu's wife called everyone to the evening meal. The meal included seafood (fish and shellfish), peccary, some meat the men didn't recognize, boiled seaweed, and fruits in abundance. Zamimolo took small portions of fish, peccary, and the meat he couldn't identify. Linpint did the same but added some clams. They took seaweed and fruit. This new land, they agreed, did provide wonderful food.

Linpint saw Ta and asked him about the meat he could not identify.

"Oh, that's spiked-tail armadillo." He noticed Linpint staring blankly at him. "You know the tan animals that are huge and look like turtles. They have either a spiked-tail or a fat tail. They seem well protected. You have to spear them through the neck and into the shelled area.

"I saw one of those on the hill just before we heard your men shout." Linpint was really interested to taste the meat now. "Thank you for telling me what it is and how to kill one."

"It may keep you from hunger someday," Ta said with a gentle smile. Ta was an older man and had been the one to receive the message from the other group of Kapotonok as to what to tell these young men if they asked about dark-skinned men. He was curious that they didn't ask. He did not know that they respected joining, and believed what they'd been told without question. Olomaru-mia had joined another. That was irrevocable.

Zamimolo looked for Ba but didn't see her anywhere.

Several men with Chief Paaku headed towards Zamimolo and Linpint. "Are you ready to observe our drum message?" he asked.

"Yes," they both replied at the same time.

The men climbed the nearby small mountain. It didn't take long. The path was well worn. The top was free of trees. A man stood in front of a huge log that reclined on two smaller logs that lay on the ground crosswise to the big log. It kept the big log dry on the bottom. The internal part of the log had either rotted or been removed. Linpint and Zamimolo assumed it had been carved out, because the ends were intact. Strips of wood lined the top of a rectangular hole that ran the length of much of the top of the log. Two very strong looking sticks thicker than a man's wrist extended from the hole in the drum. The man at the drum was dark as night. He wore a leather skin tied at the waist. It was made of what looked like cat skin, clued by the paws that dangled from it. Zamimolo had never seen a man so dark or a skin like that. He wondered where the man had been, because he had not seen him.

The Chief went to the man at the drum and told him what he wanted to send. The man listened carefully. He repeated the message word-for-word. Then all sat. The drummer began to beat on the drum. The sound was monstrous. At first, it sounded as if each blow was the same as the one before it, as if the man were simply counting. That lasted for a while. It was a call to the next drum that soon a signal would follow. Then, the drummer began to beat out the message in varying bursts and rhythms. He stopped and all were deadly silent. Even the forest was quiet, eerily quiet, as if even the animals knew what was happening. From far, far away, Zamimolo and Linpint listened carefully. The drum returned the first strokes that sounded like counting and then suddenly the message beat began. When it stopped, the drummer repeated to the Chief what had been sent. It was exactly what was supposed to have been sent.

Zamimolo and Linpint were ready to stand but realized they had not finished. They remained seated in silence, wondering what would happen next. The silence seemed to last for a terribly long time. Then, when they least expected it, the beat that sounded like counting occurred afar off. Then, a different beat on the drum. It was long. The drummer looked at the Chief. He said, "Lomah will join Linpint. She will be here in two days. With her come Dop and Kumoha. They defer to your leadership." The Chief stood and bowed to the drummer who turned and descended the mountain on the other side. The other men stood.

"Our drummer lives to himself. He remains in this place when we leave to go north. We didn't know why he came here. He just arrived and taught all of us the use of the drum. He was Alitukit, he explained one day, but for some reason he and one other were banished from their land forever. They have no names, since they are banished. We gave them the right to live on this land forever. They ask for nothing but to be left alone. Each night they climb hills to drum if there is cause. If not, they descend the hill. If no one is here at night, they wait until darkness before descending to be sure there is no message to send. We are not the end of the drum line. It follows the edge of the sea way north and way south. It is new to us. I hope it will last. The drum signal reaches us in the north. If someone is born or dies, we know. We always have at least one person learn the drum signals."

"This is a very useful communication tool. There is so much that is new and useful here. Will you share this with my People."

"Of course, they may even want to participate."

The men headed down the small mountain. It was time to go to their sleeping places. Women had prepared a lean-to for Zamimolo and Linpint. After the day they'd had, they were ready.

Mechalu and Olomaru-mia sat side-by-side on a fallen tree trunk in the shade of trees at the top of the last hill before descending to the valley that would take them to the sea where his people lived. Their backpacks balanced on the tree trunk. His arm was around her. Her toes toyed with her hat on the ground by her feet.

"See that purplish colored area where the water empties into the sea far to the right?" Mechalu pointed to a place far on the horizon.

"I see it," Olomaru-mia replied.

"That is where we will live."

Olomaru-mia was quiet. She realized how soon she would join Mechalu. At that point, her old life would be gone to her, even if Zamimolo found her. Joining was a sacred thing.

"You fear?" he asked, mistaking the reason for her silence.

"No, Mechalu. There are just so many feelings swimming in my belly."

"Let me help. Here's what you need to know right now. When we arrive, my people will be very excited for many reasons. They'll know I survived my trial."

"What do you mean trial?" Olomaru-mia asked.

"To be fully men, we have to travel alone to the west sea where we arrived at the beginning of time on this land. We have to go without weapons except for a small knife. We must survive by making whatever we need along the way. While on this trial, we have to find something that is very special to us, something that no other man can ever touch. It should reflect things that are not common to the place where we live. What I found on my trial, Olomaru-mia, is you. No man can ever touch you, except me. Any man who touches you will die. You are the most remarkable find of anyone of our people ever."

"What if I have sons, Mechalu? Will they be able to touch me?"

"Of course they can touch you, until they become men."

"When does a boy become a man?"

"When he returns successfully from a trial."

"Has anyone ever returned unsuccessfully?"

"No, Olomaru-mia. Some men have decided to join someone in another village and remain there. That is acceptable. Occasionally a hunter goes off and eventually dies. We have found bodies twice. To live in our village, however, a man must have a successful trial."

"What if someone accidentally touches me?"

"Olomaru-mia, there will always be a large space around you. There is no accidental touching. Touching for any reason at all results in death. You will be very carefully avoided by men."

"But women can touch me?"

"Yes, of course. In fact when we get home, the people will know that you are my special find. The first thing that will happen is that the women will take you to a small hut they keep for preparing young women for joining. You will go with them and they will prepare you for night. You must obey them. At a huge feast that night, we will join. We will go to my hut while the people feast and celebrate. A very old woman will sit within the hut the first night."

"Why will she be there?" Olomaru-mia asked.

Mechalu laughed. "Her function is to assure that I am not overly rough with you, and that you do what you are supposed to do from what they teach you in the hut."

"I have already been instructed in the ways of being a woman," Olomaru-mia gently protested.

"Then, you'll have to endure it again. Maybe there are some cultural differences. I do not know."

Olomaru-mia steeled herself to whatever else would follow.

"They will bring you to me at the fire circle. You will wear a feather cape. Keep it tightly held against you while there. You will stand while Chief Uvela says words that join us for this life. In our life joining cannot be undone for any reason."

"Sometimes I've seen people unjoin if the woman has no children or they don't get along well and both want to separate. You mean that cannot happen?"

"We don't permit it. It would offend the Creator of All. You have to swear to join the other for life when you join. That oath is irrevocable."

"I see. Ours is thought to be irrevocable, but sometimes it's revoked."

"Our people are called the Nola Nola. It's the name of a weapon we use. This is mine," he showed her the thick stick about as long as her arm that he carried along with his spear.

"Why are your people named after a stick?" she asked, genuinely curious.

"It is our strength. Back to what you need to know. After we join, be careful to avoid looking eye-to-eye at any of the men. If there are complaints that you are seducing them, I would be ordered to beat you. Be sure to stay with other women at all times. Some men will be jealous of me and may try to create problems. In time that will pass. But heed my words. Be careful. Always stay where many can observe you. Never wander off alone."

Olomaru-mia was becoming uncomfortable.

"Don't worry, sweet Olomaru-mia. My mother will care for and protect you. Her name is Ahma. "

"Your people lie?"

Mechalu wondered for a moment why she asked such a question. "My people lie just as other people lie. It is not something people do often. Most of the time it's done to make a person look good when they've done something the Creator of All would disapprove or to avoid punishment. Sometimes people do it from jealousy to hurt someone else. Everyone knows that the Creator of All knows our thoughts, so it's stupid to lie, but sometimes people do stupid things. Sometimes they appear to get away with it if they escape punishment. We believe the Creator of All knows and they are punished now or later. I'd rather be punished by my people than the Creator of All."

"I understand. With my People, most of us would cut out our tongues rather than lie. We are trained to accept punishment when it's due—not run from it, as it clears away our wrongdoing."

"That's an interesting way to look at it, Dear One." He squeezed her to him, and with his free hand, he turned her face towards him and he kissed her, growing increasingly passionate. Olomaru-mia did not respond immediately, but soon the passion overtook her and she participated with passion of her own, given with abandon of all the past. She found herself yearning for him intensely. He broke the bond abruptly. "Tonight we will finish the moment we just began, and it will be part of our life for as long as we both live. Olomaru-mia, I love you with every part of me." His voice was a bit hoarse.

"Mechalu, I want you," she said filled with emotion and truth. Olomaru-mia could not tell him that she loved him. She was uncertain. That she'd be his wife was clear. That she'd have moments of passion with him, she knew. But love. Love was a special word to her. She couldn't say that word yet. It would have to wait."

Mechalu took her desire for him as love. He was overjoyed. He could barely wait to reach home. The two stood, gathered their backpacks, weapons, and Olomaru-mia put her hat on her head. They trekked fast all day. Sometimes they had to go out of their way to avoid large grazers they did not want to aggravate or a basking snake. Occasionally they stopped to drink water or eat some fruit. As the evening began, Mechalu could see the slight valley that led straight to his village. Very soon, the lookouts would see them and report the presence of two people. Hunters would leave the village to meet them.

As they rounded a bend, they heard shouts and men began to trot towards them, weapons in hand.

Mechalu shouted slowly and very loudly his own name three times. At that the hunters broke into a run. Mechalu ran to meet them, telling Olomaru-mia to remain where she was.

The men greeted Mechalu with great warmth and then the greeting stopped as all stared at Olomaru-mia. The men had never seen a human with such light colored skin. She was dressed oddly and wore a greenish brown hat. Mechalu explained very fast what she was and the men were speechless. The sun created a golden aura around her where her hair hung very long. Mechalu ran to her, and taking her by the arm, he led her to the group. Men stepped back instantly to avoid any possibility of a touch. Olomaru-mia kept her eyes downcast to avoid eye-to-eye contact. She had not forgotten Mechalu's warning.

Hunters went before them, and a few followed them to the village. The Nola Nola all stood outside curious to see what person Mechalu had brought home. As soon as they realized this was his special find, they marveled. This very pale person was framed in lovely gold hair. She fascinated them. They gawked.

Mechalu introduced her to Chief Uvela and told the Chief he intended to join with her that night. Chief Uvela called Ahma and told Olomaru-mia to go with her. Olomaru-mia went with her immediately. Four women gathered around them and all of them went to a hut, the one Mechalu had told her was the place they prepared women for joining. They told Olomaru-mia to leave her backpack just inside the door. She had to step up to enter the hut. The floor was raised of packed earth. She shrugged off the backpack, and then they led her first to the privy outside and then back inside the hut. The hut was large compared to some of the other structures. Once inside, they removed her hat, foot sun protection, and her tunic. Olomaru-mia was horrified, having no idea why they did what they did, but she had promised to obey. They made her lie down. She became alarmed. The women forced her legs apart and checked.

"She is a virgin," Ahma said softly. She lifted a breast, "And look at these nipples. They are pink!" she remarked with interest.

Olomaru-mia was outraged as they examined her and made her lie still on the skin. She had no outlet for the outrage, so she had to let it dissipate.

Then, a very old woman began to speak. She wanted to know whether Olomaru-mia understood her. Olomaru-mia replied that she understood well. The old woman began. She explained what was expected in joining and Olomaru-mia listened carefully. Everything she heard was the same as what she'd been taught. Ahma came and kneeled at her side. While the old woman talked, Ahma began to paint her. She painted dots on her forehead in three parallel size-increasing lines. She painted waves on her cheeks. She painted two dots on her chin.

The old woman began a singsong chant and then announced. "You will listen carefully to the story of the Fountain of Life and the Sacred Hot Springs." She reached for a small hide covered drum. She beat the drum with a stick and timed her words to the rhythm of the drum. "Long ago before we traveled to this new land, there was a huge storm in our old land. A large bird that could not fly saw a glowing form before it. The form slowly placed a small white rock on the ground and then another. 'Eat the rocks, for they are seeds,' the glowing form said, 'Follow me.' The large bird was fascinated. He began to eat the white rocks. He followed along watching the glowing form and then looking at the ground. His craw was filling and he slowed down. After following the rocks and eating every one, he came to the sacred hot springs. He inserted his beak and drank from the hot spring. He began to tingle all over. His form changed. He was man. The form he'd followed changed into woman. Then he saw the sacred hot springs had also changed. It was part of the woman. He also saw the change in himself. The seeds had transformed into a white fountain of life. The woman smiled at him. Knowledge filled his mind web. The fountain of life must enter the sacred hot springs to create life. They joined and from their joining, life of people began." Her words stopped but the drum and humming continued for a while.

The story fascinated Olomaru-mia. Her People had no tradition even close to this.

Moving down to her chest, Ahma painted white dots under one breast circling it to the breastbone with more dots, then going over her breast and arching down to end in a white dot at her navel. Then she did exactly the same thing with the second. She painted both nipples, using more paint than she had for the dots. She took Olomaru-mia's left arm and painted dots from the shoulder to the wrist. Then she did the same with the right arm. She went back to the navel. She painted a trail of dots from the navel over the hipbone and above the pubic rise to her leg on the opposite side from her hipbone. She repeated the pattern on the other side. She spread Olomaru-mia's legs apart, and painted the dots down the front of her leg and up the inside of her leg to her labia, repeating the design on the other side.

"Olomaru-mia, now you must lie totally still. This has to dry completely. It will take some time."

"Why have you painted me?" she asked.

Ahma and the other women chuckled. "Probably the first thing Mechalu will do with you when you come to his hut is to lay you down. Your passion will begin with kissing no doubt, but then, he must remove every dot from your body with his mouth before he can do anything else. He cannot even visit your well until you are dot free. Be responsive, but do not help him in the removal of dots. Do you understand?"

"I understand what you've said but not why."

"This effort makes him very aware of you as a person, not just a way to relieve sexual tension. It also increases your desire of him while he removes the dots. It forces both of you to be patient. Does that help you to understand?"

"I think so," Olomaru-mia thought of some women who complained that the night they joined, sex occurred so fast that their new husband fell asleep, while they were still wondering what joining was all about. This would, she reasoned, definitely slow things down.

When Ahma realized that the dots were all dry, she helped Olomaru-mia get to her feet without chipping off the dots. She covered her with a long robe that came to her knees. It was made of bird feathers of bright colors. She held it together as Mechalu had told her to do.

"Keep holding it tight like that until you and Mechalu come to his hut after you're joined. When he asks for it, release it."

"I will," Olomaru-mia promised.

Ahma left the hut and let the Chief know the joining could begin. She noticed that food had been placed on servers at the edge of the fire circle. The Nola Nola had prepared to feast well and celebrate this night. The Chief told her to bring Olomaru-mia.

Finally, Mechalu and Olomaru-mia stood face-to-face in front of the Chief. All the Nola Nola stood attentive, watching the two join.

Chief Uvela said, "Mechalu, have you discussed with Olomaru-mia the meaning of joining in the Nola Nola tradition?"

"Yes," he replied.

"Mechalu, in front of the Creator of All, do you join with this woman, Olomaru-mia, until death?"

Mechalu replied, "Yes."

The Chief said, "Olomaru-mia, in front of the Creator of All, do you join with this man, Mechalu, until death?"

"Yes," she replied keeping her eyes downcast.

The Chief said, "You are joined. You are free to leave for your hut to feast upon each other while the rest of us feast on the bounty of this land."

Mechalu put his arm around Olomaru-mia and led her to a fairly large hut with a skin flap dropped down across the entryway. Sure enough, a very old woman sat just inside the entryway. Her face was downturned and she appeared asleep, but Mechalu knew his grandmother was anything but asleep. He knew he'd better do everything exactly as he should or everyone in the village would know about it and tease him.

Mechalu stood behind Olomaru-mia. "I've got the cape, Olomaru-mia. Let your grip on it go, now, so I can remove it."

Olomaru-mia released the cape. Mechalu took it from her shoulders and laid it carefully on the skin on the floor. He knew exactly how to fold the cape. Carefully, he folded it, knelt beside it, and rolled the skin to protect the cape. He returned to her and turned her towards him. He stood there for quite a while looking at first one part of her and then another as fire light played on her white skin. He smiled to himself when he realized what a painting his mother had done. He wondered whether all paintings were the same.

"Olomaru-mia, my wife," he said with tremendous emotion.

She looked directly into his eyes and said, "Mechalu, my husband."

He led her to the bed made from the furred skin of a young sloth. The furred skin rested on sand. There were some soft hair-free skins tossed on the bed. Mechalu bent down, circled her in his arms, and kissed her gently. He pointed to the bed and she stepped onto the furred skin. Mechalu removed his clothing and joined her. They spent much time kissing until he finally broke free and began to remove the dots from her forehead. The rule was to start at the top and work down. While removing the dots, his hands caressed her in every place he could reach where there were no dots. With extreme care, he followed the rules. After Mechalu removed the dots from her face and arms, he pulled her down on the furry skin. The dots, Olomaru-mia discovered quickly, didn't remove with great ease. She began to wonder how long this would take. Quickly she reasoned that the question was not a reasonable one. She gave herself over to the event. She felt herself responding and did not attempt to check responses in any way. She was now joined. She must, therefore, be joined, she reasoned. She let herself flow with the flames of passion that were being set and fanned, generously contributing flames of her own.

The next day villagers smiled at Mechalu and Olomaru-mia. The word was out. The old grandmother wished her joining night had been like that one.

Chapter 3

It was well past high sun when the huge dugout boats made their way from the coast up the inlet that Linpint pointed out as the one they traveled to make their first camp. They beached on the sand and Zamimolo and Linpint looked about. They finally found what they sought—a pile of rocks near the last camp. It pointed north.

At the same time atop the well-secured hill north of the boat arrivals, the People had been following the advance of these strangers since they spotted them.

Zamimolo and Linpint rushed to find a suitable place to set three fires in what would appear to be a straight line, running east to west, each fire separately visible to any viewers from the north. The young men didn't know exactly where the People were, but they knew that hunters would monitor the last camp watching for their return. He explained to those traveling with them that they needed to set signal fires to assure the People recognized them.

Chief Paaku looked at Linpint and asked, "What can we do to expedite making the signal?" Framed by the sunset from Linpint's perspective, the Chief was an imposing bronzed, well-fleshed figure. His hair was cut so straight at the bottom, level with the lobe of his ears, that it paralleled the horizon. He was a man of few words, efficient, yet acutely aware of what was best for his people. He was as much a part of this land as the night bugs, the day birds and monkeys, and the strange large animals, Linpint thought.

"We need to gather materials that will burn," Linpint replied. We need to create a working ember so we can start the fire in the east first, and from that one, the other fires. Zamimolo and I will draw circles in the sand and if the Kapotonok will gather dry wood and reeds to place in the circles, we would be grateful."

"We have an ember," Chief Paaku said quietly, surprised that anyone would think to travel anywhere without one, but revealing no thoughts whatever by his facial expressions. "Kapotonok," he called in a loud voice, "We need material for three fires. Please look for dry wood and reeds to put in the circles Zamimolo and Linpint will draw. Let's do this quickly."

To Linpint and Zamimolo's amazement, all scattered for the task, even the people who brought them to this place in the boats helped. The women participated. Suddenly they both found themselves showing people where to put the materials that would burn. Before dark they had materials that would burn well and be visible from a distance.

On the hilltop the Wise One, called out, "Are all People now in safety?"

Golmid replied, "All are here except Rustumarin, Grakumashi, Colitoba, and Uilo. They went to gather shellfish. Numing has run to bring them to safety."

"Thank you, Golmid. Let us continue to assure quiet. Keep children silent." The Wise One pulled a furred skin around his shoulders. He had chilled easier recently and often went about wearing a skin around his shoulders. He tied it with the short leather tie that went through holes in the skin. He returned to the southern observation point after checking to be sure the other observation points were manned.

Children heeded the warning about silence without question. They knew the loss of Olomaru-mia. They went to sheltered areas to watch the adults. They could see the tension and smell the fear. There were no infants or very young children among these immigrants yet.

Grakumashi, Rustumarin, Uilo, and Colitoba quietly ascended the mountain carrying their shellfish. The sun had almost vanished below the horizon. The women went to the gathering place and the men went to the southern observation point.

"Anything new down there?" Rustumarin asked.

"Look," Tokatumeta said in a hushed voice. "It looks like they're starting a fire."

As they looked, a second fire began far enough to the right that the fires would not be seen as part of a single fire. Then a third one.

"Linpint and Zamimolo!" Rustumarin shouted. "Golmid, Grakumashi, Jup, come with me to welcome them."

The four men took torches and carefully wended their way down the mountain on the north side. They rounded the hill and headed straight for the fires.

Back on the hill the women were racing about to put together food to feed numbers of people. They had an idea that their numbers had almost doubled.

"Look," Zamimolo shouted from fireside. "They are coming!"

"Your people have sent men to come for us?" Chief Paaku asked.

"Yes. They will be here soon and then we can follow them to where they live. They will probably have food ready for us by the time we arrive."

The four men walked boldly into the camp, the fires waning, since there was no longer a need for them. Men and women were already covering the fires with sand. Zamimolo and Linpint's People hugged their two men in greeting. Golmid's face fell as he realized that Olomaru-mia was not with the men. He had hoped to see his daughter again, despite warnings from the Wise One that he'd not see her again. He had to comfort himself with the Wise One's assurance that her life was good. Zamimolo introduced the People to those he brought with him.

"We invite all of you to our home," Rustumarin said. "Please follow us." The group followed the People to the mountain and up the winding path that ascended it to the top.

The Wise One was the first to greet the strangers at their mountaintop home. "Thank you for accompanying Zamimolo and Linpint. Each of you is welcome. Please, place your spears against the wall here. We will prepare food for your bellies and water to quench your thirst. After you are comfortable, we will talk. The girls here will show you where to sit at our gathering place." With minimum noise or confusion, all strangers were seated in an internal ring in the gathering place, and young girls of the People served the group. Only very quiet talk occurred during the meal. Slowly, stars began to appear in the dark sky and the noise of the forest and lowland, muted as it was by distance, rose as a comforting sound. A couple of tree frogs had made their home near the living area of the cave, so their calls were very loud. Some adults assumed the children had brought them to the caves, because they were interested to know more about them. The People had learned that as long as the night noise was there, the noisemakers were not alarmed at a change in the environment. Silence became the new alarm for the People. As the group finished eating, young girls showed the guests how to dispose of their remaining food and rinse out and drain bowls. Since there were not enough bowls to go around, young girls and boys had to wait until bowls were washed and available for them to use to eat. They viewed this wait as a way to show hospitality and graciousness to the visitors. Sometimes young ones would fight over the honor of giving up a bowl to a visitor.

When all had eaten, the Wise One took his seat at the head of the group. Chief Paaku was surprised to see an ancient one with a leather loincloth and a skin wrapped around his shoulders lead the People. Usually their leaders were among the fittest, able to lead hunters in war when needed.

"We welcome you to our food and fire. We are part of a larger People most of whom remain back across the western sea, where the land is not as warm as it is in this place. Some of us decided to move here to make a life where it is not so cold and where food is plentiful. We wish to live at peace with our neighbors. We are interested to know what brings you here. Whoever will speak, let him sit here," the Wise One pointed to a place to his right side.

Chief Paaku stood, claiming the place. The Wise One stood facing the Chief and held up both hands out from his own face palms outward. It signified that he was unarmed. The Chief put both of his palms against the palms of the Wise One. He and the Wise One both lowered their heads. Then the Chief stepped back and seated himself.

He turned and looked back at the Wise One. The Wise One nodded, and the Chief began. "I am Chief Paaku of the Northern Kapotonok. We came to this land at the beginning of time from the lands to the west from where you came, then to islands between the lands, and then here. We have lived here so long that only a few of our old land stories remain."

"We met Zamimolo and Linpint when they tended our wounded hunters and notified us of the death of one of them. They are good men and we are fortunate to know them. When we learned that Zamimolo was pursuing an abducted girl with help from Linpint, our Wise Man made it clear that the girl had already joined her abductor. He assured Zamimolo that her life would be good. As with our Kapotonok, it seems that the People also take joining seriously as a sacred act, not to be overturned for any reason."

"We offered to travel here to return Zamimolo and Linpint that they may live their lives well, and we came with the hope of finding wives and husbands for our young people. I have Lomah of the southern part of the Kapotonok," he held his hand towards her and she lowered her head. "She and Linpint plan to join, if they can secure your permission. Then, there is Kumoha of the southern part of the Kapotonok," he motioned to Kumoha who lowered her head, "who seeks a husband and Dop of the southern part of the Kapotonok," Dop lowered his head, "who seeks a wife. I have brought two of my children, Ba and Kolpatin," he motioned towards them. "Ba seeks a husband and Kolpatin, a wife."

"We want to live in peace with you. We also want to make available to you, if you are interested, the means by which we communicate through distance. I will not discuss the drums now. Take time to discuss this with Linpint and Zamimolo to see whether your People would find this to your advantage. Then we will talk on this further. While we are here, if there are questions about this land, we will be glad to share our knowledge of the land, the animals, and the people who live here. Whatever help we can provide, we will do so gladly. We come in peace and hope to establish an agreement to live in peace with you." The Chief remained quiet.

"That is all you have to say?" The Wise One asked.

"Yes. That is all I have to say."

"We need time to use our mind webs to consider your offers. For the rest of this night we can get to know one another. Let us visit for a few days and then talk again of these things. We will have music."

Tokatumeta brought his drum and Uilo her flute. Meninkua brought her ancient eagles-beak rattles. Tokatumeta began and the others joined. The Chief was delighted. The music was in rhythm with the sea and it reached him at an emotional level, surprising him. He had thought these people were somewhat backwards, yet their music was expertly timed and exquisite.

Olomaru-mia opened her eyes and realized there was new light of the day visible through the smoke hole. The scent of newly cut wood from which their hut was constructed stung her nostrils in a way she enjoyed. The astringent nature of the scent made her think of cleanliness. It certainly seemed to deter the accumulation of biting insects. She rolled over to her right and realized Mechalu was not there. She hadn't noticed his going out. She smiled. How she had hated him in the beginning. Now, she had to admit, she really had grown to love him. She still had bouts of conscience where she felt as if she betrayed Zamimolo. Olomaru-mia was comforted that somehow the Wise One would calm Zamimolo's concerns and make him know that she was well cared for and had joined another. Zamimolo would find a wife, Olomaru-mia felt certain, and she had to adjust to the demands of the winds of change. Mechalu had repeated he'd be a good husband, and he had kept his word. Olomaru-mia already suspected that she might be carrying a child. The very idea brought waves of joy to surround her with warmth. For many cycles of the four seasons, she and Zamimolo had dreamed of having many children. Perhaps, she would realize that dream, although with another. She ran her hands across her belly. How she hoped her suspicion was accurate.

Olomaru-mia raised up on an elbow, kneeled, stood, and reached for her tunic. She slipped it over her head. It was becoming too short. Women of the Nola Nola only wore short skirts, but Olomaru-mia was not comfortable in just a skirt and her tunic was becoming shorter with her own recent spurt in height. She had let Mechalu know she needed new skins for a longer garment to cover her skin from the sun. She took the comb Mechalu had made her. Carefully she combed her hair.

There was a shadow at the entryway. Ahma entered.

"Mechalu asked that I tell you he has gone hunting. Come with me this morning to gather berries. There are some growing nearby. Bring a container and meet me at Kiahmuha's hut." She didn't wait for a reply but slipped out of the hut as quickly as she had entered. Olomaru-mia finished combing her hair and pulled it back, holding it in place with a tie of leather. She picked up a wooden bowl that Mechalu's grandmother had given her, but put it back down, not wanting to stain it. She picked up a woven grass bag that a woman whose name she'd forgotten had given her, thinking it would do well. It had a strap that went over her head. It would give her two hands for picking berries. She put on the sun protection she had for her feet and her hat and went to find the women.

"There's the lucky girl," Tuna said flatly, unsure whether to pout or sneer so she tried both, wanting to make Olomaru-mia feel uncomfortable.

"Tuna, how can you call her a lucky girl?" Albigrimpa, Ahma's sister, said sharply. "The poor girl was abducted and taken far from her home in a new land, very different from any she's ever known. What are you thinking? She's had to learn to love an abductor. You are acting inappropriately."

"I'm thinking that if Mechalu hadn't found her, he'd be here for me. He used to like me."

"Stop the self-centeredness!" Flukua, Tuna's mother said, scowling. "The truth is more likely that if he hadn't found her, he'd still be on his test of valor. If you aren't going to control yourself, stay here!"

Tuna's face burned with the rebuke. She really had adored Mechalu, but she had no reason to think he even knew she existed. Not once did she respond to her advances. Never did he steal glances at her during meetings. She knew all those things, but she had allowed herself to dream. She hadn't planned to make her disappointment so public, but the words were out before she controlled them. Tuna thought for a moment of what it might be like to be abducted. The thought was terrifying. Olomaru-mia had survived it—to thrive. Tuna reckoned there was something to be learned from Olomaru-mia.

"Is everyone ready?" Ahma asked trying to return pleasantness to the berry picking.

Everyone nodded.

"Then let's be off," she said a little too loud.

Olomaru-mia felt a bit odd wearing the hat and having been discussed as if she weren't there, but the day was lovely, and berry picking was a way of fitting into the society in which she had to live. She didn't want to appear self-centered. If this is what Wisdom had in mind for her, she wanted to fit in well.

Tuna caught up to her and asked, "Why are you wearing the hat and the things on your feet?"

Olomaru-mia smiled at her. "My skin is so pale that the sun burns it. I have to keep it covered so it won't burn, blister, and peel off. The sun's damage is painful."

"You look like a spirit with that pale skin. I'm glad mine doesn't burn. I really like the color of your hair."

"Thank you, Tuna. That is kind of you to say."

"Are you going to cut it like we cut ours?"

"No. Mechalu likes it just as it is. He told me not to cut it."

"You always do what he wants?"

"Except for the abduction, we haven't really disagreed on anything. He has been kind and I would like to please him. Do you know what I find appealing about you?"

Tuna stopped walking, staring at Olomaru-mia's face. "You find something appealing about me?" Her expression displayed her disbelief.

"Yes. Your eyelashes are long and they frame beautiful brown eyes. And your white teeth shine like snow when the sun shines on it."

"What's snow?" Tuna asked, walking again to keep up with the others.

"In a very cold place, when rain falls, the rain turns white. It lands on the ground as a substance you can pick up with your hand. Snow doesn't flow like water. It's more like sand, but it weighs less than sand and holds together better. If you put snow in your mouth, the warmth of your mouth turns the snow to water, and you can swallow it. The cold makes rain turn to snow. A particle of snow is tiny, like a grain of white sand."

Tuna studied her carefully and then laughed aloud. "You fooled me! I almost believed you."

"Tuna, I don't lie. What I've told you is true. We used to have to wear furs to protect our skin from the cold. We had tunics like this with fur covers for our legs, feet, arms, hands, and heads. We had furs to wrap around us after all that. Part of the year is cold and the other part of the year is warm. It is very different here. I understand that it's always warm here. Where I lived the change is great."

"I thought you were teasing me. You must have looked like beasts!" Tuna laughed.

"I have been taught that teasing is mean-spirited. My People don't tease. And yes, dressed in all that fur we did look like beasts—warm beasts!" Olomaru-mia laughed lightly thinking of how they'd look to people who never felt the bite of cold weather.

"You must have come from far away."

"I did. We had to cross the great sea to the west to get here. It took many, many days. Where I lived and this place are so different. I'm still trying to adjust."

"You came over here on a boat like our ancestors?" There was awe in Tuna's voice.

"Yes, Tuna, some of my People decided to move to a warmer place."

"Some are back there with the snow?"

"Yes. But, the snow is only there when it gets cold. It melts when it's warm, and rain is just rain the rest of the year. How do you measure a year?"

"I don't know. It happens in the village to the south of us. They send us notice of when the year changes in the middle of the hottest time. We have a great feast. Nobody really understands it at all in our village. It comes on the longest day of the year. On that day we add a year to our age. Then the days get shorter, but they all seem the same to me. Some of the boys go to the village to the south to learn to be men. They learn counting and things girls don't know. Some of them learn to determine the longest day and the shortest day. That's all I know about it."

"How interesting," Olomaru-mia said. She was learning a lot about these people from someone she initially thought disliked her. Without seasons, she considered, there was little need to take much count of it other than to determine the age of a person. Olomaru-mia wondered if they did that. "Tuna, how many years have you lived?"

"Three hands."

"We are near the same age. I have lived three hands and one year."

"So that means you were alive a year before I was born."

"Good, Tuna. That's right."

"Did you know Mechalu is four hands?"

"No, I don't think we ever discussed it."

"The Nola Nola sent him to the south and he studied there. He can count and knows things we don't know. He also went to the Alitukit to learn more. It took a long time. Then, he had his trial of valor. He was gone a very long time for that. He is a good man."

"Thanks for sharing that, Tuna. There is so much about the Nola Nola I don't understand. You've taught me a lot today. Is this the place where the berries are?"

"Yes. The best ones are over there near the rock pile, but you must look carefully to be sure there are no snakes. Stay with me and I'll look out for you."

Olomaru-mia noticed that the other women were at a location nearby, busily picking berries. She smiled at Tuna. "Thank you, Tuna. You're a good friend."

"I didn't want you to be here at first. I wanted you to go away. I wanted Mechalu, but he never was interested in me. I like you Olomaru-mia. You tell me about things that interest me a lot. Like snow. You will be my friend?"

"I'd be glad to be your friend, Tuna. And you'll be my friend?"

"Yes!" Tuna beamed showing her beautiful white teeth, which fit together perfectly. Her smile was lovely when she used it.

Not until Olomaru-mia filled her bag with berries did she stop picking. She chose a rock for sitting, after checking carefully that no snake was lurking under the overhang. It was very hot and she had to shade the rock before she could sit there. The women picked berries up a slight rise by a creek that exited the mountains from where they lived. From there they had a great view of the sea. The berries were at their peak. Olomaru-mia had to take care not to squeeze the berry bag. Sweat rolled down her back and between her breasts. It formed under her hat on her scalp, soaking her hair anywhere it came close to her skin. She found sweat to be a common body function in this land, and she didn't care for it. She yearned for the cool forests she had known. Forests in this land were cooler but they were far from hospitable to Olomaru-mia. She felt the need to bathe frequently and the only close source of water was the sea and a secluded lake some distance up the hill in the forest, where Mechalu had forbidden her to go unless he accompanied her. Salt water was not good for bathing in Olomaru-mia's opinion. She longed for a lake nearby.

Women began to gather to head back to the village. Berries almost overflowed the containers. The evening meal would be delicious, and there would be enough food to last for another day at the least. Tuna joined Olomaru-mia when she finished gathering berries. She really was fascinated with Olomaru-mia. She had never seen anyone with pale skin, green eyes, and gold hair. To be considered her friend made Tuna feel proud of herself. She wanted to learn the difference in the world she inhabited and the one Olomaru-mia had left. Olomaru-mia had so much she could teach her, Tuna felt. Of all the Nola Nola, Tuna craved to learn anything new to her. Often she wished she'd been born male so she could have gone to the place of learning in the south.

"Wise One," Chief Paaku said quietly, "We have not discussed the need to establish peace between us. This land has many good people, but some make war. They live to the northeast. They are called the Alitukit, and they want to be sure that no one comes near what they consider their land. At times when they think we have trespassed, they will come to make war. We have tried to make a peace agreement with them, but they refuse. They seem to distrust everyone. None of us understands why. We have an agreement with all the other peoples along this part of the narrow land between the two big lands. We keep guards at the places they could approach us. If the Alitukit come to make war, we send the word by the drums and people gather to help us fight them—before they arrive. It is a very effective way we have to keep them from doing us harm. They take no captives. At least not yet. They kill their victims and cut off hair from the very top of their heads, hair with the skin attached."

"Why cut off someone's hair?" the Wise One asked. "That's a desecration."

"I think that's why they do it. It turns the belly of those who see it. It instills fear. They take it with them when they leave."

The Wise One cackled. "They wouldn't get much from my head!" He paused and then continued, "Taking skin with the hair is even more revolting."

"I agree. One of the things I'd like to do, if you decide to join in peace with us, is to train your hunters to fight in war so they'd be prepared. In some ways hunters are always prepared, but with the forest there are ways to appear almost invisible. There are other things that differ in war from hunting. We've had to learn. Having little forest where the Alitukit live, they are not wise to the forest. It helps us. It is obvious that your men are unfamiliar with the forests that we have here. They are not alert to the dangers. We can also teach them what they need to learn to be safe here. We would be glad to do that while we remain here."

The Wise One let himself sit on a log. "You are very kind, Chief. We need to take up the peace agreement at council, but I am sure we will agree. We would, I am certain, look with great favor on your offer to train our hunters."

Below them Lomah and Linpint sat side-by-side on a log at the edge of a small fall of water. His arm was around her shoulders and she was smiling at him. Further down by the creek, Kumoha and Numing shared shy glances while they spoke of little things. Kumoha was definitely attracted to Numing, but was having difficulty feeling comfortable in letting him know it. She had promised to join a man of the Kapotonok whom she adored, but he had died on a hunt and left her broken hearted. For a long time she had no desire to join with anyone. She felt awkward. Numing realized she was having some difficulty, so he asked her to discuss it with him. Kumoha found a great release in sharing her old pain, and from the sharing, she grew greater respect for Numing.

Dop from the southern Kapotonok was smitten with Kada. She was equally interested in him. They had found a place to hide in the grass at the bottom of the mountain to explore pleasure they might have in the future. Not far away, Mix, a rower, and Mimiputash were sharing the same activity in a small area where brushy trees grew.

Ba and Zamimolo walked along the beach sand towards the north where they were gathering seaweed in grass baskets.

"It's just so soon. I had my heart so set on Olomaru-mia. Changing, something I have to do, is just so hard. I don't know if my belly is receptive."

Ba laughed gently, placing her arm around his back, her fingers gentle on his skin. "Your belly might not be receptive, but another part of you is not so hard to please."

Zamimolo turned to her and held her in his arms tightly. He kissed her. "If anyone can take my mind from Olomaru-mia, it's you, Ba. I'm sorry I'm such a poor lover. I have been told that time changes these things. I wish it would move faster."

"Are you suggesting I find someone else?" she asked, running her fingers through the hair on his chest.

"I don't know. You are so sweet and kind. I would probably hate myself if I suggested you find another. I still feel sharp pain where Olomaru-mia is concerned. Two Wise Ones now have told me that she has joined another, and we won't see each other until our hair is white. My Wise One told me that I have to accept that this is the winds of change—a disruption in life caused by Wisdom to which I must adjust. I don't want to adjust. I actually want to throw myself to the ground, weep, and beat the ground with my fists as a small child, but it wouldn't help me anymore than it helps a small child."

"Zamimolo," Ba laughed her lighthearted laugh again, "what would Olomaru-mia think? Hasn't she already had to adjust to the winds of change?"

"Of course, you're right, Ba. It hasn't been easy for her. At least my People surround me. You are here, beautiful and sweet as that fruit we had this morning, causing me to face truth and stop feeling sorry for myself. You have been good to me, Ba."

"Zamimolo...."

"Call me Zami," he said. He let out a sob and surrounded her with a very tight hug. "I will be a good husband, Ba. Will you join with me?"

"I will," she said and they lost themselves in each other.

In the next few days the People and the Kapotonok spent days in warrior training, having agreed to peace and mutual support in war. Golmid and Linpint both agreed to learn the drums, and they prepared to go with the Chief when he left to learn what they must know to do it well. Both wives were invited to accompany them, but after much discussion, both decided to remain at their mountain home. The men would stay with the virtual hermits near the camp of the Northern Kapotonok until they learned. Eventually, the People would build a drum on their mountain.

The young ones who chose to join with the People all agreed to remain with the People, because the numbers of the People were so small and they knew so little of their environment. To their amazement the young women who joined with a man of the People were asked to wear a tunic to cover themselves more fully.

Olomaru-mia walked about arching her back, her belly protruding hugely. Ahma had already told her she carried twins. It was not unusual among the Nola Nola to have twins. It conferred a special potency upon the father. If both infants lived a moon there would be great celebration. The rippling along her spine was visible and Ahma walked over to her.

"Your time has come, Daughter."

"I thought that must be what was happening, Mother," Olomaru-mia replied. "This is a hot day."

"Well, my dear, it's made worse by the garment you wear."

Mechalu had brought her the softest skins his friends and he could make. She had sewed them together making loose sleeves and a yoked neckpiece that could be untied to her belly to free her breasts so her infants could suckle. The garment fell between her knees and ankles. It covered her well and did protect her skin. With the growing size of the twins, it was clear that she needed either to give birth or make a larger garment soon.

"It would be good for you to walk, but stay close. The birth hut will be ready by the time you are prepared to give birth. Tell Mechalu, so he'll be among the first to know."

"Do you know where he is?" she asked realizing she had no idea where her husband was.

"I saw him with Oscola and two friends walking towards the sea. There they are by the shore, if I see well. Look how lovely green the hills are, my Daughter. We have had good rain."

"That's a long way to walk in my condition, isn't it?"

Ahma looked at her in silence. Then she smiled a wistful smile. "Daughter, the first one can take much time. Walking will be good for you and the infants. Let me give you food and water to carry with you. The infants may not arrive until tomorrow."

"Thank you, Mother."

"Don't forget your hat and foot coverings, my dear."

"I will remember."

A short time later Mechalu saw Olomaru-mia walking down the hillside. He told the others he'd return. He sprinted up the hill to her.

Mechalu was slightly irritated. He had told Olomaru-mia to stay in the village in his instructions to her at the very beginning. He had no plan for her to disobey him.

He arrived just slightly winded. "What are you doing outside the village, my Wife?"

"At the advice from your Mother I have come to tell you that it's time." She knew he was unhappy with her, but it didn't matter.

"Time for what?" he asked without thinking.

"For the infants to arrive."

Mechalu felt as if all his blood dropped to his ankles. "Then, what in the name of the Creator of All are you doing down here?"

"Mother said a good walk would be beneficial, and that you should know the time has come."

Mechalu was beside himself. He was prepared to be angry but not for this moment, though he knew it was approaching. It was hard to contain anger and joy in the same body.

"We've got to get you back to the village," he said, reaching for her.

She backed away from his hand, "Mechalu, she said it would probably be tomorrow. I was wondering whether there are any crabs down here."

"You are hungry for crabs—now?" His thoughts went from anger to joy to crabs. He was certain he'd never understand the thinking of a woman.

"I could eat an entire boiling bag of crabs!"

He looked at her in shock. She'd been eating a lot more recently, but that was far too many crabs for one person to eat. He thought she was exaggerating, but he walked with her back to the beach. There were always crabs at the beach.

"Oscola, Vilminit, Mintopointin," he shouted as they neared the others. "I am about to become a father and my wife hungers for crabs."

The men laughed heartily. Oscola, Mechalu's older brother, rolled his eyes. Oscola had already experienced fatherhood. Mintopointin's wife had several moons to go before their first would be born. Vilminit had no wife or children. Eagerly the men set about finding crabs. Vilminit started a fire and Olomaru-mia carefully handed him the boiling bag using extreme caution to keep her distance. She went to search for hand-sized rocks to place beside the fire. She remembered the seaweed and gathered some of that.

It was dusk when they returned to the village. Ahma watched Olomaru-mia carefully. She was obviously progressing in the work of getting the infants out. She didn't seem very hungry at the evening meal. Ahma had to laugh when she heard why.

As night fell, Olomaru-mia and Mechalu went to their hut. They undressed and cuddled as well as they could. Olomaru-mia felt greatly comforted by his presence. Finally, Ahma came into their hut to see how birth was progressing. She looked at the birth opening and it was getting some significant size.

"Daughter, it's time to go to the birth hut," she said firmly.

Olomaru-mia looked into Mechalu's eyes not wanting to leave him. She got up with his help and followed Ahma. She was definitely ready to get this task finished. Mechalu followed them from a distance. He wanted to be certain there was no problem between his hut and the birth hut. He worried about his wife's carrying twins. He wanted all to be well but especially for her to do well. He adored her. He had never been more proud.

At the birth hut there were numbers of women, all of whom Olomaru-mia now knew. The old grandmother sat where Olomaru-mia was supposed to put her head. She was surprised that the old woman had a soft cushioned skin nestled in her crossed legs. That was for her head. Olomaru-mia complied with all the expectations. First, she removed her tunic and lay down with her head in the grandmother's lap. Ahma put a soft skin over her so she didn't chill. The pains were very uncomfortable now. After a while Ahma checked her again. She said nothing so Olomaru-mia wondered what the progress was. She continued to have pain after pain and it was hard to control not shouting out, or, worse, saying something awful that she knew she was not supposed to think, let alone say aloud, ever. How she wanted Mechalu!

Quiet as a mouse, Tuna crawled over on her hands and knees. She took Olomaru-mia's hand and held it. She whispered, "If it hurts really badly, let some of it go into my hand. I can take pain and would gladly share with you. Just squeeze my hand hard and it'll take some of your pain away so I can share with you." Tuna's face was so endearing. Olomaru-mia had another severe contraction. She squeezed Tuna's hand hardly aware of how strong a squeeze it was. The grandmother watched Tuna's face. Tuna used a cloth and wiped the sweat from Olomaru-mia's face. The two looked at each other sharing. If she couldn't have Mechalu, Olomaru-mia was glad Tuna was there. She would tell her how much it meant after this ordeal was over.

When Olomaru-mia saw that Wisdom had returned color to the land, she gave a loud shout, and the first boy was born. Ahma tied a strip of leather around his wrist. Shortly after that in quiet, the second boy was born. Both infants were perfect and healthy. Each had a small dark spot on the lower back. Olomaru-mia knew the spots would disappear after a short time. This mark that accompanied birth was common among the People. The Nola Nola had never seen it. Very quickly, the infants suckled. Olomaru-mia was glad she hadn't had three of them.

Albigrimpa, Alma's sister, had made a basket to hold the two of them. It was lined with mosses and overlaid with a soft skin. The women wrapped the infants' bottoms in soft skins stuffed with mosses and laid them to sleep.

Ahma placed a soft skin over them. Kiahmuha cleaned Olomaru-mia and helped her move to a clean place to rest. Then she gathered all the remaining material from the births and put it into a fire, which burned outside. Quiet fell on the birth hut.

Tuna crawled over to the basket and looked into the little faces of the infants whose births she'd just witnessed. They were tiny but perfectly formed. She lifted a tiny hand and examined the detail. Such perfect fingernails! Some of the women said they looked like someone; some, another. Tuna looked hard but could see no resemblance to anyone living or dead in either face. She was unsure whether they really looked like people. The boys did not look alike. They looked wrinkled and had skin that seemed to want to peel off.

A shadow crossed the entryway. Mechalu had been permitted to see Olomaru-mia and the infants. He came in quietly. He stooped over Olomaru-mia who was asleep. He reached down and put his arms around her and she immediately awakened.

"Have you seen them?" she asked.

"I came to you, first," he replied squeezing her.

"Go look and tell me what you think."

Mechalu broke his hold on Olomaru-mia and went to the basket around the far side of which Tuna had curled herself. There, side-by-side lay two tiny people sleeping peacefully. Their faces were wrinkled and their hands were very small. "I will name the first boy, Pipto, and the second boy, Token.

He turned to Olomaru-mia. "That gift is almost as great as your giving me your love." He lay beside her, slipping his arm beneath her neck. He knew the moment he saw her from the mountain viewpoint she'd be his. It all came true. And, she'd finally told him she loved him. He was a new father of twins! He wanted to shout and shout and shout. Instead, he rolled over on his side, kissed her, advised her to sleep when she could, and he left. It was time to tell his father, Chief Uvela.

As days passed, Olomaru-mia had many children arrive to see the twins. She began to tell the children stories. She longed to hear the stories, and she remembered many of them well enough to tell. She told ones that were designed for children. Occasionally, she'd tell one that the Wise One told at council meetings. She was certain she didn't have all the words right, but she did the best she could. There was something comforting to her to hear them, even if they were not perfectly delivered. She found it interesting that others, older children and adults, would come to hear the stories when she started to tell them. Sometimes someone would ask her to restart at the beginning.

Older Nola Nola discovered quickly that the stories were not for entertainment but for living. They were fascinated. The stories seemed endless.

Olomaru-mia realized one sunny afternoon, while she told stories to children and some adults as she suckled her little ones, that her life was good. It wasn't that she hadn't been happy. She had. She just recognized that her life was good. Certainly, she missed the People from the past. She never expected to see them again, but she had a good life. She lived among good people. Wisdom had blessed her even as had been the case in Ki'ti's time when they had to move to avoid the huge volcano. They had been blessed with a solution to their dwindling numbers by joining with Mol and Minguat. It was happening again. She could apply the story to herself. She was finding completeness with these strangers, learning a different way of living, and she contributed to their completeness in return. Finally, Olomaru-mia's questions dissolved. She had faced the winds of change. Wisdom had indeed set her among a strange people for a reason. She looked at her infants. Somehow, she knew that there was destiny awaiting them. She did not fathom what—only that.

The Chief came to Olomaru-mia in the afternoon. He stood before her tall and straight. His muscles bulged. He was strong at his age. Olomaru-mia stood up.

"No, no, Daughter, you need not rise," he said as she stood before him.

She wasn't about to sit back down, so she stood there relaxed but wondering why he was there.

"Tonight we praise Mechalu as father of two healthy sons, since it has been a moon since they were born. For the Nola Nola, it is a large celebration. There is a celebration for any father of a moon's age infant, but this is larger, since there are twins. You will attend the celebration with the twins. We start when the sun sinks behind the mountain to our west. That one," he pointed. "You must be there at your place when the sun sets. The twins must be with you. Please feed them before arriving so they will be more likely to be quiet if filled."

For some reason Olomaru-mia couldn't identify, she wanted to laugh aloud at the Chief, but she didn't dare. He'd have had Mechalu beat her, she thought. Because she was untouchable as a prize of valor, the Chief couldn't have done it even if she laughed at him, but he could order it done. Nevertheless, the drive to laugh was hard to keep down. She didn't know what was so humorous, but the need to laugh permeated her whole being. She wished mightily that he'd leave. She stared at the ground to make sure her facial expressions didn't give away her thoughts.

"It will be so," she finally managed to say with a strong voice.

"Thank you, Daughter," he said and left.

Olomaru-mia almost shouted as she felt a tapping on her shoulder. She was unaware anyone was near. It was Tuna.

"I saw that," Tuna grinned with glee.

"Saw what?" Olomaru-mia said shocked.

"For some reason you wanted to laugh and you did a really great job of covering it."

Olomaru-mia looked at her wordlessly.

"My friend, you know your secret is safe with me. What did you find that made you want to laugh?"

"I honestly don't have any idea," Olomaru-mia admitted. "I just don't know. I feared that he'd make Mechalu beat me if I laughed."

"You have learned the Nola Nola well!"

"But why? I don't understand that way at all. It keeps people from being themselves. It fosters pride."

"If you don't learn anything else, Olomaru-mia, learn that pride is very important to the Nola Nola."

"But pride goes against everything I was taught. My People view pride as something that goes counter to the way of success. Pride and success are as far apart from each other as day is from night."

"To my people pride is the deserved result of success."

"I think I will never understand that, my friend, Tuna."

"Well at least get the idea in what you call your mind web. Put it there firmly. It is fundamental to our way of being and cannot be taken lightly. Be careful never to destroy someone's pride."

Olomaru-mia walked over to Tuna and hugged her.

"I must tell you my secret."

"What is it, Tuna?"

"You know Coshiga, the traveler who has been here a few days?"

"I have seen him."

"We have spent much time together. He has asked me to travel with him to his people high in the mountains on the west side of the great land to the south. I have told him that I want to do that, but that I will desire to return here, for this is my home."

"Are you thinking of joining him?" Olomaru-mia asked, feeling she should be surprised, but she wasn't in the least.

"Yes."

"What will you do if he chooses to remain with his people?"

"I will be stuck. But I believe him when he says we can return here within the measure of a year."

"Oh, Tuna, I will miss you so much!"

"I will miss you also, my friend, but if anyone here understands me, it is you. I think you know why I do this."

"Yes, I do, lovely Tuna. It will give you an opportunity to see part of the world."

"That's exactly it, and, Coshiga is wonderful to me."

"Will you join before you leave?"

"Yes. After the Chief initiates the celebration for Mechalu, our joining will be announced. I go through what you experienced, cape, dots, and all."

"Tuna, as happy as you are, I am happy for you. I wish you'd known him longer, but I'll have to admit, I am happy, and I had no time to get to know Mechalu. He told me right away how things would be, and they were. You could think all the time we trekked, I had time to get to know him, but I knew him as a cruel abductor, not one to love. Occasionally he struck me and I feared him much. Later he explained that he did that so I'd obey him, not give us away, and keep us safe as we made our way to the Nola Nola. My life is good here. I couldn't be happier. I think part of the secret of happiness is to make it a purpose to love the one you join, every day, all day, for the rest of your life. It's not about him and not about you, it's about the two of you together, and you have to work all the time to keep it good. If you do that, it will be wonderful."

Tuna came over and hugged Olomaru-mia. "I will share that with Coshiga. I would like us to have that purpose. I need to do some things, Olomaru-mia. I can hear one of your little ones fussing."

So could Olomaru-mia. She touched Tuna on the shoulder lightly and walked quickly to her hut. She could see a storm forming behind the mountains. Clouds were about to pass over the sun, hiding it from view. How, Olomaru-mia wondered, would she know when the sun sank, if clouds covered it? Her thoughts drifted off as she lifted Pipto first, and then Token to her lap. She untied her tunic and lifted first one and then the other to feed at the same time. Both were very hungry. They were growing but their growth seemed very slow to her.

Ahma entered her hut. "Daughter, when you have finished come to the council. We do this evening's events now, because a great storm brews in the mountains."

"I just began. It will take some time."

"I know. Come when you have finished."

Olomaru-mia rested while the babes filled their bellies. It was another happy time for her. It was a wonder of Wisdom, she thought, that the body of a mother could feed her offspring. It was a special bonding, a giving of herself. Strength and vitality flowed from her into her offspring to cause them to grow and thrive. It was in some ways a great mystery. When the infants finished, she cleaned their wrappings and laid them in the basket. She hurried to the council seating. The meeting had already begun, so she quietly and unobtrusively took her place behind Mechalu. Ahma smiled at her.

Chief Uvela smiled broadly at the Nola Nola. "We now honor Mechalu, potent father of two lusty sons who have lived a moon. Mechalu, will you now, before us all, name your sons?" It sounded like a question, but it was a command.

Mechalu rose. "Yes, my father, Chief of the Nola Nola, I will name my sons." He lifted Pipto from the basket and held him above his head. Looking at the sky, he said in a loud voice, "Creator of All, this is my first son. His name is Pipto. Please watch over him all his days. May he serve you and his people with pride."

Olomaru-mia had not known in advance what he would say. She was horrified at his prayer for pride. She held her arms out to receive Pipto. Mechalu gathered up Token.

Mechalu returned to the place of honor and lifted Token to the sky. He began, "Creator of All, this is my second son. His name it Token." At that moment, Token let out a very loud shout, unlike common baby noises. He raised his hand skyward as if reaching for the Creator of All. A huge hissing noise rose from the sky hushing the Nola Nola to silence. No one moved. A great light appeared. To the view of the onlookers, the brilliant light arched over Token and landed somewhere behind the mountain with an explosive noise.

The Chief walked over to Mechalu and said firmly, "The Creator of All is well pleased. He has selected a son of yours, or maybe both, for greatness. You must not spoil these children but rather make them know all they must know. You will send both of them to the School in the South even as you and Oscola were sent. Then, they must go to the Alitukit. I expect great things from them. I have for you something special as a reminder of this auspicious event." The Chief went into his hut and after a while he emerged with a treasure, his special necklace, made from teeth drilled and hanging from a thin but strong strip of leather, a single knot between each tooth. The teeth were from the largest peccary boar the Nola Nola had ever found. The Chief put the necklace around Mechalu's neck and embraced him briefly around the baby that lay in his arms silent now, after his great outburst. Mechalu took Token to the basket wondering what would become of this son who seemingly called a meteor. He felt convinced that the Creator of All had special things in mind for his sons.

Oscola was seething. His brother had the best valor prize and now the greatest honor, the peccary tooth necklace! Even the Creator of All seemed to participate. At least Oscola reminded himself, he was the oldest male and would become the next Chief. Nothing would change that. In addition, the Chief, his father, had said to send his son, Ghumotu, to the School of the South and to the Alitukit School. There was no real difference, he reasoned, except for the meteor. Even he, he admitted, couldn't change that.

Winds blew stronger and the rain began to fall. Quickly Tuna in the feathered cape was ushered to the council. Olomaru-mia smiled wistfully as she could finally observe this ritual as a spectator. She hoped Tuna's night would be as wonderful as hers had been. Mechalu offered Olomaru-mia a hand to help her stand up. He carried the basket to their hut and they got inside just before the greatest amount of rain began to fall.

Once inside, Olomaru-mia looked at her children. At least Token had been spared the prayer for pride. She would try to teach her children her ways as well as the ways of the Nola Nola. Both her children needed Wisdom. She'd tell the stories and hope that they understood. She would tell the stories as if their lives depended on it. She felt safe telling the stories. The Nola Nola felt it was good entertainment for the children. She would do nothing to change their understanding. What she understood at this point is that if the Nola Nola truly understood the purpose of the stories, she'd be forbidden to tell them and she'd probably be beaten with a nola nola stick for having told them. The Nola Nola would have to listen carefully to many stories, but beneath it all was the strong teaching against pride, a quality upon which their governing status was built. She'd have been seen as teaching sedition. She would be very careful and very determined. She had learned to love Mechalu now and bore him no ill will; she adored her children; she still, however, resented having been abducted. This would be the expression of her revenge. Oddly, she felt that Wisdom would not view this as revenge, but rather as something mysteriously connected with the winds of change. Something acceptable, because it was Wisdom's way.

Ba and Lomah were lounging in the gathering place while they nursed their infants. Ba and Lomah expected the men to name infants, and the People relied on women for that. Finally, both asked Zamimolo to name their sons, since Linpint was still away learning the drums. Zamimolo had no experience naming infants, so he asked his mother, Meninqua, for assistance. Infants needed names. Often infants didn't survive. To die before being named was unthinkable. Meninqua thought for quite some time. Finally, she suggested several names for males: Ekuktu and Pah, solid old names, and Gnaha, which meant man of the salt sea, and Ventumoko, which meant steady and sure, and some others. Zamimolo chose Gnaha for his son and Ventumoko for Linpint's son. The mothers accepted the names without question, looking at their named infants' faces and repeating their names.

Days later a shout rang out from the east facing lookout point. It was high sun and at the edge of the forest the lookout had seen two men. Zamimolo ran to the lookout point and was certain it was the return of Linpint and Golmid from their time at learning the drum communication. He almost ran into Jup, Golmid's son, as they both raced to descend the mountain so they could greet the returning men. Zamimolo thought in all his life he'd never run so fast. Sure enough, Linpint and Golmid had returned.

The men arrived at the mountaintop, laid down their burdens, and went to find their wives. After warm greetings, Lomah led Linpint to where their son slept.

"What's his name?" Linpint asked, curious, his breath touching the side of her face. His belly caught at the sight of the infant. He and Linpint had new life. It was precious. He had so much to teach this little one. He wondered whether he was up to it. He wanted desperately to be a father the People would approve. He wanted to be a father that his son would approve. He touched the little hand and it grasped his finger. The infant opened his eyes and smiled.

"His name is Ventumoko," she said quietly.

"I like it very much," he said as he pulled her to his arms again.

"I didn't name him," Lomah admitted. "The Kapotonok men name their babies, so Ba and I didn't know how. We asked Zamimolo to name them. He went to his mother for help and then he came up with the names."

Linpint hugged her tighter. "The name is a good one! Next time, we'll both think together, and maybe we can do as well." She squeezed him tightly. How she had missed him! She hoped he was home for a long time now.

Although no council had been called, everyone came to the gathering place and seated themselves wherever they could find space. Golmid and Linpint were eager to share.

Golmid began to tell about the Alitukit, very dark skinned people to the northeast of them. "The drummers are Alitukit. They are banned from ever returning to their home. They helped set up the drums all along the land."

"Why?" the Wise One asked.

"You just don't ask that question," Linpint replied. "They are very private about what they will tell and what they won't discuss. With them you have to be very careful."

"They are people of incomparable knowledge. They made me feel like a child learning to walk while they were white haired adults," Golmid said.

"What do you mean?" the Wise One asked.

"They know when events in the heavens will take place. One day one of them told us that we would see meteors that night. We thought that was an interesting thing to say, but we didn't really believe him. That evening we saw meteors, numbers and numbers of them. It was a real show in the heavens. Those men knew we were about to see something spectacular—before it happened. I don't know how they knew." Golmid was clearly awed.

"I think we saw the same event, but nobody here expected it," Tokatumeta laughed.

"The men also play music. They have instruments that we've never seen. The music they play is unlike anything we've ever heard. It sounds like life growing and slowing and growing. I don't know how to explain it, except to say it's like hearing life." Linpint was still feeling the same emotions he felt when he first heard the music. It reached his emotions deeply, without entering his mind web for any analysis.

"I can't make sense of the music any clearer than Linpint did. It was very emotional. It can make your spirits soar or set you to weeping." Golmid looked around. The blank faces made it clear that the People didn't understand any better than they had.

"Might we visit them to hear their music?" Tukyatuk asked, curious.

Linpint explained, "That's the part I find frustrating. They tell us that they are there to teach us how to use the drums. Once we learn, we need not return. Between the two of us, we can train our People to build and use the drum. We have no more need of them. They see people who need them until that need no longer exists. They are not looking for friends."

"Now, here's something astonishing. I fell when I leapt to avoid a snake," Golmid said, "and in the fall I hit my head on a rock. It caused me to sleep an unwanted sleep. See this scar? They cut a hole in my head and removed remains of bleeding in the skin under the skull. It had caused pressure inside the bones of my head. They sewed it back. Shortly after that, I waked up. Once I was awake and recovered, they showed me what they removed. Now, I'm fine. I don't know how they knew what the problem was or where it was. We cannot see into a head."

"I watched what they did," Linpint said. "I feared for Golmid's life, but he was sleeping a sleep that could not be stopped. This worked. I never saw people more careful about what they did. They were so careful to be clean. I asked them how they knew what to do. Their response surprised me. They asked me, 'Don't your people analyze your animal kills, the injuries of your people, and the conditions of the internal parts of bodies when people die unexpectedly? We know because we examine life intensely.'"

"Oh," Golmid exclaimed, "one night we heard the drums from the south tell of the return of someone named Coshiga. He brought his new wife to visit his people in the southern tall mountains. Her name is Tuka or Tuna, something like that. They drummed out that it snowed in the mountains. Someone from the north wanted to know if Coshiga had seen the golden girl. I think that person from the north was one of the Alitukit. They are part of the drums, even though they don't want anyone to come on their lands. That's where the drums originated. I think they thought Tuka or Tuna was a golden girl, whatever that is. Coshiga said he'd seen her."

Suddenly the Wise One understood who the golden girl was. It had to be Olomaru-mia. Where Tuka or Tuna lived must be where Olomaru-mia was living, he reasoned. The Wise One determined not to ask questions or appear interested, because he did not want to incite Zamimolo again, and apparently, Zamimolo had thought nothing of this drum talk, or maybe he wasn't even listening. Even Linpint appeared to have seen no connection. Even her father, Golmid, hadn't seen the connection. The Wise One couldn't believe that the others hadn't seen the connection of the golden girl with Olomaru-mia, but he was quick to seize the opportunity to ask, "Where did these Alitukit originate?" Shifting to another subject could help to reduce the importance of the golden girl subject.

Golmid was surprised at the change in subject but said, "The best I can make of it is that they came from a large land, equal in size to the land below this narrow stretch of land, but on the far side of the ocean to the east."

"That's what I got of it, too," Linpint said. "They told us there are people all over the earth. Once, before time, land was of one piece, they say. Then, it broke apart according to their stories. They would like to return to their land someday, but they fear the massive separating waters. That's why the Alitukit are still here. They fear death at sea if they tried to go back. They have been here—using their word—forever. Their ancestors were traveling along the west coast of their big land and a storm blew them here. Their hope is that the land will move back to one piece. They aren't sea boatmen, so they don't know how to return to their land. They will sail near the shore, but never far out enough that they couldn't swim to shore. They have great fear of the sea."

"If they returned to their home across the sea, it wouldn't be what they hope for. All their people are gone. Their land has made great changes." The Wise One seemed far away.

"They don't seem to have any shipbuilding going on except for the little boats Zami and I saw in the eastern sea." Linpint said.

Zamimolo looked up, "Those things couldn't cross the sea!" He felt comparatively like a trained mariner to make the comparison.

The talking continued on and on, the People never tiring. Finally, women brought out food for the evening meal. Linpint was slow to respond as he held his infant, and it clutched his finger. He looked dreamily at Lomah. How delighted he was to be a father. Lomah stood up and went to get food for Linpint. The infant slept, and she went back to get food for herself.

Suddenly a shout came from the northern observation point. The older men raced to the place to see what caused the alarm. Far to the north, there was a boat at sea. Only those with the best far vision could see it. Zamimolo and Rustumarin agreed to assist on the night watch. They hoped it was a boat from their People.

Day brought the assurance that their People were arriving on one of the routine trips they made to assure the People who migrated were faring well. For safety, only a certain number of People were permitted to meet the boat. The People would escort the boatmen to their mountaintop home for a feast. Some hunters had gone out as soon as there was light enough to see to provide plenty of meat for the occasion. There was much bustling about and excitement.

Rustumarin, Tukyatuk, Tokatumeta, and Kih went to meet the boatmen. They stood waiting where the boatmen could see them as they approached through the waterway. Men who knew each other waved in greeting. A few boatmen secured the boat while the others and a single passenger went ashore.

"Who is this?" Rustumarin asked regarding the young boy.

"This is Pikotek, the People sent him as a student to learn from your Wise One. Someday you may need him. They say he knows the stories well. He has lived for thirteen years."

"Welcome, Pikotek," Rustumarin said in a loud voice. "We do need you!"

"Thank you," the young man replied, clearly not knowing what to do with himself.

"Let's head for home," Tukyatuk shouted.

After a brief interchange, two boatmen decided to remain with the boat.

The morning meal the women provided was huge. It was a feast! The boatmen who ascended the mountain were delighted, and Numing and Grakumashi packed up more than two portions and carried the food to the two boatmen who remained behind to guard the ship. After leaving the food with the grateful men, the People ran back to their mountain home. It was a beautiful clear sky day with a very gentle breeze. The morning's hunt had been exceedingly successful. Their drum learners had returned. They had a replacement for their Wise One. All seemed wonderful. Large birds soared overhead. There were many grazers in the valley. The bugs were definitely not quiet.

"Pikotek," the Wise One said, "I will want to test you. You understand that?"

"Of course. I will do my best, Wise One." He was frightened from the sea voyage and meeting all these People he knew when he was much younger. The new country was like nothing he ever saw. He hoped he still had a mind web that functioned. He picked at the food rather than fill himself. He was anxious about doing well when tested.

"No time is better than now," the Wise One said, and showed the young man to a place that had been carved out of the hill to provide a curved room for quiet within. After both were seated, the Wise One said, "Start with the story for burials."

The young man began and did not miss a word. The Wise One had him telling stories all day. Never did he miss a word or fail to recount correctly the meaning of the stories.

When the evening meal was announced, they left the little room. The Wise One said in a very loud voice. "I have tested Pikotek all day. He has missed nothing. People, you will have a Wise One when I leave this life to be with Wisdom. Guard him well. For the first time since his arrival, Pikotek smiled.

Hutapska walked over to Pikotek. "Welcome to our new land, Pikotek. Come with me," she said, "I'll show you how to serve yourself for the evening meal."

He followed, surprised at their shared traits. Both had thick, straight, black hair and deep blue eyes. They were not related.

"Take a bowl here. It doesn't matter which one if you choose one of these. Those are for the old people. They want a bowl of their own."

Pikotek smiled and chose a bowl from the general set of bowls.

"To stay healthy you are expected to eat meat, fruit, and greens. Sometimes we have nuts and food from the sea that is meat or greens. Adults will check when you're not looking to make sure you eat of all the groups of food. Be sure that you eat properly."

"Thank you," he looked at her not knowing her name.

"I'm so sorry, Pikotek, I forgot to introduce myself. My name is Hutapska."

"Thank you, Hutapska," he said and smiled.

"You'll have to work with the Wise One day after day. It's pretty hard to become a Wise One, I'd think," she said as she placed some camel meat in her bowl. He did the same. "This is camel meat. It tastes better than that meat over there, which came off a strange looking animal. It's called a spiked-tail armadillo and it looks like a turtle from someone's worst nightmare."

Pikotek looked at her to assure himself that she was serious. He put in his mind web his desire to see one of the spiked-tailed armadillos.

They moved to the greens. There was a large variety mixed with other vegetation they'd learned was good to eat. Pikotek chose a small amount of the different choices so he'd know what he preferred for the future. The fruit astonished him. There was every color of fruit one could imagine. He chose a wide variety to teach himself what he favored.

"Come sit with me, if you like, Pikotek. I want to get to know you," Hutapska offered.

"Thank you, Hutapska," he replied following her. She was making him feel comfortable and at home. He was grateful.

"What did you think of the sea crossing?" she asked.

"I was terribly sick at first from the rolling boat. I didn't want to leave all I knew, and it had been so long since I saw any of you. I knew, however, that the Wise One here is advanced in years and that I had to be available if he needed a replacement. That was, according to my Wise One, why I was born. Without option, I came. I must be obedient to Wisdom."

"What do you think of our food?" she asked.

"It is all delicious. I've never tasted food so good. The fruit is wonderful!"

"Fruit grows here all the time," she assured him. "This is a dangerous place," she added. "The first night we were here an abductor stole Olomaru-mia."

"I remember her. She had that reddish, golden hair. She was stolen?"

"Yes. That's before we knew when bugs and frogs get quiet, that's an alarm. We didn't notice. Here you have to learn to listen carefully to the bugs, frogs, birds, monkeys, and other things. There is more danger here than back home. It's also warmer and has better food. Meat doesn't dry well. Bugs get into it. But meat is available all the time, instead of just in some seasons, so we don't have to keep as much dried meat."

Pikotek tried to add all the new information to his mind web. Then he said, "Olomaru-mia was going to join with Zamimolo. What happened to him?"

"He got really mad. He followed as far as he could but lost the trail. He never found her. Our Wise One said they'd meet again when they have white hair. He told Zamimolo that she has a good life. Zamimolo was very angry. He tried to find her to bring her home. I think he wanted to kill the abductor."

"I can understand that, but it's wrong. Very wrong. The winds of change are operating in this. It's obvious. Wisdom expects us to bend with the winds of change. Is he still looking for her?"

"He joined Ba of the Northern Kapotonok. They live here. They just had a baby. I think he's making the best of a bad thing, but I think he'd still like to kill the abductor. I'm no Wise One, though, so what do I know?"

"I think, Hutapska, my little friend, you know much way beyond your years."

"I am not young," she said indignantly, "I'm short."

At that, he laughed for the first time since he left on the sea voyage. "My dear Hutapska, pardon my laughter, but you delight me. How many years have you lived on this earth?" he asked.

"Twelve," she replied. "And you?" she asked.

"Thirteen," he said.

"You have been so kind to me, Hutapska, is there anything I can do for you?"

She looked into his eyes, deep down to his soul. It startled him and then he found it pleasant. Still fixing him with her gaze, she said, "If you ever decide you'd like to join please consider me first, for I find your soul pulling on mine with a great strength."

Suddenly, Pikotek had no desire to laugh. Still caught gazing into her eyes, he replied, "I will do that, Hutapska, for I feel the same pulling—like a fish being pulled on a hook."

"Yes," she whispered. "Would you like to walk down below?"

"That would be wonderful," he replied. They took their bowls to rinse out, left them to dry, and walked down the mountain path.

"Wait a moment," Kih called out. "If you two want to walk, that's all right, but one of us must accompany you for safety. I can follow and will not intrude. Pikotek is our future Wise One. Our future Wise One is a treasure of the People and must be protected in the same way the Wise One is protected." Neither Pikotek nor Hutapska knew the rule, since neither was old enough to have seen a Wise One being taught. Kih and Latamala, his wife, both followed the two as they walked in the salty breeze on the tallest dune. Youthful, hand-in-hand the two walked, talking of the new land, the sea crossing, whatever passed their mind webs. They felt a kinship closer than family ties. They did not understand the feeling, but they felt bound together.

The sun had sunk below the mountains to the west. Children and some adults had gathered to listen to Olomaru-mia tell stories from her old land. Even the small children seemed fascinated by the stories, though they could not understand them well. Olomaru-mia liked to think it was the way the stories were told that held their interest, almost as if the stories were sung. She began.

"This is a very, very old story. It is the story of Kukuk-na and Timkut-na. Timkut-na and Kukuk-na were hunters. They had trekked far looking for meat to feed the People. It was a time of little rainfall and meat was not easy to find."

"The men went where they had known deer to gather. There were none. They went to places where trees grew in groves providing shade from the sun for animals. There were no animals there. They went to the highlands where they'd found grazers. There were none in the highlands. They went to the lowlands and found nothing. Hunger was everywhere, but they were determined that they would not let their People starve."

"Kukuk-na and Timkut-na were exhausted. They looked for a place to sleep. Wisdom was sucking color from the land fast. Below them was a grove of trees and they stumbled towards it. Timkut-na was the first to arrive. He noticed a spring that had not dried up. He kneeled and began to drink, for his thirst was great. Suddenly he felt a hit on his hand. A serpent had been harboring in the grass beside him, and it bit his hand. He noticed it was a cobra." Olomaru-mia paused. "That snake doesn't live here. Cobras are poisonous." She continued, "Timkut-na cursed himself for being so careless. Kukuk-na arrived. He saw what had happened, and Timkut-na showed him the direction the cobra had gone. Kukuk-na found the snake and killed it. He looked for others and found none. There was no cure for the bite. Either Timkut-na would live or die."

"Kukuk-na tried to make a lean-to from what was available. He helped Timkut-na put out his sleeping skins so he could lie down. He made a fire. He handed Timkut-na a piece of jerky, but the hunter declined. He wasn't hungry. Kukuk-na ate it. Timkut-na's hand was beginning to hurt severely. He became nauseated and vomited, but there was nothing in his stomach to get rid of but a little water. His eyelids were drooping and his hand and arm were swelling. He was in obvious pain. Kukuk-na agonized over his friend. He kept the fire going and watched Timkut-na carefully. Timkut-na slept fitfully. When Wisdom restored color to the land, Kukuk-na saw that Timkut-na was struggling to breathe. He saw him breathe his last."

"Kukuk-na took the digging tool Timkut-na carried in his backpack and dug the best he could to bury his friend. When he had him in the hole and covered by dirt, he still needed to find more dirt to cover him. He did not want any animal to dig the man up. Slowly he brought more dirt and covered the body. Then he found rocks and covered the mound. In the distance he heard what sounded like voices. He thought it was just his being alone and starving that caused him to hear things that weren't there."

"Kukuk-na sat by the lean-to and wept. He wept because his People hungered. He wept because there were no animals to feed his People. He wept because he and Timkut-na were starving. He wept because Timkut-na died. He wept because he was alone."

"The voices came closer. Kukuk-na didn't notice. It was two hunters from his People. They had found meat. They came to call the hunters home."

"This story is the reason we always check thoroughly for snakes and spiders when we look at a place to stop. Even if you are terribly tired, you must look to be certain that the place you are planning to stop is free of harmful living things. Timkut-na died because his thirst was more important than his safety."

122

Ghumotu, Oscola and Fimolamo's first child, was seven years old. He loved the stories. He could hardly contain himself. "Olomaru-mia, please tell the story of the dippers. I love that story best," he said with so much enthusiasm that Olomaru-mia was delighted.

"Of course," she smiled at him. "Remember that Notempa is a very tall mountain," she said and began the next story.

"Notempa was the greatest of the great ones. He had long white hair and a fierce face. Clouds would gather at his head and hang up there making ovals in the sky. The People had been visited by two Others called traders. They brought beautiful shells from the salty water. The shells were large and made wonderful dippers or food holders. They were shiny purple inside. Some of the People wanted dippers, but the traders told them they had to trade something for the dippers. Some of the People thought they should just be given the dippers for their hospitality. The People knew that Wisdom required them to show hospitality. Strangers were to be taken in and cared for well, so not to anger Wisdom. Hospitality required no return gift. It was to be freely given. While the disputes over the trading occurred, Notempa fumed. Smoke arose from his head and the smoke smelled like bad bird eggs. Many times Notempa fumed, letting the People know that they were supposed to remember hospitality."

"While the People argued with the Others, Maknu-na and Rimlad went hunting. They didn't like the squabbling over the dippers. They ranged far to the north, farther than they normally went. They could see Notempa in the distance. One day they saw that the ash had become a great billowing gray cloud, so much wider than the previous slender reddish ash clouds they had seen recently. It rose high into the clouds. Notempa shook the land and made a great noise that they could hear even where they were. They could see the cloud still rising but parts of the cloud were falling back to the earth from the sky while other clouds were racing down the face of Notempa and coming right at them. The cloud came toward Maknu-na and Rimlad at great speed. They were terrified. They could feel the warmth of the cloud coming at them. They could hear it. They grabbed reeds and jumped into a pond to try to save themselves from the wrath of Notempa. They submerged themselves in the pond and only the reeds kept them breathing. Both expected to die."

"After a long time, the air seemed to clear and they raised themselves from the pond. The whole landscape was the same color. An ugly gray. It was hot and smelled awful. They looked at Notempa. Notempa had been so angry that he had blown his own head off. No more white hair, just an empty place cut off at the neck."

"Rimlad and Maknu-na looked at each other. They knew that their group of People was gone. They could not have survived the horrible down-rushing hot smoke they'd seen. Why had they been spared? They wondered. They walked as far north as they could to get away from the terrible fury of Notempa. The air hurt their breathing passages. The ash burned their feet, legs, and arms with its caustic quality. They pushed on. When one would tire, the other would urge him on. They feared Notempa and they didn't want to die. They found animals covered in ash, dead, and they ate raw meat from those animals."

"On the third day they found a group of the People. They were taken in and cared for well. The People at first had thought they were ghosts of the dead because they were ashy colored from head to toe. But they washed up and were given clean clothing and food and what they wanted most, water. They had bad coughs, but those finally went away. The People gave them good bedding and let them sleep. They were treated differently from the way their People had treated the traders of the Others. They were shamed."

"They were asked to live with the People who took them in. They accepted the invitation. The air didn't clear from the explosion for a long time. There were many years of very cold weather. The People had to make clothing for cold weather. Sometimes people would have a toe or finger turn black and fall off. If it got too bad, they would die. One man cut off his black finger and took a white-hot stick from the fire and touched the sore place with it. His hand healed very well."

"For years along with the cold weather they also had beautiful sunsets. The colors of brilliant orange and red and purple and yellow were like none they'd ever seen. But the cold didn't last and the sunsets were only there briefly. They learned of Notempa's wrath when People failed to offer hospitality to travelers. First Notempa would get very hot and explosive and then he would cause the world to turn icy cold. Never again would the People fail to offer hospitality freely to those who were traveling. After a long time passed People said that Notempa's head was growing back. He would not forget the People. That was all a very long time ago."

Olomaru-mia looked up. Ghumotu was staring into her eyes.

"Olomaru-mia, what is the white hair? I know what a mountain looks like, but I do not understand the white."

Olomaru-mia removed her hat. "Mountains are different from place to place. The mountains we have here are long, fairly low running mountains. Sometimes mountains are shaped more like my hat. They are wide at the bottom and rise like a dirt mound. They are not mounds of dirt, though. Ash and, sometimes, fiery red material from under the earth rise up through these mounds and come out onto the land. Sometimes these mountains rise very high. When they rise very high, it is colder at the top of the mountain than it is at the bottom. In very cold places, when it rains, the rain becomes very cold and it falls to earth solid, not liquid, and it becomes white, not clear. White rain is called snow. In high places where it is always cold, the mountains may have snow on the top all year. The person who told that story first must have thought that the snow looked like white hair on someone old."

"I want to travel so I can see mountains like Notempa, well mountains like Notempa before he lost his head," Ghumotu said contemplatively. "Olomaru-mia, why did the sky turn brilliant colors? Our sky is colorful and brilliant as the sun leaves us for the night, but we had no explosion of a mountain here."

Olomaru-mia thought. "I think that the ash from the volcano makes the air a little dirty. I think that the colors look like what you have, but for some reason you get beautiful sunsets without dirt in the air. I do not really understand it. The dirt in the air made the temperatures much colder than normal for a while. I don't understand that either, but I know it's true."

Vilminit said, "I think I have a dipper like the one you describe. Have you ever seen one?"

"I saw one once. The one I saw was purple. I understand they can be different colors."

"Let me get mine." Vilminit went to his hut and returned with a beautiful turquoise colored shell.

He held it out to Olomaru-mia so she could take it but not touch him.

She examined it while children circled her to look at the beautiful shell.

"This is a dipper, but the color is different from the ones I've seen. This is very beautiful, Vilminit." She carefully handed him back the shell.

"This is one of my treasures. I found it far north from here in the western sea. A man I met told me how good the meat was. He and I went diving and we found several of them. We brought them up and ate them that night. I kept my shell. He discarded his."

"I love what the sunlight does to the colors," Olomaru-mia said while Vilminit allowed a few children to continue to examine it while he held it.

Ghumotu gently touched the inside colored part of the shell with his forefinger. He looked up at Olomaru-mia. "I can see why the People wanted them. I'd want one too, if I were fully a man." He looked at Vilminit. "What do they taste like?"

"They taste a little like clams, only they taste better than clams, I think." Thoughts of the taste of the shellfish and his time diving for them came back to him forcefully in memory. He remembered the beautiful light skinned girl with the black hair with a blue shine. Her pale blue, almost gray, eyes burned forever into his memory. She had chosen to spend one night with him. He wanted to spend every night with her for the rest of time, but that was not her desire at all. He was glad to have what he could have.

Vilminit slowly turned and carried the shell back to his hut where he placed it among his few things. Just looking at it for a moment was enough to bring back all the memories.

Children dispersed to do the chores that were assigned to them before the evening meal. Olomaru-mia sheltered herself in the shade and readjusted her seating to make herself more comfortable. She had already given birth to three children and was close to having her fourth. She wondered whether it would come before the dawn of a new day.

A shadow deepened across her legs. "How is it coming?" Ahma asked.

"You always know," Olomaru-mia smiled at her mother-in-law. "How do you know?"

"It's the way you carry yourself, Mia," she said, using the shortened version of the name she used with Olomaru-mia when the two were alone together.

"I can tell you I feel awkward this time, Mother."

"This one is large. It's just one baby, but a large one."

"Does it take longer to give birth to a large one?" Olomaru-mia asked.

"I don't think so," her mother-in-law said smiling. "This light tomorrow, it'll be all over."

"I hope so," Olomaru-mia laughed. "Is the evening meal ready?"

"Yes, of course, that's why I'm here. Take my hand," Ahma offered to help her up.

Olomaru-mia got up and walked slowly to the gathering place for food. She wasn't very hungry, but she thought it would be a good idea to eat.

As she was serving her bowl, Olomaru-mia noticed some commotion at the far end of the group of people and some got up from their food and began to walk fast toward the southwest. Her curiosity grew as she sat on a log and picked at her food. Suddenly she saw a few people and the unmistakable face of Tuna, whose body looked much like hers, ready to bring a new life to the world. After the greetings, Tuna sought her out. Flukua brought her daughter a bowl of food and Tuna and Olomaru-mia settled side-by-side to chat.

"I saw snow," Olomaru-mia. "It was exactly what you described. I knew what it was the moment I saw it. It's beautiful! I saw the western sea that you crossed in a boat. While we were there, we experienced a fierce earthquake, harder than what we've ever had here. The mountains were huge! Oh, Olomaru-mia, travel is wonderful!"

Olomaru-mia tried to follow her friend as she moved from one thing to the next. She was delighted to see Tuna so happy.

"How near are you to the birth of your baby?" Olomaru-mia asked.

"From the pains, I'm thinking it should be here by tomorrow," Tuna said with a grin.

"We may have our babies at the same time, then," Olomaru-mia said.

"Wouldn't that be wonderful?" Tuna mused as she gently stroked her bulging belly.

As darkness began to fall, Mechalu and Olomaru-mia gathered their three children, the twins, Pipto and Token, and their younger sister, Ahmu, and headed for their hut. The children were ready for sleep. During the night Olomaru-mia felt the first pains. She silently slipped out of the hut and headed to the larger one where she would give birth. There she found Tuna already laboring. By the light of the new day, each had an infant girl. Where Ahma had predicted that Olomaru-mia was carrying a very large infant, the baby had been born of normal size. Olomaru-mia and Tuna were both delighted. Ahma gently teased Olomaru-mia about too many crabs.

Weeks later Mechalu and Olomaru-mia walked down to the sea to gather crabs. Olomaru-mia had a grass sling that fitted over a shoulder to carry the new infant. The day was just slightly breezy and it was not too hot. Mechalu and Olomaru-mia were enjoying each other.

"My husband, there is something I would like to know," Olomaru-mia said softly.

"Anything," Mechalu replied.

"I know that you went south to learn and then went to the Alitukit to learn more. What did you learn in those places that you couldn't have learned at home?"

"Why do you want to know those things?" he asked.

"I am just curious. I know you plan for the boys to go there. I'm interested to know a little of what they'll be learning, and why they must leave home to do it." Olomaru-mia looked out to sea. The sea was calm and incredibly blue. A small lizard slithered through the vegetation at her feet.

"Here, we learn basic counting. We learn to add and remove quantities. In the south the numbers are far more complicated. We learn to project what quantities may be needed for very large projects. If, for example, you wanted to build a tower for signal communication that would be taller than the trees, how many of a certain size stones would you need to complete the task? We learn the different stones' qualities and what is useful for what purposes. Some people learn to carve stones. I didn't learn that."

"I have not seen buildings made of stones. Are there any of them in the south?"

"Yes, and much more distant to the south, there is great need for the towers, for the forests are very thick. Communication there is very difficult, if you cannot rise above the trees."

"And what did you learn from the Alitukit?"

"Ah, that's a different matter. The Alitukit look to the future and want to be able to determine future outcomes. I knew that there would be some falling stars near the time of the naming of our twins, but I was uncertain of the day. The Alitukit would know the day precisely. They would have castigated me for being lazy minded in my imprecision."

"That sounds awful."

"It wasn't personal. They treat all the same. They expect perfection. They strive for it. They are actually brilliant people. They tolerate us to the point where we become ineffective. For me it was with zero. You see, there is a manipulation of numbers that focuses on partitioning quantities. Let's say that you have two papayas. You have six children who want papaya. How do you distribute the papayas?"

"You're asking me?"

"Yes."

"I cut up the papayas into thirds and give each child a third."

"Right. Now, our number partitioning became more complex. Suppose you had seven children who wanted papayas and you had two papayas. What would you do then."

"I see what you mean, if I had to partition it equally among them. What I'd normally do is cut the papaya into small pieces and give a small piece to each child. Other children or older people could have some as well."

"The Alitukit would not want that for an answer. They want precision." Mechalu looked off into the distance leaning on his nola nola. "I told you I failed when dealing with zero. In theory, you can partition zero. You could say that zero partitioned by seven is zero. How would you partition out nothing? In practice, that's nonsense. The problem is that I could not theoretically or in practice partition a number such as seven by zero. The Alitukit call it dividing by zero. I could theoretically divide zero, although that's absurd, but I could not divide a number by zero. I couldn't reason how to do it, so I failed, and they sent me home. I know of no non-Alitukit, who was taught by the Alitukit, who got past that point. They told me I thought too small. That's what they tell those who can't figure out how to divide by zero. They said that our minds learn how to learn in only one way, while they use a variety of different means. They say that our way of learning works until we reach dividing zero and by zero. We have to learn differently to grasp that and our prior learning interferes by telling us it's impossible. They say the brightness we have grows to a certain point and then needlessly extinguishes itself."

"It sounds as if you learned all that you could learn. Why didn't they just teach you how to do it?"

"They teach up to that point when someone has difficulty. All the rest came so easily to me. When I got to that point, they gave me time to reflect and ponder the problem. I just couldn't find the answer. They assured me there is a solution. Sometimes I'd feel I was approaching it, and then I'd lose it. They say it's so simple. It wasn't simple to me! All I can guess is that it requires a different type of thinking—one I lack, just as they said. For a long time I felt terrible failure. I don't feel failure now. I am convinced that if there was a need for me to know, I'd be able to figure it out. I learned to understand the basic working of the night sky, to predict meteor showers and the appearance of comets and when the sun or moon would be blocked out, to determine the shortest and longest days of the year, and to use complicated numbers. I could build structures to tell us that, but the School of the South provides us that information. It's foolish to duplicate the effort for what we'd get from it, which is basically when the new year begins. I learned to communicate using the drums. We don't use them here. We can hear them from time to time, but we choose not to make known what happens here. We guessed long ago that the Alitukit use the drums to know what we are doing, but they share almost nothing. We decided not to participate. We listen to hear what others have to share, but we are silent. We are distant from drums so we don't always hear them."

Olomaru-mia leaned against a rock that jutted from the sand near the shore. Mechalu skipped stones across the surface of the sea. She untied the yoke of her tunic so she could feed her daughter. She rested her thoughts as the infant suckled. She considered how Mechalu had learned things she'd never dreamed. Her sons would have that opportunity, she realized. What privilege to learn complex knowledge, she reasoned, even if it would not be used immediately or perhaps ever. Sometime, there might be a need for the information. Of all the Nola Nola, she knew well that truth.

Olomaru-mia looked at the face of her daughter. How, she wondered, did a girl like Tuna arise—a girl who wanted nothing more than to have the education that bright boys had. She wondered whether it was wrong to seek after knowledge. She wondered how to teach girls in the culture of the Nola Nola. Perhaps, she'd have no need to know, but if her girl children hungered after knowledge, how could she help them? In her culture, it would have been easy. Knowledge was available to all, except spiritual knowledge, which Wisdom apportioned to the Wise One and those who were learning to become Wise Ones. It would be good to be prepared, she thought. But, how?

Chapter 4

Pikotek lay on his bedding. His body was burning from fever and Hutapska, who knelt beside him, kept wiping his forehead and placing damp cloths on his chest. Gimel and Gifi were watching her three children. Hutapska thought back over the last several years. She adored Pikotek more than life itself. She had been drawn to him from the moment she saw him, and the graveness of his injury frightened her. They had just recently moved to these new, wonderful caves, but a snake on their travel north had bitten Pikotek, and nobody knew what kind of snake it was or what to do for the bite. The bite appeared to be infected. Linpint had run to the two Alitukit men who taught him the drums to see if they knew of something that would help. He had been gone for three days. Hutapska's hope for his recovery grew each day Pikotek lived.

"Hutapska, you must eat something. Here's some fruit. Are you managing to get plenty of water into him?" Meninkua asked.

"Thank you, Mother," she replied, "I am getting water into him. Much water, but the water is not extinguishing the fire that burns in him. I worry."

Meninkua knelt beside her daughter. Gently, she placed her hand on Hutapska's shoulder. "I know. But, he is still living. Most poisonous snakebites take the lives of people they bite in a single day. Keep your hope. Even though he appears to sleep, his body knows your hope through your hands. Be careful what your hands say."

"I am doing my best. I wish Linpint would return. I have trust that the wise Alitukit will have found something that helps in snakebite cases like this."

"All of us feel the same way. If there were no help from them, Linpint would have returned by now. If there is anything you want or need, daughter, call for me."

"Thank you," Hutapska said with her eyes remaining on Pikotek's face.

The new cave system was one that a north Kapotonok had shown some of the hunters when they trained them in warfare. It was north of their former cave and part way up a mountain. It was an extensive arrangement of habitable cave areas strung along a central access way in the shape of a cylinder. The Kapotonok said water used to run underground through the cave system. They explained that long ago the land lifted up as it does sometimes after earthquakes. The cave size was far greater than they needed, but they had discovered that their numbers grew fast. The council decided to move to the location because it was an excellent choice and had plenty of room to expand. Pikotek lay in the second large area where most of the People slept. It had a small hole that opened to the sky. The hole let in light and let out smoke from the hearth fire. The first area was the gathering place for eating and where the People held council. It opened wide to the outside.

A gentle flow of air moved through the cave system along the central access way. Pikotek's bedding was not in the flow of the air but near it.

"How is my father?" Pomodaw, their first child, asked.

"There is no change, my son," Hutapska said flatly, putting her arm around the six-year-old.

Pomodaw stared at his father, who was alive but seemed to be somewhere else. He kept grasping the single shoulder strap of his tunic and squeezing it. He stood with his weight on first one foot and then another, as if he had more to say, but decided to remain silent.

There was some commotion at the entrance to the second cave area. Linpint walked directly to Hutapska with two gourds in his hands. His brow was wrinkled with vertical lines. He dispensed with greeting and knelt beside her. Pomodaw withdrew quickly to the side of the cave to watch from a distance.

"This is a substance to put on the wound itself. First, wash the wound. Remove all the pus and dead skin. Then put this on and wrap a cloth around his leg not too tight. Do that twice a day. Then, this gourd has a powder they made. Keep the powder dry and cover the gourd that contains it. Moisten your finger and stick it in there. Put your finger with the powder on the side or back of his tongue and give him water. Get all the powder on his tongue. Do this twice a day for ten days. Keep giving him a lot of water. Keep putting the wet cloths on him. Cover his body with wet cloths from his shoulders to his knees. That is all they told me. Do you have questions, Hutapska?"

"No, I understand. Thank you so much, Linpint."

"I just hope it works. He is our future Wise One. You need him as a husband. We need him as a leader."

Hutapska immediately began to clean the wound and pry the dead skin away. A task that once might have sickened her became one that carried hope. She was meticulous in her approach to the work. Having gently wrapped the wound, she put her finger into the water bowl and then coated it with the powder. She put it into Pikotek's mouth. She managed to transfer the powder from her finger to his mouth, but it wasn't as easy as she expected. Carefully, she transferred all the powder her finger contained to his mouth.

Linpint found Colitoba, the most knowledgeable person about plants that cure. He explained to her about the plants that the Alitukit made for Pikotek and how they made one into a paste and the other into a powder. He had sample plants. She had seen and knew where to find the plant with the shiny leaves that carried hanging green flower-like structures. The hanging flower-like structure had a triangle base with curved leaves appearing between the points of the triangles, and a rounded bud with a top that looked like worms. She had occasionally seen the elongated plant that grew stems with leaves one behind the other and carried an odd attachment that looked as if it could catch water in a rain. That attachment had a bright red pointed spire that rose from the top. She knew about the thin-stemmed plant that grew a flowering stem along with a leaf from the same bud area. The two discussed the two things the Alitukit had given him until Colitoba had the process clearly fixed in her mind web. The plants were ones that the People had seen and recognized. She would need some honey and wax. If Pikotek needed more than what the gourds contained, she was prepared to make more. She also kept the information in her mind web in case this need arose again.

The People in the cave had come to live more quietly since one of them lay so sick. No one suggested the hush—it just came naturally. From time to time, they would look to see whether Pikotek had moved, but he seemed to remain in the same position day after day.

Later that night, well after the evening meal, Golmid and Linpint climbed the mountain to listen for the drums. So many days had passed without a drum message, they had begun to question the value of making the daily climb. The message was short. It told of several birds—they interpreted the drums to say terror birds—moving through the lowlands from north to south. They were at the northern reaches of the Northern Kapotonok land. Golmid and Linpint looked at each other with blank stares. They lacked understanding of the message. The term terror bird made no sense to them. They hurried back to the caves and a quick council meeting.

At the meeting, Linpint told what the drum message said, and he noticed that Kolpatin blanched.

Finally, Kolpatin cleared his throat and said, "The terror birds are terrible predators. They are taller than we are. They have huge beaks that can tear a person apart. They don't fly but rather run around on the earth. They can run much faster than we can. They eat meat, and they would see us as food. It would not be wise for any of the People to be alone. Preferably, at least six hunters should be together when two of these birds are present. If there are large numbers of them, we must think of climbing trees to avoid them. Children should not spend time in the lowlands until danger is past. It's possible we'll be beyond their pathway, since they do prefer the open spaces and they track usually more to the east of us. It is good to have warning that they are nearby. They usually don't come through this narrow strip of land we inhabit, preferring to remain way to the south or north of us where in both places the land is much larger and more open, but occasionally, they do come through. I have seen them twice. Once a single one that our hunters killed and we ate, and another group of four from which our hunters wisely hid. The one I saw that we ate killed one of my people. I was very young, but I saw it. We ate it, in retaliation, I think."

"How do they taste?" Zamimolo asked. "Sorry, but my curiosity is caught."

Ba hit him in the side with her elbow, and gave him a disgusted look.

Kolpatin smiled, "They taste better than a spiked-tailed armadillo to me, but not as good as well-cooked camel." At that the group chuckled. Each thought to himself how great it would be to have terror bird for the evening meal sometime. It seemed more of a grand challenge than the terrifying reality Kolpatin reflected. Something to share with future generations. Kolpatin knew the birds were named appropriately. "If they come here, you may change your mind about eating them, and just try to avoid their knowledge of where you are. Whatever you do, if you see them, don't lead them to the cave."

Kumoha began to clear away the food from the evening meal that had remained out for the People to eat.

Kada asked her, "Did you ever see one of those terror birds?"

"No, when they are out, my people hide or leave the area completely. They are not something to treat lightly. They are terrible predators. I'd rather go up against a big cat than one of those birds. How is Mop doing with the slingshot now?"

"He finally learned to hit what he was aiming at. Apparently, when he'd let the stones fly, he'd shut his eyes. Inrusk discovered what was happening and taught him to keep his eyes opened. That made all the difference."

Slowly the People went to unroll their sleeping skins and prepare for night. From some sleeping areas, the night sky showed the uncountable stars. This night was so clear that stars filled the skies in abundance. Zamimolo thought as he drifted off to sleep of luminescent salt water. The cave quieted gradually for a while, until finally all but the guards slept.

The Wise One raised himself up on his elbow and looked out at the early return of light beyond the hills he could see from his sleeping skins. He had not felt well for some time. He decided that he would turn over the responsibility of Wise One to Pikotek as soon as the young man recovered. Of all the People he was the only one certain that Pikotek would actually recover. He and Hutapska had been joined for almost ten years and Pikotek had a solid understanding of being a Wise One. He wondered why he had held to the responsibility for so long instead of turning it over to Pikotek a year or two ago. At eighty-one, he was exceptionally old. He felt his age. He tried to rise, but found the task beyond his ability. He found that peculiar. For a moment he lost his vision. He supposed he'd shut his eyes without realizing it. His mind web became confused. He returned to his resting place with a bit of a thud. His eyes no longer saw but instead lost their focus hold and rolled oddly; his jaw muscles fully relaxed into a strange, unlifelike drop.

It was Uilo who found the Wise One. Her wail awakened everyone in the cave except Pikotek. Meninkua and Colitoba immediately began the necessary steps to prepare the body for burial. They laid out a skin and washed the old man carefully. They tied his jaw shut and closed his eyes. Colitoba cradled his head in her arms briefly, as she mourned. All of the older People were stunned. For all purposes at that moment they had no Wise One. The thought was unnerving. It raised questions. How did the People, in the absence of a Wise One, properly perform a burial? Tukyatuk began to go from person to person asking whether anyone knew the story for burials. Jalutui, Folifilo's youngest daughter, said she knew it, but she was only seven years old. Surely, she overestimated her storytelling ability, her mother thought.

Colitoba called Jalutui over and asked her to tell the story. Jalutui was frightened that she had said something wrong in admitting she knew the story, but she knew she knew it. She sat with Colitoba by a tree on the side of the hill above the cave. Looking directly into Colitoba's eyes, instead of unfocusing her eyes on some indefinite point as Wise Ones did, she began:

"In the beginning, Wisdom made the world. He made it by speaking. His words created. He spoke the water and the land into existence, the night and day, the plants that grow in the dirt, and the animals that live on the dirt, and those that live in the water and in the air. Then he went to the navel of the earth. There he found good red soil and started to form it into a shape with his hands. He made it to look a little like himself. Then he inhaled the good air and breathed it into the mouth of the man he created. The man came to life. Then he took some of the clay left from the man and he made woman. He inhaled and breathed life into her. Wisdom created a feast. He killed an aurochs, skinned it, made clothing for the man and woman from the aurochs, and then roasted the aurochs for the feast. The man and the woman watched carefully and quietly to see how he killed the aurochs, how he skinned it, how he made clothing from its skin, and how he roasted it. They paid good attention and they were able to survive by doing what they had seen done."

"The People were special and Wisdom pronounced that the man was to treat the land and the water and the animals and the woman the way he wanted to be treated—good. And the same was true of the woman. And it went well for a long time. But Wisdom hadn't made the People of stone. He had made them of dirt, knowing that they shouldn't have lives that would go on too long for they might get prideful and forget Wisdom. That is good because People should not be without Wisdom. They would die."

"That is why the People return to Wisdom when they die. They are placed in the earth and Wisdom knows. When Wisdom hears of a death of the People, Wisdom waits until the grave is filled back. He waits until it is dark. Then he causes the earth to pull on the spirit of the dead to draw that person's spirit back through the dirt of the earth to the navel from which all People came, the navel of the earth where the red clay for making the first man was. The dead spirits depart for the navel of Wisdom. That is where they reside for all time. All People's bodies return to the dirt. But their spirit, that essence of the person made by the One Who Made Us, is pulled back to Wisdom in the place where first man was made, and Wisdom keeps all those he chooses with him there, safe and loved. There is a cycle Wisdom made: a cycle from the navel to the navel. He keeps the spirits of those whom he chooses and he destroys those whom he hates. Wisdom hates those who hate him, those who ignore him, those who would be hurtful to him or the land or water or to those living things Wisdom made including People."

Jalutui exhibited another difference in telling the stories. When the Wise Ones said the stories, they almost sang them. Jalutui spoke it in words that sounded as if she were talking with a good friend. It was the same story but told a little differently. As far as Colitoba knew, she knew the story perfectly. She hugged the young girl and went to find Tukyatuk. Colitoba admitted to herself that she liked the eye contact and Jalutui's telling the story with feeling in her words.

The men had found a level place in a meadow on the mountaintop not far from the drum. The drum was about the length of the height of a boy age twelve. It sat in a hut without walls with a carefully made roof of palm leaves laced with other vegetation to keep the drum dry. They chose flat land near the drum for their first grave. The men began to dig right away. As soon as the grave was finished, the People walked solemnly up to the meadow and gathered in a circle around the grave. A few men carried the camel skin that held the body of the old man. He had become so withered that he was lighter than most of the women. They gently handed their light burden to men who were standing in the hole, so they could place the body in the hole appropriately. Many of the People had gathered wildflowers from the meadow, not wanting to go to the lowland where they might encounter a terror bird. Then, as they had done from the beginning of time, they began to speak, rotating around the People who edged the grave, each telling of the special meaning of the deceased to them. When each finished his or her words, they added their flowers to the grave by tossing them into the open hole. Over time, People had taken longer and longer to tell of the special meaning the deceased had to them, as if a short amount of words meant that the deceased was a lesser person. It took quite a long time for the circle to complete. Then, Jalutui began. She spoke from her heart, for she had loved the old man. She told the story in a way no one had heard it told, but the words were the same, and all recognized it. Back in the cave, Hutapska watched over an immobile Pikotek.

Slowly people began to return to the cave. It was a very quiet time. Many of the older people wondered about Jalutui and her knowledge of the story. Did she know other stories, they wondered. Was she to be a Wise One? None of those thoughts passed the mind web of the young girl. She simply knew that story and told it. Afterwards, she felt very tired, but she didn't understand why.

That evening the men outside heard the drums. They told that the terror birds had passed through the Northern Kapotonok land and had entered into the Southern Kapotonok land. There were ten terror birds. Golmid quickly went to the cave to alert the People. He was surprised that flightless birds could move that fast through such a large territory. All of the People were urged to return to the caves.

When Hutapska got up to get her evening meal, she thought she detected some movement from Pikotek. She stared at him carefully, but saw nothing else and assumed she'd been mistaken. She returned with some camel and some fruit, not much of either. She sat there and picked at her food. Suddenly she felt movement beside her. Pikotek's hand had touched her side. She was so startled that she dropped her bowl and didn't realize it. She had crouched down to hug Pikotek. Her joy was boundless. He was terribly weak, but he was clearly living and functioning in his mind web. Colitoba brought some camel broth and cleaned up the meat and fruit Hutapska spilled. Hutapska slowly fed Pikotek the broth and struggled to keep her joy controlled.

Pomodaw came slowly to his mother's side. He looked at his father while his mother put her arm around his waist.

"Is he going to be well?" Pomodaw asked in a very small voice.

"I am going to be very well," Pikotek said with as much smile as he could create.

Pomodaw jumped and then recovered enough to grin at his father. "I'm glad!" he said and left to be with his friends.

That night the council met to discuss what they should do with the terror birds so near. It finally came down to agreement that all would stay at the cave and they would be very quiet. The drums would tell when the birds had passed out of the Southern Kapotonok's land and from that message on the drums, it would be a short while before the terror birds cleared their land. It could be days before the next drum to the south reported. They would keep silent and remain hidden in their caves while there was danger. Once the far south drums reported the birds, they'd feel safe. Otherwise, some of the terror birds might be lurking nearby. The People could not spare the loss of a single person.

As the days passed, Pikotek improved daily. He heard of the storytelling by Jalutui, and he asked her to come to him to tell some stories. Jalutui was uncertain whether she had somehow offended the Wise One by taking his place. Before he could begin testing her, he had to assure her that what she did was a very good thing, not an offense at all. He asked her to tell the story she had told when they buried the Wise One. She began and continued through to the end. He noticed immediately what the others had noticed. She did not use the sing-song method of traditional storytelling. She spoke directly to the listener as if the listener and she conversed. She told the story with significant and appropriate feeling. As he listened, Pikotek thought how much easier it was to learn the sing-song method than to speak directly to the listener as if in conversation. He also realized how much easier it was on the listener to follow the story the way Jalutui told it. He marveled at her youth.

He had her tell story after story and he realized that she was destined to become another Wise One. He was twenty-three and Jalutui was seven. It surprised him that she was so close in age to him, but he also realized that he was not to question Wisdom. There would be a reason for Jalutui's becoming a Wise One. He definitely had a responsibility to teach her. As soon as the council met, he shared the information with the People. After having heard her, no one was surprised. It meant keeping watch over another Wise One, but the People would not question that responsibility. They had great respect for Wisdom and the memories were given by Wisdom. What Wisdom chose to do, they would support wholeheartedly.

Terror birds reached the land beyond the Southern Kapotonok border, the drums sounded out one night. Because the Kapotonok killed one of them, only nine crossed into the southern lands. The People felt a great sense of relief as they continued on with their lives with less apprehension.

"You think you're so important!" Oscola, quite red in the face, railed at his brother. "You got the best trial of valor, the peccary tooth necklace, two sets of twins! In addition, you still have a body of a young man, not one like mine. Oscola's hands started at the front middle and smoothed around his great girth to the sides. Just wait until I am Chief!"

Mechalu looked at his brother as if he'd never seen him. They were at the edge of the sea, having gone to gather crabs. "You are my brother. I do not set myself up against you. What is the meaning of this?"

"Don't tell me you don't take great pride in having found the golden woman or having received of our father the peccary tooth necklace. Don't tell me you didn't glory in your knowledge when we were sent to school and all the information came to you so easily, while I struggled so hard. Don't tell me you aren't plotting to become Chief when Father dies."

"What's the matter with you? I have no interest in becoming Chief. I know that's yours. You are my brother. I love and respect you. I fully expect you to become my Chief. I am a hunter! I've always seen myself as a hunter. It's what I do." Mechalu was dumbfounded. He had no suspicion that his brother held anything against him.

"It's just like you to act so innocent." Oscola was snarling. Sweat was dripping from his body and his face was puffy and red. It was hot but not hot enough to cause so much sweating, Mechalu thought.

"Let us sit in the shade and discuss this, Oscola. I am trying hard to understand what I've done to give you these ideas. Truly, I do not think better of myself than of you. I have looked up to you all my life. Something has gone terribly wrong, and I'd like to fix it, if possible."

Oscola joined him in the shade of some palm trees. "When we were children, you'd be recognized in the School of the South over and over for having figured out things easily. You'd stand there in all the praise, smiling as if you were the Chief. At the Alitukit School you had the same response but you hid it better there. Don't tell me you weren't delighted to have showed better than I did."

"Stop, Oscola. I had to figure things out just like you did. When someone praised my effort, I wasn't competing with you. I was solving a difficult problem. My interaction was with a problem, not you. I never put you down. Always, I considered you a little better than myself, because you are my older brother. I esteem you. I always have. I have seen the teachers praise you. I didn't take your smiles then as your raising yourself over me. You have me totally confused."

"Father expects your firstborn twins to become men of renown. He's never said that about Ghumotu or Too."

"Oscola," Mechalu said calmly and straightforwardly, "I cannot control what our father says. I think he was overcome with the meteor. We went to the Alitukit School. He never did. A meteor is a meteor, not a messenger. I can control what I think and how I feel—not someone else. I do not want our being brothers to be torn apart because our father thinks a meteor's a messenger. I love you and have great respect for you. It would break my heart if you continue to think evil of me, for I have no evil intent towards you. I know that often brothers quarrel, but I thought you and I were special in that we loved each other."

Oscola looked at Mechalu and really saw him. His anger had dissipated. The day was hot and he was very irritable, but he no longer carried ill will towards Mechalu. He believed what Mechalu told him. He could see the truth in Mechalu's face. Mechalu's face had always shown his true feelings.

"Then, maybe I was mistaken, my brother. Your words have calmed my heart. Shall we go now and gather many crabs?"

"Yes. Let's do it. Thank you for discussing this with me, Oscola."

"And I thank you," Oscola said, meaning it. He felt exhausted, uncomfortable.

Olomaru-mia was busy at her hut getting things ready for the return of Pipto and Token. They had been at School in the South, would be returning for about thirteen days, and then would leave for the land of the Alitukit. She wanted to enjoy every moment she could while they were at home.

She looked up. "Tuna, how are you?"

"I'm fine, Mia. It looks like we're going to take another trip."

"Where will you go this time?"

"We go east then south along the eastern seashore to the mouth of the enormous river."

"Will you take all your children?" Olomaru-mia asked.

"No, they'll stay with my parents. My parents love having them. I expect I'll have this one while we travel," she said rubbing her belly. "Coshiga just loves to travel, and so do I. I tease him about itchy feet. They're very itchy right now. On both of us."

"You did hear the drums about the terror birds, didn't you?"

"Oh, yes, but we'll be far away from them. No worry."

"Ah, Tuna, I do worry. I know both of you know this land, but it's only the two of you."

"Mia, my lovely friend, we'll be fine. I promise."

"When will you leave?"

"In the morning early. We want to get into the rhythm of walking before it gets terribly hot."

"I'll miss you."

"We won't be gone that long, and when we return, there will be so much to share." Tuna turned with a smile and headed towards her own hut.

Olomaru-mia watched her go, wondering at her friend who could pull up from responsibilities to take off for adventures with only one other person. She agreed with Tuna that the grandparents loved the children and cared for them, but she felt that there was something missing in parents who could just leave their children for countless days. She couldn't understand it. What she did know is that Tuna and Coshiga were happy people and their children adored them.

Oscola and Mechalu headed up the path with large bags filled with crabs. Olomaru-mia saw them from the covered shelter where she sat out of the sun in front of her hut. She salivated just thinking about the crabs. Of all the food new to this land, Olomaru-mia loved crabs best. The firm white meat was mild and delicious, and it took minimal time and effort to prepare. The men had an enormous number of crabs. She'd be able to eat them greedily.

At the top of their climb, Oscola was struggling to breathe. He asked Mechalu to carry his crab bag to the women while he went to his hut. Mechalu realized finally that Oscola was having a problem that had more to do with how he felt physically than how he and Mechalu did in school. It struck Mechalu with a pang of fear for his brother. He would talk with his mother in confidence.

There was some commotion at the top of the hill. Many years ago Mechalu had descended that same hill with Olomaru-mia, when he returned to his people after his trial of valor. Mechalu quickly handed the two bags of crabs to the women who were standing near the fire, and he ran up the hill. The sight of Pipto, Token, and Ghumotu rewarded his run. His two boys ran to hug him. Ghumotu looked for Oscola, but he couldn't see him. He continued walking down the path to his hut. Pipto was on one side of Mechalu and Token on the other. The three walked strongly to their hut, while their friends and older people lined the way welcoming them home.

At their hut the hugs shifted from Mechalu to Olomaru-mia. The boys had grown so tall. They were taller than Olomaru-mia, but not quite as tall as Mechalu. They might easily pass his height at their age, a fact not lost on their father.

"We have brought you something, Mother," Pipto said. "They grow on the top of the mountain where our school is," Token continued the thought, while Pipto pulled out a white crystal from a soft piece of leather. "This is now yours, Mother," Pipto said watching the sparkle in his mother's eyes.

"It's beautiful," she murmured. "What do you mean they grow there?"

"They appear on the surface of the top of the mountain, just like flowers," Token said.

Pipto could not contain himself, "We asked one of the masters if we could bring you one, and they said we could, because they *grow* there."

"The place where you have your school must be a very unique place."

"When we have some time to slow down, we'll tell you all about it," Token said. "You won't believe it. Nobody prepared me for that place! When you see it for the first time and people tell you it's necessary to climb to the top, you're sure it's impossible. Can we go talk to a few of our friends before the evening meal?"

"Of course! We'll talk later." Olomaru-mia looked at Mechalu quizzically.

He sat beside her and put his arm around her. "The school is located at the top of a tall mountain that has sides that go straight up. The mountain looks like an incredibly huge tree trunk that the top has been sliced off flat. It's very, very difficult to climb up and go down. Once there, it's as if you were in a different world. I won't spoil it by sharing it with you. I know the boys want to do that."

"There is so much about you and your earlier life that I don't know."

"If you'd lived here all along, you'd not know much more. Most of my life has been involved in learning away from here. There are only three places where a young person can go to learn more than what's passed on right here. One's the School in the South, up high on a mountain. The other is in the land of the Alitukit, again on a mountain. Not all boys go away to school. It depends on whether the family can do without the child's help and whether the child has the curiosity of mind to make it worthwhile. Boys sent who waste the time of the masters are sent home alone. The third place is wherever the boy goes for his trial of valor."

"Has anyone been sent home that you know?"

"No. My father has carefully made the decision on whether the children go or remain at home. Just because parents want to keep the child here or want him to go, it matters not unless my father agrees. He will not send just any boy. He will send the ones who are bright and show a desire to learn things. He observes them from the time they're born. He refused to let a friend of mine go, and I was unhappy about that. Later, I discovered that the father of the boy became very sick, and he was needed at home. My father must have seen the illness coming on. That friend later died from a sloth slashing. Some places let the families decide. I'm not certain which is the better way."

Olomaru-mia snuggled against Mechalu. He looked at her with a wicked grin, "Let's make another set of twins."

"Now?" she asked.

He was on his feet and extending her a hand, "Now!" he replied, still grinning. They disappeared into the hut.

Ghumotu had entered his hut to find his father lying on his sleeping mat drooling and looking strange. He seemed happy to see Ghumotu, but smiled a strange crooked smile. He also seemed to be very unhappy that he wasn't functioning well, and he couldn't speak so that his son could understand. Ghumotu ran to find his mother. She was with the women in the cooking area. Ahma, Oscola's mother, understood the problem and she followed Fimolamo and Ghumotu. By the time they reached Oscola, he was struggling to breathe. Finally, he seemed to give up and shortly afterwards, he stopped breathing. Oscola died young. It was a complete shock to all but Ahma, who had seen a few people die in this manner. Ghumotu was undone. He loved his father and the loss was terrible. He assumed that the loss would mean that he would no longer be able to continue his learning with Pipto and Token. His life had gone from delight in the early part of the day to complete dismay before the evening meal. Fimolamo was distraught. Immediately women arrived to help prepare Oscola for burial.

Some of the men raced off with digging tools to the area where the Nola Nola buried their dead. In hot climates people did not wait to bury their dead. The job was completed and the men came to get the body of Oscola. It took a while to find Oscola's prize of valor. The prize of valor had to be buried with the man whose prize it was, since no other man was permitted to touch it. His was a seashell from the waters of the western sea. His son, Too, found it, climbed into the grave, and placed it in the hand of his father. He climbed back out and stood beside his mother. All the people gathered at the grave and the Chief said a few words:

"Creator of All, this is my first son, Oscola, who died too soon. A man should not have to bury his child. Take his body and his spirit and give them new life in your eternal land, for he was a good son and a good husband and father. I will look after his widow and children, so that his son may continue his learning. Do any others wish to speak?" he asked, his voice cracking. No one spoke up.

The group disbanded and returned to their homes. The men who had dug the grave filled it back and placed stones on the top of it. Instead of a normal evening meal, people went to take food that was set out and they returned to their huts to eat instead of gathering together. It was such a shock that light conversation was beyond thought.

After they ate, Pipto and Token asked if they could visit Ghumotu. Olomaru-mia and Mechalu agreed immediately. The boys went. Token was concerned that Ghumotu would want to take care of his family instead of going on to school, and they wanted to encourage him to continue with school. Mechalu remained silent. He knew that once the Chief said something—that was the end of it. Ghumotu really had no choice in the matter, but he felt his boys were doing what they should do, so he remained silent.

"Do you think we made twins?" Mechalu asked Olomaru-mia.

"Dearest, I have no idea. That was not the best way to end lovemaking."

Mechalu hugged her. The little faces of their children appeared in the light of the fire of their hearth. The little ones were happy children. The older ones were struggling to understand how a man they'd known all their life could be alive and well one minute and dead the next. Many of the children had never seen death. Mechalu looked at the children. "Death comes to us all, little ones. It is not something to fear. You simply leave this life for another one with the Creator of All."

"I'd rather just stay with you," the youngest said.

Mechalu and Olomaru-mia smiled. What could they say to that?

The next morning things were slow. All gathered for the morning meal, but words were slow to form and be spoken. The sun shone brightly but the day was somber.

In the shaded area in front of the hut, Olomaru-mia sat with the two boys after the morning meal. "Tell me about your school life," she asked.

"Oh, Mother, I could not have imagined it!" Pipto said, his voice awe tinged.

"It's a huge flat topped mountain where we went. It rises up from the ground looking like a tree trunk without limbs with a top that that got sliced off. We had to get to the top."

"Was it very tall?"

"It made the mountains here look like little hills. It rises into the clouds." Token was lost as he envisioned it. "Water falls from the top and there are many places where water falls."

"We had to climb the only path that goes up to the top. It took us all day. We had to climb over rocks that were lying jumbled and some would roll when we stepped on them. It was a time you don't look down. You just keep going up. It is like no place on earth. Once you are there, you are certain that you're in another place on another earth."

"What do you mean?"

"There are plants and animals there that are no place else. Nothing that grows here or in the nearby forest grows there. The things that grow there don't grow here. There are plants there that eat bugs! Beautiful blossoms curl around bugs and devour them. You can see the plants move!" Pipto was trying to put the place into some form for sharing, but the images he remembered came so fast that he had difficulty.

"And the rocks. Don't forget the rocks! Rocks up there are formed like animals or people. They sit on narrow props of rock. It's as if you're being watched up there. Huge rocks balance on the tiniest of points. It's beyond imagining!" Token was reliving the scene.

"The school and our places to sleep lie in a great tube that was once an underground waterway. It was spooky to think that where we slept once water ran through there fast. You could see it on the walls of the cave. The cave is huge!" Pipto added.

"We bathed in pools of water that lay on the surface up there. The rocks in the pools are smooth and they form strange shapes just as the ones on the top of the mountain do. The water is very clear. You'd love one of those pools for bathing. Mother," Token stopped, looking at his mother's hair, "You've got lots of white hairs among the gold ones."

Olomaru-mia smoothed her hair back. "It happens to all when we get old enough. Someday yours will whiten." She had not been aware of the white hair. She'd check for herself when no one looked.

Token looked into her eyes, "The masters are strict. They expect us to act maturely and to do exactly what they say. The threat of being sent home alone frightens many kids. We both just wanted to learn, just like Ghumotu. I wanted to come home once because I felt unhappy. It rains there almost every day. I wanted sun, the sea, and my people. I got over it. One of the masters told me it's not unusual for that to happen, but that it would pass. One of the masters' wives brought me some sage and told me to put in in my sleeping skins. It had a wonderful calming effect.

"We had lots to learn. Once they sent us out for three days to the lower levels. I had to watch leaf cutter ants and Token had to watch army ants. We had to do that for the whole three days except when we slept."

"I was afraid to sleep for fear the army ants would get me in my sleep," Token admitted.

Pipto was so excited to share that he couldn't contain it any longer. "When we got back we had to tell all the others what we observed. Two of the learners didn't observe much so they had to repeat the experience. I told about the leaf cutters and how they carried leaf pieces they'd cut down—the leaves were huge compared to the ants—and they carried the leaves under the ground where the leaf changes form. Apparently, they eat the material the

146

leaf changes into. We have to go out and gather our food each day. These ants bring home the material that grows what they will eat. They have stored food. If they couldn't cut leaves for a while, they'd still have food. It's right there available to them when they want."

"My ants were courageous or vicious, depending on how you look at it. They attack as a group. It's as if the entire group was a predator. They attack what moves. If a living thing stays perfectly still, the ants don't attack. Instead of eating plant material, these ants eat meat! I've seen them stand on their back legs and fight as tough as any man, maybe tougher. They don't have a leader. They just all know together exactly what to do and they do it. I get chills about it and sometimes bad dreams," Token admitted. "I think we could learn from them how to fight wars."

Pipto lay on his back with one leg propped on the bent knee of the other leg. He chewed a piece of grass. "We wondered when we left here why we had to carry a furred skin and a plain one. One night it got so cold up there that the three of us used my furred skin to lie down on and we covered with Token's furred skin over our plain ones. We slept well that night, but some of the others had a cold night. Ghumotu didn't have a furred skin. That surprised me."

"It may be that Oscola had been struggling for some time. He may just have forgotten about sleeping skins when he helped his son pack for school," Olomaru-mia said, wondering.

"Well, Ghumotu never got left out. He's our friend," Token said.

"I'm glad you boys looked out for him. You will become good men."

Dragonflies buzzed by. One landed for a moment on Pipto's knee.

"The best part of the experience for me was getting to work the pieces of stone. We had some sandstone and we carved it into shapes. That was fascinating how you can pull an image out of a lump of stone."

"What did you carve?" Olomaru-mia asked.

"I carved a conch shell," Pipto replied. "The masters liked it so much they kept it."

"That's wonderful, Pipto. I had no idea you would carve stones."

"I didn't either. I would have thought that was not manly somehow, but I discovered it is clearly a manly thing. It takes hard work to do that. You need muscles. You have to see what it is you want to give life in the stone, and then you have to free it. It takes much planning."

"Did you carve, too, Token?"

"No, Mother, I spent most of my time on math. They show us various ways of computing numbers and I was fascinated. There is a way of using cords, knots, and loops that I wanted to master. I spent much time doing that."

"So some things you have to do all together and some are spent on things you choose."

"You either choose them or the masters choose them for you," Pipto added. "If Token had chosen something else, the masters would have kept him at math. He's really good at it!"

"Token, you didn't tell me that," Olomaru-mia said quietly, wondering what his response would be, if any.

"I was afraid I might appear to boast. I enjoy math. It absorbs me. I should not be praised for something I enjoy so much."

Olomaru-mia wondered whether her prayers to Wisdom to keep Token from pride had worked. He certainly didn't exhibit the pride that was arrogance, a trait that looked good on no one.

Mechalu stormed into the peaceful area, clearly upset.

"What is it my husband?" Olomaru-mia asked, alarmed.

"I have been with my father. Since Oscola died, I am now to become Chief when my father dies. I never wanted that job."

"Isn't it an honor?" Olomaru-mia asked. Her youngest daughter fell into her lap.

"Maybe for some people. It's one I never sought and didn't want. Now, I'm stuck with it. I have to look at things differently. I will be trained starting now."

"Well, my dear, the Winds of Change turned my life upside down and I am happy. I hope that the same will be said of you."

He rolled his eyes at her and said nothing.

"I trust the masters carefully honed in on your hunting skills," Mechalu said touching each of the boys on the shoulders. "Let's get up now and find out. Mia we'll only be gone a short while."

She smiled at him. It had crossed her mind since she heard that the Chief usually stayed home in much the same way as the Wise One of the People remained at the cave, that would not make Mechalu happy at all. How could he hunt?

The boys were up and had their weapons ready. Mechalu told Pipto to get Ghumotu to join them with his weapons. The three boys accompanied Mechalu up the path into the forest. Later they would come down the same path carrying four peccaries. They would have a feast that night.

During the days that remained for the boys to be at home, Mechalu kept the three of them busy. He carefully included Ghumotu, knowing that his mother was not doing well following Oscola's death. The Chief had determined that Ghumotu would go to the Alitukit School. Mechalu wanted to keep Ghumotu's focus on that instead of pity for his mother and a desire to remain to comfort her. That would be the Chief's function, not her son's. The Chief had spoken. Mostly they would go hunting during the day, returning only late in the evening. When they returned, they took care to prepare the animals for the women's use. They butchered the animals and prepared the skins for use or disposal.

The Nola Nola had acquired a large number of skins that were finished to incredible softness. Some had the fur left on and some were fur free. They also had stored a large number of coconuts, fruit, and other items. These were gifts they gave the Alitukit when the boats would arrive to gather the boys for the school. The boats would arrive seven days following the solstice.

The day of the solstice dawned. Mechalu had planned to take the boys hunting again. They did not have a large solstice celebration, but they did put out special food the women prepared and they would have music and dance following the evening meal. Olomaru-mia asked them to gather crabs and other seafood for the feast, rather than return to hunt forest animals. She wanted to join them and bring the other children. Mechalu could see no reason not to accommodate her wishes, so he agreed. The other children were delighted to be included. Pipto and Token had been the center of the family. The children knew the older twins were only there temporarily, but they felt pushed aside during their visit. This day they would be included.

Mechalu and Olomaru-mia had eight children. The twins were twelve years of age, next was a girl, eleven, named Sima, then a boy of nine named Mohu, a girl of eight named Poa, twins of six years named Azom and Snar, and a girl of four named Maisy. They had occasionally lost a child through miscarriage and one toddler died of snakebite. The children had skin color between the darkness of Mechalu and the lightness of Olomaru-mia. Sima and Poa had light colored hair, though not the gold of their mother. The other children had dark hair. They were exquisitely lovely to see. They were well-behaved children of the Nola Nola.

It came as a shock to Olomaru-mia to return from the privy to find Mechalu beating Sima with his hand instead of his nola nola. She knew better than to interfere, but she was horrified. She had to wait until he finished. Then she looked at him, horror plain on her face.

149

She looked at Mechalu still holding Sima by the arm. She was sobbing, clearly in pain. He said, "She refused to accompany us. When I told her she had no alternative, she cursed the Creator of All and said that you and I love only the boys. She has lost control of her mind and her mouth."

Olomaru-mia had no idea how to respond, so she stood there expressionless. She had seen a few women beaten, but rarely a child. She was acutely aware that the females were the sex most frequently beaten. She wanted to protect Sima, but she didn't want to be beaten.

Mechalu looked at Olomaru-mia and said, "Tell her she has no choice when I tell her to do something."

Olomaru-mia knew what he said was true, so she said calmly, "Sima, daughter, you were wrong to go against your father. When he tells you to do something, you must do it. He will not tell you to do what's wrong. You know that. You are wrong to think that you are not loved. We do love you. We love you enough to assure that you obey." Then Olomaru-mia looked at Mechalu. "Did she tell you why she didn't want to go?"

"I don't care why she didn't want to go. When I tell her she's going, that's the end of it. You know that, wife." His manner was brusk.

Olomaru-mia knew she needed to talk with Sima, but now was definitely not the time. It would be good to choose a time when the boys were with Mechalu hunting. She could give Sima no sympathy now. They had to go to the sea to gather seafood. Olomaru-mia started to feel guilt for having asked to gather seafood, but stopped herself. Sima had asserted herself in a situation she knew could only bring a negative reaction from Mechalu. Olomaru-mia realized that it was not her place to carry guilt. Olomaru-mia's only consolation was that Mechalu had not used his nola nola on Sima. She would likely have been left with broken bones. She could see from Sima's face that Mechalu had injured her physically, but the spirit that caused the outburst still thrived. She could see it in her daughter's eyes. Sima wept, but it seemed to Olomaru-mia, it was more from fury than acceptance of correction. He hadn't broken her spirit. Olomaru-mia knew she had to find a way to reach her daughter as soon as possible. She knew Mechalu well enough to know that he had warned her. If she persisted, he'd use his nola nola, and she might be deformed or disabled from what Mechalu would see as correction.

They carried many bags to the sea. The other children had seen Mechalu beating Sima, and they were slightly fearful and wary that they might do something wrong. The lightheartedness that the family usually experienced had disappeared and in its place was a foreign somberness. As they descended the well-worn path, Mechalu who walked in the front put both his arms out to the side, the signal for all to stop and remain silent. He pointed to a depression in the land below. All looked in the direction he pointed. They could see three glars grazing below. Glars were as tall at the shoulder as a man, and they were longer than a man is tall. They were heavy animals with a rough coat. They were stocky like elephants and had significant teeth but nothing like the tusk or large ears of an elephant. They grazed but also enjoyed gathering greens from lakes.

Mechalu turned to face his family. "Return home. Sima, you are to go into the hut and remain there until I free you. You leave for no reason whatever. You will do as I say?"

"Yes, Father," she said stiffly.

"The rest of you tell every hunter to come quickly and quietly."

The family went quickly and very quietly back to the village. Sima went to the hut as she had said she would, while the others notified hunters about the glars and their need for speed and quiet. Then they went to their hut where the children played in the covered place where Olomaru-mia usually spent her days protected from the sun. Olomaru-mia went inside the hut where it was hot to talk to Sima.

"My daughter, what caused you to be so disrespectful? You know you are loved."

Sima glared at Olomaru-mia. "You don't love us equally. Pipto and Token get all the attention and praise. And in this place girls are worthless."

"Slow down, Sima," Olomaru-mia said. "First, the boys have been gone for almost three years! During that time, because you are the next oldest, you have received a lot of attention, because you are special and because your help is needed with the younger ones. Second, during those three years, the boys got no attention from us at all. Third, use of the name of the Creator of All wrongly is something that disappoints me in you. You know better. Moreover, the rules and ways of doing things of the people among whom we live is harsh for women and girls. You've known that all your life. To anger a male or go against his pride is a sure way to bring pain to yourself, if not outright broken bones or disability for the rest of your life. What were you thinking?"

"Maybe it's time to change how women are treated."

"Well, if that's your goal, you surely started the wrong way to bring about change. The first problem you have is a total disregard for the Creator of All. That has to turn around."

"The Creator of All is a joke that people use to keep us in line."

151

Before she knew what she was doing, Olomaru-mia slapped Sima's face hard. After a brief pause where she collected herself, Olomaru-mia said, "If you wish to find out how wrong you are, I'll have Mechalu take you blindfolded and naked to the forest to a very remote place. After seven days of being there alone, he will return for you alive or dead. However, you will find the first thing you do is to call to the Creator of All for help. You'll find out how real the Creator of All is." She looked into Sima's eyes. The girl was still holding onto her arrogant pride. Olomaru-mia, having already lived where males and females were equal, had already realized that for the Nola Nola it was acceptable for males to show arrogant pride and full power over women and children, while it was totally unacceptable for a woman to do the same.

"I just wanted to go with Too to the waterfall. We were going to swim. Everyone has taken care of Ghumotu, but Too has not been doing anything but looking out for his mother. I thought it was a good time for him to do something."

"Your thoughts were good, my daughter; your timing was terrible; your attitude, indefensible."

"I told Father what I told you and he refused to let me tell Too the plans had been changed. He got furious that I refused him."

"That was your first mistake. You would have been wise to explain that, of course, you'd accompany the family. You could have said that you made plans with Too and wanted to let him know of the change in plans. You could have asked whether he could accompany us to the sea. Instead, you came out fighting with disobedience and arrogance, my daughter. What did you expect your father to do?"

"I didn't think." Sima rubbed her arm where the bruise was already forming. "I was just angry and tired of the boys getting to do things like go to school and hunt, while I take care of children, cook, make things."

"That's clear to me, but did you learn anything?"

"I learned that girls get poor treatment here."

"Sima, I am ashamed of you. Have you ever truly been unloved, gone without food or shelter?"

Slowly and begrudgingly Sima replied, "No."

"Why is obedience a thing to rebel against? When you are a mother, you will expect your children to obey you."

"I don't want to be a mother."

"Sima, that's a subject for a discussion another day. Right now we are dealing with your disobedience."

"But it's all tied together. Look at Tuna. She has a lot of children, but she's free to go about on adventures with her husband. They are happy. He doesn't beat her."

"Tuna is married to a man who is not of the Nola Nola. He lives here, but he is a man who does not have to follow our customs. You do not have that luxury."

"It isn't fair."

Olomaru-mia grabbed Sima by the hair and held her head firmly so that she had to face her. "Get this straight for the rest of your life. Look at me! Life isn't fair. Say it," she demanded.

Sima said, "Life isn't fair."

Still holding her head firmly, Olomaru-mia continued, "I was abducted. I had to learn to love a man who abducted me. Someday try to imagine that. I came from a People where males and females were equal. Life ripped me from my only security and brought me here. On the way Mechalu treated me harshly. I found out later that he was trying to keep my trackers from finding me. He brought me so far from my People that I couldn't find my way back to them. Since then he has treated me exceptionally well. You have to learn to make the best of what happens to you in life. You choose to be happy or miserable. Nobody ever makes that choice for you. Your circumstances change, but you and you alone control your happiness. I am happy, or was until I discovered my own child disrespecting the Creator of All and her father. I'll be happy again, even if you choose to remain a disobedient, arrogant child and end up broken, disabled, or dead. I am trying to save your life." She let go of Sima's hair.

"You think that my father would kill me?" Sima seemed jarred by the information.

"I don't think Mechalu would ever intend to kill you. I do think that if he beat you with a nola nola stick, you could die from the injuries. He certainly didn't want to beat you today. Your disrespect and disobedience left him no choice. When Mechalu does a job, he doesn't do it part way. If he's going to beat you, you will get the full beating. For him to beat you with his hand today instead of the nola nola was a warning. He's never had to beat you. If he has to beat you again, there is no question. He'll use the nola nola and he won't be gentle about it. You could die. Your rebellion is suicidal."

"Mother, I don't want to die."

Olomaru-mia could see that finally Sima began to understand. She looked into her daughter's eyes and saw fear. Clearly, she had reached her daughter in some fundamentally necessary way. "I am glad to hear that. I don't want you to die. I want you to live, join with one you love, and have a wonderful life. Sima, until now you've been respectful and obedient. It is not a hard thing to do. Stop comparing yourself with other people. You have one life to live. It is yours. You know only a small part of the life of any other person. To make comparisons is vain. Simply be the best you can be and never wish to change places with anyone else. A person you see in the day may face a terrible life at night. You never know. You must remember that when you wish for something, sometimes the Creator of All grants that wish, and sometimes it results in something very undesirable. Just be you. Live the life that is uniquely yours. You will not change the Nola Nola. You will become a mother and have many children. That is your life. Your choice is to make your life happy or sad. You do that alone. No one can affect that but you."

"Mother, I'm sorry I disappointed you today. I am truly sorry."

"I know, my daughter. You need to tell your father and the Creator of All. Get straight in your belly and do what is right. You will have a good life, sometimes wonderful, sometimes sad, but overall very good. First, you have to get right with yourself. Respect and obedience are things you must make part of you."

"I have learned much today. Thank you."

Olomaru-mia reached out to her daughter and hugged her. Sima was a good child, but she did have some work to do on herself. Olomaru-mia hoped that the other children had seen enough and heard enough to learn a lesson from what happened that day.

When the men had taken the three glars, they let the women know and many of the women went to the lower land to help with the skinning and butchering. They would feast that night and have plenty of jerky smoked and set aside for lean times or for traveling.

Mechalu still fumed about Sima. When he returned to the hut before the evening meal, he saw her sitting there.

"Father, may I speak?" she asked.

He ignored her. He changed the leather strip he wore threaded through a narrow band of leather around his waist. He stood in the hut looking at everyone. "All of you may attend the feast and dance—except Sima. Sima you are still confined."

"My husband," Olomaru-mia said calmly, "Sima should go to the privy."

He looked sharply at Olomaru-mia and said, "You accompany her and see that she speaks to no one."

"I will," she replied.

"The rest of you come with me," he said.

Olomaru-mia gave Sima a hand. Sima took it and got to her feet. "Mother what must I do?"

"First, do not leave this hut. Be obedient. When he has come home, sat, and relaxed a little, go to him and kneel. Say nothing. When he recognizes you, say that you are sorry for your disrespect and disobedience to the Creator of All and to him. Tell him it will not happen again. Then keep your mouth closed."

"I will, Mother."

Olomaru-mia and Sima's attention was distracted by the atmosphere of the cooking area. There was great joy and the place moved with excitement. Food would be wonderful that night and the women had gathered plants that they had left untouched for a long time. Some of the plants were to flavor the meat and as they began to cook, the savor was causing people to salivate. Sima tried to keep her eyes downward and hurry with her mother to the privy and back to the hut. She was embarrassed following the beating and wanted to get back to the hut to avoid being seen.

It was almost dark when Olomaru-mia entered the hut. Sima was on her bedding sitting cross-legged. She had been weeping, Olomaru-mia realized, but she didn't say anything about it.

"I brought you some food, Sima. It is good."

"I don't deserve any," Sima said almost in a whisper.

"Don't be silly, my daughter. I have brought you food. I expect you to eat it. To fail to do so would be disrespect. Do you understand?"

"Yes. Mother, I understand. I am not hungry, but I will eat from respect."

"Very well, my daughter. I'll return for your bowl soon."

Sima picked at the food. She was frightened not to eat it. If she failed to eat and her mother told her father, she could be beaten. She made herself eat everything in the bowl. Her mother had brought her some greens that tasted awful, but she forced them down. She put the bowl aside. Punishment was harsh for disobedience and disrespect, she discovered. It seemed to go on endlessly. She had never felt so alone. And then, she realized her mother thought she was not alone. Sima for the first time in her life said out loud, "Creator of All, if you're there, come to me and comfort me, for I am alone and scared." Sima felt a warmth run through her body. It was a new feeling to her and she observed it. It was comforting. Her tears stopped and she smiled. This comfort remained. She laughed a tiny laugh from deep inside. "You are real," she said in a whisper. "I'm so sorry I offended you today. Please stay with me." For the first time since the beating, Sima relaxed.

True to her word, Olomaru-mia returned after eating her evening meal to get the bowl she'd taken to Sima. She was surprised to see Sima in a better condition. "What has changed, Sima?"

"He is real," Sima whispered.

"What are you talking about?"

"I talked to the Creator of All. He is real. He is comforting me after what I did today."

"Of course, he's real."

"I always thought he was something adults made up. I'm so glad he's real."

Olomaru-mia shook her head and left the hut. She wondered where children got some of the ideas they had. Of course, the Creator of All was real. Olomaru-mia knew him by the name Wisdom. Without Wisdom, Olomaru-mia knew well, she would probably not be alive.

Well after dark Olomaru-mia returned to the hut with Poa, Azom, Snar, and Maisy. Quickly the children unrolled their bedding and prepared for sleep. Later Mohu and Pipto came home and prepared for sleep. Finally, Mechalu and Token arrived. While Token was unrolling his bedding, Mechalu grabbed Olomaru-mia by the wrist and said, "Come."

She followed him asking why when they were outside.

"We are going up the hill to make more twins."

"I thought we already did that," she said.

"Then we'll do it again and again. Look at this night. Did you ever see such a night for making twins?"

Usually Mechalu was so very gentle, but this night he was direct, demanding, and forceful. Olomaru-mia was uncertain what she thought of this approach, but the two flowed together as always without missing a beat. His need and her willingness met in an explosion for the both of them. Differences melted as snow in summer. They were one, had been one for a long time, and would continue as one. She assumed they would return to the hut, but she was pleasantly surprised with Mechalu's continuing demand. How she adored this man, her captor. He still had surprises for her. He pulled the leather strip off that held her hair back. He ran his hands through it. "Look at that in the moonlight!" They lay there together in the moonlight her extremely white body reflecting the light of the moon. "You excite me beyond words," he said huskily, and again they connected explosively.

He gave her his hand and pulled her up. Instead of leading her to the hut, he went uphill onto the path that led to the small lake. When they reached the lake, he picked her up and walked into the water with her. They lay at the water's edge and again merged as one, this time gentler. Finally, Mechalu rinsed the earth from Olomaru-mia's hair and they walked back to where they had discarded their clothing. They dressed and returned to the hut. Sima slept.

In the morning, Mechalu waked with Sima kneeling beside him.

"What is it, Sima?" he asked.

"Father I am sorry that I disobeyed and failed to respect you and the Creator of All yesterday. It will not happen again."

"Sima, that is good. I do not want to hurt you, but if you disrespect or disobey me or the Creator of All again, I will beat you with the nola nola stick. You will not be spared. You do understand that?"

"Yes, Father. I do understand."

"You are now free to come and go from the hut."

"Thank you." She left quickly.

Token slipped out behind her.

"Sima, wait."

She waited but was anxious to reach the privy quickly.

"I talked to Too. He understands what happened, and at first, he felt responsible for your beating. I tried to make it clear that it was not something for which he should feel guilty. The wrongdoing was yours. Sima, Too really cares a good deal for you. Do you know that?"

"I thought we were good friends," she said honestly.

"Sima, I think he has a love for you that a husband has for a wife. Would you receive him as a future husband?"

"I have never thought about that. Can I tell you on the way back from the privy?"

"Of course."

Sima realized she was about a year from the age at which many girls of the Nola Nola joined. Too would not be going to the school that his brother attended. Too was a very good hunter but was not singled out as a leader. Others were already identified. He was two years older than she was. He was tender and gentle. He would not likely beat her for pleasure as sometimes occurred. Sima realized that of all those with whom she might join, he was a very good choice.

Token joined her on the walk back to the hut.

"I would very much like to consider him as a future husband, Token."

"Then, he will soon be talking to Father."

"I'm not woman yet."

"These things are decided long before a girl becomes woman. I think this will go well. Just whatever you do, be respectful and obedient."

"I will."

"Are you significantly hurt, Sima?"

"No. Of course, I hurt, but nothing is broken or dislocated. My pride got hurt badly, but I learned a lot. I was stupid to be disrespectful, desiring disobedience over obedience."

"I'm glad Father didn't use the nola nola."

"I, also, Token. How is it that you and Pipto never have been beaten?"

"It's so much easier to be obedient and respectful. I expect to be punished if I am disrespectful or disobedient. Did you think he wouldn't punish you?"

"I just exploded. I didn't think."

"You better learn that lesson fast."

"I have."

He put his arm around her and they went back to the hut.

Later in the day, Sima went to bring water from the spring at the edge of the forest. When she turned to pick up the bag, she was face-to-face with Too.

"I talked to your father," he said looking more confident than she had ever seen him. "He said we are free to join after you become woman."

"That is wonderful, Too. You will be a great husband."

"You will be a very special wife, Sima. I have loved you a long time."

Sima stared at him. Finally, she said, "I love you, Too," and she meant it.

Too carried the bag to the women's cooking area. Then she and Too slipped off to the waterfall to be alone. Each of them looked at the other with very different eyes. They no longer saw the boy and girl bodies they were so used to, but rather the bodies of a future spouse. They drew together to hug, kiss, and touch what they had previously considered off limits. They found a new joy in each other that carried them beyond their pain with hope for their future.

A few days later there was much busy work in the village. The boat from the Alitukit was due that afternoon and they were preparing their gifts for the masters of the school. They were also making certain that the three boys who would be going had everything they needed. Their bedding and clothing were double and triple checked by women. For the masters there was fruit of every kind available, a huge supply of jerky from the glars, skins with and without fur attached, nuts, honey, and containers of herbs.

All of the material had been carefully transported to the edge of the sea. The boys were excited at the prospects of the boat trip and the new school. They knew this education would be a lot more difficult than any they had encountered. They expected it to last for about four years.

"Token, I wish you a wonderful trip and a profitable learning experience. When you return, you should be an uncle." He grinned. "And I thank you again for talking to your father for me."

"I think you are the best person for Sima. I love her dearly, Too, and you are a special friend whom I treasure. For me this is the best bond I could hope to make. Take good care of her, and, Sima, respect and obey him."

Sima glared at him.

"Don't start doing that. Get your thoughts arranged right," he reminded her.

Sima realized he meant well, so she calmed herself. She was still very sensitive about how females were treated and the fact that her father or Too, or her brother for that matter, were free to beat her for disrespect or disobedience, but it didn't work in reverse. Olomaru-mia had told her to get used to the fact that life wasn't fair, but she wasn't sure that even in a lifetime, she would be able to get used to it.

Suddenly there was some commotion down the beach. Someone had seen the boats. There were three of them. They had red sails and moved swiftly. As they approached, the signs painted on the sides of the boat became clear. The strange markings meant nothing to them. One of the boatmen got off each boat and came to where the Chief stood. The Chief introduced the boys and each was told to board a different boat. The Chief then told the boatmen that they had some gifts for the masters. The boatmen directed the men where to load the gifts.

Too stood behind Sima who watched her brothers board different boats. She would miss Token so much. Too put his arms around her. She loved Pipto, but she and Pipto did not share the same relationship she and Token did. Pipto was more apt to be short with her and authoritarian, where Token took the time to understand and look out for her best interest.

"I wonder why they have to be on different boats," she said.

"They may want them to get to know others right away and not depend on people they already know well," Too replied, wondering the same thing himself.

Shortly after all the gifts were boarded, the boatmen got back on board their boats and the Nola Nola pushed them back into the deeper water. The time with the boys had ended and it would be a long time before they saw them again.

Too put his arm around Sima and they began to climb the hill to home. Mechalu touched Olomaru-mia's shoulder and pointed to the pair. Olomaru-mia smiled at him. "They will do well together," she said with a great deal of relief. She pulled a section of her hair forward to examine. She was shocked at the large number of white hairs. She wondered briefly when that had happened. Small groups began to leave the seashore and return to their homes above. From their village, they could see the boats with red sails moving north.

Zamimolo and Ba had walked to the burying grounds. Darkness would soon cover the land. His tanned face, so different from the pale face she first met attracted Ba the way it had when she first saw him. His hair was black mixed with white; his eyebrows black; his upper lip hair was black; his beard mostly white; and the hair on his chest was a mixture of black and white hair. His hair color spoke of a long life they had shared. His body, built on a stocky frame, was not fat but instead muscled well from his hunting. She smiled at him.

"It has been fifteen years since I came to this land, Ba."

"Yes, it has. You keep count also?"

"I do." He smiled. "I know this land now, but sometimes I still feel like an intruder."

"You are part of this land now, Zami. How can you feel like an intruder?"

"I still remember the old country where I was born—the quiet forests, the smooth mountains. It was cold but a gentler place. We had our hazards, but I feel that here they are so much more numerous."

"Is that thinking back to Olomaru-mia?"

"Ba, in truth I haven't thought of her in a long time, but her abduction would be part of it. I think it's the different animals and the number of snakes, spiders, and other hazards and how well hidden they are. This is just to me a more dangerous place. It's necessary always to be fully alert."

"Zami, drums!" Ba held his strong forearm and looked into his eyes.

He touched her lips straining his ears to hear the message. It was unmistakable. The Northern Kapotonok were calling for assistance. There were Alitukit warriors heading to their border. "I must go," he said and they turned for home.

The People planned a rotating group of support warriors who would know to go if a request for help came. For almost fifteen years, they had kept the list, but they had not used it. Nevertheless, it was significant enough to them that they did not discard it from the disuse. They had not until this day had to use it, but each person knew whether it was his time to go if the call came. It was time for Zamimolo. He didn't hesitate but went straight to his weapons and hurried to gather what he'd need in his backpack. He met Jup, Grakumashi, Obi, and Numing. Men who were not selected for this war made torches for the men to use since dark was on them. It was time for the evening meal, but the men did not stop to eat. They carried a lot of jerky in their backpacks, and they would eat that when they hungered. Although there was no need for quiet at their cave, the men left in silence as the People watched until they could no longer see. Zamimolo did not leave Ba without a hug. He was walking into the unknown. They'd been trained to be warriors, but he'd never faced war. Eliminating all other thoughts, he returned in his mind web to the warrior lessons they'd been taught. He reviewed them repeatedly, not wanting to miss any detail. He was also as watchful as possible for hazards on the path. The memory of Pikotek and his snakebite was still clear in memory.

Ba watched him go. She was not filled with foreboding as she thought she might be, if this event ever occurred. Somehow, she had great confidence in his ability to live well in this land. She did wonder why he didn't feel part of this land, but she attributed that to his feelings of helplessness when he realized he could not save Olomaru-mia. Then she remembered he'd mentioned that he'd not thought of her in a long time. Ba loved Zami completely. She did, however, live with the ghost of Olomaru-mia. There was something magical about the girl she'd never met. She seemed bigger than life. More beautiful than anyone. Kinder and gentler than normal. Ba had never felt she could compete with the ghost, so she'd quit trying and settled for what she thought of as second best—simply being herself. Had she known the mind of Zamimolo, she'd have realized that he loved her with a fierce love that stood on the foundation of knowing how easy it was to lose someone. Ba was his rock and he clung to that rock as a limpet to a rock. In his mind web there was no first or second best. They were one. She returned to the cave to settle the children for the evening meal.

The men walked through the dark to reach their destination as soon as possible. There was barely enough light to see and the skittering of animals on the path and snapping branches off to their sides were occasionally unnerving, but the men continued. By morning they arrived at the Southern Kapotonok border. They followed the coastline north. When they reached the village where Zamimolo and Linpint had first made contact with people other than themselves in the new land, they stopped. Some men from that village had already left to help. The Kapotonok insisted they rest briefly and eat. While the men rested, the women of the Kapotonok fixed food. Before Linpint and Zamimolo were allowed to leave, the Wise One, hobbled to them. He gave five leaves to each man. "When you tire, chew one or half of one of these leaves. Don't swallow them. It will give you energy to continue on." Each man put the leaves in a place in his backpack where they would remain safely.

The Wise One hobbled over to Zamimolo pointing a bony finger at him. "The time comes closer but is not quite here. You must control your desires, for they will try to overcome you. Heed my words!"

"What do you mean?" Zamimolo asked, confused and eager to travel onward to battle.

"Your hair grows white. You will find what you sought, but it is not what you expect. Do no evil, or you will be overwhelmed with regret."

"Are you talking about war?"

"I am talking about the golden girl."

"You mean the girl I sought?"

"Yes. That one."

"Thank you, Wise One. I'll remember." Zamimolo and the others took the path that went inland towards the Northern Kapotonok lands. Not far into the walk, Grakumashi tried chewing a half leaf. He told the others of the extra energy he felt. Each man chewed half a leaf.

As they walked, Zamimolo remembered the words of the Wise One, "golden girl." Where had he heard those words? He searched his mind web as he walked through the forest. He felt occasionally as if he were close to the memory and something would happen to distract him, such as falling water where they could drink and refill their gourds, proximity to a spiked-tailed armadillo or sloth, or the forest becoming deathly quiet too suddenly.

As they arrived at a tree free hilltop, Zamimolo remembered: the drums from the south. They spoke of the golden girl. The golden girl was

Olomaru-mia. It had to be! Why didn't he realize it when he heard the message? But they didn't say where she was. Zamimolo put the information in his mind web and purposed to address it when the war was over. He could ask the question on the drums. Drummers might be able to tell where she was. It was a novel thought and he wondered why he hadn't thought of it long ago. Then, he realized that she was supposed to have joined before he knew about the drums. He had a sinking feeling. He asked himself why he still chose to pursue her whereabouts. He had to admit that once he loved her. Love wasn't something he could just end. He still loved her. Not as he did years ago. In his mind web she was still sixteen, while he was old. He didn't know her any longer, but he still loved her. Differently. Was there a way, he wondered, to stop loving? He really wanted to know that she'd had a good life and was safe. He didn't stop to think what he would do if she wasn't happy or being treated well.

Back at the People's village, the children had been playing near the path that entered the woods. Olf, Linpint's grandson, small for his age of three, had climbed upon a strange rock. He sat upon it and enjoyed seeing from such a great height. Suddenly the rock moved. He shrieked.

Chiru and Khlaput saw the little boy and realized the danger. He was sitting on the back of one of the huge armadillos near the path that went into the woods.

"I'll go for help. You watch," Chiru screamed at Khlaput, though the volume was not necessary. He took off at a run as fast as he could go.

Linpint heard Chiru and ran to meet him. Rustumarin and Ramaduku came up from the river. They followed Chiru to the place where Olf sat on the back of what they discovered was a smooth-tailed armadillo. Smooth-tailed or not, the tail of an armadillo, even if it wasn't spiked, could deliver quite a hit.

On the other side of the armadillo, unseen by any of the others was Amitu, a girl of ten years, granddaughter of Tokatumeta. Amitu was terrified of the armadillo, which she had thought to be a rock while it slept, but she was even more frightened of what could happen to Olf. When the men arrived at the far side of the beast, she ran toward the beast and grasped his great shell at the neck and pulled herself up, using the animal's neck as a foothold. Shaking, she climbed the shell to the frightened little one. At the top of the shell, she sat with Olf in her lap as if she might be calmly doing what she'd done many times. She looked at the men waiting for them to tell her what do to next. Olf had calmed.

The armadillo was aware that it was near people. It knew that it had a small weight on its back. Those things registered. It did not get defensive. Instead, the animal was trying to determine what was happening, because it was a new experience.

Linpint asked Amitu to slide the boy down the side of the armadillo so he could reach him. Rustumarin had a spear poised near the animal's head and Ramaduku had one near the tail. Amitu slowly slid the boy down and Linpint lifted him off the animal. He took Olf to a small hill and told the boy to stay there. He returned to Amitu.

"Slide down the side of the animal, Amitu. I'll be here to pick you up just like with Olf," Linpint said, noticing the beast was starting to move. "Be quick!" he said trying not to show his concern in his voice.

Amitu began her slide. The shell was rough, and the animal moved quickly in a shift to the side Amitu had slid down. No one realized the armadillos could move that quickly. Khlaput noticed the animal's movement and ran for Olf. He picked up the little one and headed for the forested area where trees were too close together to allow the armadillo to enter at that point.

Rustumarin held his spear against the neck of the armadillo to keep it turned away from Amitu. As soon as her feet hit the ground and Linpint saw she was standing securely, he let her go and she raced home. Ramaduku ran to the other side of the armadillo and poked it with his spear. It caused the armadillo to head toward the path that went into the woods. Finally, with some prods and thrown rocks, the men got the animal to go down the pathway that would take it to the lower land it used, if it chose to continue on the path.

Khlaput came out of the woods with Olf and they walked home.

"Wait," Linpint called to Khlaput, "Who was watching over Olf?"

"I think he came with his mother," Khlaput said. "I haven't seen her for a while," he added.

Linpint looked for Achi, his daughter-in-law. He didn't see her anywhere. He returned to the cave, but Achi was not there. He went to a lookout point and did not see her anywhere. He called to his son, Lamitun.

"Where's Achi?" he asked his son.

"I have no idea. She went with the women earlier to look for bird eggs."

"She may have been with Olf just before he climbed on the back of the smooth-tailed armadillo, but she hasn't been seen since," Linpint said with concern.

"My son did what?" Lamitun couldn't believe his son had climbed onto the back of an armadillo.

"That can hold for a moment, son. The problem now is that your wife is missing."

"You're serious?"

"Of course."

Lamitun immediately began to gather as many men as possible for a hunt for Achi. He found fourteen men and they immediately spread out in the area between the cave and forest to search. If not found, they would go through the forest. They searched for quite some time before Tukyatuk whistled three times. Tukyatuk was down in a deep arroyo not far from where Olf had encountered the armadillo. Under an overhang that shielded Achi from view above, she lay with a twisted leg. Tokatumeta brought a stretcher and they placed the unconscious woman on the stretcher. The leg that remained whole was swollen. The men quickly found two marks showing a snake had bitten her. They assumed it was poisonous due to the swelling of the leg.

Lamitun was horrified. He quickly unrolled her sleeping skins and prepared a soft place for her. Uilo told the children that they were to come to her in the cave, not trouble their father while he looked after their mother.

In all the confusion of the day, no one seemed to notice Amitu squatting in a quiet area of the cave, until Meninkua passed by her and stopped. She noticed that Amitu was shaking.

"Are you sick, Little One?" she asked.

Amitu shook her head, signifying the negative.

Meninkua squatted down beside the trembling girl. "What's causing you to shake?"

"Armadillo," was all she'd say.

Meninkua hadn't heard about the armadillo, so she didn't understand.

"Are you cold?"

Amitu nodded her head affirmatively.

Meninkua went to find a skin to wrap around the trembling girl. She saw Jalutui and asked her if she knew why Amitu was shaking.

"She climbed on the back of the smooth-tailed armadillo to rescue Olf, who climbed up there. She's probably terrified. Where is she?"

"She's back there near the herbs. I'm going to get a skin to wrap around her."

Jalutui walked back to the shivering girl. She sat beside her and pulled the girl into her ample lap. "Shhhhhhh," she murmured, "You're safe now." Jalutui's arms surrounded Amitu confirming her words.

Amitu slowly, almost imperceptibly, began to relax. Meninkua returned with a furred skin that was not too heavy but would provide good comfort as well as warmth. Gently she laid it over the girl who lay on Jalutui's lap and legs. Meninkua went to the herb keep and took a pinch of some leaves she'd mixed and kept in gourds. She put the herbs in a gourd and poured some hot water on them. She carried the gourd to Jalutui and said, "Get her to drink all of this. It'll calm her."

Meninkua returned to the herb keep and took the snakebite paste and powder. She also gathered some straight pieces of wood and soft leather strips stored nearby for setting broken bones. Meninkua was the acknowledged bonesetter. She'd worked with Colitoba for years to learn the use of herbs and had become proficient. She had been on her way to get the supplies for Achi. Achi was still sleeping, and Meninkua wanted to do the painful work of setting the leg right, while the young woman was still sleeping.

While Meninkua worked on the broken leg, Folifilo passed by.

"Wait," Meninkua said.

Folifilo stopped and asked, "Are you talking to me, Meninkua?"

"Yes. Your granddaughter is back by the herbs with Jalutui. She was the one who rescued Olf this morning by climbing on the armadillo and lowering him to Linpint. She is shivering in the back of the cave and Jalutui is comforting her. She is very shaken. Odd, isn't it, that sometimes our heroes are shaken badly by the very events that caused them to be heroes."

Folifilo nodded at Meninkua. "Is she okay?"

"I think she'll be fine, but she needs some patience, understanding, and comfort right now. I think she's terrified of the armadillo but was more frightened for Olf."

"Thank you, Meninkua. I'll go back to see what, if anything, I can do." She walked down the tube-like cave structure to the place where herbs were kept. She thought to herself that when she was Amitu's age, she'd never heard of an armadillo, spiked-tailed or smooth. Life seemed so much simpler then. She smiled to herself as she remembered slogging through the snow, covered in furred skins. Maybe it wasn't all that much easier.

She squatted down near Jalutui and Amitu. Her granddaughter smiled weakly.

Folifilo took Amitu's hand and felt the chill. "I hear you were a real hero!" she said brightly.

"I was terrified for me and for Olf. He was too young to leave alone on the armadillo. I didn't have time to think what to do."

"You made the right decision."

"When I got back here, I really fell to pieces like a rock that shatters when it falls from a high place. I'm trying hard to put myself back together."

"You just rest there until you feel better. Don't keep reliving it. It's behind you. Olf is fine—thanks to you. You are fine. The men chased the armadillo down the path through the forest in the direction of the lowlands."

"Thank you, Grandmother. "

"You're welcome, Little Hero."

Folifilo got up and headed for Meninkua. She wondered how Achi was doing.

Meninkua told her, "Achi awakened briefly and seemed concerned for Olf. She said she fell after the snake bit her. It was clear she remembered nothing else but worry for Olf. I told her Olf was fine, and the girl fell back into unwanted sleep."

"Is there anything I can do?" Folifilo asked.

"I've just finished up. Would you watch her for a while?"

"Gladly," Folifilo said seating herself to watch over the young woman.

To the north Zamimolo, Jup, Grakumashi, Obi, and Numing were entering the village of the Northern Kapotonok. Chief Paaku came running to meet them. They stood there with their mouths hanging open. The men in the village were painted. Some had feathers in their hair. Most were without clothing.

"Come quickly, so we can get you painted," the Chief said.

"Why the paint?" Grakumashi asked slightly offended by the idea.

"Remember when we taught you how to hide in the forest?"

"Of course!"

"The paint adds to the camouflage. We don't have time to show you right now. Just trust that it does. At least you don't have tooth white bellies any longer," Chief Paaku laughed.

The men suddenly had lines and dots of various colors covering their skins. They agreed to go without clothing to keep their clothes from becoming ensnared in the foliage, giving away their positions.

"We must hurry," shouted a warrior from a group of Kapotonok who had arrived from farther to the north than those on the thin band of land that connected the two large landmasses.

All gathered and a man of great height stood solemn before them. "I am Chief Aton from the far north Kapotonok. Thank you for your support. There is a large group of warriors from the Alitukit. They are furious because they are missing animals they penned. They accuse the Kapotonok of taking them or setting them free. The Kapotonok did neither. They have forty warriors. They are well skilled and fight furiously, but they do not know the forests and jungles. They lose interest quickly when they encounter snakes in trees or wild boar or other forest animals. They lose sense of direction in the jungles, and in forests they cannot tell the source of sounds. They don't know how to track in the forests. Remember what you've been taught. We will meet them near the low land and lure them into the woods. Here we can beat them easily. They will think we are few when we are about double their number. For those of you new to war, if you see a friend killed, you have to grieve later. You cannot stop to grieve or vomit or you will join your friend. Are there questions?"

No one replied.

"Follow me."

Chief Aton led them through a mountain pass onto the small hills that led to a land the People had never seen. The People and some of the Kapotonok were halted in the forest in various locations. Right outside the lovely forested area was dry land, not as dry as a desert, but when walking across it they raised dust. Below them they could see the Alitukit warriors bunched up, noticing them. They were shaking spears and clubs, making horribly frightening noises. They suddenly sprang forth rushing up the hill beyond which the forest concealed more than half the Kapotonok and their support warriors. The best of the runners were in this forward section.

They waited until the Alitukit warriors who had just raced up a hill almost reached them and they turned and ran, fresh from their waiting, up the remainder of the hill into the forest. The Alitukit, winded and tired, pursued them with vengeance, breathing so hard it affected their hearing in the forest. Zamimolo was fascinated at how well the paint helped the men fade into the foliage. He could see the others, but if he hadn't known where they were, he would have had difficulty. He saw some of the men nearer the edge of the woods fighting and he had the urge to run to join them. He knew what his job was and he followed the directions carefully. He began to understand as he saw opposing warriors pass those who were fighting, running into the forest blindly looking for opponents they could have touched if they saw them. He realized the camouflage made it possible for him, undetected, to kill an opponent before the opponent ever knew he was there. The Alitukit clearly had no forest sense. It was a revelation to him with respect to life in the forest. He was grateful the Kapotonok had taught them to know forest life.

At one point Grakumashi stepped back, cracking a dry branch and giving away his location. Quickly he was in a fight with one of the Alitukit. Zamimolo was horrified. The man killed Grakumashi and cut the hair off the center top of his head, sticking it into his waistband. The man then walked carelessly under the tree where Zamimolo was perched. Zamimolo dropped to the man and cut his throat with his flint knife. The only sound the man made was his drop to the ground in death. Zamimolo had never seen a person killed or killed one, and he wanted to vomit, but he realized that this was war, and he didn't have time for that. He climbed back up into the tree, knife between his teeth, despite the human blood on it.

The forest war went on for quite some time, but in the end the Kapotonok were successful. Two men from the Alitukit escaped the forest and ran fast back to the dry land from which they had come. The Kapotonok dragged first all the bodies of the Alitukit to the top of the hill where the Alitukit could see them. If they wanted to bury their dead, they would make it easy for them. Zamimolo found the man who killed Grakumashi and carefully gathered the piece of scalp the man had removed from Grakumashi's head. He attached it to the waistband of his friend's leather waistband. Then, they took their own dead and carried them to the Kapotonok village. There they buried them with great solemnity, worthy of warriors who had fallen in battle.

The People remained with the Kapotonok for seven days to be sure the Alitukit didn't return. Zamimolo was not injured. Grakumashi would remain buried in the land of the Kapotonok. Jup had a fairly deep cut on his leg that was healing well. Obi and Numing had bruises and scrapes but nothing serious. They considered, having seen the war, that they had done well. They learned well from the experience. The Kapotonok intentionally hadn't put them in the front of the fighting, because they were unseasoned. They ached for Grakumashi.

When it was time for the People to return home, Chief Paaku and Chief Aton went to Zamimolo with two wrapped packages.

"Give this to your People for the valor of Grakumashi. He gave all he had for us and we are grateful," Chief Paaku said, handing a package to Zamimolo. The package contained a flat disk of gold hammered by a wooden hammer. "This is a representation of our Maker," he said. We form it from the gold we find. "It will bring your People good fortune."

Zamimolo was astounded. "For Grakumashi's valor," he said.

"Yes," Chief Paaku replied.

Chief Aton walked over to Zamimolo and handed him the other package. "This," he said, "is for the wife of Grakumashi. It is a crystal from a mountain far, far away to the north. It grows near the red striped mountains in the north. You can see that it is flat and is formed of many, many crystals packed tight together like leaves, one atop the other. See, you can peel them apart and each alone is flimsy. Together—very strong. It shows what happened here. When many stand together, there is far greater strength than a single one or just a few could ever be."

Zamimolo ran his fingertip over the smooth crystal. It was a strange object and like the disk, it was something to treasure. He rewrapped it carefully and placed both of the objects into the backpack. He and the others left for home.

As they walked home, Zamimolo remembered the old Wise One's warning, "Do no evil or you will be overwhelmed with regret." It had to do with Olomaru-mia. He thought again about using the drums to locate her, but he wondered whether that was wise at all. He had his life, and she had hers. It might be best to leave it all alone. If they met somehow later on, then that would be something he hadn't pushed to make happen. That might be best. He also knew that Ba was insecure about his feelings for the girl.

Days later, there was much excitement when the men emerged from the path in the forest. They were obviously short a man, and it wasn't long before Dimutenka realized her husband was missing and Rustumarin and Uilo realized their son was gone. Their grief began before they even heard what happened. A council meeting formed immediately. Zamimolo brought both packages.

He held out the disk so everyone could see it. "This was given to the People by the Kapotonok to revere Grakumashi's valor. It is made of gold hammered with a wooden hammer to represent the Maker, their equivalent of Wisdom. I suggest that Pikotek keep it for the People. Maybe he could display it somewhere. This second package is for Dimutenka. It is a crystal made of many, many crystals. It shows that many together are always much stronger than one alone. It comes from far away to the north beyond where the narrow land goes to the large landmass. The crystals grow near the red striped mountains." He handed the crystals and the wrapper to Dimutenka.

Dimutenka looked at him with a blank stare. She didn't know what to do with the crystal and didn't want to be responsible for it. "Perhaps Pikotek could display this with the disk," she suggested. Pikotek took it and laid it beside the other gift.

The council broke up after each person had his or her words to say about Grakumashi, and, then, Pikotek told the graveside story.

The People somberly went to their evening meal and then to sleep fully realizing that war exacted painful losses. It was good to stand together, but it had to be done knowing some would not return. It was an awful thing—sometimes needed—but truly awful. The death of one of the People, like the crystal showed, didn't affect one person but all of the People as pulling one of the slivers of the crystal out of its midst would affect the whole crystal. It would take time for them to realize that if they and others had failed to come to the Kapotonok's assistance, the Northern Kapotonoks as a whole people might no longer exist. They would continue to help their friends but with much greater understanding.

Chapter 5

Mechalu and Olomaru-mia's oldest children, twins, Pipto and Token, and their cousin, Ghumotu, along with two other students of the Alitukit, Hoft and Kit, were studying for the examinations that would soon try their knowledge from three years of study. Their success on the examinations determined whether they continued their education at the school for another year. They sat on a bluff overlooking the sea where the wind played lightly with their hair as they worked to hone their skills.

Token, his thin body showing the strains of fatigue, said plaintively, "I just struggle with the drums. I can understand them much better than I can play them."

"That's because the way you learn to hear and the way you learn to drum are two different things. I think you keep trying to learn the things the same way," Hoft, an Alitukit, said gently. "You want people to tell you what you need to learn, and then that amazing memory of yours stores it forever. But, you don't listen to your own body or spend time exploring in your thoughts how things are—learning for yourself."

"What do you mean?" Token asked, surprised at the thought.

"Well," Hoft replied, squinting his eyes to reduce the amount of sunlight entering them, "When you listen to the drums, you hear the rhythm of songs we've been singing, you hear the patterns of thought that carry meaning. Think of the ways of calling to friends over long distances in a field. You'd know what they were saying, even if you didn't get every word. Sometimes you get the meaning from the way it's said. You learn this through sound without hearing each word. Then, when you drum, you have to get the rhythm right. The meaning can change by the length of a pause between drum strikes, the place where you strike the drum—either the high tone or the low tone. And, if you don't know the fixed expressions that are a huge part of the communication process, you're in trouble. But, Token, you know the fixed expressions perfectly. Where you need work is on the part you learn through moving your body, not listening to others with your ears. Use your right knee for the low tones, your left knee for the high ones, your hands as the drum sticks, and let's work with this."

Token sat up straight. Pipto was fascinated because he had the same trouble Token did, though it was not as obvious.

Hoft said, "Drum the message that the Nola Nola of your geographic area are having a celebration for the birth of twins in two days."

Token thought it through. There was a fixed drum expression for each of the Nola Nola, one for celebration, one for birth, one for day, and the pauses expressed the numbers in this communication. He tapped out: Tap-tap (high tone)-tap-tap—pause—tap (high tone)-tap (high tone)-tap (high tone)-tap—pause—tap-tap-tap-tap-tap-tap—pause—tap-tap-tap-tap (high tone)-tap (high tone)-tap (high tone)—pause—tap.

Kit said, "It's the rhythm. Your taps are unequal, and you missed the pauses. You drummed: Nola Nola, celebration, one birth, one day, when what you wanted to communicate was Nola Nola, celebration, two births, two days. It should have been this way, now listen to the beats for the pauses. Tap-tap (high tone)-tap-tap—pause—tap (high tone)-tap (high tone)-tap (high tone)-tap—pause + pause—tap-tap-tap-tap-tap-tap—pause + pause—tap-tap-tap-tap (high tone)-tap (high tone)-tap (high tone)—pause—tap. Each tap in the expression gets the same length until you come to the pauses."

"It's helpful to think of a heartbeat when you want to learn rhythm. The heartbeat's the natural rhythm we're born with. It's hard to hear your heartbeat unless you've been running, so let's think about walking. I have an idea. Try walking and walk as if you're trekking. Keep the time the same for each footfall. Now shout out 'tap' with a high voice for the high tones and shout out 'tap' with a low voice for the low tones. Say pause for the pause and where you need two pauses, say pause … pause. Get the feel of the rhythm. Come on boys, let's do this with him." Kit was aware that Pipto had the same difficulty. He knew that for himself, it was easier to learn a song, if he sang and danced together. It helped him with the rhythm. He hoped this would help his friends.

For a long time the boys walked in a large circle using their voices and footfalls to sound out the drumbeats and their silences and footfalls to display the pauses. Little by little they began to make it part of themselves. They increased the twins to triplets and two days to five. Ghumotu found it easier than the other two boys did. Token realized that for the first time rhythm made sense to him. Up to that point, it had been something he didn't understand and didn't know what about it he didn't understand. To realize there was rhythm to his heartbeat and walking gave him something he could connect with the needed learning. It involved precise timing, something he'd never understood clearly. The circling and giving voice to the beats helped immeasurably with the skill that had escaped him.

The Nola Nola boys thanked the Alitukits after the lesson. The Nola Nolas felt that they had enough time to practice for improvement before the Masters examined them. They decided they'd retest themselves in two days.

"Token," Ghumotu said, "Will you stay a little longer and help me with math?"

"Of course," Token replied. "How can I help?"

"I'm doing well enough with multiplication, but dividing is bothering me, especially when we have to divide long numbers. I don't want to have to discontinue learning here, but I am really slow on that area of knowledge."

Token took a piece of charred wood and went with Ghumotu to a place where the rock was smooth. They talked long enough for Token to discover that where Ghumotu had trouble was when the number didn't divide evenly. He talked about the need to include the number obtained from dividing with either the lower number or higher number. They were expected to round up or down, not have a remainder. Their lesson was completed a lot quicker, because with Ghumotu, he simply didn't understand what the masters had told him about the reasoning to arrive at the correct rounding up or down answer.

Where many young people would have time for recreation, the students of the Alitukit were not provided time to play. They had responsibilities whether it was gathering driftwood from the sea down below, going to the deep hole for water, or running errands down the mountain to the villagers, there was always a chore that needed to be done. They worked hard. Once chores were finished, there was always a need to practice spear throwing and slingshot, running quickly, creating a song they'd sing to the whole group when they left the school. Sometimes they'd be assigned to accompany a hunting party. Any time not assigned was to be used to study to perfect skills.

Ghumotu, walking back to the school with Token, asked, "Have the Alitukit asked you probing questions about our people?"

"Yes. I know that my father said we don't do the drums because the Alitukit want to know more about us and share nothing, so I have been guarded in what I tell them."

"I've done the same. They seem curious about your mother. They've heard her called the golden girl and they ask where she came from, who are her people, what is the color of her skin, what is the color of her hair, whether she's fertile, and who is her god? I don't know the answers to all those questions, so I tell them they're asking the wrong person," Ghumotu said, adding, "Sometimes, I lie."

"They've asked me a little, but not that much. When one of them questioned me, he seemed to want to know who the Chief was, what his strengths were, whether he was a good hunter and warrior, and who would be the next Chief." Token scratched his elbow and upper arm. A bug had bitten him and the area of the bite was swelling a little.

"They definitely want to know a lot."

"Yes. I feel uncomfortable when they start asking those questions," Token admitted.

"I think you need to make yourself relax and answer as you can and when you don't know, just say you don't know."

"That's what I've done, except I try to think what use they might make of the information. When they wanted to know about the next Chief, I overemphasized what a great hunter and warrior my father is. He is, but I thought that if they thought he was very strong, they'd be less likely to attack us."

"Or," Ghumotu said, "More likely to try to get rid of us as a threat to themselves."

"I never thought of that," Token said. "That's a little scary."

"Well, they realized you were talking about your father."

"True." Token said feeling a small sense of relief.

As they arrived at the school's entryway that led to the underground caves, Master Gu called Token.

Token went to him and stood silently before him with his head bowed.

"Token, you have become too thin. I suspect that worry over the examinations has affected your appetite. For a time, I expect you to eat more than you normally would eat. I want to see some fat return to your bones. To become too thin leaves your body nothing with which to fight, if a sickness comes upon you. Remedy it."

"Yes, Sir," Token said. The last thing he'd thought about recently was food.

"Go now and get a large snack. And I'll watch tonight to see that you eat a full dinner."

"Yes, Sir," Token replied and quickly went to get a snack. He found some meat from the night before and some fruit. He took some of both.

As soon as he finished eating, Master Lipin called to him.

He went to the Master and stood with his head bowed.

"I am glad to see you eating. Have you been ill?"

"No, Sir."

"Then, how do you explain this too thin body of yours. You have failed to take good care of it."

"Sir, I have been studying and somehow food hasn't seemed very important."

"You cannot expect to function, if you fail to care for yourself. I notice you've not neglected to breathe. What happens to a fire when the wood is consumed?"

"The fire goes out, Sir."

"And so will the life from your body, if you fail to care for it properly. You must feed it as you feed a fire."

"Yes, Sir."

"Make sure to take care of your body."

"Yes, Sir."

"Today you will go to Master Theu to work on making spear points. You will do sedentary work until you get some fat on your body."

"Yes, Sir." Most of the students hated to do sedentary work, but Master Theu had some different ways of making spear points that interested Token, so he was not uncomfortable in the least at the shift in his chores.

Ghumotu and Kit had been sent to the seashore to gather any driftwood they might find. There were not many trees in the upper area of the mountain, since many had been gathered for fires countless years ago, and no new tree growth had occurred for a very long time. Atop the mountain was flat grassland. Sometimes, as an alternative to firewood, they would gather animal dung from the grazers that used that grassland. Sometimes they had to go great distances to gather wood. They would not gather it from the lower levels of the mountains, because there it supported the wildlife they hunted. The Alitukit had learned long ago that overharvesting trees was not in their best interest. Driftwood was a gift.

The path to the seashore was a winding one. It took quite some time to reach the bottom. Carrying the logs up would be an even longer process.

"Kit, look down there! There's a whole pile of them we couldn't see from above." Ghumotu was delighted to have found such a large amount of wood.

"Wonderful! I'll get there before you do!" Kit shouted back as he began to run toward the driftwood.

Ghumotu ran alongside his friend, both equally paced. They reached the pile at the same time, winded. Quickly they gathered what they could carry, hoping that they might make several trips to the woodpile. They took as much as they could possibly lift to carry uphill on the steep, winding path. The boys were in good spirits and laughed as they climbed the hill. When they reached the top, they saw Master Alikuat. They became serious quickly.

"Have you boys found a good source of wood?" he asked raising one eyebrow as he often did.

"Yes, Sir, we have," Kit replied quickly. "There is much driftwood in a pile just east of the base of the path."

"Put that on the firewood pile and I'll gather some help for you," he said.

The boys were quick to comply. Of all the Masters, nobody wanted to cross Master Alikuat.

Token sat in the sun as it began to go down, working an arrowhead of bone. Hoft joined him and the two enjoyed the remaining heat of the day.

"What do you make of the water tours we've had recently?" Hoft asked.

"I understood nothing when we went to the falling water to the north or the ones to the west on this mountain. When we went to the hole in the earth where there is much water, I still failed to understand. I found it odd that the sea was not included in our trips. Then, I began to wonder whether the trips were for us to examine water or something else." Token held the beautiful spear point with two fingers, seeing it in his mind attached to a shaft. He laid it carefully on the soft piece of leather in front of him and picked up another piece of bone, twisting it and examining it for soundness.

"All this time I've been focused on water. If that's not what we're supposed to examine, no wonder I'm having a tough time," Hoft said, his voiced tinged with irritation. "It would be so much easier, if they just told us what they wanted us to discover."

"I'm thinking that the lesson is for us to discover what they want us to discover. I'm thinking that water by itself is too easy."

"I'm wondering what falling water and water in a hole would lead us to discover, and it still bothers me that the sea wasn't included. Maybe it's just water that contains no salt." Hoft sat with his legs folded, his arms held tightly around his legs. He stared far out over the trees to the place where the land began to flatten. "If it's just water with no salt, we have another thing we didn't look at. Our cave here. It used to flow with water under the ground. The falling water and the water that used to flow in our cave moved. The water hole doesn't move."

Token looked at Hoft. "I'm not sure about that. When we've been swimming in that water hole, the water is fresh. If it didn't move, how could it be fresh?"

"I hadn't considered that!" Hoft said with renewed enthusiasm. "Maybe it's part of a conduit like the school cave we live in used to be. This could get interesting."

Token looked out over the treetops at the setting sun. "After we finally learn what we're supposed to discover, it usually is a fascinating thinking experience. It wakes up our ability to think for now and for the future, but it's one of the hardest things I've had to do since I arrived here. It's easy to learn facts when a human communicates them. It's quite another thing to try to comprehend what the world is trying to tell you about the laws of nature. We had a little of this at the Kapotonok School of the South near where we live. I can remember having to observe ants."

"Ants?"

"Yeah. I had to watch army ants and Pipto had to watch leaf cutters. We had to go back to explain to the Masters what we learned. If we didn't learn enough, we'd have to return to the observation. Army ants will not attack unless there's movement. I learned that and didn't have to return to the site to learn more. While I was observing, I was afraid to sleep for fear that I'd move in my sleep. They fight fiercely and devour their prey. They eat meat! We got to hear the explanations of the other students, so I learned from Pipto that the leaf cutters carry leaves that weigh more than they do, and they store them underground where they turn into a food they can eat."

"I don't think we have those ants here," Hoft said thoughtfully. "I'm glad we don't have army ants!"

"I've never seen them except at the base of the huge mountain. Our school was on top of that mountain."

"We had some lessons like that where we had to go out into nature and do certain things. I've had to go out and spend three nights on Bald Rock, a huge rock where nothing grows. You can see far away out to sea from there. We were not allowed to eat, but we were given a small water bag. Some of the people who were sent on that trip came back describing visions, but I didn't have any. I just hungered and thirsted. Couldn't get my mind off being alone at night and with no protection."

"That must have been a frightening experience."

"Actually, I did learn that it wasn't as frightening as I thought it was, while I was going through it. I've been frightened by worse things." Hoft leaned back against a large rock and looked at the sky beginning to darken.

Token put his hands on the sides of his head in frustration. "Water! I'm still wondering. We'll be examined in a few days. I'm sure they'll ask one of us what we've reasoned about the water. It has to be a law of nature—but what law? I still come up with no understanding," Token said feeling frustration that he might not have an answer by the examination.

"There's the whistle calling us to the evening meal. Let's go. I'm starved!" Hoft said.

Token carefully wrapped his spear points, laid them on a ledge, and joined Hoft for the walk to the area of the cave where they ate. This night it smelled wonderful. The school had some excellent cooks, volunteers from the village lower down the mountainside.

That night Token lay on his sleeping skins looking towards the small amount of light coming from a hole in the roof of the cave. Little bits of dust or vegetation floated in the air, visible in the shaft of light. He could hear his heart beating. He listened to the steady rhythm. All the beats were the same, and it was like walking when each step was measured as the one before it. He wondered how he had managed to live for so long without ever understanding the rhythm of the body. He felt he had learned something huge from his friends. He felt he could apply that knowledge to the drum well enough to pass that part of the examination. He wondered whether all human hearts beat the same way. He fell asleep thinking of water.

A few days later Token awakened with a sense of dread. It was the day of the examination. He had studied and knew he could not study more and do any better. He knew what he knew to that point. It bothered him greatly that he still failed to grasp the significance of the water tours.

He got up and went outside. The mountaintop across from the school displayed clouds of mist rising from the land. It was a beautiful sight to see the white and green. Then, the thought struck him that he was looking at water. Sun made water rise off the land in the form of mist. Clearly, water moved a lot! He thought on the movement of water. Water tried to find the lowest place. It would race to find the lowest place. He felt he had found a part of the reason for the tours, but not the whole reason. It was better than nothing. Water ran to the lowest place. That, he thought, was a law of nature, like some of the other laws of nature they'd begun to explore. He'd grasped a law of nature! In the day, the mist rose to the sky, only to fall back down as rain. That stopped him. What made the mist rise? Mist rising was an effect. What was the cause? He knew the sun drew it. What, then, was the cause of the water running down to the lowest level? Suddenly it occurred to him that the sun drew water to it, and the earth somehow drew water as close to its inner part as possible. Somehow, the earth could hold the water to itself, so it didn't fly off to the sun. Maybe the sun was too far away to draw the water all the way to it. He was elated. He felt he had gained an insight. Water flowing downhill wasn't the law of nature. The law was that the earth drew water to it. The thought thrilled him. He wanted to shout out what he'd understood, but he knew to keep his own counsel on examination day. He whispered "Thank you," to that being his mother called Wisdom and his people called the Creator of All. In his mind, he had been given the gift of understanding, so he did not credit himself with fully identifying the answer he sought. His joy lay in the understanding, not arriving at it.

Token joined the others at the morning meal. All ate in silence, the weight of the day hanging heavy in the air as storm clouds on mountains. As soon as they finished eating, they washed out their bowls and put them in the proper place. When all were finished, the students and the Masters walked solemnly to the examination area.

The Masters all sat in a straight line at the highest point in the room. The fourth year students sat in the row closest to the Masters, the third year students behind them, the second year students in the row behind the third, and the first year students at the farthest distance from the Masters. Token could hear his heart. He knew the procedure. First, the Masters would examine by year in school, starting with the fourth year students. Later they'd randomize their student selection. He felt safe for the moment.

Master Lipin called first one and then another of the fourth year students to the drum. They were each given a different message to communicate. The messages were complex and tried even the knowledge of the older students. Each passed.

Then, Master Lipin called the third year students. When he called Pipto, Token felt his own heart was no longer beating a nicely paced rhythm. He was next. Pipto passed. Then, Token heard his own name. He rose on shaky knees and went to the drum. He was so nervous that he had to ask Master

Lipin to repeat the message he was to communicate. He heard the message and reminded himself to drum to the beat of his normally beating heart, not the one that was racing wildly. He took a deep breath and holding the drumsticks, he tapped out the message.

"Well done," Master Lipin said, though Token struggled to hear it over the beating of his own heart. He returned to his seat with enormous relief that his toughest challenge was over.

There was quite a variety of questions directed at the students. It took the largest part of the daylight hours. Everyone paid attention, because if they advanced, they might get the same question someday. Master Gu told a second year student to tell how long the Alitukit had studied the heavens at night. He answered correctly that they had studied the skies for over 100,000 full cycles of the seasons, not all in this place. Master Theu told two other second year students to see who could immobilize the other first. Some were surprised when the wiry smaller youth successfully pinned the larger one to the ground and held him there. Master Bognuru told a first year student to push his straight body up from the ground forty times using his arms without stopping to rest. The young student succeeded. Master Alikuat told Pipto to divide 10714 by 30. Pipto answered correctly, rounding down. Master Theu told a fourth year student to fashion a spear point from something in the examination area, using two rocks provided by the Master. The young man spotted a rock embedded in the cave wall. It would flake well, and he succeeded in performing the task. He had no protective leather, and he cut himself, but he was successful. Master Gu told a second year student to knock a rock off a piece of driftwood using his slingshot in two tries. He did it on the first try. Students had to remain attentive because there was no way at this point in the examination to know when a Master would call his name.

The day went on with six of the seven fourth year students dismissed for lack of ability to divide by zero. Masters asked each fourth year student whether they could divide by zero. Only one replied affirmatively. That one person, who affirmed that he did, was taken from the room by Master Alikuat, who examined him where the other students could not hear the answer. When they returned, Master Alikuat announced in his deep voice that they had a fifth year student. He also announced that this was the first time in thirty-three years that they'd had a fifth year student. All the students noticed that the only one who made it to fifth year was an Alitukit.

The Masters began to examine the third year students. When Token's name was called first, he rose, somewhat startled, and walked to the place where they had to stand before the Masters to reply to their questions. His knees were not as steady as he'd like, but he was doing well enough, he thought.

Master Alikuat stood to face him. Of all the Masters, he was the most threatening.

"Token, you were given a tour of falling water and the water hole. Why did we choose to provide you with those tours?" Master Alikuat returned to his seat.

Token was not surprised that he'd gotten the question. Only one person would get it and he'd had what he thought was an understanding that morning. He tried to shake off the nervousness and apply what he'd learned. "I struggled to understand the meaning of the tours. At first I wondered why the sea was omitted. Then I realized it must have something to do with more than salt in water. My first assumption, then, was that it must have to do with a law of nature. I have been pursuing this question and running into trees, until this morning I had a breakthrough in understanding. I saw the mist rise from the hill across from our largest entryway. It occurred to me that water moves."

There was slight laughter behind him.

"Silence!" Master Alikuat snapped. "Continue," he nodded to Token.

"Then, I realized that the sun draws the mist upwards. I reasoned that water lost to the sky ultimately rains back down. All water seems to race to the lowest spot it can find, as if the earth itself draws it to its core. The earth is stronger in its drawing power than the sun, because the mist that rises does return to the earth. It doesn't leave earth for the sun. So, I think I understand a law of nature. The sun and the earth both draw water, but the earth is the stronger, probably because it is closer, and water will run to the greatest depth it can find on the surface of the earth. Waters do not lose their places on the earth because the drawing of the earth holds water down. The law of nature is that the earth has holding power so water does not leave for the sun."

Master Alikuat looked at Token. He smiled—something most students had never seen him do. He asked, "Do you think that the drawing of the earth holds you down, so you don't rise up as mist?"

Token wasn't prepared so he reasoned as quickly as he could. He took a deep breath and said, "Yes, Sir."

Master Alikuat looked almost through Token. He asked, "Is there any way you can identify to overcome this law of nature?"

This time Token took longer to reply but his nervousness was gone. "Sir, the birds, bugs, and some fish have a way of overcoming this drawing by flying, but they seem limited in how high and how long they can fly. Volcanoes can spew ash high into the sky, but it also returns to earth. I would have to reply that there is limited ability to overcome this law of nature with our present understanding." Token had forgotten his fear and had relaxed, thoroughly fascinated in the pursuit of the analysis.

The room was totally silent. Token stood before the Masters, his mind soaring into areas he'd never considered.

"Outstanding, Token. You may return to your seat."

Token snapped back to the scene and returned to his seat.

At the end of the examination, each of the six four year students who failed to advance had time to sing their farewell song. Most of the songs were songs of gratitude and a bit sad. One of the students added a little humor which caused the Masters to smile and the students to laugh, as he wove a rhyming experience into the lines. He sang seriously until the middle of his song where he inserted, "alertness and acuity taught by Master Alikuat helped me identify a predatory long-toothed cat—before it could spring to bite me." Finally, a day later the Alitukit Masters sent two Kapotonoks from the second and first year groups back home. Otherwise, all remaining students advanced.

Zamimolo and Ba had taken a long walk to the seashore. The day was hot and they enjoyed walking by the salt water. They walked hand-in-hand, occasionally embracing in the surf.

"It has been twenty years since we joined, Ba. That's a long time."

"It has been a long time. At first, I wondered whether we would last."

"Why? Did you not trust me?"

Ba looked into his face framed by white hair on his head, face, and chest. She adored him as much, if not more, than when she fell in love with him, and it showed on her face. She had only once shared with him her insecurities regarding Olomaru-mia. She had just put them aside and tried hard to ignore them. "I trusted you not to run after anyone but Olomaru-mia. She's always been like a ghost to me, Zami, someone just too beautiful, too perfect, too kind. I thought of myself as second best."

Zamimolo brushed the loose white hair from her face and put his hands on her shoulders. "Ba, from the time we joined, you've been the only woman I ever wanted. I knew Olomaru-mia had joined and was no longer available or even reachable. I have never thought of a competition between the two of you. You are you, and I adore you. No one could have been a better wife than you. How long have you had this idea of second best? I can't believe you've been thinking that. How long, Ba? How long?"

"It's not a big thing, Zami," she tried to assure him.

"How long?"

"Since we joined," she said truthfully.

He pulled her to his chest, his hands still on her shoulders. Then he pushed her back a small way so he could see her face. "Ba, I don't know whether to weep or laugh. That is so incredible! Haven't I shown you repeatedly how much I love you? Haven't I said it enough?"

"Zami, I know you love me. I just thought if you ever saw her, you'd love her more. I allowed myself to doubt. You never gave me a reason to doubt."

"It hurts me terribly to know that you were insecure. Will you please drop it now? Can't you see what's real?"

"I'll try, Zami. Because of the age of the thought, it makes it seem more real."

They resumed walking but much slower.

"Do you carry other insecurities that I don't know about?"

"No," she replied, "that's the only one I have."

"You still have it?"

"Okay, it's the only one I **had**." Ba hoped she could eliminate that old insecurity as her words voiced the idea. It wasn't something she'd thought much about, but it had always been there. "You have never heard more about her?" she asked.

"Oh, back when we helped the Kapotonok at war, there was the old man with the Southern Kapotonok, their Wise One, who told me to control myself in meeting her. I didn't understand what he meant, and I still don't understand. I realized I could probably have found out where she was by the drums, but I never pursued it. She and I don't even know each other. What difference would it make?" He paused. Then he answered his own question, "None. None whatever."

"I didn't know that."

"Ba, it wasn't important. I'd have shared it, if it had importance. I just didn't think about it. We have a life here. I've been busy living it. You cannot truly live if you keep dragging things up from the past."

Ba wondered again, checked herself, and let it go. Zami had told her she had nothing to be insecure about, so she needed to live as if his words were true. She believed they were true words.

"Let's sit on that log and watch the sun on the water for a while," he suggested.

Using the root structure, they climbed up on the huge tree trunk that was resting on the sand. The tree had been a giant. They looked far out to sea.

"Am I seeing something on the horizon, Zami, or are my eyes just getting old?"

"Where?" he asked.

"Out there about three fingers from the shore."

Zamimolo stared off into the distance. For a little while, he saw nothing. Then he thought he saw something. Then he was sure he saw something. "Your eyes are definitely not getting old," he said. "There's a boat out there. Is it time for a boat again? It seems early to me."

"Is it one of our boats?" she asked.

"You mean the Kapotonok boats?" he asked.

"No, no, no," she said watching the little speck, "I mean the boats that come here from your People across the sea."

"I can't see it well enough to know yet. Let's head back so that we can see it from a better height."

The two got up and walked swiftly back north up the beach heading for home where they could see the boat easier from the top of the mountain. When they reached home, they realized it was time for the evening meal. Both were very hungry and ready for the good food they knew they'd enjoy from the savor that floated through the air.

When the evening meal finished, Zamimolo, Ba, and a few others climbed to the top of the mountain to view the boat.

"Sure looks like ours," Golmid said.

"It's sailing, so it has to be ours," Tokatumeta agreed.

"Well, tomorrow, we'll have guests," Zamimolo added.

The small group watched for a while and then returned to the cave.

By morning it was clear that the boat was theirs, and it was almost at the offshore spot where they anchored. No longer could they use the mooring spot they used before the move to the newer cave. It was too far to the south. A few years ago, the men had built a large pile of rocks at the shore's edge just above the high tide mark as a sign for the boatmen. Women scurried to be certain that there was plenty of food for the morning meal and adequate containers for all to eat at one time. They sent a few of the older girls to gather more fruit. A greeting party of men gathered and headed towards the anchorage to be there to meet the boat.

A few men stayed on the boat but the rest of them swam to shore. They introduced the new members of the crew and then they headed for the cave. There were no new immigrants. Eagerly they ate the morning meal, fully enjoying the fruit of this land. Then the boatmen and the People met in council. A hush came over the cave as all wanted to hear the news.

Macrumak, the leader of the boatmen, cleared his throat. "We were sent early. A cobra recently bit the Wise One, and he went to Wisdom. There was no one training as a Wise One replacement. The People ask whether you have a Wise One or someone being trained as a Wise One, who can come to fill this great emptiness and continue the stories. They are desolate in the absence of a Wise One."

Pikotek looked at Jalutui. Jalutui looked like a spooked camel—eyes wide open and fearful, staring straight ahead. She realized that it was likely she'd be chosen to leave her home, travel by boat to a people she didn't know, and transplant herself to a land where it was very cold to become a Wise One. The very idea struck her with terror. Pikotek was their Wise One. He'd come from that land far away. She had to hope he'd wish to return.

Rustumarin said, "We have a Wise One, Pikotek, who came from there. We have another, Jalutui, who is learning and is probably fully able to serve as Wise One. What will have to be determined is which one of these People will go. I suggest we take a time for thought. Let us gather again after the evening meal to determine who will go. Perhaps one will volunteer. We will not leave the People desolate when we have a person who can fill their need for a Wise One. Wisdom has provided us with two. They and we each need only one."

The meeting adjourned and the People were very quiet wondering whether one of the Wise Ones would volunteer to leave or whether it would come to having to make a choice between Jalutui and Pikotek.

The Wise One and Hutapska, his wife, went for a walk by the sea. They talked for a long time. They still had young children. A voyage with small children could be very difficult. When People decided to come to this land, they were excluded if they had small children, because of the dangers of boat travel. Both were aware of that. They concluded that it only made sense for Jalutui to make the move.

In the cave Jalutui was with her mother, Folifilo. Both of them were acutely aware that it only made sense for Jalutui to leave, but both grieved over the choice. Jalutui could not control the stream of tears that left her eyes as she held onto her mother.

"Why does it have to be me? The Wise One came from there. He knows how to live there and he knows the People. I don't know either."

"My daughter, you must control yourself. This is a Wisdom thing. Your life will not be a bad one. This is just something you will have to do. Look at Pikotek now. As Wise One he has come to find Hutapska and they have children. He has been a good Wise One for us. You don't see him weeping and objecting."

"I don't see him volunteering."

"Jalutui, he has small children. You cannot be so mean spirited that you'd have him separate from either his children or his wife and children, so that you wouldn't have to move?"

"I understand that, Mother. It's just that my belly rips apart thinking of having to leave."

"So does mine, but it would be a lot easier if you could bring yourself to volunteer rather than have to be pushed with all of us and the boatmen knowing that you objected so strenuously. What you do now is embarrassing. Think of how this looks when you think of Wisdom. Are you honoring Wisdom?"

Jalutui sat straight up. Put that way, she could see clearly what she had to do. Did it please her? In no way. But she knew what Wisdom wanted her to do and she could refuse People, but not Wisdom. Her mother was right—this was a Wisdom thing. She berated herself. She should have seen that.

Jalutui got up and walked to the top of the mountain. She had been born in this warm land. It was her home. She felt utterly alone with the single exception of Wisdom. She was about to leave for a place that got so cold People had to wear animal skins with fur left on them. She was about to leave for a place where she knew no one. The pain was overwhelming. And worse, she had to volunteer for it. She walked back to the cave. She saw Rustumarin and told him she was volunteering to go. Then she turned away from him abruptly, and ran to her sleeping skins and lost more tears. It felt as if she couldn't bear it any longer, but she knew she could not let Wisdom down.

At the council after the evening meal, Rustumarin announced that Jalutui would be leaving and that the boat would depart in the morning. After the meeting, Pikotek thanked her. She said, "Wise One, it is Wisdom I have to satisfy before myself. I do not want to do this, but when I think of what Wisdom would want, this is the only solution."

"Jalutui, you are ready to be Wise One. You'll be a good one. I once stood in the place where you now stand. I was terrified at a crossing of the sea, of moving to a new place, of being with People I didn't know. Remove your fear, Jalutui. When Wisdom asks something enormous of us, the reward is also enormous."

"Thank you, Wise One," she replied automatically. "I will hold that hope in my belly to comfort me."

At the council meeting, Tokatumeta, Jalutui's father, announced her volunteering to leave to serve as the People's Wise One across the sea. He was torn between grief and pride over his daughter's leaving. He knew there really had been no choice, but it was so much better for her to have volunteered. After the council adjourned, a few People brought something small as a remembrance to Jalutui. She placed each gift into a grass bag she'd take with her. Each came to say farewell.

Quietly, the People settled down to sleep. The boatmen had returned to their boat, expecting Jalutui to join them in the early morning. They felt strange trying to sleep on land. Jalutui fell to sleep as tears escaped the boundaries of her eyes. She ached from the separation even before it occurred.

When the sun began to rise Tokatumeta waked Jalutui. He gathered her few things. Jalutui went with Tokatumeta down the winding path that led to the salt water. There was just enough light to see. The walk seemed so much shorter on this morning. She swam to the boat and boarded, shivering from the cool water. The boatmen took her things and placed them in a small hut that they must have built just for her. They gave her a skin to dry the water from her shivering body. The small hut attached to a much bigger, longer hut behind the first sail. The hut was still showing traces of green from its construction. Jalutui stood on the deck and waved to her father. Then, she turned and faced west. She had to change her entire perspective and assumed the quicker she did it, the better. Her first effort would come from surviving a sea crossing for which nothing could prepare her.

Tokatumeta saw her turn and realized what she was doing. He turned and began to walk the winding path up the mountain to their cave. He knew Jalutui would leave a great empty place in the bellies of many of the People. Her laughter and happy disposition would be sorely missed. He turned to look back at the boat before entering the wooded forest. The boat had already begun to sail to the west. He did not see Jalutui.

The Wise One began to speak to the adults quietly but with a small sense of urgency. He wanted to know whether any of them or their children knew the stories. What he sought was a new Wise One. When he discovered that no People currently knew any of the stories, he asked that they watch the young ones to see who might develop into a Wise One. He knew that the younger they found the new Wise One, the easier it was to train them. All the People would be watching for signs of knowledge of the stories in the young children.

A loud scream went up from the lower area to the east. From the lookout point, Linpint could see a spiked-tail armadillo attacking his son, Ventumoko. His friend, Gnaha, Zamimolo's son, was trying to distract the beast. It kept pushing Ventumoko with its head. Ventumoko had lost his spear and was trying to run, but it was clear that his right leg gave him difficulty. Linpint didn't wait but turned to run to his son as fast as he could. He stubbed his toe on a rock, but that didn't slow him down. Several other hunters were already nearing the attack area.

Gnaha had speared the beast in the front leg several times and the wounds gushed blood, but the beast didn't seem to notice. It was as if one huge animal was totally obsessed with Ventumoko, and nothing else existed. It moved so much faster than most People thought it could. Ventumoko had come very close to the ravine where they had already had some accidents. Gnaha realized that Ventumoko was purposely leading the animal to the ravine. Ventumoko ran as fast as his right leg would allow and leaped off the edge of the ravine to a small ledge that stood out from a crack in the ravine wall. He threw himself into the crack. The spiked-tail armadillo had gained too much speed to stop and it fell into the ravine bellowing as it went over the ledge where it landed upside down in the ravine, incapable of righting itself.

Gnaha raced to Ventumoko, forgetting the armadillo. Ventumoko had a nasty gash on his leg. It was deep. Gnaha pulled his friend to his feet and helped him stand on the ledge. He asked one of the hunters to bring rope to haul him up to the level ground. The hunter brought the rope and two men came quickly with a stretcher. Hunters hauled Ventumoko up the edge of the ravine and eased him onto the stretcher. Linpint gazed at him with concern. The wound looked awful. Other hunters took the life of the armadillo and butchering would soon occur.

Back in the cave, a few women set to work cleaning Ventumoko's leg. They knew how important it was to get the wound as clean as possible, so they were vigorous in their efforts regardless of Ventumoko's protestations. After pouring cooled water that they'd boiled over the wound, they filled the gash with the salve that the Alitukit men had taught them to use to heal the snakebite and added a generous amount of honey to the wound and surrounding area before wrapping it with soft skins. Fortunately, they thought, the bone was intact.

Men set up roasting spits and there was some festivity associated with the kill. It had been a long time since they'd had a meal of armadillo.

Kih, Zamimolo's older brother, walked down to the path that led from the flat upper level to the far lower level where the men went to hunt. The armadillos when they came to this upper level used that path, because they wouldn't fit between the trees. Kih stood looking down the path. There had to be, he reasoned, a way to prevent armadillos from coming through that pathway. He spent a large part of the day pondering various ways to prevent their access. Finally, he had reached some potential solutions, and he decided to hold them until the council meeting. He entered the woods to gather some mushrooms to add to the night's feast.

The men built a smoker to smoke the meat they couldn't eat. They constructed it from tree trunks overlaid with vegetation. They hung meat on horizontal branches tied to the inside of the tree trunks. They would store it as long as possible in a dry part of the cave. Jerky made from armadillo wasn't their first choice, but it was acceptable food. Having spent time living through long winters, the older People were acutely aware of the need for some stored food.

The young boys and girls who were practicing with slingshots under the watchful supervision of Tukyatuk were attracted by the delightful fragrance coming from the smoker. They had to concentrate with extra effort not to become distracted.

In the shade of a great oak tree, several young women sat weaving mats. Ba had taught them how to make things from the leaves of some of the local plants, leaves known for having lasting ability. They made mats for sitting and for placing under their bedding skins to give longer life to the skins. They made sleeping mats thicker, to provide extra comfort on the ground.

The evening meal was a great success. Several of the People chose to return for more food. After the cleanup from the evening meal, the People gathered for the council meeting.

The Wise One opened the meeting, "Tonight our number has reduced by one. May Wisdom comfort and reward Jalutui in her new life and give her a safe, uneventful sea crossing. We have a serious injury. May Wisdom cause Ventumoko's injury to heal quickly. Now, who would speak?"

Kih spoke out, "I would speak."

The Wise One nodded to him. He was interested. Kih was usually a very quiet person, rarely ever speaking at council meetings.

Kih said, "Today, after the accident I walked to the path to the lower level and examined it. The path provides access to armadillos and other large animals who cannot reach our living area through the trees. I wondered how we might prevent them from using the path while keeping it for our use. I have two thoughts. We could dig a trench and fill it with tree trunks, which we would stand on end, refilling the trench once the tree trunks stand. We'd probably have to hold them upright with ropes, while we refill the trench. We could leave an entrance wide enough for us but not for them. Or we could bring large numbers of plants we dig up from the forest and place them to grow on the path so it would be a strip of forest they wouldn't be able to fit through."

"What a great idea," Rustumarin said, forgetting to wait for a nod.

Some of the other hunters were as enthusiastic as Rustumarin, and the discussion became lively.

"I prefer the idea of the trenches with the standing tree trunks," Golmid said. "It would require more hard work, but it would be done. If we planted trees, we'd have to care for them until they were secure, and some might not live."

"Golmid, eventually the trees would rot and the trench would have to be redone. Planting trees, once they adjusted, would not require another effort," a voice interrupted.

"I'm in favor of the trenched tree trunks," Remu said, joining in.

"Let's raise our hands if we prefer the trenched tree trunks," shouted Tukyatuk.

"All but three hunters signified that they preferred the trenched tree trunks," The Wise One said. "Kih, since the idea was yours, will you lead the group to build the trenched tree trunks?"

"Yes. Any who will participate meet me after the morning meal in the area of the top of the path, ready to dig."

At least ten hunters indicated willingness to be there.

"Is there any other who would speak?"

No response came, so the meeting closed.

The next morning the men hurried to the top of the path. They had numbers of digging tools. Kih walked several man lengths onto the path heading towards the hunting level. He took some thin rope and tied it to a tree. He walked with the rope to the other side of the path and tied the rope to another tree. The rope gave a straight line for the trench. The ground was hard, so they broke it up by pounding short, thick spears into it. By high sun, they had made a noticeable trench about the depth of the height of a twelve-year-old boy. They decided to dig a long trench before beginning to place the tree trunks. A number of other men consulted with Kih about the diameter of the tree trunks and the length, and they went off to the forest to harvest tree trunks.

Men who were not participating, women, and children were fascinated. As they worked at their chores, they watched the progress of the trenched tree trunk barrier. Men from the forest had returned with a large number of tree trunks. The tree trunks were the length of one and a half men. The men removed all the roots and limbs. They piled them up near the trench.

It took two days to dig the trench. There was much excitement to see the men mark the opening and then begin to place the tree trunks into the trenches. They did hold the trunks vertical using rope. Refilling the trench could not begin for the first tree trunk until five other tree trunks had been lowered into the trench and held vertical with ropes. Refilling the hole was not as easy as it seemed. Putting the earth back was one thing; getting it tight enough to hold a tree trunk, quite another. When they had ten tree trunks positioned and five were refilled, the men realized they needed a support. They went to the forest and took two more trees, cutting off the limbs and root structures. They returned and at the end of the trench, they placed one tree trunk so that the top of the tree trunk tied to the standing tree trunk and its base rested on the ground on the cave side of the trench. On the other side, they tied another tree trunk with its length going down the path to the lower level. Men dug holes and inserted the bottoms of the bracing trees into the holes. The men tightly tied the tree tops to the tops of the first tree in the trench. If a man looked down the line of tree trunks, the supports would have formed a triangle with the ground as its base. They took heavy poles and tamped down the refilled dirt to steady the tree trunks. They continued. As they worked, they found that every ten to twelve tree trunks needed to serve as a brace point if the barrier would be strong. To keep the tree trunks lined up well, they tied a slender tree trunk with rope to each of the tree trunks horizontally on the inside of the barrier. Once the barrier was set up, it was strong and made an entry width of two men standing side-by-side. Even a young armadillo would have difficulty getting through that opening. They felt they were finally free of invading armadillos.

The very next afternoon to the horror of all, Golmid spotted a mature sloth on the path. Never had anyone seen a sloth on the path or upper level. It was frightening and with one whistle, all the People gathered in the cave and watched from the observation point. All were silent as they watched.

The enormous sloth browsed treetops on the path seemingly unaware of the barrier. When it reached the barrier, it reached down with one of its horribly sharp-clawed forelegs and touched the barrier. It bent down to smell the barrier. It turned and went back down the path to the lower level and disappeared. The People were greatly relieved. After all their work, they knew the sloth had enough power to destroy the barrier had it chosen to do so. It took some time before People returned to the upper open level, even though they knew they were safe from the sloth.

Later that evening, Linpint and Yu, his son who was learning to hear the drums, climbed to the top of the mountain to listen for any messages that might come. That night there was one. Linpint and Yu heard the drumming to the south of them. It never was as strong as the drums from the north, but they could hear it well. The message began, "to all ... meeting ... search wives and husbands ... ten days ... Bekwaboati." Linpint had listened carefully. He heard the drumming repeat. After the second time, the drummer signed off. Linpint began to beat out the message. He was having difficulty with the last word, not positive that he knew what it meant, but he simply repeated what he'd heard. He repeated the message and signed off. He could hear the message pick up to the north. He and Yu went back to the cave.

Council was about to begin, so they took their seats and waited until it was time to speak. When the Wise One nodded at Linpint, he told what he got of the message. He didn't know what Bekwaboati was and it seemed neither did any of the others. He decided he'd travel to the Southern Kapotonok, their closest neighbors, to see what he could learn. Zamimolo agreed to accompany him on the brief trip. They'd leave at first light.

When light appeared in the east, Linpint and Zamimolo gathered their backpacks and spears and headed for the new barrier and the path that went down from it. They moved rapidly and were in the level area quickly. From there they'd pass hills and follow rivers to reach the coast and shortly afterwards arrive at the home of the Southern Kapotonok. Women had packed jerky from the armadillo and Linpint hoped the trip was very short, since that was his least favorite jerky. Zamimolo didn't much care for it either. Both picked a papaya on the hillside and ate it as they walked.

Parrots colored the trees and the monkeys made a thunderous noise in the early daylight. Off to the south side, something large moved slowly in the trees. The men didn't take time to check to see what it was. They moved rapidly. There was no reaction from the animal they'd heard. A squealing peccary raced across the path followed by several very small ones. The men took time to chuckle at the little line of peccaries.

Linpint paused, smelling a snake, and there near his face was a snake coiled among the branches in a tree. He pointed it out to Zamimolo. It was a mottled green-brown triangular headed snake. The two pressed on. Mist rose from the higher hills they crossed and they had to take more care to look for hazards. Finally, just before the sun began to set, they began their descent to a river that would take them directly to the Southern Kapotonok.

"I hope they have something really filling for the evening meal," Zamimolo said to Linpint, slightly breathless from a slipping slide down a hill where the mud had turned to wet clay. He walked over to clean his feet in the river.

"I'd like filling and tasty," Linpint laughed. "This jerky is awful."

"Well, it's better than nothing."

"I'm not sure about that. I've only eaten half a stick."

"You must be very hungry!"

"Well, I've been grabbing fruit from time to time. That makes a difference."

"The sea is beautiful, and look how calm it is!"

"Hardly a ripple, Zami."

"They're north of us, right?" Zamimolo asked, momentarily disoriented.

"Yes. Let's go."

The two began to walk quickly across the river and then straight to the sea and then they turned left and began to walk in the sand.

It was not long before the lookouts for the Southern Kapotonoks spotted them and strode to meet them.

Chief Hirmit hobbled out using a bent stick to steady himself. "It is Zamimolo and Linpint, friends from long ago. How are you?" he asked.

"Both of us well, and you, Chief Hirmit?" Linpint replied.

"Doing well, doing well. Come, it is time for the evening meal and we have camel cooked as none other cooks it, so that even the Maker would want to join us."

Linpint and Zamimolo followed the old man and others to their village and put their weapons in the weapons keep. They sat where the women showed them. Soon the women served each of them huge portions of camel and vegetables and fruits. They talked about unimportant things while they ate, such as the weather and how many animals were up or down in count this year as compared to other years. The women remained silent.

When the meal was finished, the women collected the serving platters and the men began to talk of other things of greater import: how were Lomah, Kumoha, and Dop. Had they had any more children? The Chief told them that their Wise One had gone to the Maker during the last year, but they'd probably heard it on drum talk, which, they agreed, they had.

"Now," Chief Hirmit said quietly, "Tell us why you came."

"It has to do with the drums. We had a message from the Bekwaboati to the south. It spoke of what sounds like a gathering where people who need to find wives or husbands could choose from those who are not closely related. The idea sounds great, but I'm not sure I got the message right."

"You got it right. It will take place now in nine days. You have some people who want to go?"

"We have some, who might want to go, but it takes place so soon and we have no idea where it is."

"Ah, you need to contact the Northwestern Kapotonok, the people who took you by boat back to your campsite when you first arrived and got lost in the mountains. They usually stop along the west seashore to pick up any who want to go to the wife/husband event. Bekwaboati is on the west seashore of the big land below this narrow strip of land. I will send Ti with you. Ti may want to find a wife. Ti will lead you to the Northwestern Kapotonok. You will leave just as the light arrives to the morning sky."

"Thank you Chief. That's very helpful. I think there will be some who wish to go from the People. I hope we can make it in time."

"Use the drums. Go up with Tomarghi and send your message this evening. Then, you'll know."

Linpint and Zamimolo had forgotten that they were able to use the drums as well as forward messages. Linpint went with Tomarghi who was right beside him as the Chief spoke, and the two of them went right to the drums. Tomarghi asked what Linpint wanted to send.

"Do any People wish to attend wife/husband search in the south in nine days?"

Tomarghi sent the message from the Southern Kapotonok to the People. Linpint watched as he sent the message seemingly without any effort at all. The two waited. They waited for quite some time. Finally, the drum sounded from the People. This was the first time Linpint had heard the drum from his People. The drum said that five People would like to attend the event.

"You'd better be ready to leave with Ti. It sounds like there is a lot of interest among the People."

"We'll be ready. Thank you for the drumming, Tomarghi. You are an expert."

"Far from expert, but I manage to do well enough. If I can help, you are welcome."

As darkness came, the men set their sleeping skins on the soft sand and quickly fell to sleep near the fire. In the morning Ti touched them gently on the shoulder and each waked quickly to prepare for another day of trekking through the forest. The Southern Kapotonoks provided them with food to eat during the trek, and it far surpassed the taste of the jerky the People made.

It took all day but by evening, they had arrived at the village of the Northwestern Kapotonoks. Ti was a person they knew, so they spoke to him directly first.

"We are here, Tam," Ti explained, "to see if we might accompany you in your boats to the wife/husband search at Bekwaboati. I want to go and Linpint and Zamimolo of the People have five they would like to take."

"It will require an additional boat, but, of course, we will be glad to provide boat space if they are willing to row."

Linpint nodded in the affirmative when Tam mentioned rowing.

Tam looked at the men from the People. "That is your rock pile on the shore?"

"Yes," Zamimolo replied.

"We will pick up your people in two days—early—at sunrise. You will be ready?"

"Yes."

"We have space for seven."

"We will have no more than that."

"Very well," Tam directed them to the fire with his hand. "Come, join us for our evening meal."

The three men were glad they'd arrived in time to eat. The trek had been hard and tiring. Ti was one who moved quickly through the forests making hardly a sound but moving far faster than either Linpint or Zamimolo normally moved. That evening the men feasted on fish of a variety of types. There were many fruits and some greens, mostly from the sea. The taste was wonderful.

After they ate, they prepared to sleep. Tam told them a man would take Linpint and Zamimolo home the next morning in one of their smaller boats. They were glad not to have to wait for two days. The man who transported them home warned them to take rope and skins to make shelters to keep them dry when it rained. He explained that there was little place to accommodate as many travelers as would come to Bekwaboati.

Arriving back at the cave, Zamimolo and Linpint were interested to know who would be going to the Bekwaboati. It was afternoon so each went to find their wives.

Ba came running when she saw that Zamimolo had returned. He caught her in his arms and for a moment, they did not speak.

"Ahah, wants to go, Zami, and it scares me."

Zamimolo looked into her eyes. "She is a grown woman, and she is not satisfied with her options here. We've known that for some time. Just as you did, she needs to search for what she would have. She's so much like you. Of all your daughters, she reminds me most of you. She may find no one there. Alternatively, she may do what you did, move to a different place. What's important is for her to find her way in life. She's strong willed and strong minded, Ba. Leave Ahah her freedom, as your father left you yours."

"I have no choice, but it doesn't make it any easier. Was your trip a good one?"

"It was fine. We have to do something about the jerky. Linpint really hates it, and I don't like it either."

"Is it just that it's armadillo, or is it the way we make jerky?" Ba asked.

"I think it's the way it's made. Years ago, it used to taste good. Now, I'd rather just pluck fruit, but I eat it so not to be wasteful. Who else wants to go?"

"Linpint and Lomah's son, Ventumoko, Tokatumeta and Folifilo's son, Nob, Golmid and Colitoba's daughter, Picota, and Tukyatuk and Meninkua's son, Tas."

"I thought Ahah might want Ventumoko, but something happened to end their interest in each other after he was injured by the armadillo," Zamimolo said quietly. He liked Ventumoko.

"Well, we had better get things gathered for our daughter."

"What do we need to gather?" Zamimolo wondered aloud.

"She needs a new tunic. Hers is too short and stained. Who would want a woman with a stained tunic?"

"Oh," he laughed, "certainly she needs a stain free tunic!"

Ba ignored his pleasantries and looked seriously at him. "She also needs a bag to carry whatever necessary things she may need."

"All that's women's work. Is there anything I need to provide?"

Ba smiled. "No, my dear, nothing but yourself. You will accompany her?"

"Of course, Linpint and I already decided to make the trip with the young people."

"Where are you going?"

"Have you seen the drawing of this thin strip of land that connects the two huge lands, one to the north and one to the south?"

"You know I've seen it," she said pretending offense.

"It's a little way down the shoreline from the place where the big land to the south joins the smaller land where we live. Down there is a very large cove. It opens to the south. It is there that Bekwaboati serves as a large, safe anchorage for boats going north and south. I understand it's a large village."

"You will watch out for Ahah, won't you?"

"Of course, I'll be as careful of her safety as I can possibly be. She's our daughter."

"I'd better get that tunic ready," Ba said, turning away and heading for the place in the cave where they stored skins.

There was excitement as the young people prepared for their trip to Bekwaboati. Many of the people they'd already met would be there, but there would also be others from the far south in the big south land and some from the big north land. Boats would be heading north and south along both seas. Others would use paths in the big land to the south to reach the place of the gathering.

Zamimolo, Linpint, Ventumoko, Nob, and Tas gathered to decide what to carry to make their accommodations. They understood that most of the travelers stayed in a wooded area just east of the village where the land leveled off half way up a mountain, where trees helped support lean-tos made of skins. They wanted to enjoy the time spent, so they planned to carry plenty of skins, ropes, and sleeping skins—enough for all seven of them.

When the day of departure arrived, all travelers were ready. Family members looked at their young ones, wondering whether they'd ever see them again. Each strongly hoped that the lives of the young people would be good ones.

Very early, the boats from the Northwestern Kapotonok arrived. The transfer of People and goods was a quick one, and the boats were on their way. The People had their emotional farewells the night before travel due to the suspicion that sadness on departure day would cause the travel to fall into difficulty. Anyone who might weep or show sadness remained at the cave on departure day.

Chapter 6

Excitement on the boats increased as they rounded the point of land to make their way to Bekwaboati. There were two major inlets facing south. The second one to the east led to Bekwaboati. The occupants of the boat could hear the people before they could see them. In the experience of those who previously had attended one of these events, not even they had ever seen so many people in one place at one time.

The Northwestern Kapotonok told the newcomers to follow their lead. Before they could participate in the event, they had to establish their camp and set up their shelters. It took a good while to climb the hill to reach the area where people set up shelters. When they reached the area many others were busily arranging their camp sites. Ahah and Ventumoko took the rope and tied the ends to two sturdy trees. They tied rope to two other trees parallel to the first one. The skins would easily fit the ropes and provide enough covered space for the seven of them.

"This is so exciting," Ahah said to Ventumoko while they began to set up their shelter, a skin tent.

"It really is. I heard from Ti that there isn't much to the gathering until the evening. They make a large fire and those interested in meeting others have to introduce themselves to the large group. That way you see people introduce themselves and begin to see who might interest you. I feel a bit outside of myself here. I don't really feel comfortable just walking up to a stranger for the purpose of getting to know her. I think I will have to learn quickly, if I want to find a wife here."

"I know what you mean. I felt comfortable until we arrived, and, then, I saw the huge number of people here. Suddenly I feel very small."

"I guess you have something to learn also."

"Yes, Ventumoko, I have to learn just like you do."

"Can I help with those bundles?" Picota asked them.

"Of course. We're just putting the things under the tent area we tied off. Here comes Linpint with skins for the tent. Looks like Zamimolo is right behind him with more."

"You didn't waste any time," Linpint boomed out. "Why'd you pick this place where it's so open?"

"We chose this one because of the breeze. If there are bugs tonight, the breeze might help us have fewer of them."

"Good thinking for people who haven't traveled much."

"Thank you, Father," Ventumoko laughed. The People joked about Linpint's always being ready to travel somewhere.

The men began to place the skins on the ropes arranging them to make a secure tent that would protect from rain. When the tent began to droop, they'd prop the ropes with branches they either salvaged from the ground or cut down. The young people gathered armfuls of dried grasses to make a barrier between the sleeping skins and the ground. Ahah wanted to bring some mats made of strong leaves for ground protection from home, but they were too heavy to carry along with the skins. Gathering dried grasses was the best they could do, but the dried grass available was disappearing quickly so the young people hurried to gather a good supply before the grasses near them were gone. More dried grasses were available to the north, but it required a good walk over rough ground to reach them. Tas collected wood for hearth fires and stacked a pile in front of the tent opening. When all had finished, they gathered at their camp to prepare for the evening by combing their hair and picking their teeth.

Inside the tent, leaning against a tree trunk, Linpint said, "I think we should go as a group to the meeting tonight. We should present ourselves as orderly People. We will see together what the meeting shows us. Then, if it's advisable for us to split our group, that will happen. You are here, after all, to meet people. Then, we will meet back here at night. I do not want anyone in our group to spend the night anywhere except our tent. Is that clear? Be here when the sun is no more than half way below the sea."

"Father," Ventumoko laughed, "You really think we could find someone that quickly?"

The other young People laughed.

"I am not trying to entertain you. Before you left, you agreed to obey Zamimolo and me. I am holding you to that agreement."

"I'll be here, Father," Ventumoko said.

"I'll be here," the other young People each acknowledged, more serious.

"Good, then our People should look good to others. Let's go down now," Zamimolo said. He was as eager as the young People to see what this meeting would bring.

When they reached the lower level where the evening's events would occur, Zamimolo was surprised. The people of the village at Bekwaboati had prepared a long table of food for the people who came to the event. There was a lot of roasted peccary, some camel, some seafood, and lots of greens and fruits. The variety was widely selected and there was a seeming overabundance of food. All were invited to eat when they arrived. The interaction among people who didn't know each other was pleasant. People introduced themselves, knowing that it was unlikely that the other person would remember their names. It was a social event, however, and people were interested in the interaction with those they'd never seen, even if they felt somewhat awkward and retiring about it.

A young girl with very long black hair that shone almost as blue walked up to Tas. "Are you here for the search?" she asked, her eyes looking directly into his."

"Yes. I'm Tas," he replied somewhat surprised, until he remembered that he was at the event to meet people, and he was glad she was forward.

"I'm Kib. My home is far, far south where the snow covered mountains rise above the land."

"I'm Tas," he repeated and groaned silently to himself at the repetition. "My People came from across the sea where it was very cold to find a warmer place. We now live on the narrow land that connects the two big lands."

"You must have many colorful birds," she said with a smile.

"We do," he said, realizing that she was having as much difficulty talking to him as he was in talking to her. Birds! he thought, smiling to himself.

In another place, Picota, Ahah, Ventumoko, and Nob were clustered, somewhat anxious about their decision to attend the event. Each was eating the wonderful food that had been set out for them, wondering whether they should have come. It was just awkward.

A loud whistle sounded and a voice called to all to come to assemble at the meeting place. The People gathered and went to the meeting place together. They sat either cross-legged or kneeling, sitting on their heels. All were eager to hear what the speaker would say. Those who accompanied the young people, such as Zamimolo and Linpint, stood on the outside perimeter, watching.

A short, man with skin the color of a rain soaked tree trunk and a smile showing gleaming white teeth stood before the gathering. He raised both his arms to quiet the group. A hush fell on the group. He began, "I am Ta, Chief of the Bekwaboati. All of us live in great lands where there is much distance between us and little opportunity for small groups of people to find others with whom to join, others who are not related in some way. This meeting is to add health to the people who live in these great lands. We can find people who are appealing to us in different ways, people we'd otherwise never meet. Each pair that comes from this meeting will have to decide where they will choose to live. This is a special time. When you come together to talk, keep in mind that you are here for a reason. Look for someone who has the characteristics you find critically important. If you go to hunt for a wife or husband, you don't chat about the weather."

Several young people laughed audibly. They'd already chatted about things that had no import on wife/husband selection.

"Look into how the other lives, what they believe, who are their friends and enemies. Find out whether the other person is calm or spirited, helpful or wants freedom from helping others, gentle or rough, self-effacing or arrogant. These things matter. You only have seven days for your selections, so you must choose quickly, but remember to be careful. Whatever it is that you choose to do, it's a significant choice that can affect you for the rest of your life. Choose wisely. Now, what we will do here is have each person who is searching come forward one at a time. Tell the group your name, something about yourself, and repeat your name at the end. You'll have a little time to think what you'll say, while I continue with the news. Skirim has just counted the people here. There are seventy eight people who came here. That's the most we've ever had. You should find a great variety to help you make your selections. This is not a time to be shy. Listen carefully to each young person as they introduce themselves. Look at them. Is there something that draws you to that person? If so, make a note to remember their names."

"Each day for seven days, we'll provide food in the evening just as we did this evening. You have to provide your own morning meal. We have privies set up on the hill behind the large rock and over by the dead tree stump that stands with half its roots exposed to the air. Down on this level there are

204

privies to the far south, over by the palm trees down there where I'm pointing, and back behind the dwellings that are set over there where I'm pointing. You're free to make your own, but with this many people, it is critical that you make sure to cover your leavings. Also, if you eat at your camp, be sure to put any bones in your hearth fire. Don't throw them out where someone could step on them."

"Finally, unless there are reasons to provide you information, there will be no more meetings. If there is a need to share information, a local drum will sound. If that occurs, please come quickly."

"Now, the moment you've all been waiting for. You'll begin to introduce yourselves. After your introduction, go to Skirim. She'll give you a string with a seashell attached. That lets all know that you're one of the searchers. Do not approach anyone in your search who doesn't wear the stringed shell. There are plenty of people here for one reason or another who are not searching. Leave them alone. Finally, when you find the person who will be your wife or husband, return the stringed shell to Skirim. Now, I'll go over here by Skirim, and each of you who is searching, come up and introduce yourself when you're ready." Ta walked over to the table where Skirim had the stringed shells. He sat down and leaned against a tree.

A young man stood and walked to the front. "I am Bul of the Nola Nola. I went south to school in the land of the Nola Nola on the high straight mountain, then finished four years at the Alitukit School, completed my trial of manhood, and now seek a wife. We live in a beautiful valley by the sea where I hunt and participate in making our village a good place to live. I seek a strong, healthy wife who will bear many happy children. I want to live in my village. My name is Bul." He smiled at the group, turned, and went to get his stringed shell. Picota was fascinated by him. His dark color appealed to her and his self-assured ease in talking to the group made her remember his name, Bul. His smile warmed her. He returned to his seat at the far side of the gathering place from her.

Another young man rose and introduced himself. He was not as at ease in front of the group as Bul, but he was handsome and many of the young women were drawn to him. One after another, the young men and women introduced themselves. Those who were shy found that listening to others made their introductions became clearer to construct. For a few, it would be agonizingly painful to speak to the large group, but somehow they each managed to give a name and some personal information. A few of the young women were so quiet that their voices could not be heard at all.

When Picota went to speak, she found that her fear seemed to vanish because Bul was looking at her with amazing interest. She said, "My name is Picota. My People live on the narrow piece of the connecting land. My parents and I made the sea voyage from a cold land to the warm land where we live now. I have no memory of it. I seek a husband who is gentle, kind, likes children, and is a good hunter. I also look for someone who can laugh easily." Looking at Bul, she added, "It wouldn't hurt if he is pleasing to look at. My name is Picota." She smiled at the group, lingering her smile on Bul, and went to get her stringed shell.

Ventumoko followed her. As he spoke, Ahah became increasingly uncomfortable. She saw some of the women looking at him, and it bothered her. She tried to reason herself out of what she considered absurd jealousy but found it terribly difficult. He had every right to be a searcher. She had, after all, rejected him.

It was her turn. She rose and stood before the group. She looked at the sea of faces and saw Ventumoko as he returned to his seat. "I am Ahah," she said firmly. "I am from the narrow connecting land and live among the People. I search for a husband who will be kind, gentle, a good provider, and who delights me just to see his face in the morning, all through the day, and at night. I know how to do the things wives do in a community. I'm a good worker." She had prepared other things to say, but she looked at Ventumoko again and said, "My name is Ahah."

Ventumoko looked at her wondering why she seemed so uncomfortable. In another part of the large group, a young man named Kowotiach was attracted to Ahah and wanted to meet her as soon as the meeting adjourned. Ahah returned to her place after taking the stringed shell. She suddenly realized she had been at the meeting listening carefully, and she had seen no one she wanted to get to know. Ahah was horrified. She hoped soon to see someone who would attract her. She began to wonder whether something was wrong with her.

The introductions seemed to go on forever but finally the searchers were fewer and took longer to come to the front to share information—until there were no more. As soon as the young people began to realize the introductions were over, they tried to get close to the person who impressed them the most. Ahah turned to ask Ventumoko something only to face a tall very handsome young man with dark tanned skin and dark brown eyes.

"As soon as I heard you speak, I wanted to meet you," Kowotiach said, smiling.

"Hi," she replied coolly. "What's your name?"

The young man realized quickly that she hadn't been impressed enough to remember his name, so he carefully told her syllable by syllable, "Kowotiach."

"If I remember right, you live to the far south, and your people have been here for a long, long time. Is that right?"

"You may have me mistaken for someone else. I live just on the large land to the north. My people have been here longer than memory, but the history is that we came from the sea to the west. We make boats from large trees that are hollowed out carefully, and we travel the waterways of the rivers. At some times, such as these events, we come out to the sea. Tell me about you. You were born in this land, is that right?"

"Yes, I was born here but my parents were born across the sea where it was cold. I am glad to be here. I'm sorry that I confused you with someone else. There are so many people here that it's hard to keep all the stories straight." Although she talked with Kowotiach, her eyes followed Ventumoko until she could no longer see him.

Kowotiach realized she was preoccupied, but he wasn't ready to give up. He found Ahah beautiful, her white skin so unusual that he could not keep his eyes from it. Her blue eyes were the color of sky, something he'd never seen in eye color and her long, brown, loose curly hair captivated him. He kept talking and she responded, but not in the way that a smitten woman would, at least not the ones he knew. He tried every approach he could think of, but none of them really seemed to hold her attention for long. He began to wonder whether he should seek a wife elsewhere. Then a loud noise occurred, and the earth began to rumble and move beneath their feet. Some people were knocked off their feet. Kowotiach fell to his back and Ahah tried to help him up only to fall on her side near him. The quake lasted for what the people at the search event felt was a very long time. They'd find some camp tents needed to be fixed and some trees had fallen over, but the table with all the food remained standing though many people near it were on the ground.

People began to get up. Kowotiach helped Ahah rise to her feet. Once she stood, another rumble sent her back to the ground. Her arm hit a rock and it began to swell. What looked like a great plum hung from her forearm near the elbow, evidence that she bled inside the skin. Finally the size of it remained the same, so that those who understood could reason the bleeding had stopped and she would be alright. There were two people who cured the sick and injured. They went to the gathering place and Ta whistled. He called any who were injured to come to the gathering place.

"Here," Kowotiach offered, "Let me help you to the gathering place."

"I'm fine, thank you."

"Ahah, is there nothing you find appealing about me?" he finally asked, having exhausted his thoughts on how to appeal to her.

"It's not that. I'm worried about the people I know."

"They are with others. If they're injured, you'll see them come down here to the gathering place."

"Thank you Kowotiach. Right now, I'm just a little frightened and I want to find my People."

Kowotiach left her. He wished he could find the way to reach the part of her that would be open to love, but he had no idea what to do. He considered that at another time he might try again, unless he'd found someone else.

Without thinking, Ahah climbed up the hill to the camp. Their tent was still standing. Trees near it were all standing. She bent over to enter the shelter of the tent, knelt to pull a skin from her backpack, and sat while she wrapped it around herself. She was shivering. She pulled it tightly around herself.

Ventumoko had seen her scrambling up the hill alone, so he followed, not too close. He wondered why she was alone. When he saw her shivering in the tent, he joined her.

"What it is, Ahi?" he asked her using his teasing name for her which meant dragonfly.

Instead of answering, she held her arms out to him. He was thoroughly confused. She began to weep. Ventumoko was concerned, because Ahah had always been so self-assured. He had no idea what to do, so he simply sat there and held her. The sun began to lower itself to the horizon. Ahah has ceased crying but still seemed shaky. Ventumoko noticed the swollen arm and was instantly nauseated by the looks of it, and then began to ask questions about it.

"It is not that bad," she said. "It feels tight where it's swollen, but there is no huge pain. I have been so wrong, so very, very wrong. Tonight I discovered how wrong I've been."

"Ahah, what are you talking about?"

"When I saw the women looking at you when you introduced yourself, I had a strange feeling. I have never been jealous or mean spirited, but I wanted to throw all of those who looked at you into the sea. I wanted to run up there, grab you, and run into the woods with you."

Ventumoko couldn't help but laugh. "And once you got me into the woods, what then?"

"I didn't think that far. Ventumoko, I think at that moment, certainly when I stood to introduce myself, I didn't want anyone else but you. I certainly didn't want anyone else to have you. I don't know why I didn't see it until I got here, but my fear of losing you is huge. Have you found a wife yet?"

"Ahah, I think I have found a wife. If you will swear by the name of Wisdom that you'll never change, you can be sure that I have found a wife in you."

She put her arms around his neck and the two of them cuddled in the tent alone with the brilliant sunset overhead. She felt safe and right for the first time since she'd told him that she rejected him.

"We have something we must do, Ahah," he said.

"What's that?"

"We have to go take our stringed shells to Skirim," he said with a smile. "And I'd feel better if someone took a look at that arm."

The two got up and hand-in-hand walked back down the hill to the gathering place.

Later that night Linpint and Zamimolo arrived at the tent and checked on their young people. They were missing Picota. With some alarm, they decided how they would search and just as they were about to leave to search, Picota returned with a young man named Bul.

"We were just going to search for you Picota. The sun has already set and you just got here. You were to be here before it reached half way below the horizon."

"I'm sorry. Let me introduce, Bul of the Nola Nola. We were talking and I couldn't see the sun. We were so involved in our talk that I didn't pay attention to the sun."

"Bul, our rule is that Picota must be back at the tent before half the sun has gone below the horizon." Linpint stood there with a hand on his left hip.

"I'm sorry. If she will be with me tomorrow, I assure you it will not happen again."

"Where are the Nola Nola?" Zamimolo asked.

"On the big land to the south at the top middle," he explained with an easy smile.

Zamimolo couldn't help himself. He liked the young man.

"So you're the one who went to school in two places?" Linpint asked.

"Yes. It was a great opportunity. It also was very hard work," Bul replied.

"We had to help in a war against the Alitukit. Do they war with your Nola Nola?" Zamimolo asked.

"They are a strange people who usually keep to themselves. They are so distrustful that sometimes, I think, they war when it's not a good idea. They have a group of men who are brilliant, but they keep most of their brilliance to themselves. We think they invite us to school to teach us, so they can learn about our people and what our plans are. We have to answer questions sometimes that make us uncomfortable. From schooling we gain information that is valuable to us. We've even thought of teaching our own Nola Nola, but we just don't have the fullness of the knowledge they have. We could hurt more than help if we tried to do it ourselves. So, we take it as we get it. The students are away from the fighting. Wars usually involve borders, and the school is far inside the borders. We Nola Nola are too distant from them for them to worry about borders with us."

Bul took a deep breath. "Picota," he said quieter, "Will you meet with me tomorrow?"

She looked into his eyes and replied, "I will be here. You may meet me here after your morning meal. I would like very much to spend time with you."

"Until morning, then," he replied. "It was nice to meet you," he said to the older men but tried to include all with his glance. Then, he was gone.

"He seems to be a good choice, Picota," Linpint said with a smile.

Picota smiled and remained silent. She had already concluded, if no negatives appeared while they grew to know each other, she wanted Bul for her husband, even if it meant living with his people.

Zamimolo saw Ventumoko sitting in the far back of the tent with Ahah right in front of him, leaning against him. His arms were around her. She had no stringed shell.

"What is the meaning of this?" Zamimolo asked.

"It's my doing," Ahah replied quickly. "When I saw Ventumoko looking at the women there, and saw them looking at him, it made me realize that I've been a fool. I've loved him all along—just didn't realize it. I don't want to lose him to anyone." She looked over her shoulder and leaned back so she could see his face. Her hands held his, which still were held together as his arms circled her. They smiled at each other.

"Well, that's interesting," Linpint said, stupefied. "Never would I have expected this."

"Me either," Zamimolo echoed.

The camp settled down with each finding his or her bedding.

When the sun was up, Nob, Tas, and Picota were eager to see what the day would bring. Picota took extra time combing her hair and picking her teeth. Picota used some of the water from the water gourd to wash her face, since there was no bathing lake nearby. Ahah made the morning meal by boiling water and pouring it over grains they'd rolled flat on stones and portioned into pouches for quick meals. Tas ate his quickly and left to find his new friend, Kib, who lived far south by the snow-covered mountains. Nob still wondered whether he'd find anyone so he headed for the large gathering place. Ventumoko and Ahah left to replenish the firewood supply.

Linpint looked at Zamimolo while he finished eating. "It looks like Ventumoko and Ahah are settled, Picota and Bul seem well matched, Tas seems taken with the girl from the south, but I wonder about Nob."

"He seems like a fish out of water, flopping and twisting, unsure to find his place. I'm not sure what's wrong."

Down at the gathering place, Nob looked around but only saw a small group of young men talking. He decided to join them.

"Hi, come join us," one called to him.

"Thanks. I don't seem to be doing very well here," Nob admitted.

"It depends on what you want," another said.

"Yes, I'm supposed to find a wife, but I'd rather explore this land, and a wife with children would be a burden. I want to be free to travel all over this land and learn more about it. That's what we've been talking about," a tall young man with dark wavy hair and blue eyes said with enthusiasm. "I cannot find anyone interested."

"That sounds exciting," Nob admitted. "You are seriously talking about not joining with a wife but instead traveling the country and living from what you hunt each day or so?"

"Exactly!"

"That sounds like a dream come true. I would love to spend my life that way."

"My name is Po. I come from the Nola Nola. Why not become an adventurer with me. If either of us wants, later is a time for joining with a woman, after we've satisfied our desire to explore."

"Well, Po, my name is Nob. I come from the People and we are not long in this land. I know very little about how to survive here, although I've been learning since I arrived. I might be a burden."

"If you're willing to learn, you'd be no burden but rather someone with whom to share the land and what it has to teach. I've lived here all my life. I've been to the Nola Nola School, called the School of the South, and the Alitukit School. I've done my trial of valor alone and been successful. That taught much about this land, but the knowledge I gained is not wide with respect to this entire land. I want to know more."

"When do you leave, Po?"

"I'm ready to leave as soon as I find someone who wants to take the same journey."

Without further thought, Nob said, "I'm ready."

"Do you want to get your supplies and meet back here as soon as you have them?"

"Yes!" Nob said. "I do need to turn in this stringed shell and tell the elders in our group. Then, I'll return here."

"I will be here when you return," Po said.

The others were shocked that two people looking for wives would depart to journey through the large land to the south. To them it was preposterous, but interesting. They kept standing together talking, hoping some girls would come to the same place and notice them.

Nob arrived back at the camp and found Zamimolo and Linpint had gone somewhere. Ventumoko and Ahah had returned with arms full of wood, so he told them his plan.

"You cannot leave without talking to Linpint or Zamimolo," Ahah said horrified.

"That is due respect for elders," Ventumoko said.

"For the first time in my life, I know what I want to do. I'm going. Please ask that they not follow me. I am a man, not a child. I am doing what I want to do."

Ventumoko and Ahah watched him leave. They were horrified, saddened, and slightly fearful of the reactions they'd get from Linpint and Zamimolo, but they could not stop Nob.

Nob found Po at the gathering place and the two left immediately heading southeast for the mountains on a small path Po knew led to the interior.

When Zamimolo and Linpint arrived back at the camp, they learned about Nob. Both were furious, but they realized there was no way Ventumoko and Ahah could have stopped him, short of tying him up. They also realized there would be no way to track the young man, even if they thought they should.

"This is a strange trip we've taken," Zamimolo said aloud, more in reflection than to any of the other three. "We come here with five people searching for a wife or husband. Two of ours found each other, two are about the reason they came here, and one has gone off on an exploration of this land. How strange we must look to others!"

"Zami," Linpint said sharply, "I don't think anyone at this gathering is interested in our group—individual members of it, yes, but the group as a whole, no."

"You're probably right," he conceded with a nod to Linpint. "You two are also right. There was nothing you could have done to stop him." His shock was subsiding and self-control returning.

By the seventh day it was decided that Picota and Bul would join when they reached the land of the Nola Nola. Tas planned to leave for the far south to join with Kib. They would travel by boat on the sea. Zamimolo, Linpint, Ventumoko, and Ahah would trek with Picota to the land of the Nola Nola to attend her joining with Bul.

When they awakened on the eighth day, the sun was shining in a clear sky. To reduce the weight of their backpacks, Linpint and Zamimolo chose to leave their tent skins with the Bekwaboati for their elders or widows. Their gesture brought them great goodwill, for it was unexpected and something for which the recipients were tremendously grateful. They began a trek through the mountains to the west. Fortunately, Bul knew the way through the mountains and was familiar with the signs of danger. For days they'd trek to the north and finally find lower ground that would eventually take them to the land of the Nola Nola.

On their trek only once did they come near a long-tooth cat. Bul spotted it and led them out of its danger circle, as he called it. There were a few snakes and one stomping elephant angry over something, but otherwise the trek was uneventful and quite beautiful. With four hunters, they ate well each day.

When at last they approached the land of the Nola Nola, Bul stopped at a high point of the land and picked up a conch shell. He put it to his mouth and blew on it. The People were startled at the amount of noise it made. Before long people at a very far distance began to come toward them. When they came together in the valley, Bul threw his arms around his father, Coshiga, and his mother, Tuna.

Bul made the introductions of the elders and others, leaving Picota to the last. "This is the woman with whom I will join. Her name is Picota. These are her People. They will stay to see our joining ceremony. Will you make a place for them?" he asked his parents.

"Of course, by tonight there will be shelter provided. Welcome to the land of the Nola Nola," Coshiga said, extending his open hands palm out to each of the male People. Each of the men held their hands out in the same manner until they touched palms.

213

Tuna was stunned. She looked carefully at Picota. Picota looked just like Olomaru-mia except for the color of her hair. Tuna couldn't wait to tell Olomaru-mia. Her friend would be sitting under her shelter from the sun. Bul had used the word People, which is the same term Olomaru-mia always used when talking of them. They had to be of the same group. The resemblance was her clue.

Coshiga led the people to the village gathering place to meet Chief Uvela. The touching of palms from outstretched arms occurred again. They were led to the council place where they could sit and talk of the trip and the wife search for Bul and Po, who had not returned. Bul let them know that Po had decided to explore the big land and would not soon return.

While they were meeting Tuna ran over and sat by Olomaru-mia. Without a word but gesturing with her eyes and the tilt of her head, she asked Olomaru-mia whether anyone was in the shelter.

"No one," Olomaru-mia said aloud.

"Mia, Bul has brought home his future wife. She looks exactly like you except she has brown hair. Her skin is white like yours. She has blue eyes. She wears clothing that covers her."

Olomaru-mia felt anxiety pour over her like overspray from a waterfall. She asked, "Is she alone or accompanied?"

"There are two men with her. They'll be there for the joining ceremony. The next morning they'll leave."

"Tuna, can you possibly find out the names of the men with her?"

"That's easy. When they were introduced to us one of the elders was named Linpint. The other name is something that starts with zzzzzz and ends with olo like the front part of your name. I can't remember it. The third is young and his name is Ventu- Ventu-something. There's another girl, too."

Olomaru-mia covered her face with her hands. "There's no way I can avoid this, my friend. Zamimolo is the man with whom I was to join. I cannot just hide until they are joined and the strangers leave. This is awkward." She paused. "Tuna, can you help here? Can you tell the one named Zamimolo that Olomaru-mia lives here, and for her safety, she asks you please do not acknowledge knowing her. Assure him I have a happy life."

"I will do it, Mia. I will keep this secret until my death. Fear not."

Good to her word, Tuna kept watch and on his way back from the privy, she caught up with Zamimolo and conveyed Olomaru-mia's messages.

"You are serious that it could be unsafe for me to recognize her."

"Yes, customs here are different. She has had a happy and very good life, but if there were a challenge because of her knowing you, it could be a terrible thing. The Nola Nola could go to war over something less."

"Tell her I'll keep my knowledge to myself. I will also tell Linpint to fail to make the connection. Tell her to relax. We would do nothing to hurt her. Which one of these men is her husband?"

"Thank you," Tuna said with a smile of relief. "Her husband and abductor is Mechalu." She slipped away and back to calm her friend. She trusted Zamimolo to be good to his word.

Zamimolo didn't see Olomaru-mia until the evening meal. Despite the white hair and additional weight she'd gained, he would have known her anywhere. Instinctively, he wanted to race to her, embrace, and kiss her. He knew how inappropriate that would be. Her eyes went straight to his, and in his face he assured her he would not give away that they knew each other. He thought to himself that the old Southern Kapotonok man's warning must have something to do with the need for them not to know each other. He had seen Mechalu and, despite his preconceptions, he found the man to be a good leader and a kind and thoughtful man. He could find no fault with him except what he had done long, long ago.

Observing her sitting at her place to eat, Zamimolo noticed children coming to Olomaru-mia and they clearly loved her. Some were obviously her children; others were clearly not, but they all demonstrated a fondness for her that showed. He found that touching, and it made him realize she had contributed much to this group of children. Much of what she contributed was openly returned. Part of his belly ripped apart. Then he remembered Ba's feelings of second best. Ba surely wasn't second. He felt part of the winds of change. For some reason Wisdom let him see for himself that Olomaru-mia was happy and loved. He tried to ease himself but found it increasingly difficult.

Olomaru-mia was studying Picota. Olomaru-mia only knew what she looked like from her image reflected from water. The water image was never very clear. The girl had pale skin like hers, hair like hers, and eyes that weren't brown. She clearly was attracted to Bul, and he to her. Olomaru-mia's eyes locked onto Picota's left hand. Colitoba, Olomaru-mia's mother, had a knuckle that was frozen. Try as she might it would not bend. Olomaru-mia had the same trait. And, she noticed, so did Picota. Olomaru-mia again felt the icy feel of the waterfall overspray. She had to be looking at her sister. Olomaru-mia felt that the winds of change were swirling around her. It was not a comfortable feeling, and she wondered whether it ever was comfortable when they blew. So much was awkward. While the icy feelings washed over her, little children were choosing to sit in her lap or lean against her shoulder. They distracted her back to her life with the Nola Nola and she responded to them as usual: tickling some, talking to some, hugging some, brushing through the hair of some with her fingers. Adults would ask her a question or say something to her. It was as if two different realities existed briefly, and it disturbed her. She was happy in her life.

The arrival of Bul and Picota came too late in the day to permit them to join that evening. Instead, the joining ceremony would take place the next day. Darkness had begun to descend on the little village. Mechalu came over to Linpint and Zamimolo.

"Would you like to accompany me on a hunt early tomorrow?"

"That sounds wonderful," Ventumoko replied, assuming he was included, while Zamimolo and Linpint nodded their enthusiasm.

Immediately, Mechalu readjusted his thoughts to include Ventumoko. "Then, at first light we'll go!" he said, glad to be going on a hunt. He decided to go to the mountains of the west since no one lived there and they only rarely hunted in that place.

Quiet settled on the village one hut at a time. The hut made for Zamimolo, Linpint, Ventumoko, and the two women of the People was large and as well done as the huts the Nola Nola used. After they left, Bul and Picota would use it.

Early, just before first light, Zamimolo had gotten up, unable to sleep. He went outside and climbed a gentle slope a little distance to the northwest behind the gathering place. There was a narrow path that looked to be an animal trail. Certainly it wasn't one that was well traveled. He heard a noise behind him, and he slipped into the trees hoping to remain undetected. Zamimolo observed Mechalu walking quietly on the path. He had no weapons. He went to the end of the path, a large rock protruded from the land. It overlooked a deep valley. Mechalu stood on the edge of the rock promontory and began to sing. He moved his feet almost imperceptibly. He sang in words that Zamimolo had never heard from anyone. Zamimolo was utterly fascinated. He almost held his breath. Mechalu's song took a while. He sang with his eyes closed and his arms raised to the sky. His head was elevated so that if his eyes were opened, he'd be looking at the sky. He sang in the spirit language of the Alitukit to their god of the sky. Their god, he was convinced, was the source of his great luck. Master Alikuat had taught him in his fourth year about their great serpent sky god. Students who weren't Alitukit were not taught of this god. He never understood why Master Alikuat had taught him, but he was pleased with the great luck it brought him. He sang with his whole heart, carefully, so none other could observe. Then, when he finished, he fastened his opened eyes on the view of the sky and smiled. Mechalu finally lowered his arms, turned, and walked back down the path home. Zamimolo waited and then went back down the same path, but instead of turning off where Mechalu did, he walked further south and exited at a very different place.

At first light the hunters shrugged on their backpacks, secured their knives to their waistbands, picked up their spears and assembled at the gathering place. They headed to the mountains of the southwest. It was a bright day with no clouds. Gin and Mur of the Nola Nola decided to accompany them. As they approached the forested slope, the shadows brought a dark contrast to which their eyes had to adjust. There was the usual forest noise that indicated that the inhabitants knew people were entering their place, as alarms went out in warning.

The men were careful to step gently to avoid cracking twigs while they kept alert for snakes, spiders, and any other danger. They used their noses to smell for anything unusual. They looked in places where there were no leaves for tracks. At the top of the first hill, Mechalu gave a hand signal to halt. He pointed to a meadow at the top of the next hill. The men looked, but only Ventumoko could see the colorful creature walking man-like in that meadow. It was yellow and red and had a beak like an eagle, a beak large enough to be seen from a distance. He had never seen anything like it. The men squatted down to observe. Finally, Zamimolo and Linpint saw the object but their eyes were not sharp enough to see the detail. Whatever it was, it was big.

Mechalu was dumbfounded. "You won't believe what we might kill!"

"What is that?" Ventumoko whispered.

"It's a terror bird and it has some problem. Notice there are no other terror birds with it. They run in packs. This one keeps moving in circles. We might be able to kill it. No one among the Nola Nola has killed a terror bird in my lifetime. They are out of place to be here. They belong much farther to the south. Let's go."

Mechalu didn't ask whether the others wanted to kill the terror bird, he just took command of the group of hunters. They all quickly stood up and followed him. They descended to the valley and quickly ascended the hillside to the meadow. The bird was still there. At the edge they squatted down and watched the bird carefully. Mechalu used his hand to show them to stay in position and be still. He stood with a slingshot at the ready. He flung some pebbles to the bird's left. Clearly, the bird heard the sound. By doing this several times to the right and left of the bird, Mechalu and the hunters realized the bird could not see from its left eye. To see what was on the left required the bird to turn its head far to the left and possibly have to move its position as well. Anyone to the left of the bird had a reasonable opportunity to spear the bird. They realized its beak and the claws on its feet were something to be reckoned with.

Seen up close, Zamimolo and Linpint could see why they had been warned about the destructive capacity of these birds. Seeing one was something. Finding ten of them together, a human stood little chance against them—unless, as they'd been told, they could climb a tree. Now, there were six hunters and one terror bird. There was a definite chance of success.

Mechalu cleared the leaves off the dirt at their feet. He showed the position of the bird with a pebble. He showed a position to the right side of the bird. He pointed to himself. The men of the People were impressed that he put himself in the greatest way of harm. Then with pebbles, he showed each individual his position. Ventumoko, the least experienced hunter was placed on the bird's left side between the legs and tail. Using hand signals, Mechalu showed how each would creep around the border of the meadow and then at his waving signal, they'd all begin a slow approach to the terror bird. Once he whistled, all were to shout and approach the bird for the kill. His request for questions yielded no response. He gave the signal to circle the border of the meadow.

As they began to circle the forest, the bird appeared somewhat anxious. It began to look around to see whether it could identify the environmental difference it detected. It lowered its head and swung it from side to side. It shook. Then, it began to rattle its beak by clamping the upper and lower parts of the beak together. The sound ran shivers down the backs of the men. The bird was preparing to defend itself or take the initiative to fight. So far they didn't think the bird had seen them.

Linpint was in position and while crouched down he marveled at the bird. Its red and yellow plumage was extraordinary. The brownish red on its back was good camouflage. The red plumage of its chest and under wings, if those little appendages could be called wings, was a brilliant contrast. The bird could raise red and yellow feathers into a huge crown on its head or leave the feathers flattened, horizontal to the ground. He knew the Kapotonoks stood in awe of these birds, and faced with just one, he did too.

Finally, all saw Mechalu waving. They began their approach. The bird spotted Mur. His position was just to the left of the front of the bird. The bird sprang into a run, clicking its beak loudly. Mur had never seen a terror bird, let alone had one charge him. He froze. His mind could not process fast enough the information needed to respond. While the bird charged, the men began to shout and follow, spears raised and ready. They raced to the bird and while the bird literally bit Mur in half ripping apart his midsection, every one of the men buried their spears deeply into the bird. They killed a terror bird at the loss of a man. There was no celebratory afterkill. The men went to Mur and determined he was in fact dead. Since, Ventumoko and Gin were the youngest of the men, they were given the grim task of carrying Mur's body to the village for burial and calling the aid of other hunters to come butcher and carry home the meat for eating.

With great respect, Ventumoko and Gin carefully gathered the halves of Mur's body and traveled as quickly as they could to comply with Mechalu's orders. They both felt a strange combination of sadness at the loss of Mur mixed with amazement tinged with joy that they'd participated in a terror bird kill. They moved very quickly back to the village.

When they arrived back at the village, grieving began and a burial group was formed to dig a grave. The young men managed to get four other young men to bring their hunting gear to go with them to bring the meat to the village. It was early enough that the women hadn't begun to cook meat for the evening meal, so they decided to wait for the bird meat. They spent the morning gathering greens and fruit to accompany the meat.

As Mechalu, Zamimolo, and Linpint stood by the terror bird, Zamimolo said, "I don't know whether the Nola Nola collect trophies, but I would very much like for each of the People to have a claw from this bird. There are enough claws for each hunter to have one. It would make a good ornament to tie on a piece of leather around the neck."

"I agree," Mechalu said. "Let's begin to cut them out now. I'll gather for my people and you gather for yours."

The men set about cutting claws from the bird.

Hunters returned with arms loaded with strong grass bags into which the meat could be put to make it easier to carry. By the time they arrived at the kill site, the bird had been bled and its gut removed. Carrion-eating birds were arriving drawn by the scent. Far in the distance, a long-tooth cat let out a horrible growling, screeching noise. The men knew they had limited time before there would be war for the remains of the bird. The hunters quickly carved off as much meat as would fit into the bags. Hunters would begin the trek home as soon as a bag was filled. They did not try to take all the meat from the bird—only what could be consumed by the Nola Nola and guests before it spoiled. The rest would feed wildlife in the forest. This went against what Zamimolo and Linpint had been taught, but this was a different land. Meat spoiled easier than back where it was colder and their caves made it possible to dry and keep meat well.

The hunters finally loaded meat into the last bag and they headed off as a group, leaving behind the great bird who lost his life because he lost his eye. As Zamimolo walked with the burden down the trail, he thought again that he was among the fortunate to see such a creature and participate in a kill. He in no way wanted to have the opportunity again. Zamimolo had seen what it did to Mur in the blink of an eye. The bird was truly well named.

Back in the village, Mur had been put to rest in the place of burial. The driftwood was his valor prize. He found it on an island in the western sea to which he'd swum to explore. It was shaped incredibly like the head of a seabird. The Chief placed it in Mur's hand. The Chief spoke briefly about the man Mur was, and then the grave was covered and they returned to the village. When the hunters were all back, people gathered to hear the men tell of the hunt. Women took the meat, cleaned it, and put it on skewers to roast. There would be a feast that night despite the grieving. Picota had gone to be painted with dots by the women of the village.

Zamimolo noticed that Mechalu left for the little densely wooded hill that was part of the slope down to the sea. It was the place where Zamimolo had observed Mechalu singing before the light appeared on the day of the hunt. He decided to follow to see what he could see. He noticed that Mechalu walked up to the stone promontory. He watched as Mechalu raised his arms to the sky, shut his eyes, moved his feet slightly, and began to sing. He was fascinated. What Mechalu did was exactly what he'd done the last time he observed him. Zamimolo found the fire that had been kept an ember in his belly was expanding to flames. Here was this man who had stolen Olomaru-mia from him and her People. He brought her to this place where she had to adjust to a different life. Mechalu definitely had Olomaru-mia's love now. However, despite her current happiness, Mechalu had hurt him, her, and the People by his selfish act of the past. Hatred rose from his gut and made a bitter taste in his mouth. He wondered how this man dared to exhibit such happiness, confidence, power, after having done what he did. Zamimolo hid carefully until Mechalu had returned home. Then, he turned and went back to the village trying to stifle the rage that was rising. Later when he saw Mechalu back in the village, Zamimolo walked back to the place he'd seen Mechalu singing. He stood on the same spot where Mechalu sang. Mechalu had stood at a dropoff that was far deeper than Zamimolo expected. Zamimolo realized that the drop was from their level almost to the level of the sea, as if a great shock had split off part of the land and changed a slope to a sheer drop. It unnerved him. He wondered why Mechalu chose that place to sing whatever song he sang. He wondered to whom the song was addressed and what it said.

The village gathered for the feast of terror bird. It had been cooking ever since the meat arrived and the people were eager to try this new meat. Only a few women were hidden away in the women's hut, while Picota was being prepared for the joining ceremony. Ahma and Tuna carried food to those in the hut. All of the people enjoyed the meat, whether it was because of what it was or the way it was seasoned and the flavor of the meat itself, no one could say. It was just delicious. Of course, the starchy roots and the greens along with ripe fruit served with it added just the right mix. Nobody was doing much talking during the evening meal. They spent their time eating and returning for more.

Finally the joining ceremony began. Picota came out led by the women. She was wrapped in a beautiful, brightly colored feathered cape. Zamimolo and the other People were fascinated by the dots painted all over her face and legs, which was all they could see. The two had a brief joining ceremony conducted by Chief Uvela, where they agreed to remain together for life, and they left for their temporary hut. Despite the earlier burial, musicians brought their instruments and soon began to play and there was much music and dancing to celebrate the joining.

"Let's try it," Ventumoko said to Ahah, pulling her up by her hand.

"I don't know how to do this," she demurred to no avail.

Somehow the beat of the music pulled them in and they danced. There was no preplanned step to the dance of the Nola Nola. They did what the music led them to do. They could feel it leading, directing the movement of their bodies, arms, legs, and feet. The two dancers from the People fit well among the Nola Nola dancers. To the fascination of Linpint and Zamimolo, they danced unto each other as well as part of the group. There was light laughter as people who didn't dance chatted among themselves. Off to the side, Olomaru-mia told stories to the children. Occasionally a child would drift off to dance and then return. Mechalu danced for a while and then he went to sit by Olomaru-mia. Zamimolo observed her stroking him, and his hands on her. Were it any other people on the world, he'd have smiled a knowing smile. For these two people, he could not smile.

Zamimolo intentionally began to drink more water than normal. As the Nola Nola began to head for their huts, he downed more water and headed for his hut. Linpint observed the behavior. At first Linpint thought he drank to be sure to arise at first light, so they could get on the trek home. They knew how to find the village of the Southern Kapotonok by following the seashore, so the earlier they got up the better. The trek would take them days. But Linpint was troubled by something he could not fully grasp, so he also drank more water than normal.

A good while before first light, Zamimolo and Linpint awakened. Zamimolo took his spear and left the hut. He went to the place he exited the hill beyond where Mechalu would enter it. Zamimolo climbed the hill up the path he could just barely see. Linpint, without Zamimolo's knowledge, followed him. Zamimolo hid off the path just before the promontory. He hardly breathed. Linpint saw him, having moved quickly not to lose sight of him. He hid lower down the path. In a short time Mechalu came up the path. He made noise that no hunter would make, not interested in game or feeling a need to conceal himself. He reached the promontory and began his song and dance. In extreme silence with sweat beading his forehead, Zamimolo swiftly crept up behind Mechalu, lifted his spear with both hands, and rammed him at the base of his skull, sending Mechalu flying over the dropoff. He went without a sound. Linpint was horrified. He watched Zamimolo, whose eyes were bulging, walk back down the path, spear in hand. He walked fast back to the hut. Linpint, who had come without a weapon, followed at some distance. He had learned what he came to learn, but not anything at all that he wanted to know. He stopped at the privy. He was sickened. Part of him understood the rage Zamimolo had carried for so long. Part of him could not fathom his carrying it for so long. He couldn't grasp how Zamimolo could have acted on his rage. Had it, yes. But for so long? Acted on it after all that time? It was all wrong. Somewhere, he was convinced, there came a time for forgiveness. Something had gone terribly wrong. Zamimolo should have forgiven Mechalu long ago. Soon, they would arise to go home. Linpint longed for home. He had to adjust to what he'd seen. He struggled. His mind web wasn't designed to work problems like this one.

At first light, the People gathered checking to be sure they had all their supplies. They headed down to the seashore where they'd trek west until the shoreline turned to the north. They'd follow the shore until they arrived at the Southern Kapotonok village, from where they'd know the way home.

Zamimolo thought he'd have lost his animosity toward Mechalu once he was dead, but he didn't feel any real release. Instead he felt guilty for any unhappiness he might have caused Olomaru-mia, something Zamimolo hadn't considered until the deed was done. He headed home with one enormous question that rested on his shoulders as a mighty burden: had he done the right thing? Way down deep Zamimolo had a sense that he should not have done what he did, but he kept pushing that suggestion away. He was confident that in time the burden would lift.

Ahah and Ventumoko walked along having no idea that one of their members had committed murder that morning. All seemed lighthearted and adventurous as they walked hand-in-hand along the seashore. It was a beautiful day. Linpint carried a burden also. He had spied on his friend. That was acceptable but not often done. His burden was knowledge of what occurred. There was no one to tell. To talk to Zamimolo he reasoned would avail nothing. It wasn't something that could be undone, and he knew Zamimolo well enough to feel certain that when he thought on what he'd done, it would bother him until he died. Linpint purposed to say nothing about his knowledge, because he could not see in any way revealing it would make anything better for anyone. He wished he hadn't followed his friend. He grit his teeth realizing that it is not possible to unknow something.

They made progress along the seashore. By the evening meal, all were feeling the effect of the sun on their faces and skin. Living in the mountains, they had sun, but there were plenty of trees that gave them shade, so they were not exposed all day. The older men had begun to tan since their migration, and both the younger ones had skin slightly darker than their People parents had. Nevertheless, the sun had done some damage. They decided to camp to make some protection for their skin before continuing on. Ventumoko decided to see whether he could find some crabs while Ahah made hats from long leafed plants that grew nearby. He carried the one grass bag he had in his backpack, and a stick he found in the treed area where they planned to camp. The stick would hold the crab until he could grab it at the back leg to avoid being pinched. Linpint discovered that he could wrap his bedding cover around his shoulders to keep the sun off. All he needed was to poke two holes in the covering so he could tie it with a piece of leather and not have to hold it with his hands. It would add no weight since he already carried it. The others chose to make their coverings serve both purposes also.

Ventumoko returned to the camp later with a bag full of crabs. He had pulled off the pinchers, because they were hanging up in the grass basket. Ahah was delighted. She carried the boiling bag to a small fall of water at the base of a rock hill and filled it. Zamimolo had started a fire and she hung the bag on a tree branch. She took the bent wood tongs and lifted hot rocks to place in the boiling bag.

They sat around the fire with their sun-protection problems solved and ate.

"These crabs are delicious!" Ahah said holding one in her left hand while digging out meat with fingers on her right hand.

"When we first ate them," Linpint said, "I couldn't believe we would eat such a hard, ugly thing. "They no longer look ugly to me. I really like them. Thanks, Ventumoko."

"You're welcome, Father," he replied with a grin.

"What do you young people think of all this traveling?" Zamimolo asked.

Ahah looked up. "I am so glad we've had the opportunities we've had. Traveling to see different parts of this land gives us such a bigger view of what this place is where we live. Being in the villages of other people makes me realize that people are very similar but there are some unexpected and significant differences. Seeing the terror bird and actually eating meat from one is an experience I'll probably never have again. It's been wonderful. And sharing it with Ventumoko is even better." She smiled, leaning against him.

"I'm glad you can see the value of some adventure," Linpint said. "Some people don't want to leave the comfort of home, and they miss a lot that way. I think it odd that the Nola Nola have their young men go off alone from one sea to the other with just a knife, to find their prize of valor. I would think some young men would be afraid to venture into the wilds of this place alone. I would think that some would fall victim to predators."

"Chief Uvela told me that they lost about two young men every five years. That is an enormous sacrifice," Zamimolo said. "I think it a very unwise practice."

"Well," Ahah said, "That must have been what the abductor of Olomaru-mia was doing. Do you think he could have been Nola Nola?"

"Very possibly," Linpint answered quickly, uneasy at his intentional deception. "Or, there may be more people on the big land to the south who do the same thing. We'll probably never know."

"I can't wait to get home to drill out my claw. It's a large object to wear around my neck, but I'll manage," Ventumoko said, smiling.

"Now, don't you go boasting, Son," Linpint said.

"I won't, Father," he promised, "I know that this claw is mine because someone died."

"That is Wisdom speaking," Zamimolo said.

"Is that a boat?" Ahah asked.

"Where?" Zamimolo asked.

"Out there far to the right."

"Oh, I see it," Ventumoko said.

"Cover the fire quickly," Linpint said. "We have no idea who these people are. I've heard there are some people who capture people to sell as slaves for rowing. They live on the east side of the big land far to the south, beyond what they call the big river. We need to conceal this camp site and move up the hill to hide."

Before he finished, Ahah dumped cooking water on the hearth to quench the fire while Ventumoko buried crab shells and the evidence of a fire. Zamimolo swept footprints from the sand, and the People carefully gathered their things and slipped into the forest. They watched. The boat came nearer. It was a large boat made of two carved-out logs attached by crosspieces. It had a large red sail and on the sides there was white painting that meant nothing to the People. They watched as the boat seemed to be traveling the shoreline observing. By nightfall it was well past them. For the night they remained in the forest for safety.

Olomaru-mia's concern began to grow. Mechalu was gone before she arose, and it was late enough that women were preparing the evening meal. When he left on hunting trips he took his spear, backpack, and other items that remained in the hut. She rarely left the protection of the hut, because it was so important to Mechalu, but she got up and went to find the Chief.

"Mechalu has been gone since before first light. His hunting tools remain untouched. Have you seen Chief Uvela?" she asked Ahma.

"He's over there with Dooderido and Bul. Are you worried, Mia?"

"Yes, I am. This has never happened since we've been here. Thank you, Ahma," she said and walked over to where the men were talking. She stood before them until the Chief looked up. He knew she was there, but he did not choose to acknowledge her presence quickly.

"Yes, Olomaru-mia. What is it?"

"Mechalu left this morning before first light as he often does. Usually he returns for the morning meal, but today he did not. I thought he might have gone hunting, but his spear and backpack have not been touched. As late as it is, I worry."

"Olomaru-mia, Mechalu is a competent man. He can take care of himself. If he hasn't returned by council meeting, we'll discuss hunting for him, but you can be sure he'll be here."

She lowered her head to him and thanked him, not at all comfortable that Mechalu would be back by the council meeting. She turned and went back to her hut.

At the council meeting the Chief noticed that Mechalu was not present. Even he became moderately alarmed. He said to the council members, "Mechalu went out before first light without his hunting gear. He has not returned. Do any of you have information that would explain this?"

The Nola Nola looked around at the faces of each other. This was indeed unusual.

At length Quigmot, Tuna and Bul's brother, said, "I have seen him outside before first light. I followed him once, as have some of the other people my age. He goes to the hill over there." He pointed to the west. "He stands on a rock at the end of the path, holds his arms to the sky, and sings a song that has strange words. He dances. He does that with his eyes shut. It's fascinating."

"I've seen it," Kumonib added.

"I have also seen him do that," Too added.

Older adults looked at the young people and then at each other. What was Mechalu doing up there? They wondered about him. Some mused that too often they thought they knew someone only to discover something unexpected that made them wonder if they knew the person at all.

The Chief was aware that there was a dropoff on the hill to the west. That's why children were warned carefully of the dangers and told until they reached the age of thirteen, they were not allowed to go there. He said, "After the morning meal, I will meet with those of you who wish to search for Mechalu. It is not clear that he has met with harm. There are other reasons he might be missing. We will search after the morning meal." With a sense of dread and contrary to the assurance he tried to project, the Chief had an uneasiness that Mechalu breathed no longer. He ached deep in his bones that he'd lost one son and had just lost another.

Olomaru-mia was heartbroken. She had come to love Mechalu with a deep and abiding love. If anything had happened to him, she would be devastated. She wondered if he were dead how she could continue to live. He was her life. The news of his dancing and singing with his eyes shut by a dangerous dropoff startled her. Why do such a dangerous thing? It wasn't like him. Before the meeting ended she picked up Lah, took Kenu by the hand, and returned to her hut. She hugged the children and put them into their sleeping places. Somehow, deep down inside, she felt an emptiness, a virtual certainty that Mechalu would not return alive. She had felt it all day. Mechalu was predictable. This was extremely far from his normal behavior. She wept silently in the hut, alone.

Her other children came bursting into the hut. Once inside they went to their sleeping places. Mohu, her fifteen-year-old, came to her, knelt beside her, and whispered, "Is Father dead?"

Olomaru-mia put her hand on the boy's shoulder and whispered back truthfully, "Son, I don't know."

"Do I have your permission to search for him?" he asked.

"That is up to your grandfather, Mohu. Ask the Chief."

Mohu crawled over to his sleeping place and lay there wondering. His older brothers were gone on their trial of valor. He was the oldest son at home. He felt much responsibility. There were eight children presently in the hut. He wondered if he had the ability, if his father had died, to take care of all those children. It was overwhelming. He had already begun to prepare for his trial of valor. He fell asleep with worry in his thoughts.

Olomaru-mia lay down. She could see the form of Mohu. She knew he understood fully the possibility that his father was gone. She knew he recognized his responsibility in such a case to the family, while his plans were to leave soon for his trial of valor. Her heart ached for him. She prepared herself for the winds of change. She could feel the breeze blowing. She knew that before the end of the next day change would sweep upon them and all would have to adjust. She fell into a fitful sleep.

After the morning meal, the Chief assembled all who were willing to search. He accepted Mohu, as Olomaru-mia was sure he would. He sent Mohu with a group of men who went southwest. He sent a larger search group to the land below the dropoff. He decided to wait to see what the searchers would report before sending others in different directions. He told all groups to return by high sun. Coshiga climbed the hill to the west. He found the trail that was little used. He followed it to the promontory where Mechalu went in the mornings before the sun rose. He stood on the rock and looked down. He could see the body of Mechalu. It lay on the rocks below. There was no movement.

Coshiga wondered why anyone would stand on that rock to sing and dance with his eyes shut. It seemed as if he asked for a fall. Mechalu seemed to have better sense than that. He shook his head. Coshiga saw some of the searchers and called to them. They looked up.

"On the rocks directly below me," he called and pointed down.

It took some time for the men to get there, but they found the body. They examined it. He lay on his back. The back of his head, neck, and his back were badly damaged from the impact with the rocks.

"He died fast," one man muttered.

It was not easy, but the men took Mechalu's body by the arms and legs and carried him to more level ground away from the rocks. Instead of going for a stretcher, the largest of the men, Rur, picked up the body and carried it across his shoulders. They headed back to the village.

Grieving began when the men approached the village. Very quickly a group of men began to dig. One ran to the southwest to call in the searchers.

Chief Uvela looked at Rur who had just laid the body near the Chief's hut. "Will you do it?" he asked.

Rur looked back, remembering. "You get the children out of the way."

"Ahma," the Chief said, "Bring his children here, all of them."

"What about Olomaru-mia?"

"Tell her someone will come for her and to wait in her hut."

Ahma left to do his bidding.

After the children gathered, Rur went to Mechalu's hut. He entered.

Olomaru-mia was startled. "What is it Rur?"

Rur looked at her and shut his thoughts to what he had to do. He said, "Mechalu's body has been found. You are a prize of valor. You must be buried with him. We don't bury people alive." With those words, he put his large hands around her throat and strangled her. She did not defend herself. Rur then lifted her body in his arms and carried her to the Chief's hut and laid her beside Mechalu. The Nola Nola were aghast. No one, certainly not the women, dared to say anything that showed disapproval. It was almost too much for Ahma. She loved Olomaru-mia dearly and had just experienced the death of her son. She was overcome at what the Nola Nola had done to Mia.

228

She was certain they could have let her live. They could have found a way. She was very careful, however, not to let her thoughts show. Olomaru-mia and Mechalu's children were stunned at the sight of both their parents lying dead before them. They suspended emotion from lack of comprehension and understanding. It was too much to grasp the meaning of such an event.

Some of the people headed for the hillside to the east. There were some flowers blooming and for some people, flowers would be added to the grave before it was filled in. Others without a word realized they could express something by adding flowers to the grave, so they quickly joined the gathering. They would return one by one with arms full of colorful flowers. Even Ahma participated.

Tuna knew that Lah, Kenu, and the youngest twin boys were walking about unsupervised, so she took on the responsibility of watching them. She dried her eyes and looked after the youngest children as an honor to Olomaru-mia. She'd weep later.

Mohu returned from the search to find not one but both his parents' bodies ready for burial. He was horrified.

"Who did this evil deed?" he demanded.

The Chief grabbed him by the arm and pulled him into his hut.

"Silence. You do not sit in judgment here. Olomaru-mia was Mechalu's prize of valor. The prize of valor is buried with the man who owns it. We don't bury people alive, Mohu. You are about to leave for your trial. Be careful what you choose."

Mohu was stunned. He stared at his grandfather with his mouth partly opened. He knew the prize of valor was buried with the dead man, but those things were not living, breathing people loved by their children. What manner of people were the Nola Nola, he wondered. He was born to them but didn't feel part of them at that moment. He felt utterly foreign.

"I will take care of the children to see that each has a suitable home. It is not your responsibility. You will leave in seven days for your trial. Prepare for that."

They walked solemnly to the burial ground. A deep grave was dug. Mechalu's body was laid in the ground first with his head to the west and his feet to the east. Olomaru-mia's body was next to his. Someone had circled Mechalu's arms around her and put her hand on his side. As people arrived, they tossed their flowers down onto the two who lay there together. There was palpable grief, but unlike the typical burial, no one permitted their crying to raise a noise. Women had a legitimate reason, fearing if anyone thought they wept for Olomaru-mia or felt it unfair that she had been killed, they might be beaten.

Chief Uvela stood before the open grave looking at the flowers that completely covered the bodies of Mechalu and Olomaru-mia. He looked up to the sky. "Creator of All," he said, "This is the second son I've buried. If I've done something wrong, show me, so I can stop these unnatural deaths from occurring. Keep us safe. From this day no young man on his trial of valor is permitted to abduct any other person." He could say no more. He loved Olomaru-mia and to see her and Mechalu gone together was tearing him apart.

After the ceremony, the Chief went from family to family until he had divided up the children, all except for Mohu, who would remain at Mechalu's hut until he left for his trial.

The little group returning from the wife/husband search finally reached the village of the Southern Kapotonok. Ti had already returned with a wife, Qi. They arrived in time for the evening meal. This brought good laughter to the group as if Linpint and Zamimolo liked Kapotonok food so well they always arrived in time for dinner. It wasn't far from the truth.

Ventumoko and Ahah were surprised at how at home their parents were in this village the two of them had never seen. Everyone appeared to know them and like them. Each was shown to a place to sit and they were served food on great leaves. The food was wonderful: boiled fresh fish just caught in nets and roasted peccary, vegetable greens boiled and served in coconut shells, and a wide variety of colorful fruit. The trekkers filled themselves almost too full.

"Ti told us about the search. Did it go well for your People?" Chief Paaku asked, his voice cracking, age showing.

"These two we brought from home decided they really wanted each other," Linpint commented, followed by laughter from the Kapotonok while Linpint pulled a fish bone from his mouth. "Picota found a man of the Nola Nola and we went with her to his village. That is where we were before we arrived here. Tas found a wife and left for the far south, and Nob. What can I say about Nob? He seemed not to fit well. He didn't know what to do. He met a young man who wanted to adventure through the big country to the south, and Nob decided to accompany him."

"Some men are designed for adventure and exploring. They seem unable to remain confined to a village. The allure of the big land to the south is strong. You two have some of that desire for adventure in you. Those are the people who bring understanding to others of things in this land we don't know—if they return," the Chief said.

The people chatted until dark and the Chief gave them a place to sleep in a tent shelter next to his hut. After the morning meal, they left on the path that would take them over the mountains to home.

When the People arrived back home, they went through the armadillo barrier and many raced from the lowland and cave to meet them. Some wondered why Ahah and Ventumoko had been unsuccessful.

Ventumoko found Lomah and hugged her.

"Why is it, my Son, that you are here with no wife?"

"Mother," he chuckled, "Ahah is my wife!"

"No," she said with mock disbelief. "That is a good source of humor. The two of you had to go that distance to know what everyone here has known for years?"

Ahah arrived and overheard the conversation. She added, "It took my seeing the hungry eyes of others on Ventumoko for me to realize how I loved him and how jealous I was of others who might want to take him from me. I was terribly blind, but I see much clearer now."

Lomah hugged her. "Welcome home, Daughter," she beamed. "Ba," she called to Ahah's mother, "Welcome your son."

"Oh, no, you took that trip to discover that you were meant for each other?"

Ahah hugged Ba and replied, "Yes, Mother. I was slow to see what was right before me."

"I'm glad you finally saw. Welcome home, Ventumoko."

"Thank you, Mother," he said using that term for the first time with Ba. "We had a wonderful trip, saw so much of the land, and are very happy to be home."

"Where is Picota?" Colitoba called as she waddled down from the hill where the cave was located.

Linpint sprinted to her and told her, "Picota found a very good man of the Nola Nola. He wanted to remain with the Nola Nola. She decided to join him to live there, so we accompanied her there to be sure all was well. She joined with Bul the night before we left. She lives on the big land to the south on the central part of the north by the sea."

"Does she appear happy?"

"Colitoba, Picota seems very, very happy."

"I will miss her."

Linpint put his arms around her. "She will miss her People, but she will be happy among the Nola Nola with Bul." Linpint wondered whether he should tell her about Olomaru-mia, but he decided he'd better discuss it with Zamimolo before sharing that information.

Later Zamimolo and Linpint walked to the burial ground. The view from there was the best in the area. They listened for the drums. There was no sound that night.

"I had an awkward thought when Colitoba came to ask about Picota. I did not tell her about Olomaru-mia. Should we share that?" he asked.

"I don't think so. For some reason, Mia didn't want us to recognize her, so that may hold true for all the People. She'll eventually realize that Picota is her sister, but she'll handle the information however best for the two of them. I think we should leave things of the past to the past." Zamimolo walked over to a smooth rock and climbed to the top of it. He threw his arms wide as if to embrace the sea.

Linpint leaned against a tree and wondered why, after what he'd seen Zami do, he asked him for counsel on anything. Then he realized that Zami was still Zami, regardless of what he'd done. Before the trip he depended on Zami. There was no real reason not to do the same after the trip. He felt confused, and momentarily covered his face with his hands. Inwardly he wanted to scream out to Zami asking him why he did such an evil deed. It still sickened Linpint. But, Linpint reasoned, he'd done evil deeds in his life, so he really had no right to consider himself better somehow. He also knew that Mechalu had pushed Zami to the ends of his coping with life for a long time. He thought how Ba saved Zami from himself, bringing him to life in some ways. Their life was good. He thought how he had spied upon his friend. Had he not done that, he'd never have known. Was his knowledge what soured his present view? Linpint knew Zami had no desire for any other murder. Zami had been sober on the trek from the land of the Nola Nola to their home. His normal lighthearted, natural humor absented itself in silence. The young people didn't seem to notice the change, but Linpint and Zamimolo knew each other very well. Linpint could hear Zami speaking. Some of the words were clear to him.

Zamimolo stood on the rock and opened his heart to Wisdom: "I have done evil in your sight, Wisdom. I killed a man for something he did far in the past. I hated him for a long time, since he stole Mia from me. There was no need for me to murder. Mia was happy with him and he seemed a good man. Who was I to take his life? That is what the old man warned me against, and I didn't understand. Wisdom, I hurt Mia by doing that. I didn't think at the time that I would deprive her of a husband. The last thing I wanted to do was deprive her of happiness. Wisdom, I ask you to forgive me for murder. I ask you to take good care of Mia. She deserves all the good that life can bring. Forgive me for hurting her." He drew his arms close to him, put them to his face, and wept. He got to his knees and continued to weep. He'd held it in since the murder. Finally, he'd acknowledged his evil to Wisdom. He hoped to bury his evil at the burying ground. He flattened himself on the rock that still retained heat from the sun.

Linpint didn't know whether to leave or remain there. Because Zamimolo had no apparent sense of his environment, Linpint decided to remain to watch over him. Finally, Zamimolo returned to a kneeling position. He threw his arms wide again and looked to the sky. "Never again will I murder. I swear upon my own life, Wisdom, I shall never murder again." Slowly, he got to his feet and turned, realizing that Linpint was there.

"You heard?" he asked.

"I heard some of your words, Zami. The wind blows here, so I didn't hear all. I understand what happened."

"I feel like a broken man, unfit somehow."

"Zami, you did something evil. You've determined never to repeat it. You've asked Wisdom for forgiveness. You have done all you can do. You have responsibilities in life. Take them seriously. Go to Ba. Treat her well. Do good for your People. Wisdom has forgiven you."

"How do you know?"

"Because you're still among us—healthy."

"Oh."

"Let's go back."

The two began the walk to the cave.

It had been two years since the great wife/husband search. Linpint and Numing were at the Southern Kapotonok village when a boat appeared on the horizon. Many watched to see whether it appeared to be a threat. It came toward them. The boat had no sail. It was made from a tree trunk that had been burned and dug out and burned and dug out until the huge tree trunk made a large boat that could be rowed. The boat continued towards them. The occupants took a rock that was tied by rope to another rock and tossed one of the rocks over the side of the boat. That anchored the boat, so that the occupants could leave the boat and come to shore, knowing the boat would not drift off. Leaving the boat was one very dark skinned person, one with dark tan skin and one a little lighter, and one with very pale skin. Linpint recognized Picota.

Chief Hirmit, very old but still well, hobbled from his seat to hold his hands open and out in greeting. The greeting was returned by the man with the dark tan skin.

"Welcome to our village," Chief Hirmit said, his voice firmer and far younger looking than his body.

"Thank you," Coshiga said.

"I am Chief Hirmit, Chief of the Southern Kapotonok. Our land runs from the river north of here all the way to the place where this narrow land connects with the big land to the south. We are part of a large group of people who live from places in the big land to the south to the big land to the north. We have lived here since our ancestors crossed the western sea. That was before time."

"I am Coshiga, traveler and now part of the Nola Nola. This is my wife, Tuna. The small woman with the very dark skin smiled. This is my son Bul, and this is his wife, Picota. We come here searching for the leaves to chew that keep one from fatigue when traveling. Are any available here or do you have some for which we could trade?"

The Chief made it clear they would discuss that soon. He asked about weapons and they assured him their weapons were on the boat.

Picota recognized Linpint and Numing, but she did not show it to them, except with her eyes. Meetings like this were formal and all were to be silent until the initial formalities concluded.

At length the Chief led all of them to the gathering place. He served them fruit and nuts. The food was finally removed and the Chief asked what they had to trade.

"I have a clear crystal of great beauty," Coshiga said and then asked, "Do you have a supply of the leaves we seek?"

The old Chief nodded.

"I would like to see the crystal," the old Chief said, his eyes fixed on the sand.

Coshiga looked at Bul. He said nothing.

"I'll get it, Father." He stood up and trotted off to the boat. He returned with a small leather wrapped object. He didn't know whether to hand it to his father or the Chief.

"Hand it to the Chief, Son," Coshiga said smiling.

Chief Hirmit opened the wrapping and looked at the crystal inside. In all his years he'd never seen anything like the crystal. He held it up to the light and then tasted it. He didn't understand it, had no idea how or where it originated, what its use might be, but he wanted it. Coshiga observed him as he studied it. He had been a trader. He knew how to determine the interest of someone studying an object.

"We have leaves in supply that we dry. They fill pouches when we trek. Chewing them keeps us filled with energy."

"I need a pouch this size," Coshiga showed with his hands. "For that I will trade the crystal."

"That's almost all we have," Chief Hirmit said plaintively.

Coshiga sat patiently, looking at the Chief. He said nothing. For quite some time no one made a sound.

Finally, Chief Hirmit looked at Tomarghi, "Get a new pouch and fill it as he showed. I will have this crystal."

Once the exchange was made, the people gathered in different groups and talked before the Nola Nola would leave. Linpint saw Picota at the water's edge and he walked towards her.

"Picota, are you well?"

"Yes, I adore Bul. I am so happy we found each other. How are the People?"

"They are fine. How are Chief Uvela, Mechalu, and Olomaru-mia?"

"That's a sad story. The Chief is not well. Mechalu had a place where he used to sing and dance on an outcropping on a hill. He'd do it with his eyes shut! Apparently, he went there and while he had his eyes shut, he fell and died. In addition, long ago it seems Mechalu abducted Olomaru-mia. He was on his trial of manhood and he had to find a prize that showed he was a man. He abducted her for his prize of valor. The problem with that choice is that when a man of the Nola Nola dies, his prize of valor is buried with him." She paused. Tears fell down her cheeks.

Linpint's stomach sickened.

Picota wiped her tears and continued. "One of the Nola Nola killed her so she could be buried with Mechalu. They killed her, because they don't bury people alive. The children were separated among the villagers to raise. I understand that Olomaru-mia was greatly loved. She was the storyteller. Nobody talks much about her or Mechalu because it brings too much sadness. Linpint, she was my sister."

"I know," he replied. "I will not ever share this with the People." Linpint wanted to retch, but he controlled himself. He did not want her to see the turmoil that raged within him. In many ways he wished he hadn't asked. Why, he wondered, did he seek after information that later turned into burdens for him?

"Nor will I, if I ever see them again," she whispered.

Bul joined Picota and Linpint. "I remember you," he said. "How are you?"

"Doing well, and you?" Linpint affected a lighthearted spirit that he did not feel.

"Couldn't be better. We're off on a journey with our traveling parents. They've been everywhere. This time we're heading north to explore the big land to the north. Fortunately, I went to the Alitukit School, so they know me. They won't give us trouble for passing their land."

"I wish you a good trip."

"Thank you. I'm sure we'll have one. Coshiga loves to travel, so this time we decided to go with him. We're enjoying it so far."

Linpint watched them wade out to the boat and get in. He watched as they rowed along the shoreline. True to his word, he did not share the information about Olomaru-mia with Numing. Some knowledge was to be a burden, and he reasoned this was another one of those.

That night, Linpint lay on his bedding on the sand with the starry sky above him. He tried to make sense of Mechalu's abduction of Olomaru-mia and Zamimolo's murder of Mechalu. He and Zami knew Mechalu had been murdered. He and the Nola Nola knew Olomaru-mia had been killed. Only he knew the whole story. The Wise One of the Southern Kapotonok knew it all, but he was dead. When he and Zamimolo died, he hoped none of the People would ever know what happened.

He wondered whether he should tell Zamimolo what he learned from Picota about Olomaru-mia. For a long while he let his thoughts stop racing through his mind web. He relaxed. Finally, he knew. He wouldn't share that horrifying news with Zamimolo. What would be the point? Zamimolo already had burden enough over what he'd done. To add this might be a burden he could not endure. Linpint purposed to carry the burden himself. People would continue with no need to hear this, no need for this story to spread the evil by sharing the thought that murder was an option, no need to vilify Zamimolo's name for all the ages. The deed was evil on the part of both men. Best if it were left unspoken. By leaving it unsaid, it also would not give others birth to the idea that they might do what Zamimolo had done. Some day that idea would be born among the People as it had with Zamimolo, but he would not be the one to spread it now. Zamimolo's idea a few years ago on the rock at the burying ground was a good one. Bury the knowledge in the burying ground. Linpint made a burying ground in his mind web. He would bury it there and live his life according to Wisdom's plan—for the good of the People.

Bibliography

Achilli, A., Perego, U.A., Bravi, C. M., Coble, M. D., Kong, Q.-P., Woodward, S. R., Salas, A., Terroni, A., Bandelt, H.-J., "The Phylogeny of the Four Pan-American MtDNA Haplogroups: Implications for Evolutionary and disease Studies," *PLoS ONE*, 3(3) e1764.

Adovasio, J.M., Page, J., *The First Americans: In Pursuit of Archaeology's Greatest Mystery*, Modern Library, Imprint of Random House, 2003.

Ao, H., Deng, C, Dekkers, M. J., Sun, Y., Liu, Q., Zhu, R., "Pleistocene environmental evolution in the Nihewan Basin and implications for early human colonization of North China," *Quaternary International*, 2010.

Bae, C., "The late Middle Pleistocene hominin fossil record of eastern Asia: Synthesis and review," *American Journal of Physical Anthropology*, supplement yearbook, 143(51), 2010.

Bae, K., "Origin and patterns of the Upper Paleolithic industries in the Korean Peninsula and movement of modern humans in East Asia," *Quaternary International*, 211(1-2), 2010.

Bailey, S., "A Closer Look at Neanderthal Postcanine Dental Morphology: The Mandibular Dentition," *The Anatomical Record*, 269, 2002.

Bailey, S. E., Wu, L., "A comparative dental metrical and morphological analysis of a Middle Pleistocene hominin maxilla from Chaoxian (Chaohu), China," *Quaternary International*, 211(1-2), 2010.

Bailliet, G., Rothhammer, F., Garnese, F. R., Bravi, C. M., and Bianchi, N. O., "Founder Mitochondrial Haplotypes in Amerindian Populations," *The Journal of Human Genetics*, 54, 1994.

Balter, M., "Child Burial Provides Rare Glimpse of Early Americans," *ScienceNOW*, Feb 2011.

Banks, W., D'Errico, F., Dibble, H., Krishtalka, L., West, D., Olszewski, D., Peterson, A., Anderson, D., Gillam, J., Montet-White, A., Crucifix, M., Marean, C., Sánchez-Goñi, M., Wohlfarth, B., Vanhaeran, M., "Eco-Cultural Niche Modeling: New Tools for Reconstructing the Geography and Ecology of Past Human Populations," *PaleoAnthropology*, 2006.

Bannai, M., Ohashi, J., Harihara, S., Takahashi, Y., Juji, T., Omoto, K., Tokunaga, K., "Analysis of HLA genes and haplotypes in Ainu (from Hokkaido, northern Japan) supports the premise that they descent from Upper Paleolithic populations of East Asia," *Tissue Antigens*, 55, 2000.

Bengston, John D., *In Hot Pursuit of Language in Prehistory*, John Benjamin Publishing Co., The Netherlands, 2008.

Benson, L., Lund, S., Smoot, J., Rhode, D., Spencer, R., Verosub, K., Louderback, L., Johnson, C., "The rise and fall of Lake Bonneville between 45 and 10.5 ka," *Quaternary International*, 235(1-2), 2009.

Boeskorov, G. G., "The North of Eastern Siberia: Refuge of Mammoth Fauna in the Holocene," *Gondwana Research*, 7(2) 2004, available in English in ScienceDirect, November 2005

Bogoras, W., *The Jesup North Pacific Expedition, Memoir of the American Museum of Natural History, Volume VII, The Chukchee*, Leiden, E. J. Brill, Ltd., Printers and Publishers, 1975 (reprint of the 1904-1909 edition). This publication is routinely referred to as *The Chukchee*.

Bolnick, D. A., Shook, B. A, Campbell, L, Goddard, I, "Problematic Use of Greenberg's Linguistic Classification of the Americas in Studies of Native American Genetic Variation," *American Journal of Human Genetics,* 75(3): 2004.

Bonnichsen, R. Lepper, B., Stanford, D., Waters, M., *Paleoamerican Origins: Beyond Clovis,* Center for the Study of the First Americans, Department of Anthropology, Texas A&M University, 2005.

Borrell, B., "Bon Voyage, Caveman," *Archaeology,* 63(3), May/June 2010. (possibility of seafaring by *Homo erectus* at 130,000 ya)

Bower, B., "Asian Trek," *Science News,* 171(14), 4/7/2007.

Bower, B., "Ancient hominids may have been seafarers," *Science News,* 177(3), 2010.

Brantingham, P., Gao, X., Madsen, D., Bettinger, R., Elston, R., " The initial Upper Paleolithic at Shuidonggou, Northwestern China," in *The Early Upper Paleolithic beyond Western Europe,* Ed. By Brantingham, P, Juhn, S., and Kerry, K., 2004.

Cannon, M. D., "Explaining variability in Early Paleoindian foraging," *Quaternary International,* 191(1), 2008.

Carmel, James H., "Homo sapiens and Neanderthals lived in peace, say researchers," The Times, United Kingdom, http://www.thetimes.co.uk/tto/news/world/middleeaste/article3552845.ece, 2013.

Catto, N., "Quaternary floral and faunal asssemblages: Ecological and taphonomical investigations," *Quaternary International,* 233(2), 2011.

Catto, N., "Quaternary landscape evolution: Interplay of climate, tectonics, geomorphology, and natural hazards," *Quaternary International,* 233(1), 2011.

Chauhan, P. R., "Large mammal fossil occurrences and associated archaeological evidence in Pleistocene contexts of peninsular India and Sri Lanka," *Quaternary International,* 192(1), 2008.

Chen, C., An, J, Chen, H., "Analysis of the Xionanhai lithic assemblage, excavated in 1978," *Quaternary International,* 211(1-2), 2010.

Chen, X-Y., Cui, G-H., Yang, J-X., "Threatened fishes of the world: *Pseudobagrus medianalis* (Regan) 1904 (Bagridae), *Environmental Biology of Fishes,* 81(3), 2008.

Chlachula, J., Drozdov, N., Ovodov, N., "Last Interglacial peopling of Siberia: the Middle Palaeolithic site Ust'-Izhul', the upper Yenisei area," *Boreas,* 32, 2003.

Ciochon, R., Bettis III, A., "Asian *Homo erectus* converges in time," *Nature,* 458, March 2009

Cione, A., Tonni, E., Soibelzon, L., "The Broken Zig-Zag: Late Cenozoic large mammal and tortoise extinction in South America," *Rev. Mus. Argentino Cienc. Nat.,* n.s., 5(1), 2003.

Coppens, Y., Tseveendorj, D., Demeter, F., Turbat, T., and Giscard, P., "Discovery of an archaic *Homo sapiens* skullcap in Northeast Mongolia," *Comptes Rendus Palevol,* 7(1), Feb 2008. Note: The findings are that the skullcap shows similarities with Neanderthals, Chinese Homo erectus, and West/Far East archaic Homo sapiens. Dating is possible late Pleistocene.

Corvinus, G., "*Homo erectus* in East and Southeast Asia, and the questions of the age of the species and its association with stone artifacts, with special attention to handaxe-like tools," *Quaternary International,* 117, 2004.

Coxe, W., *The Russian Discoveries Between Asia and America,* Readex Microprint Corp., 1966, copy of Coxe's document from 1780.

Cremo, M., Thompson, R., *Forbidden Archaeology: The Hidden History of the Human Race,* Unlimited Resources, 1996-2011.

Delluc, B., Delluc, G., "Art Paléolithique, saisons et climats," *Comtes Rendus Palevol,* 5, 2006.

Demske, D., Heumann, G., Granoszewski, W., Nita, M., Mamakowa, K., Tarasov, P., Oberhänsli, H., "Late glacial and Holocene vegetation and regional climate variability evidenced in high-resolution pollen records from Lake Baikal," *Global and Planetary Change,* 46, 2005.

Derbeneva, O. A., Sukernik, R. I., Volodko, N.V., Hosseini, S. H., Lott, M. T., and Wallace, D. C., "Analysis of Mitochondrial DNA Diversity in the Aleuts of the Commander Islands and Its Implications for the Genetic History of Beringia," *The American Journal of Human Genetics,* 71(2): 2002.

Derenko, M., Malyarchuk, B., Grzybowski, T., Denisove, G., Dambueva, I., Perkova, M., Dorzhu, C., Luzina, F., Lee, H. K., Vanecek, T., Villems, R., and Zakharov, I., "Phylogeographic analysis of Mitochondrial DNA in Northern Asian Populations," *The American Journal of Human Genetics,* 81, November 2007.

Dickinson, William R., "Geological perspectives on the Monte Verde archaeological site in Chile and pre-Clovis coastal migration in the Americas," *Quaternary Research,* 76, 201-210, 2011.

Dillehay, T. D., *The Settlement of the Americas: A New Prehistory,* Basic Books of the Perseus Books Group, 2000.

Dixon, E. J. and G. S. Smith, "Broken canines from Alaskan cave deposits: re-evaluating evidence for domesticated dog and early humans in Alaska." *American Antiquity,* 51(2): 1986.

Doelman, T., "Flexibility and Creativity in Microblade Core Manufacture in Southern Primorye, Far East Russia," *Asian Perspectives,* 47(2), 2009.

Elliott, D.K., *Dynamics of Extinction,* John Wiley & Sons, New York, 1986.

Elston, Robert G., Brantingham, P. Jeffrey, "Microlithic Technology in Northern Asia: A Risk-Minimizing Strategy of the Late Paleolithic and Early Holocene," *Archaeological Papers of the American Anghropological Association,* 12 (1) 103-116, 2002.

Erlandson, J., Moss, M., Des Lauriers, M., "Life on the edge: early maritime cultures of the Pacific coast of North America, *Quaternary Science Reviews,* 27, 2008.

Etler, D., "The Fossil Evidence for Human Evolution in Asia," *Annual Review of Anthropology,* 25, 1996.

Etler, D., "*Homo erectus* in East Asia: Human Ancestor or Evolutionary Dead-End?" *Athena Review,* 4(1) [Cannot locate year. The author is from Department of Anthropology, Cabrillio College, Aptos, California.]

Etler, D., Crummett, T., Wolpoff, M., "Longgupo: Early Homo Colonizer or Late Pliocene Lufengpithecus Survivor in South China?" *Human Evolution,* 16(1-12), 2001.

Fell, B., *America B.C.,* Artisan Publishers, 2010.

Fiedel, Stuart J., "Older Than We Thought: Implications of Corrected Dates for Paleoindians," *American Antiquity,* 64(1), 1999.

Finlayson, Clive, *The HUMANS WHO WENT EXTINCT, Why Neanderthals died out and we survived.* Oxford University Press, 2009.

Fitzhugh, W., "Stone Shamans and Flying Deer of Northern Mongolia: Deer Goddess of Siberia or Chimera of the Steppe?" *Arctic Anthropology,* 46(1-2) 2009.

Flam, F.: "Red hair a part of the Neanderthal genetic profile" *The Philadelphia Inquirer,* October 26, 2007.

Flannery, T., *The Eternal Frontier,* Atlantic Monthly Press, New York, 2001.

Forster, P., Harding, R., Torroni, A., and Bandelt, H. J., "Origin and Evolution of Native American mtDNA Variation: A Reappraisal," *The American Journal of Human Genetics,* 59(4): 1996.

Froehle, A., Churchill, S., "Energetic Competition Between Neandertals and Anatomically Modern Humans," *PaleoAnthropology,* 2009.

Gilbert, M. T. P., Jenkins, D. L., Götherstrom, A., Naveran, N. Sanchez, J. J., Hofreiter, M., Thomsen, P. F., Binladen, J., Higham, T. F. G., Yohe, R. M., II, Parr, R. Cummings, L. S. Willerslev, E., "DNA from Pre-Clovis Human Coprolites in Oregon, North America," *Science Express,* April 2008.

Gilligan, I., "The Prehistoric Development of clothing: Archaeological Implications of a thermal Model," *Journal of Archaeological Method Theory,* 17, 2010.

Gladyshev, S., Olsen, J., Tabarev, A., Kuzmin, Y., "Peleoenvironment. The Stone Age: Chronology and Periodization of Upper Paleolithic Sites in Mongolia." *Archaeology Ethnology & Anthropology of Eurasia,* 38(3), 2010.

Goebel, T., Waters, M., Dikova, M., "The Archaeology of Ushki Lake, Kamchatka, and the Pleistocene Peopling of the Americas," *Science,* 301(5632), 2003.

Goebel, T., et al, "The Late Pleistocene Dispersal of Modern Humans in the Americas, *Science,* 319, 1497, 2008.

Goldberg, E., Chebykin, E., Zhuchenko, N., Vorobyeva, S., Stepanova, O., Khlystov, O., Ivanov, E., Weinberg, E, Gvozdkov, A., "Uranium isotopes as proxies of the Lake Baikal watershed (East Siberia) during the past 150 ka," *Palaeogeography, Palaeoclimatology, Palaeoecology,* 294(1-2) August 2010.

Golubenko, M. V., Stepanov, V. A., Gubina, M. A., Zhadanov, S. I., Ossipova, L. Pl, Damba, L., Voevoda, M. I., Dipierri, J. E., Villems, R., Malhi, R. S., Beringian "Standstill and Spread of Native American Founders," *PLoS ONE* 2(9): eB29. doi;10.1371/journal.pone.0000829.

Goodyear, Albert C., "Evidence for Pre-Clovis Sites in the Eastern United States," unpublished and undated manuscript, [no longer has active link]

Grayson, D., Meltzer, D., "A requiem for North American overkill," *Journal of Archaeological Science,* 30(5), 2003.

Grove, C., "Ice-age child's remains discovered in Interior," *Anchorage Daily News,* 2/24/2011

Hall, R., "Cenozoic plate tectonic reconstruction of SE Asia," from Fraser, L., Matthews, S., Murphy, R., (Eds.), *Petroleum Geology of Southeast Asia,* Geological Society of London Special Publication 26, 1997.

Hapgood, C., *Maps of the Ancient Sea Kings,* Adventures Unlimited Press, 1966.

Hardaker, C., *The First American: the Suppressed Story of the People Who Discovered the New World,* New Page Books, 2007.

Haynes, C. V., Jr., "Younger Dryas 'Black mats' and the Rancholabrean termination in North America," *National Academy of Sciences of the USA,* 2008. (See also: for photographs http://www.georgehoward.net/Vance%20 Haynes'%20Black%20Mat.htm)

Henry, A., Brooks, A., Piperno, D., "Microfossils in calculus demonstrate consumption of plants and cooked foods in Neanderthal diets," *Proceedings of the National Academy of Sciences,* 108(2), 2010.

Hoffecker, J. F., *A Prehistory of the North: Human Settlement of the Higher Latitudes,* Rutgers University Press, New Brunswick, New Jersey, 2005.

Honeychurch, W., Amartuvshin, C., "Hinterlands, Urban Centers, and Mobile Settings: The 'New' Old World Archaeology from the Eurasian Steppe," *Asian Perspectives,* 46(1) 2007.

Hopkins, D. M., Matthews, J. V, Jr., Schweger, C. E., Young, S. B., *Paleoecology of Beringia,* Academic Press, New York, 1982.

Huyghe, P., *Columbus Was Last: From 200,000 B.C. To 1492 A Heretical History of Who Was First,* Anomalist Books, 1992.

Igarashi, Y., Zharov, A., "Climate and vegetation change during the late Pleistocene and early Holocene in Sakhalin and Hokkaido, northeast Asia," *Quaternary International,* xxx (in process), 2011.

Inman, M.: "Neanderthals Had Same 'Language Gene' as Modern Humans," *National Geographic News,* October 18, 2007, http://news.nationalgeo-graphic.com/news/2007/10/071018-neandertal-gene.html

Irwin-Williams, Cynthia, "Dilemma Posed by Uranium-Series Dates on Archaeologically Significant Bones from Valsequillo, Puebla, Mexico," *Earth and Planetary Science Letters* 6 (1969) 237-244, North Holland Publishing Comp., Amsterdam.

Jackinsky, M., "Evidence of woolly mammoths on Peninsula grows," *Alaska Daily News,* 3/13/2011.

Jackson, Jr., L. E., Wilson, M. C., "The Ice-Free Corridor Revisited," *Geotimes,* Feb. 2004.

Jiang, Y-E., Chen, X-Y, Yang, J-X., "Threatened fishes of the world: Yunnanilus discoloris Zhou & He 1989 (Cobitidae)," *Environmental Biology of Fishes,* 86(1), 2009.

Jin, J. J. H., Shipman, P., "documenting natural wear on antlers: A first step in identifying use-wear on purported antler tools," *Quaternary International,* 211(1-2) 2010.

Johnson, John F. C., *Chugach Legends: Stories and Photographs of the Chugach Region,* Chugach Alaska Corporation, 1984.

Joling, D., "Warming brings unwelcome change to Alaska villages," *Anchorage Daily News,* 3/27/ 2011.

Joseph, F., *Discovering the Mysteries of Ancient America: Lost History and Legends, Unearthed and Explored,* New Page Books, 2006.

Khenzykhenova, F., "Paleoenvironments of Palaeolithic humans in the Baikal region," *Quaternary International,* 179(1), 2008.

Khenzykhenova, F., Sato, T., Lipnina, E., Medvedev, G., Kato, H., Kogai, S., Maximenko, K., Novosel'zeva, V., "Upper paleolithic mammal fauna of the Baikal region, east Siberia (new data)," *Quaternary International,* 231, 2011.

Kienast, F., Schirrmeister, L., Siegert, C., Tarasov, P., "Palaeobotanical evidence for warm summers in the East Siberian Arctic during the last cold stage," *Quaternary Research,* 63(3), 2005.

King, G., Bailey, G., "Tectonics and human evolution," *Antiquity,* 80, 2006.

Klein, H. S., Schiffner, D. C., "The Current Debate about the Origins of the Paleoindian of America," *Journal of Social History,* 37(2), Winter 2003.

Kolomiets, V. L., Gladyshev, S. A., Bezrukova, E. V., Rybin, E. P., Letunova, P. P., Abzaeva, A. A., "Paleoenvironment The Stone Age: Environment and human behavior in northern Mongolia during the Upper Pleistocene," *Archaeology, Ethnology, and Anthropology of Eurasia,* 37(1), 2009.

Komatsu, G., Olsen, J., Ormo, J., Di. Achille, G., Kring, D., Matsui T., "The Tsenkher structure in the Gobi-Altai, Mongolia: Geomorphological hints of an impact origin," *Geomorphology,* 74(1-4), March 2006.

Kornfeld, M., Larson, M. L., "Bonebeds and other myths: Paleoindian to Archaic transition on North American Great Plains and Rocky Mountains," *Quaternary International,* 191(1), 2008.

Krause, J., Orlando, L., Serre, D., Viola, B., Prüfer, K., Richards, M., Hublin, J., Hänni, C., Derevianko, A., Pääbo, S., "Neanderthals in central Asia and Siberia," *Nature LETTERS,* 449, 2007.

Kunz, Michael, M. Bever, C. Adkins, *The Mesa Site: Paleoindians above the Arctic Circle,* U. S. Department of the Interior, Bureau of Land Management, BLM-Alaska Open File Report 86, BLM/AK/ST-03/001+8100+020, April 2003.

Kurochkin, E., Kuzmin, Y., Antoshchenko-Olenev, I., Zabelin, V., Krivonogov, S., Nohrina, T., Lbova, L., Burr, G, and Cruz, R., "The timing of ostrich existence in Central Asia: AMS 14C age of eggshells from Mongolia and southern Siberia (a pilot study)," *Nuclear Instruments and Methods in Physics Research Section B: Beam Interactions with Materials and Atoms,* 268(7-8), April 2010. Kuzmin, Y., Orlova, L., "Radiocarbon chronology and environment of woolly mammoth (*Mammuthus primigenius* Blum.) in northern Asia: results and perspectives," *Earth-Science Reviews,* 68, 2004.

Kuzmin, Y., Richards, M., Yoneda, M., "Paleodietary Patterning and Radiocarbon Dating of Neolithic Populations in the Primorye Province, Russian Far East," *Ancient Biomolecules,* 4(2), 2002.

Lam, Y. M., Brunson, K, Meadow, R., Yuan, J., "Integrating taphonomy into the practice of zooarchaeology in China," *Quaternary International,* 211(1-2), 2010.

Lee, H., "Paleoenvironment: The Stone Age. Projectile Points and Their Implications," *Archaeology Ethnology & Anthropology of Eurasia,* 38(3), 2010.

Lell, J. T., Sukernik, R. I., Starikovskaya, Y. B., Su, B., Jin, L., Schurr, T. G., Underhill, P. A., Wallace, D. C., "The Dual Origin and Siberian Affinities of Native American Y Chromosomes," *The American Journal of Human Genetics,* 70, 2002.

Lister, A., Bahn, P. G., *Mammoths: Giants of the Ice Age,* Richard Green Publisher, 1994.

Liu, W., Wu, X., Pei, S., Wu, Xiujie, Norton, C. J., "Huanglong Cave: A Late Pleistocene human fossil site in Hubei Province, China," *Quaternary International,* 211(1-2), 2010.

Lu, X., Xiong, D., Chen, C., "Threatened fishes of the world: *Sinocyclocheilus grahami* (Regan 1904) (Cyprinidae)," *Environmental Biology of Fishes,* 85(2), 2009.

Ma, S., Wang, Y., Xu, L., "Taxonomic and Phylogenetic Studies on the Genus Muntiacus," *Acta Theriologica Sinica* VI(3) 1986. (Translated by Will Downs, Dept of Geology, Bilby Research Center, Northern Arizona Univ., 1991)

Macé, F., "Human Rhythm and Divine Rhythm in Ainu Epics," *Diogenes,* 46(1), 1998.

Marwick, b., "Biogeography of Middle Pleistocene hominins in mainland Southeast Asia: A review of current evidence," *Quaternary International,* 202(1-2), 2009.

Mednikova, M., Dobrovolskaya, M., Buzhilova, A., Kandinov, M., "A Fossil Human Humerus from Khvalynsk: Morphology and Taxonomy," *Archaeology Ethnology & Anthropology of Eurasia,* 38(1), 2010.

Meltzer, D., *First Peoples in a New World: Colonizing Ice Age America*, University of California Press, 2009.

Merriwether, D. A., Hall, W. W., Vahine, A., and Ferrell, R. E., "mtDNA Variation Indicates Mongolia May Have Been the Source for the Founding Population for the New World," *The American Journal of Human Genetics*, 59, 1996.

Mol, D., de Vos, J., van der Plicht, J., "The presence and extinction of *Elephas antiquus* Falconer and Cautley, 1847, in Europe," *Quaternary International*, 169-170, 2007.

Moncel, M., "Oldest human expansions in Eurasia: Favouring and limiting factors," *Quaternary International*, 223-4, 2010.

Mueller, Tom, "Ice Baby: Secrets of a Frozen Mammoth," National Geographic, 215, 5, May 2009

Naske, C.-M., Slotnick, H. E., *Alaska A History of the 49th State*, 2nd Ed., University of Oklahoma Press, Norman, 1979.

Neel, J. V., Biggar, R. J., Sukernik, R. I., "Virologic and genetic studies relate Amerind origins to the indigenous people of the Mongolia/Manchuria/ southeastern Siberia region," *Proceedings of the National Academy of Sciences, USA*, 91, 1994.

Nikolskiy, P. A., Basilyan, A. E., Sulerzhitsky, L. D., and Pitulko, V. V., "Prelude to the extinction: Revision of the Achchagyl-Allaikha and Berelyokh mass accumulations of mammoth," *Quaternary International*, 219(1-2), 2010.

Norton, C. J., "The nature of megafaunal extinctions during the MIS 3-2 transition in Japan," *Quaternary International*, 211(1-2), 2010.

Norton, C. J., Jin, J. J. H., "Hominin morphological and behavioral variation in eastern Asia and Australasia: current perspectives," *Quaternary International*, 211(1-2), 2010.

O'Neill, D., *The Last Giant of Beringia: The Mystery of the Bering Land Bridge*, Westview Press, Perseus Books Group, New York, 2004.

Oppenheimer, S., "The great arc of dispersal of modern humans: Africa to Australia," *Quaternary International*, 202(1-2), 2009.

Orlova, L. A., Kuzmin, Y. V., Stuart, A. J., Tikhonov, A. N., "Chronology and environment of woolly mammoth (Mammuthus primigenius Blumenbach) extinction in northern Asia," *The World of Elephants – International Congress*, Rome 2001.

Osipov, E., Khlystov, O., "Glaciers and meltwater flux to Lake Baikal during the Last Glacial Maximum," *Palaeogeography, Palaeoclimatology, Palaeoecology*, 294(1-2) 2010.

Palombo, M. R., "Quaternary mammal communities at a glance," *Quaternary International*, 212(2), 2010.

Park, S., "L'hominidé du Pléistocène supérieur en Corée, *L'anthropologie*, 110, 2006.

Pei, S., Gao, X., Feng, X., Chen, F., Dennell, R., "Lithic assemblage from the Jingshuiwan Paleolithic site of the early Late Pleistocene in the Three Gorges, China," *Quaternary International*, 211(1-2), January 2010.

Pietrusewsky, M., "A multivariate analysis of measurements recorded in early and more modern crania from East Asia and Southeast Asia," *Quaternary International*, 211(1-2), 2010.

Pimenoff, V., Comas, D., Palo, J., Vershubsky, G., Kozlov, A, Sajantila, A., "Northwest Siberian Khanty and Mansi in the junction of West and East Eurasian gene pools as revealed by uniparental markers," *European Journal of Human Genetics*, 16, 2008.

Pitulko, V., "The Berelekh Quest: A Review of Forty Years of Research in the Mammoth Graveyard in Northeast Siberia," *Geoarchaeology*, 26(1), 2011.

Ponce de León, M., Golovanova, L., Doronichev, V., Romanova, G., Akazaqa, T., Kondo, O., Ishida, H., Zollikofer, C., "Neanderthal brain size at birth provides insights into the evolution of human life history," *Proceedings of the National Academy of Sciences,* 105(37), Sept 2008.

Potter, B. A., Reuther, J. D., Bowers, P. M., and Relvin-Reymiller, C., "Little Delta Dune Site: A Late-Pleistocene Multicomponent Site in Central Alaska," *Archaeology: North America,* CRP 25, 2008.

Powell, E., "Mongolia," *Archaeology,* 59(1) Jan/Feb 2006.

Prokopenko, A., Kuzmin, M., Li, H., Woo, K., Catto, N., "Lake Hovsgol basin as a new study site for long continental paleoclimate records in continental interior Asia: General contest and current status," *Quaternary International,* 205, 2009.

Quade, J., Forester, R. M., Pratt, W. L., Carter, C., "Black Mats, Spring-Fed Streams, and Late-Glacial-Age Recharge in the Southern Great Basin," *Quaternary Research,* 49(2) 1998.

Ransom, J. E., "Derivation of the Word Alaska," *American Anthropologist,* 42, 1942.

Razjigaeva, N., Korotky, A., Grebennikova, T., Ganzey, L., Mokhova, L., Bazarova, V. Sulerzhitsky, L., Lutaenko, K., "Holocene climatic changes and environmental history of Iturup Island, Kurile Islands, northwestern Pacific," *The Holocene,* 12, 2002.

Reich, D., et al., "Genetic history of an archaic hominin group from Denisova Cave in Siberia," *Nature,* 468, 7327, 2010.

Rose, W. I., Chesner, C. A., "Dispersal of ash in the great Toba Eruption, 74 ka," *Geology,* 15, 1987.

Rudaya, N., Tarasov, P., Dorofeyuk, N., Solovieva, N., Kalugin, I., Andreev, Daryin, A., Diekmann, B., Riedel, F., Tserendash, N., Wagner, M., "Holocene environments and climate in the Mongolian Altai reconstructed from the Hoton-Nur pollen and diatom records: a step towards better understanding climate dynamics in Central Asia," *Quaternary Science Reviews,* 28(5-6) 2009.

Ruvinsky, J., "The Great American Extinction," *Discover,* 28(8) 2007.

Saillard, J., Forster, P., Lynnerup, N., Bandelt, H.-J., Nørby, S., "mtDNA Variation among Greenland Eskimos: The Edge of the Beringian Expansion," *The Journal of Human Genetics,* 2000 September; 67(3): 718-726.

Saleeby, B. M., "Out of Place Bones: beyond the study of prehistoric subsistence," Arctic Research of the United States, *U. S. National Science Foundation,* 2002.

Sattler, H. R., *The Earliest Americans,* Clarion Books, New York, 1993.

Schepartz, L. A., Miller-Antonio, S., "Taphonomy, Life History, and Human Exploitation of Rhinoceros sinensis at the Middle Pleistocene site of Panxian Dadong, Guizhou, China," *International Journal of Osteoarchaeology,* 2008.

Schrenk, F., Muller, S. *The Neanderthals,* Routledge, 2005.

Seong, C., "Tanged points, microblades and Late Palaeolithic hunting in Korea," *Antiquity,* 82, 2008.

Shen, G., Fang, Y., Bischoff, J. L., Feng, Y., and Zhao, J., "Mass spectrometric U-series dating of the Chaoxian hominin site at Yinshan, eastern China," *Quaternary International,* 211(1-2), 2010.

Sher, A., Weinstock, J., Baryshnikov, G., Davydov, S., Boeskorov, G., Zazhigin, V., Nikolskiy, P., "The first record of 'spelaeoid' bears in Arctic Siberia, *Quaternary Science Reviews,* 30, 2010.

Shichi, K., Takahara, H., Krivonogov, S., Bezrukova, E., Kashiwaya, K., Takehara, A., Nakamura, T., "Late Pleistocene and Holocene vegetation and climate records from Lake Kotokel, central Baikal region," *Quaternary International,* 205, 2009.

Smith, T., Toussaint, M., Reid, D., Olejniczak, A., Hublin, J., "Rapid dental development in a Middle Paleolithic Belgian Neanderthal," *Proceedings of the National Academy of Sciences,* 104(51), Dec. 2007.

Snodgrass, J., Leonard, W., "Neandertal Energetics Revisited: Insight Into Population Dynamics and Life History Evolution," *PaleoAnthropology,* 2009.

Starikovskaya, Y. B., Sukernik, R. I., Schurr, T. G., Kogelnik, A. M., and Wallace, D. C. "mtDNA diversity in Chukchi and Siberian Eskimos: Implications for the Genetic History of Ancient Beringia and the Peopling of the New World," *The American Journal of Human Genetics,* 63, 1998.

Stephan, A. E., *The First Athabascans of Alaska: Strawberries,* Dorrance Publishing Co, Inc., Pittsburg, 1996.

Stone, R., "A Surprising Survival Story in the Siberian Arctic," *Science,* 303(5642): 2004.

Stringer, C., Finlayson, J., Barton, R., Fernández-Jalvo, Y., Cáceres, I., Sabin, R., Rhodes, E., Currant, A., Rodriguez-Vidal, J., Giles-Pacheco, F., Riquelme-Cantal, J., "Neanderthal exploitation of marine mammals in Gibraltar," *Proceedings of the National Academy of Sciences,* 105(38) Sept. 2008.

Stringer, C., *Lone Survivors: How We Came To Be the Only Humans on Earth.* Times Books, Henry Holt & Co., LLC, New York, 2012.

Strong, S., "The Most Revered of Foxes: Knowledge of Animals and Animal Power in an Ainu *Kamui Yukar,*" *Asian Ethnology,* 68(1), 2009.

Sykes, B., *The Seven Daughters of Eve,* W.W. Norton & Company, New York, 2001.

Szathmary, E. J. E., "mtDNA and the Peopling of the Americas," *The Journal of Human Genetics,* 53, 1993.

Tamm, E., Kivisild, T., Reidla, M., Metspalu, M., Smith, D. G., Mulligan, C. J., Bravi, C. M., Rickards, O., Martinez-Labarga, C., Khusnutdinova, E. K., Fedorova, S. A., Torroni, A., Neel, J. V., Barrantes, R., Schurr, T. G., "Mitochondrial DNA 'clock' for the Amerinds and its implications for timing their entry into North America," *Proceedings of the National Academy of Sciences, USA,* 91, 1994.

Tarasov, P., Williams, J., Andreev, A., Nakagawa, T., Bezrukova, E., Herzschuh, U., Igarashi, Y., Müller, S., Werner, K., Zheng, Z., "Satellite- and pollen-based quantitative woody cover reconstructions for northern Asia: Verification and application to late-Quaternary pollen data," *Earth and Planetary Science Letters*, 264(1-2), 2007.

Tattersall, I., *Masters of the Planet, The Search for Our Human Origins*, Palgrace Macmillan, 2012

Than, K., "Neanderthals, Humans Interbred—First Solid DNA Evidence: Most of us have some Neanderthal genes, study finds," May 6, 2010 for *National Geographic News*, http://news.nationalgeographic. com/news/2010/05/100506-science-neanderthals-humans-mated-interbred-dna-gene/

Tianyuan, L., Etler, D., "New Middle Pleistocene hominid crania from Yunxian in China," *Nature*, 357, June 1992.

Tong, H., Moigne, A.-M., "Quaternary Rhinoceros of China," in English, *Acta Anthropologica Sinica*, Supplement to Volume 19, 2000.

Torroni, A., Sukernik, R. I., Schurr, Ti G., Starikovskaya, Y. B., Cabell, M. F., Crawford, M. H., Comuzzie, A. G., Wallace, D. C., "mtDNA Variations of Aboriginal Siberians Reveals distinct Genetic Affinities with Native Americans," *The American Journal of Human Genetics*, 53, 1993.

Vasil'ev, S. A., Kuzmin, Y. V., Orlova, L. A., Dementiev, V. N., "Radiocarbon-Based Chronology of the Paleolithic in Siberia and Its Relevance to the Peopling of the New World," *Radiocarbon*, 44(2), 2002.

Vialet, A., Guipert, G., Jianing, H., Xiaobo, F., Zune, L., Youping, W., de Lumley, M.-A., de Lumley, H., "Homo erectus from the Yunxian and Nankin Chinese sites: Anthropological insights using 3D virtual imaging techniques," *Comptes Rendus Palevol* 9(6-7), 2010.

Volodko, N. V., Starikovskaya, E. B., Mazunin, I. O., Eltsov, N. P., Naidenko, P. V., Wallace, D. C., and Sukernik, R. I., "Mitochondrial Genome Diversity in Arctic Siberians, with Particular Reference to the Evolutionary History of Beringia and Pleistocenic Peopling of the Americas," *American Journal of Human Genetics,* 82(5), 2008.

Wagner, D. P., McAvoy, J. M., "Pedoarchaeology of Cactus Hill, a sandy Paleoindian site in southeastern Virginia, U. S. A." *Geoarchaeology,* 19(4), 2004.

Waguespack, N. M., Surovell, T. A., "Clovis Hunting Strategies, or How to Make Out on Plentiful Resources," *American Antiquity,* 68(2), 2003.

Wang, J., "Late Paleozoic macrofloral assemblages from Weibel coalfield, with reference to vegetational change through the Late Paleozoic Ice-age in the North China Block," *International Journal of Coal Geology,* 83(2-3), 2010.

Waters, Michael R. et al., "Redefining the Age of Clovis: Implications for the Peopling of the Americas," *Science,* 315, 1122, 2007.

Waters-Rist, A., Bazaliiskii, V. I., Weber, A, Goriunova, O. I., Katzenberg, A., "Activity-induced dental modification in holocene Siberian hunter-fisher-gatherers," *American Journal of Physical Anthropology,* 143(2), 2010.

West, F. H., Ed., *AMERICAN BEGINNINGS: the Prehistory and Palaeoecology of Beringia,* The University of Chicago Press, Chicago, 1996.

Wiedmer, M., Montgomery, D., Gillespie, A., Greenberg, H., "Late Quaternary megafloods from Glaial Lake Atna, Southcentral Alaska, U.S.A., *Quaternary Research,* 73, 2010.

Woodman, N., Athfield, N., "Post-Clovis survival of American Mastodon in the southern Great Lakes Region of North America," *Quaternary Research,* 72(3), 20009.

Wu, X., "Fossil Humankind and Other Anthropoid Primates of China," *International Journal of Primatology,* 25(5) 2004.

Wu, X., "On the origins of modern humans in China," *Quaternary International,* 117(1), 2004.

Wu, X., Schepartz, L. A., Norton, C. J., "Morphological and morphometric analysis of variation in the Zhoukoudian Homo erectus brain endocasts," *Quaternary International*, 211(1-2) 2010.

Wu, Y-S., Chen, Y-S., Xiao, J-Y., "A preliminary study on vegetation and climate changes in Dianchi Lake area in the last 40,000 years," partial in English, *Acta Botanica Sinica*, 33(5), 1991.

Wynn, T., Coolidge, F. L., *How to Think like a Neanderthal*, Oxford University Press, 2012.

Xiao, J., Jin, C., Zhu, Y., "Age of the fossil Dali Man in north-central China deduced from chronostratigraphy of the loess-paleosol sequence," *Quaternary Science Reviews*, 21, 2002.

Xiangcan, J., "Lake Dianchi," *Experience and Lessons Learned Brief*, final version 2004.

Xu, J-X., Ferguson, D. K., Li, C-S., Wang, Y-F., "Late Miocene vegetation and the climate of the Lühe region in Yunnan, southwestern China," *Review of Palaeobotany and Palynology*, 148(1), 2008.

Yahner, R. H., "Barking in a primitive ungulate, *Muntiacus reevesi:* function and adaptiveness," *The American Naturalist*, 116(2), 1980.

Zang, W., Wang, Y., Zheng, S., Yang, X., Li, Y., Fu, X., Li, N., "Taxonomic investigations on permineralized conifer woods from the Late Paleozoic Angaran deposits of northeastern Inner Mongolia, China, and their palaeoclimatic significance," *Review of Palaeobotany and Palynology*, 144(3-4), May 2007.

Zhang, Y., Stiner, M, Dennell, R., Wang, C., Zhang, Sh, Gao, X., "Zooarchaeological perspectives on the Chinese Early and Late Paleolithic from the Ma'anshan site (Guizhou, South China)," *Journal of Archaeological Science*, 37(8), 2010.

Zhu, R., An, Z., Potts, R., Hoffman, K., "Magnetostratigraphic dating of early humans in China," *Earth-Science Reviews*, 61(3-4) June 2003.

Zorich, Z., "Did *Homo erectus* Coddle His Grandparents?" *Discover,* 27(1) Jan. 2006.

No author designated. "Bone fossil points to a mystery human species," *USA Today,* Mar 25, 2010. [Three types of humans lived within 60 miles of each other in southern Siberia.]

FROM THE INTERNET:

America's Stone Age Explorers http://www.pbs.org/wgbh/nova/tran-scripts/3116_stoneage.html (8/23/2010)

Ancestral Human Skull Found in China (80,000 to 100,000 ya) http://news.nationalgeographic.com/news/2008/02/080220-china-fossil.html

Ancient bison bones supports theory about Ice Age seafarers being first in Americas http://www.thaindian.com/newsportal/world-news/ancient-bison-bones-supports-theory-abo... (9/5/2010)

Archaeology of the Altai Republic http://eng.altai-republic.ru/mod-ules.php?op=modload&name=Sections&file=index&req=viewarticle&artid=20... (1/30/2011)

Archaic Human Culture http://anthro.palomar.edu/homo2/mod_homo_3.htm (9/9/2010)

Bamboo http://earthnotes.tripod.com/bamboo.htm (9/13/2010)

Berelekh Map http://www.maplandia.com/russia/magadanskaya-oblast/susumanskiy-rayon/berelekh/ (8/31/2010)

China map http://en.wikipedia.org/wiki/File:China_100.78713E_35.63718N.jpg (8/20/2010)

Chukchee Society http://lucy.ukc.ac.uk/ethnoatlas/hmar/cult_dir/culture.7837 (4/5/2011)

Chukchi Directions of time and space http://www.cosmicelk.net/ Chukchidirections.htm (4/5/2011)

Chukchi Language http://en.wikipedia.org/wiki/Chukchi_language (4/5/2011)

Cro-Magnon http://en.wikipedia.org/wiki/Cro-Magnon (8/12/2010)

Denisova Cave (Siberia) http://archaeology.about.com/od/dathroughde-terms/qt/denisova_cave.htm (8?31/2010)

Dover Bronze Age Boat http://indigenousboats.blogspot.com/2008/01/ dover-bronze-age-boat.html

Drum Talk Is the African's "Wireless," A. I. Good, *Natural History Magazine,* 1942, http://www.naturalhistorymag.com/htmlsite/master.html? http:// www.naturalhistorymag.com/htmlsite/editors_pick/1942_09_pick.html

Earliest Humanlike Footprints Found in Kenya http://donsmaps.com/ erectus.html (9/11/2010)

Face of a Neanderthal woman http://www.femininebeauty.info/neanderthal-woman (8/23/2010)

First Americans http://www.nmhcpl.org/First_American.html (8/23/2010)

Four-horned Antelope http://en.wikipedia.org/wiki/Four-horned_ Antelope (9/15/2010)

Geography of China http://en.wikipedia.org/wiki/Geography_of_China (9/3/2010)

Historical earthquakes in China http://drgeorgepc.com/EarthquakesChina. html (9/24/2010)

Historical SuperVolcanoes and Archeology Indicate Nuclear Winter Climate Models Exaggerate Effects http://nextbigfuture.com/2010/04/historical-supervolcanoes-and.html (8/20/2010)

Hominid Tools
http://www.handprint.com/LS/ANC/stones.html (8/23/2010)

Homo erectus http://humanorigins.si.edu/evidence/human-fossils/species/homo-erectus (8/12/2010)

Homo erectus http://en.wikipedia.org/wiki/Homo_erectus (8/12/2010)

Homo erectus http://www.archaeologyinfo.com/homoerectus.htm (9/5/2010)

Homo erectus Survival http://www.archaeology.org/9703/newsbriefs/h.erectus.html (9/5/2010)

Homo neanderthalensis http://humanorigins.si.edu/evidence/human-fossils/species/homo-neanderthalensis (8/12/2010)

Humans wore shoes 40,000 years ago, fossil suggests http://www.stonepages.com/news/archives/002825.html (8/27/2010)

Hydropotes inermis (Chinese water deer) http://www.ultimateungulate.com/Artiodactyla/Hydropotes_inermis.html (9/8/2010)

Ice Age Climate Cycles http://earthguide.ucsd.edu/virtualmuseum/climatechange2/03_1.shtml (1/29/2011)

Images of Neanderthals http://www.talkorigins.org/faqs/homs/savage.html (8/23/2010)

La Ferrassie Neanderthal Reconstruction http://s1.zetaboards.com/anthroscape/topic/2448167/1/ (8/23/2010)

Late Pleistocene, now-extinct fauna of the southwest http://www.saguaro-juniper.com/i_and_i/history/megafauna.html (8/22/2010)

Meet the Neanderthals http://news.bbc.co.uk/2/hi/science/nature/1469607.stm (8/23/2010)

Mousterian http://en.wikipedia.org/wiki/Mousterian

Muntjac (barking deer) http://www.itsnature.org/ground/mammals-land/muntjac/ (9/8/2010)

Neanderthal http://www.crystalinks.com/neanderthal.html

Neanderthals more intelligent than thought http://www.msnbc.msn.com/id/39324819/ns/technology_and_science-science (9/24/2010)

Neanderthal reconstructions http://www.daynes.com/en/reconstructions/neanderthal-4.php (8/23/2010)

Origins of Paleoindians http://en.wikipedia.org/wiki/Origins_of_Paleoindians (8/22/2010)

Pedra Furada, Brazil: Paleoindian, Paintings, and Paradoxes, http://www.athenapub.com/10pfurad.htm (2012)

Pompeii-Like Excavations Tell Us More About Toba Super-Eruption http://www.sciencedaily.com/releases/2010/02/100227170841.htm

Quaternary Period http://www3.hi.is/~oi/quaternary_geology.htm (8/31/2010)

Red hair a part of Neanderthal genetic profile http://seattletimes.nwsource.com/html/nationworld/2003975496_neanderthal26.html (8/26/2010)

Rethinking Neanderthals, Joe Alper, Smithsonian.com, Science and Nature, June 2003 http://www.smithsonianmag.com/science-nature/neanderthals.html?c=y&page=1

Sacred Bones, Fields of Stones, Dr. Francis Allard Earthwatch Journal, October 2002, www.earthwatch.org

Savoonga artist to explore traditional native tattoos, Anchorage Daily News http://www.adn.com/2011/04/02/1788951/savoonga-artist-to-explore-traditional.html (4/5/2011)

Shamanism in Siberia http://www.sacred-texts.com/sha/sis/sis04.htm (4/5/2011)

Shiraoi Ainu Village http://members.virtualtourist.com/m/tt/52254/

Signs of Neanderthals Mating With Humans http://www.nytimes.com/2010/05/07/science/07neanderthal.html?_r=1 (8/26/2010)

Simple techniques for production of dried meat http://www.fao.org/docrep/003/x6932e/X6932E02.htm (9/27/2010)

"Skin Deep," a program on the Smithsonian Channel with Penn State anthropologist, Nina Jablonski http://www.smithsonianchannel.com/site/sn/video/player/latest-videos/skin-deep-full-episode/2180530922001/

Solutrean http://en.wikipedia.org/wiki/Solutrean (8/23/2010)

Stone Age Columbus http://www.bbc.co.uk/science/horizon/2002/columbusqa.shtml (8/23/2010)

Stone Age Site Yields Evidence of Advanced Culture http://history.cultural-china.com/en/51History9459.html (9/5/2010)

Stone-tipped spear invented earlier than thought, researchers say, http://www.latimes.com/news/science/la-sci-hafting-spears-201221116,0,6983702.story (11/17/2012

Straight-tusked elephant http://en.wikipedia.org/wiki/Straight-tusked_Elephant (10/3/2010)

Synoptic table of the principal old world prehistoric cultures http://en.wikipedia.org/wiki/Synoptic_table_of_the_principal_old_world_prehistoric_cultures (9/8/2010)

Transmitting the Ainu wisdom http://www.town.shiraoi.hokkaido.jp/ainu-tradition/yamamaru/index.html

Umiaq skin boat http://en.wikipedia.org/wiki/File:Umiaq_skin_boat.jpg

Volcanic Ash http://geology.com/articles/volcanic-ash.shtml (8/20/2010)

Zhirendong puts the chin in china http://johnhawks.net/weblog/fossils/china/zhirendong-2010-liu-chin.html

Zhoukoudian Relics Museum http: www.china.org.cn/english/features/museums/129075.htm (9/5/2010)

About the Author

Bonnye Matthews is an award winning novelist of the series, Winds of Change, which focuses on the pre-Clovis peopling of the Americas. Her first book in the series, *Ki'ti's Story, 75,000 BC*, came out in 2012 followed by the second book, *Manak-na's Story, 75,000 BC*, in 2013. She has taught in public school at the secondary level, written self-instruction courses and a video for an insurance company, and worked in personnel for various federal government agencies where she developed a management development plan for an agency in the Seattle area. Her favorite federal work was performing personnel management evaluations of agency programs and spearheading organizational audits to conform work to desired organizational planning outcomes for an entire regional agency and various other agency departments.

Printed in Great Britain
by Amazon

67102164R00153